THE INTERROGATOR

THE INTERROGATOR

AND OTHER CRIMINALLY GOOD FICTION

EDITED BY

ED GORMAN AND MARTIN H. GREENBERG

CEMETERY DANCE PUBLICATIONS

Baltimore

❖ 2012 ❖

See page 478 for individual story Copyright information.

Cemetery Dance Publications
132-B Industry Lane, Unit #7
Forest Hill, MD 21050
http://www.cemeterydance.com

ISBN-13: 978-1-58767-336-8

Interior Design by Kate Freeman Design

For twenty-five years Martin H. Greenberg and I edited annual collections of mystery and suspense stories we thought readers would enjoy. This is the last such collection because Marty died last year. His passing was especially difficult for me because he'd been my best friend for thirty years. He was a generous, funny and knowledgeable man who took great pride in the books he edited. Speaking for Marty's wife Roz and his daughter Maj and for all the people at Tekno Books, Marty's business, I'm dedicating this to our great friend and mentor—expert on all things Seinfeld and the Three Stooges—Marty Greenberg.

TABLE OF CONTENTS

THE MYSTERY IN 2010

JON L. BREEN

FALL 2010, THE YEAR OF THE E-BOOK. THOUGH I KNOW THEY'VE been around for years, they didn't really take off as a mass-market phenomenon until portable devices like the Kindle, the Nook, and the iPad widened the potential audience. The ease of self-publishing through e-books and print on demand, coupled with the publicity possibilities of the Internet and the weakening grip of the traditional mainstream publishers, have created a kind of Wild West atmosphere in the marketplace that is confusing and frustrating for some, astonishingly lucrative for others.

Some writers in the mystery/thriller field apparently are making a good living writing directly for e-books, sometimes offered at bargain-basement prices. According to an article in the April 21, 2011 *Wall Street Journal*, John Locke (certainly not the English philosopher and presumably not the pulp magazine historian), whose novels about former CIA assassin Donovan Creed began appearing as print-on-demand paperbacks in 2009, entered digital publishing in March 2010, offering his books for $.99 each on Kindle, of which he gets $.35. With Amazon downloads increasing from 1300 in November, 2010, to 369,000 in March, 2011, his monthly take had risen to six figures. Curious about this self-made bestseller, I downloaded one of his books, *Lethal Experiment* (print: iUniverse, 2009; e-book: Telemachus Press, 2010), and found he's an entertaining writer, given to nutty plot twists and oddball humor. Not for a moment did I regret the expenditure of 99 cents or, more importantly, the time I spent reading the book. Could Locke have found a place in mainstream publishing? In the current market, it's doubtful, and with his knack for self-promotion, why should he bother?

Less cheerful news underlined the impression of a genre and a world in transition. As always, the obituary columns were all too full. I noted in last year's summary the early-2010 deaths of two MWA Grand Masters: Dick Francis and Robert B. Parker. As the year went on, we also lost novelists A.J. Baantjer, prolific Dutch police proceduralist; Eleanor Taylor Brand, creator of African American policewoman Marti MacAlister; Jon Cleary, Edgar-winning Australian novelist; A.S. (Sid) Fleischman, author of Gold Medal paperbacks for adults and award-winning juvenile novels; and Ralph McInerny, creator of Father Dowling. The toll was also high on important mystery figures in radio (Himan Brown), television (Stephen J. Cannell, Jackson Gillis), editorial work (Knox Burger, Ruth Cavin), motion pictures (Blake Edwards), comic strips (Peter O'Donnell), short story writing (C.B. Gilford), bookselling (Ed Thomas, David Thompson), and fanzine publishing (Len Moffatt). It's hard to imagine a mystery world without these people.

BEST NOVELS OF THE YEAR 2010

Before unveiling the fifteen best new books I read and reviewed during the year, here's the boilerplate disclaimer: I don't pretend to cover the whole field—no single reviewer does—but if you have a better list of fifteen, I'd love to see it.

Andrea Camilleri, *The Wings of the Sphinx*, translated from the Italian by Stephen Sartarelli (Penguin). Sicilian Inspector Montalbano is one of the best series cops to come out of Continental Europe in the past couple of decades—and the humor somehow comes through thanks to a gifted translator.

Gianrico Carofiglio, *The Past is a Foreign Country*, translated from the Italian by Howard Curtis (Minotaur). A fine piece of contemporary noir develops two apparently unconnected stories in a structure pioneered in the 1950s by Bill S. Ballinger.

Michael Connelly, *The Reversal* (Little, Brown). L.A. advocate Mickey Haller temporarily turns prosecutor in a new exhibit to strengthen the case that one of the finest writers of legal thrillers is a non-lawyer.

K.O. Dahl, *The Last Fix*, translated from the Norwegian by Don Bartlett (Minotaur). A pair of Oslo cops unravel a complex mystery in the latest from an author who may outshine some more heavily publicized Scandinavians.

Loren D. Estleman, *The Left-handed Dollar* (Forge). Detroit private eye Amos Walker may have entered the 21st Century reluctantly, but readers of great crime fiction are glad to have him.

Alan Gordon, *The Parisian Prodigal* (Minotaur). This case for members of the 13th-century Fools' Guild is notable for sparkling dialogue and fair-play puzzle plotting.

Barbara Hamilton, *A Marked Man* (Berkley). The second Revolutionary period novel with Abigail Adams as detective is more evidence that Barbara Hambly (writing as herself or Hamilton) is one of the finest practitioners of American historical mysteries.

Robert Harris, *Conspirata* (Simon and Schuster). The second of a trilogy of novels about Roman orator Cicero is a superb piece of historical fiction with plenty of criminous activity.

Faye Kellerman, *Hangman* (Morrow). Combining family saga with police procedural, as Kellerman has done in the series about L.A. police lieutenant Peter Decker and wife Rina Lazarus, could only work with the proper balance between cops and case. Kellerman manages it perfectly.

Jon Lellenberg, *Baker Street Irregular* (Arkham House/Mycroft & Moran). Of all the novels about organized devotees of Sherlock Holmes, this 1930s and 1940s spy novel may be the best.

Richard A. Lupoff, *The Emerald Cat Killer* (Minotaur). The final entry in the series about insurance investigator Hobart Lindsey and Berkeley cop Marvia Plum was worth the 13-year wait.

Nancy Pickard, *The Scent of Rain and Lightning* (Ballantine). A beautifully rendered rural background and twisty plot fuel the account of quarter-century-old murder that haunts a Kansas ranching family.

Claudia Pineiro, *Thursday Night Widows*, translated from the Spanish by Miranda France (Bitter Lemon). As Argentina's economy unravels, so do the relationships of several couples living in a gated community near Buenos Aires.

Bill Pronzini, *Betrayers* (Forge). San Francisco's Nameless Detective and his associates look into a quartet of mysteries that demonstrate the author's skill and versatility.

Scott Turow, *Innocent* (Grand Central). I'd have sworn *Presumed Innocent* didn't require a sequel until I read this remarkable update of the tangled lives of Rusty Sabich and his family.

SUB-GENRES

Private eyes. The second of Max Allan Collins's posthumous collaborations with Mickey Spillane on an unfinished Mike Hammer novel, *The Big Bang* (Penzler/Houghton Mifflin Harcourt) is far better than its predecessor. Other sleuths for hire in good form included Parnell Hall's Stanley Hastings in *Caper* (Pegasus) and Ken Bruen's Jack Taylor in *The Devil* (Minotaur).

Amateur sleuths. It was a strong year for non-professional crime-solvers, who as usual represented various day jobs: political consultant Dev Conrad in Ed Gorman's *Stranglehold* (Minotaur), chef and TV personality Billy Blessing in Al Roker and Dick Lochte's *The Midnight Show Murders* (Delacorte), art restorer Annie Kincaid in Hailey Lind's *Arsenic and Old Paint* (Perseverance), mother and daughter antique dealers Vivian and Brandy Borne in Barbara Allan's *Antiques Bizarre* (Kensington), prison chaplain John Jordan in Michael Lister's *The Body and the Blood* (Five Star), movie stuntwoman Darcy Lott in Susan Dunlap's *Power Slide* (Counterpoint), psychotherapist Dr. Daniel Rinaldi in Dennis Palumbo's *Mirror Image* (Poisoned Pen), historian Daniel Kind in Martin Edwards's *The Serpent Pool* (Poisoned Pen), and the team of British home office retiree Carole Seddon and New Age healer Jude in Simon Brett's *The Shooting in the Shop* (Five Star).

Police. There were solid cases for TV's obsessive-compulsive cop-turned-consultant Adrian Monk in Lee Goldberg's *Mr. Monk is Cleaned Out* (Obsidian), Bill Crider's Texas Sheriff Dan Rhodes in *Murder in the Air* (Minotaur), Cynthia Riggs's 92-year-old Martha's Vineyard deputy Victoria Trumbull in *Touch-Me-Not* (Minotaur), Jo Nesbø's Harry Hole in *The Devil's Star*, translated from the Norwegian by Don Bartlett (Harper), and the late Stuart M. Kaminsky's Moscow cop Porfiry Petrovich Rostnikov in *A Whisper to the Living* (Forge).

Lawyers. John Grisham extended his franchise to juvenile fiction in *Theodore Boone: Kid Lawyer* (Dutton). Pastor and attorney Randy Singer's *Fatal Convictions* (Tyndale) concerned Christian and Muslim religious conflict. Ed Gorman's Iowa attorney Sam McCain appears for (maybe) the last time in the 1960s-based *Ticket to Ride* (Pegasus). Other series lawyers in good form included Scott Pratt's Joe Dillard in *Injustice for All* (Obsidian), William Bernhardt's Ben Kincaid in *Capitol Betrayal* (Ballantine), and Margaret Maron's Judge Deborah Knott in *Christmas Mourning* (Grand Central).

Historicals. In Pierre Magnan's *The Murdered House*, translated from the French by Patricia Clancy (Minotaur), a World War I combat veteran who in infancy survived the mass murder of his family members, searches for the truth in post-war Provence. Daniëlle Hermans's first novel *The Tulip Virus*, translated from the Dutch by David MacKay (Minotaur) concerns two centuries-apart bubbles in the tulip trade. Sharyn McCrumb's *The Devil Amongst the Lawyers* (St. Martin's/Dunne) fictionalizes a 1935 Virginia murder trail in a fine return to her Appalachian series. Anne Perry's *The Sheen on the Silk* (Ballantine), more interesting as history than mystery, is set in the 13th-century Ottoman Empire. Bruce Macbain makes a sleuth of Pliny the Younger in the first-century-A.D. *Roman Games* (Poisoned Pen). Thirty-five years after the debut of Edwardian-era archaeologist Amelia Peabody, her adventures with her extended family continue to provide charm and humor in Elizabeth Peters's *A River in the Sky* (Morrow). Other series detectives from past eras included Victoria Thompson's turn-of-the-20th-century team of New York Detective Sergeant Frank Malloy and midwife Sarah Brandt in *Murder on Lexington Avenue* (Berkley) and Loren D. Estleman's 1880s U.S. Marshal in the western mystery *The Book of Murdock* (Forge).

Thrillers. Remember my catch-all definition: anything that doesn't neatly fit the other categories. Bill Pronzini's *The Hidden* (Walker) is a fine pure suspense novel about an environmentalist serial killer. Fans of Dick Francis and other horse racing specialists should hunt for Sasscer Hill's *Full Mortality* (Wildside). The versatile Michael Lister's *Thunder Beach* (Tyrus) is noirish in setting and mood but has an underlying spirituality. Two novels by Joyce Carol

Oates, *Little Bird of Heaven* (Ecco) and *A Fair Maiden* (Houghton Mifflin Harcourt/Penzler), are typically excellent in their grasp of character and suspense. Henry Porter's *The Bell Ringers* (Atlantic Monthly) is an unsettling tale of terrorism and invasion of privacy in near-future Britain.

SHORT STORIES

Single-author short story collections kept coming in 2010, including several specifically created for the e-book market, where they are offered at bargain prices: Steve Hockensmith's *Naughty: Nine Tales of Christmas Crime*, Marcus Sakey's *Scar Tissue: Seven Stories of Love and Wounds*, Chris S. Holm's *Eight Pounds: Eight Tales of Crime, Horror and Suspense*, Twist Phelan's *A Stab in the Heart: Collected Crime and Mystery Stories 2005-2009*, a pair each from J.A. Konrath (*Crime Stories: Twenty Thriller Tales* and *Jack Daniels Stories: Fifteen Mystery Tales*) and Simon Wood (*Working Stiffs* and *Asking for Trouble*), and probably others I never caught up with.

Books by contemporary authors following a more conventional publishing route were Loren Estleman's *Amos Walker: The Complete Story Collection* (Tyrus), Terence Faherty's *The Hollywood Op* (Perfect Crime), Ed Gorman's *Noir 13* (Perfect Crime), Ron Goulart's *Playing Detective* (Gryphon), William Link's *The Columbo Collection* (Crippen & Landru), Gary Lovisi's *Ultra-Boiled* (Ramble House), Richard A. Lupoff's *Killer's Dozen* (Wildside), Francis M. Nevins's *Night Forms* (Perfect Crime), William F. Nolan's *Dark Dimensions* (Darkwood), Joyce Carol Oates's *Give Me Your Heart* (Harcourt/Penzler) and *Sourland* (Ecco), Stephen D. Rogers's *Shot to Death: 31 Stories of Nefarious New England* (Mainly Murder), S.J. Rozan's *A Tale About a Tiger and Other Mysterious Events* (Crippen & Landru), Ennis Willie's *Sand's Game* (Ramble House), Jonathan Woods's *Bad Juju* (New Pulp), and a couple of Sherlockian collections: Donald Thomas's *Sherlock Holmes and the Ghosts of Bly* (Pegasus) and Ann Margaret Lewis's *Murder in the Vatican: The Church Mysteries of Sherlock Holmes* (Gasogene).

Along with its collections of living writers, Crippen & Landru added several retrospective collections to its Lost Classics series: Vera Caspary's *The Murder in the Stork Club and Other Mysteries*, Michael Innes's *Appleby Talks About Crime*, and Philip Wylie's *Ten Thousand Blunt Instruments and Other Tales of Mystery*.

Once again the two annual best-of collections—*The Best American Mystery Stories 2010* (Houghton Mifflin Harcourt), edited by Lee Child with series editor Otto Penzler; and the present volume's predecessor, *By Hook or By Crook and 27 More of the Best Crime and Mystery Stories of the Year* (Tyrus), edited by Ed Gorman and Martin H. Greenberg—agreed on only two entries: Lyndsay Faye's Sherlockian pastiche "The Case of Colonel Warburton's Madness" and Dennis Lehane's Edgar nominee "Animal Rescue." Appearing in both volumes with different stories was Doug Allyn: "An Early Christmas" in C&P's, "The Valhalla Verdict" in G&G's. As usual, G&G's had more in common with the Edgar judges, picking the winning story, Luis Alberto Urrea's "Amapola" plus three of the other nominees.

Other reprint anthologies edited by the ubiquitous Penzler included *The Best American Noir of the Century* (Houghton Mifflin Harcourt), with James Ellroy; *The Black Lizard Big Book of Black Mask Stories* (Vintage/Black Lizard); *The Greatest Russian Stories of Crime and Suspense* (Pegasus); and *Christmas at the Mysterious Bookshop* (Vanguard).

Among the retrospectives assembled by other hands were *The Best Paranormal Crime Stories Ever Told* (Skyhorse), edited by Martin H. Greenberg; *Sexton Blake, Detective* (London: Snowbooks), edited by George Mann with an introduction by Michael Moorcock; and *City of Numbered Men: The Best of Prison Stories* (Off-Trail), another extraordinary piece of pulp magazine scholarship edited by John Locke. (As noted earlier, this John Locke is apparently not the author of the Donovan Creed novels.)

Original anthologies of note included *Delta Blues* (Tyrus), edited by Carolyn Haines with a foreword by Morgan Freeman; the paranormal crossover *Death's Excellent Vacation* (Ace), edited by Charlaine Harris and Toni L.P. Kelner; the International Thriller Writers' *First Thrills* (Forge), edited by Lee Child; *Florida Heat Wave* (Tyrus), edited by Michael Lister; the Mystery Writers of America's *Crimes by Moonlight* (Berkley), edited by Charlaine Harris; *Hook, Line & Sinister* (Countryman), edited by T. Jefferson Parker; *The Dark End of the Street* (Bloomsbury), edited by S.J. Rozan and Jonathan Santlofer; Sisters in Crime, Los Angeles's *Murder in La-La Land* (TOP), edited by Naomi Hirahara, Eric Stone, and Juliet Blackwell; and *Agents of Treachery* (Vintage Black Lizard), edited by (there he is again) Otto Penzler. Also the Medieval Murderers were back with another collection of connected short stories from various periods in British history, *The Sacred Stone* (Simon & Schuster UK; Trafalgar Square).

REFERENCE BOOKS AND SECONDARY SOURCES

For me, and the Edgar selectors agreed, the secondary source of the year was Yunte Huang's *Charlie Chan: The Untold Story of the Honorable Detective and his Rendezvous with American History* (Norton), which served to counter the inexplicable hostility by some commentators toward Earl Derr Biggers and his great character. Coincidentally, Chan's creator was also covered at length in another worthwhile study, J.K. Van Dover's *Making the Detective Story American: Biggers, Van Dine and Hammett and the Turning Point of the Genre, 1925-1930* (McFarland).

The next four books belong in any mystery reference collection. Amnon Kabatchnik continued his cataloging of theatrical crime in *Blood on the Stage, 1925-1950: Milestone Plays of Crime, Mystery, and Detection: An Annotated Repertoire* (Scarecrow). An important historical collection of interest beyond the Sherlockian was *Sherlock Holmes, Conan Doyle & The Bookman: Pastiches, Parodies, Letters, Columns and Commentary from America's "Magazine of Literature and Life" (1895-1933)* (Gasogene), edited by S.E. Dahlinger and Leslie S. Klinger. The International Thriller Writers selected and analyzed the best and/or most important examples of their subgenre in the Edgar-nominated *Thrillers: 100 Must Reads* (Oceanview), edited by David Morrell and Hank Wagner. Francis M. Nevins collected several decades worth of superb critical writing in *Cornucopia of Crime: Memories and Summations* (Ramble House). (Nevins's book reminds me that in past years, due to inherent modesty and a steadfast aversion to self-promotion, I neglected to mention my own 2008 compilation *A Shot Rang Out: Selected Mystery Criticism*, also from Ramble House under its Surinam Turtle imprint.)

Fresh ground was covered in *The Boy Detectives: Essays on the Hardy Boys and Others* (McFarland), edited by Michael G. Cornelius, and in *Tied In: The Business, History, and Craft of Media Tie-in Writing* (CreateSpace), edited by Lee Goldberg, valuable as both technical manual and critical history. Though too limited and unbalanced in its coverage to justify its ambitious title, *The Cambridge Companion to American Crime Fiction* (Cambridge University Press), edited by Catherine Ross Nickerson, included some worthwhile essays.

James Ellroy continued to probe his troubled past in *The Hilliker Curse: My Pursuit of Women* (Knopf). Other studies of individual authors were *A Violent Conscience: Essays on the Fiction of James Lee Burke* (McFarland), edited by Leonard Engel; and a couple of Edgar nominees, John Curran's *Agatha Christie's Secret Notebooks* (HarperCollins) and Steven Doyle and David A. Crowder's *Sherlock Holmes for Dummies*.

Sources on criminous TV shows and movies included Ron Backer's *Mystery Movie Series of 1940s Hollywood* (McFarland), Matthew R. Bradley's *Richard Matheson on Screen: A History of the Filmed Works* (McFarland), Rafael Alvarez's Edgar-nominated *The Wire: Truth Be Told* (Grove Atlantic), and the fourth edition of *Film Noir: The Encyclopedia* (Overlook Duckworth), edited by Alain Silver, Elizabeth Ward, James Ursini, and Robert Porfirio.

A SENSE OF HISTORY

The new visibility of e-books has made it possible to build a good library of older mysteries, especially public-domain items, at very little cost. I've filled my own iPad with old-timers like E. Phillips Oppenheim, Mary Roberts Rinehart, Anna Katharine Green, Edgar Wallace, Frank L. Packard, and others, either freeing up space in my collection by getting rid of shabby old print editions or finally acquiring books that would have been difficult and/or expensive to get in their original form. But these are mostly no-frills editions, often without even a date of original publication, and for permanence, there's nothing like an old-fashioned, low-tech book.

Several prolific reprinters can always be relied upon for something worthwhile. Among the relatively obscure authors receiving deserved revival in Ramble House's vast eclectic list are Rupert Penny, whose *She Had to Have Gas* (1939 in Britain but new to U.S. publication) is a fine example of complex Golden Age puzzle-spinning, and Arlton Eadie, author of *The Trail of the Cloven Hoof* (1935). The always busy Rue Morgue Press added to its traditional mystery list Frances Crane's *The Pink Umbrella* (1943), Glyn Carr's *Murder on the Matterhorn* (1951), John Dickson Carr's *The Case of the Constant Suicides* (1941), and Catherine Aird's *Slight Mourning* (1975). The more noir-minded Stark House brought us Jada M. Davis's *One for Hell* (1952) and a pairing of A.S. Fleishman's *Look Behind You, Lady* (1952) and *The Venetian Blonde* (1963).

A newer imprint, Bruin, revived the work of David Dodge with handsome trade paperbacks of his first novel, *Death and Taxes* (1941), and his most famous, *To Catch a Thief* (1952). They also offered James Hadley Chase's *No Orchids for Miss Blandish*, combining its 1939 first edition with its 1961 revision, that famous/notorious novel's 1948 sequel *Flesh of the Orchid*, and Fredric Brown's *Knock Three-One-Two* (1959).

Academy Chicago keeps the reputation of Leo Bruce and his Sgt. Beef alive with the postmodernist 1939 novel *Case with Four Clowns*. And Penguin Classics accorded appropriately respectful treatment to Anna Katharine Green's 1878 debut *The Leavenworth Case*.

AT THE MOVIES

Though movies generally are worse than ever, at least the juvenile Hollywood studio product that clogs up the multiplexes, 2010 had some worthwhile big-screen crime. Two great directors presented adaptations of well-received novels early in the year: Martin Scorsese with Dennis Lehane's psychological puzzle *Shutter Island*, screenplay by Laeta Kalogridis, and Roman Polanski with Robert Harris's political thriller *The Ghost Writer*, adapted by Harris and the director from *The Ghost*.

And there were a few other strong English-language films the Edgar movie committee (if there were still such an award) might have considered. Best of them was the expert rural thriller about an Ozark girl's search for her vanished father, *Winter's Bone*, from Daniel Woodrell's novel, directed by Debra Granik, who wrote the screenplay with Anne Rosellini. Michael Winterbottom's adaptation of Jim Thompson's classic *The Killer Inside Me*, scripted by John Curran, was a better effort than generally reputed, though not helped by Casey Affleck's one-note performance in the central role. Three films served as unconventional vehicles for stellar actors: Michael Caine played a senior-citizen avenger in *Harry Brown*, directed by Gary Young from Daniel Barber's screenplay, while George Clooney was a professional assassin in the low-key thriller *The American*, directed by Anton Corbijn from Rowan Joffe's adaptation of Martin Booth's novel, and Robert Duvall was a 1930s Tennessee hermit who wanted to attend his own funeral in *Get Low*, directed by Aaron Shneider, from a script by Chris Provenzano and C. Gaby Mitchell from an original story by Provenzano and Scott Seeke. Ben Affleck was a triple threat in the big caper tale *The Town*: acting, directing, and adapting the screenplay with Peter Craig and Aaron Stockard from Chuck Hogan's novel *Prince of Thieves*. Christopher Nolan's science fictional mystery *Inception* explored the possibilities of dream invasion.

Subtitle readers had more to choose from, including the worthy 2009 Oscar winner for best foreign film, Argentina's *The Secret in Their Eyes*, directed by Juan José Campanella, who co-wrote it with the author of the original novel, *La pregunta de sus ojos*, Eduardo Sacheri. Jean Bruce's originally straightfaced French James Bond, Hubert Bonisseur de la Bath, as played with comic brilliance by Jean Dujardin, had a second parodic outing in *OSS117: Lost in Rio*, directed by Michel Hazanavicius, who wrote the screenplay with Jean-Francois Halin. A more serious French espionage thriller was Christian Carion's Cold War drama *Farewell*, adapted with Eric Raynaud from Serguei Kostine's nonfiction book *Bonjour Farewell*. All three film adaptations of the late Swedish journalist Stieg Larsson's best-selling Millennium trilogy were in U.S. release: *The Girl with the Dragon Tattoo*, directed by Niels Arden Oplev from a script by Nikolaj Arcel and Rasmus Heisterberg; *The Girl Who Played with Fire*, directed by Daniel Alfredson from Jonas Frykberg's script; and *The Girl Who Kicked the Hornet's Nest*, directed by Alfredson from Ulf Ryberg's script. Though the middle one was much weaker than the other two, all three were effective enough to obviate the artistic need, if not the commercial itch, to remake in English-language versions.

AWARD WINNERS

Awards tied to publishers' contests, those limited to a geographical region smaller than a country, those awarded for works in languages other than English (with the exception of the Crime Writers of Canada's nod to their French compatriots), and those confined to works from a single periodical have been omitted. Gratitude is again extended to all the websites that keep track of these things, with a special nod to Jiro Kimura's Gumshoe Site and Janet Rudolph's Mystery Fanfare.

(Awarded in 2011 for material published in 2010)

EDGAR ALLAN POE AWARDS
(Mystery Writers of America)

- Best novel: Steve Hamilton, *The Lock Artist* (Minotaur)
- Best first novel by an American author: Bruce DeSilva, *Rogue Island* (Forge)
- Best original paperback: Robert Goddard, *Long Time Coming* (Bantam)
- Best fact crime book: Ken Armstrong and Nick Perry, *Scoreboard, Baby: A Story of College Football, Crime and Complicity* (University of Nebraska Press)
- Best critical/biographical work: Yunte Huang, *Charlie Chan: The Untold Story of the Honorable Detective and his Rendezvouz with American History* (Norton)
- Best short story: Doug Allyn, "The Scent of Lilacs" (*Ellery Queen's Mystery Magazine*, September/October)
- Best young adult mystery: Charlie Price, *Interrogation of Gabriel James* (Farrar, Straus, Giroux)
- Best juvenile mystery: Dori Hillestad Butler, *The Buddy Files: The Case of the Lost Boy* (Albert Whitman)
- Best play: Sam Bobrick, *The Psychic* (Falcon Theatre, Burbank, CA)
- Best television episode teleplay: Neil Cross, "Episode 1" (*Luther*, BBC America)
- Grand Master: Sara Paretsky
- Robert L. Fish award (best first story): Evan Lewis, "Skyler Hobbs and the Rabbit Man" (*Ellery Queen*'s *Mystery Magazine*, February)
- Raven: Centuries & Sleuths Bookstore, Forest Park, Illinois (Augie Aleksy); Once Upon a Crime Bookstore, Minneapolis, Minnesota (Gary Shulze and Pat Frovarp)
- Mary Higgins Clark Award: Elly Griffiths, *The Crossing Places* (Houghton Mifflin Harcourt)

AGATHA AWARDS
(Malice Domestic Mystery Convention)

- Best novel: Louise Penny, *Bury Your Dead* (Minotaur)
- Best first novel: Avery Aames, *The Long Quiche Goodbye* (Berkley)

- Best short story: Mary Jane Maffini, "So Much in Common" (*Ellery Queen's Mystery Magazine*, September/October)
- Best non-fiction: John Curran, *Agatha Christie's Secret Notebook: 50 Years of Mysteries in the Making* (Harper)
- Best children's/young adult: Sarah Smith, *The Other Side of Dark* (Atheneum)
- Lifetime Achievement Award: Sue Grafton
- Poirot Award: Janet Rudolph

LEFT COAST CRIME AWARDS

- Lefty (best humorous mystery): J. Michael Orenduff, *The Pot Thief Who Studied Einstein* (Oak Tree)
- Bruce Alexander Memorial Historical Mystery Award: Jacqueline Winspear, *The Mapping of Love and Death* (HarperCollins)
- Hillerman Sky Award: Margaret Coel, *The Spider's Web* (Berkley)
- Watson Award: Craig Johnson, *Junkyard Dogs* (Viking)
- Lifetime Achievement Award: Martin Cruz Smith

DERRINGER AWARDS
(Short Mystery Fiction Society)

- Best Flash Fiction Story (under 1000 words) (tie): Kathy Chencharik, "The Book Signing" (*Thin Ice: Crime Stories by New England Writers*, Level Best) and Jane Hammons, "The Unknown Substance" (*A Twist of Noir*, December 27)
- Best Short Story (1,001-4,000 words): Michael J. Solender, "Pewter Badge" (*Yellow Mama*, August)
- Best Long Story (4,001-8,000 words) (tie): Sean Doolittle, "Care of the Circumcised Penis" (*Thuglit Presents: Blood, Guts & Whiskey*, Kensington) and B. K. Stevens, "Interpretation of Murder" *Alfred Hitchcock's Mystery Magazine*, December)
- Best Novelette (8,001-17,500 words): Art Taylor, "Rearview Mirror" (*Ellery Queen's Mystery Magazine*, March)
- Edward D. Hoch Memorial Golden Derringer Award for Lifetime Achievement: Ruth Rendell

DILYS AWARD
(Independent Mystery Booksellers Association)

Louise Penny, *Bury Your Dead* (Minotaur)

LOS ANGELES TIMES BOOK PRIZE

Mystery/Thriller Category
Tom Franklin, *Crooked Letter, Crooked Letter* (Morrow)

(Awarded in 2010 for material published in 2009)

EDGAR ALLAN POE AWARDS
(Mystery Writers of America)

- Best novel: John Hart, *The Last Child* (Minotaur)
- Best first novel by an American author: Stefanie Pintoff, *In the Shadow of Gotham* (Minotaur)
- Best original paperback: Marc Strange, *Body Blows* (Dundurn/Castle Street)
- Best fact crime book: Dave Cullen, *Columbine* (Twelve)
- Best critical/biographical work: Otto Penzler, ed., *The Lineup: The World's Greatest Crime Writers Tell the Inside Story of Their Greatest Detectives* (Little, Brown)
- Best short story: Luis Alberto Urrea, "Amapola" (*Phoenix Noir*, Akashic)
- Best young adult mystery: Peter Abrahams, *Reality Check* (HarperCollins)
- Best juvenile mystery: Mary Downing Hahn, *Closed for the Season* (Houghton Mifflin Harcourt)
- Best television episode teleplay: Patrick Harbinson, *Place of Execution* (PBS/WGBH Boston)
- Grand Master: Dorothy Gilman
- Robert L. Fish award (best first story): Dan Warthman, "A Dreadful Day" (*Alfred Hitchcock's Mystery Magazine*, January/February)
- Raven: Mystery Lovers Bookshop, Oakmont, Pennsylvania (Richard Goldman and Mary Alice Gorman); International Mystery Writers Festival (Zev Buffman)
- Ellery Queen Award: Poisoned Pen Press (Barbara Peters and Robert Rosenwald)
- Mary Higgins Clark Award: S.J. Bolton, *Awakening* (Minotaur)

AGATHA AWARDS
(Malice Domestic Mystery Convention)

- Best novel: Louise Penny, *The Brutal Telling* (Minotaur)

- Best first novel: Alan Bradley, *The Sweetness at the Bottom of the Pie* (Delacorte)
- Best short story: Hank Phillippi Ryan, "On the House" (*Quarry*, Level Best Books)
- Best non-fiction: Elena Santangelo, *Dame Agatha's Shorts* (Bella Rosa)
- Best children's/young adult: Chris Grabenstein, *The Hanging Hill* (Random House)
- Lifetime Achievement Award: Mary Higgins Clark
- Poirot Award: William Link

DAGGER AWARDS
(Crime Writers' Association, Great Britain)

- Gold Dagger: Belinda Bauer, *Blacklands* (Corgi)
- International Dagger: Johan Theorin, *The Darkest Room* (Doubleday UK)
- Ian Fleming Steel Dagger: Simon Conway, *A Loyal Spy* (Hodder & Stoughton)
- Non-fiction Dagger: Ruth Dudley Edwards, *Aftermath: The Omagh Bombing & the Families' Pursuit of Justice* (Harvill Secker)
- Best short story: Robert Ferrigno, "Can You Help Me Out Here?" (*Thriller 2*, Mira)
- John Creasey New Blood Dagger: Ryan David Jahn, *Acts of Violence* (Macmillan)
- Film Dagger: *Inception* (Warner Bros.)
- TV Dagger: *Sherlock* (BBC)
- International TV Dagger: *Wallender*, Series 2 (Yellow Bird Films)
- Best Actress Dagger: Maxine Peake (*Criminal Justice*)
- Best Actor Dagger: Benedict Cumberbatch (*Sherlock*)
- Best Supporting Actress Dagger: Dervla Kirwan (*The Silence*)
- Best Supporting Actor Dagger: Matthew Macfadyen (*Criminal Justice*)
- People's Detective Dagger: Christopher Foyle (*Foyle's War*)
- Hall of Fame: Frederick Forsyth, George Pelecanos
- Diamond Dagger: Val McDermid
- Ellis Peters Award Historical Dagger: Rory Clements, *Revenger* (John Murray)

- Dagger in the Library (voted by librarians for a body of work): Ariana Franklin
- Debut Dagger (for unpublished writers): Patrick Eden, *A Place of Dying*

ANTHONY AWARDS
(Bouchercon World Mystery Convention)

- Best novel: Louise Penny, *The Brutal Telling* (Minotaur)
- Best first novel: Sophie Littlefield, *A Bad Day for Sorry* (Minotaur)
- Best paperback original: Brian Gruley, *Starvation Lake* (Touchstone)
- Best short story: Hank Phillippi Ryan, "On the House" (*Quarry*, Level Best Books)
- Best critical nonfiction work: P.D. James, *Talking About Detective Fiction* (Knopf)

SHAMUS AWARDS
(Private Eye Writers of America)

- Best hardcover novel: Marcia Muller, *Locked In* (Grand Central)
- Best first novel: Brad Parks, *Faces of the Gone* (Minotaur)
- Best original paperback novel: Brian Gruley, *Starvation Lake* (Touchstone)
- Best short story: Dave Zeltserman, "Julius Katz" (*Ellery Queen's Mystery Magazine*, September/October)
- The Eye (life achievement): Robert Crais
- Hammer Award (for a memorable private eye character or series): Sharon McCone (created by Marcia Muller)

MACAVITY AWARDS
(Mystery Readers International)

- Best novel: Ken Bruen and Reed Farrel Coleman, *Tower* (Busted Flush)
- Best first novel: Alan Bradley, *The Sweetness at the Bottom of the Pie* (Delacorte)
- Best non-fiction: P.D. James, *Talking About Detective Fiction* (Knopf)
- Best short story: Hank Phillippi Ryan, "On the House" (*Quarry*, Level Best Books)

- Sue Feder Historical Mystery Award: Rebecca Cantrell, *A Trace of Smoke* (Forge)

BARRY AWARDS
(*Deadly Pleasures* and *Mystery News*)

- Best novel: John Hart, *The Last Child* (Minotaur)
- Best first novel: Alan Bradley, *The Sweetness at the Bottom of the Pie* (Delacorte)
- Best British novel: Philip Kerr, *If the Dead Rise Not* (Quercus)
- Best paperback original: Brian Gruley, *Starvation Lake* (Touchstone)
- Best thriller: Jamie Freveletti, *Running from the Devil* (Morrow)
- Best short story: Brendan DuBois, "The High House Writer" (*Alfred Hitchcock's Mystery Magazine*, July/August)
- Mystery/crime novel of the decade: Stieg Larsson, *The Girl With the Dragon Tattoo* (Knopf)
- Don Sandstrom Memorial Award for Lifetime Achievement in Mystery Fandom: Len and June Moffatt; Cap'n Bob Napier

ARTHUR ELLIS AWARDS
(Crime Writers of Canada)

- Best novel: Howard Shrier, *High Chicago* (Vintage Canada)
- Best first novel: Alan Bradley, *The Sweetness at the Bottom of the Pie* (Doubleday Canada)
- Best nonfiction: Terry Gould, *Murder Without Borders* (Random House Canada)
- Best juvenile novel: Barbara Hawarth-Attard, *Haunted* (Harper Trophy Canada)
- Best short story: Dennis Richard Murphy, "Prisoner in Paradise" (*Ellery Queen's Mystery Magazine*, January)
- The Unhanged Arthur (best unpublished first crime novel: Gloria Ferris, *The Corpse Flower*
- Best crime writing in French: Jean Lemieux, *Le mort du chemin des Arsene* (Ed. la Courte Echelle Inc.)
- Derrick Murdoch Award: Peter Robinson

THRILLER AWARDS
(International Thriller Writers, Inc.)

- Best novel: Lisa Gardner, *The Neighbor* (Bantam)

- Best first novel: Jamie Freveletti, *Running from the Devil* (Morrow)
- Best paperback original: Tom Piccirilli, *Shadow Season* (Bantam)
- Best short story: Twist Phelan, "A Stab in the Heart" (*Ellery Queen's Mystery Magazine*, February)
- ThrillerMaster Award: Ken Follett
- True Thriller Award: Mark Bowden
- Silver Bullet Award: Linda Fairstein
- Silver Bullet Corporate Award: U.S. Airways

NED KELLY AWARDS
(Crime Writers' Association of Australia)

- Best novel: Gary Disher, *Wyatt* (Text Publishing)
- Best first novel: Mark Dapin, *King of the Cross* (Macmillan)
- Best true crime: Kathy Marks, *Pitcairn: Paradise Lost* (HarperCollins)
- Best short story (S. D. Harvey Award): Zane Lovitt, "Leaving the Fountainhead"
- Lifetime achievement: Peter Doyle

LEFT COAST CRIME AWARDS

- Lefty (best humorous mystery): Rita Lakin, *Getting Old is a Disaster* (Dell)
- Bruce Alexander Memorial Historical Mystery Award: Rebecca Cantrell, *A Trace of Smoke* (Forge)
- Panik Award (best Los Angeles noir): Linda Richards, *Death Was in the Picture* (Minotaur)

STRAND CRITICS
(The Strand Magazine)

- Best novel: Michael Connelly, *Nine Dragons* (Little, Brown)
- Best first novel (tie): Josh Bazell, *Beat the Reaper* (Little, Brown); Brian Gruley, *Starvation Lake* (Touchstone)
- Lifetime achievement: Elmore Leonard

DERRINGER AWARDS
(Short Mystery Fiction Society)

- Best flash fiction story (under 1000 words: Hamilton Waymire, "And Here's to You, Mrs. Edwardson" (*Big Pulp*, November 23)
- Best short story (1,001-4,000 words): Anita Page, "'Twas the Night" (*The Gift of Murder*, Wolfmont)
- Best long story (4,001-8,000 words): Doug Allyn, "Famous Last Words" (*Ellery Queen's Mystery Magazine*, November)
- Best novelette (8,001-17,500 words): Dave Zeltserman, "Julius Katz" (*Ellery Queen's Mystery Magazine*, September/October)
- Edward D. Hoch Memorial Golden Derringer Award for Lifetime Achievement: Lawrence Block

DILYS AWARD
(Independent Mystery Booksellers Association)

Alan Bradley, *The Sweetness at the Bottom of the Pie* (Delacorte)

NERO WOLFE AWARD
(Wolfe Pack)

Brad Parks, *Faces of the Gone* (Minotaur)

HAMMETT PRIZE
(International Association of Crime Writers, North America Branch)

Jedediah Berry, *The Manual of Detection* (Penguin)

LOS ANGELES TIMES BOOK PRIZE

Mystery/Thriller Category
Stuart Neville, *The Ghosts of Belfast* (SOHO)

JON L. BREEN is the author of eight novels, most recently the comic Christmas courtroom mystery *Probable Claus* (Five Star), more than a hundred short stories, and untold thousands of book reviews and critical articles, some of which are collected in *A Shot Rang Out* (Surinam Turtle/Ramble House). Two of his volumes of criticism, *What About Murder?: A Guide to Books About Mystery and Detective Fiction* and *Novel Verdicts: A Guide to Courtroom Fiction,* won Edgar Awards, and his novel *Touch of the Past* was shortlisted for the Dagger Awards. He first contributed to *Ellery Queen's Mystery Magazine* in 1966 and still appears there frequently. He also writes regularly for *Mystery Scene* and occasionally (and non-politically) for *The Weekly Standard.* A retired librarian and English professor, he lives in Fountain Valley, California, with his wife and plot doctor Rita, with whom he collaborated on the anthology *American Murders.*

THE INTERROGATOR

DAVID MORRELL

When Andrew Durand was growing up, his father never missed an opportunity to teach him tradecraft. Anything they did was a chance for the boy to learn about dead drops, brush contacts, cutouts, elicitation, and other arts of the espionage profession.

Not that Andrew's father spent a great deal of time with him. As a senior member of the Agency's Directorate of Operations, his father had global responsibilities that constantly called him away. But when circumstances permitted, the father's attention to Andrew was absolute, and Andrew never forgot their conspiratorial expeditions.

In particular, Andrew recalled the July afternoon his father took him sailing on the Chesapeake to celebrate his sixteenth birthday. During a lull in the wind, his father told him about his graduate-student days at George Washington University and how his political science professor introduced him to a man who turned out to be a CIA recruiter.

"It was the Cold War years of the nineteen fifties," his father said with a nostalgic smile as waves lapped the hull. "The nuclear arms race. Mushroom clouds. Bomb shelters. In fact, my parents installed a bomb shelter where we now have the swimming pool. The thing was deep enough that when we tore it out later, we didn't need to do much excavating for the pool. I figured handling the Soviets was just about the most important job anybody could want, so when the recruiter finally ended the courtship and popped the question, I didn't need long to decide. The Agency had already done its background check. A few formalities still remained, like the polygraph, but before they got to that, they decided to test my qualifications for the job they had in mind."

The test, Andrew's father explained, was to make him sit in a windowless room and read a novel. Written by Henry James, published in 1903, the book was called *The Ambassadors*. In long, complicated sentences, the first section introduced a middle-aged American with the odd name of Lambert Strether, who traveled to Paris on some kind of mission.

"James has a reputation for being difficult to read," Andrew's father said. "At first, I thought I was being subjected to a practical joke. After all, what was the point of just sitting in a room and reading? After about a half hour, music started playing through a speaker hidden in the ceiling, something brassy by Frank Sinatra, 'I've Got You Under My Skin.' I remember the title because I later understood how ironic it was. Another brassy Sinatra tune followed. Then another. Abruptly, the music stopped, and a male voice I'd never heard before instructed me to put the book in my lap and describe what was happening in the plot. I replied that Strether worked for a rich woman in a town in New England. She'd sent him to Paris to learn why her son hadn't returned home after a long trip abroad. 'Continue reading,' the voice said. The moment I picked up the novel, another brassy Sinatra tune began playing.

"As I turned the pages, I was suddenly aware of faint voices behind the music, a man and a woman. Their tone was subdued, but I could tell they were angry. At once, the music and the voices stopped.

"'What's happening in the book?' the voice asked from the ceiling.

"I answered, 'Strether's worried that he'll lose his job if he doesn't persuade the son to go home to his mother.'

"'Lose only his job?' the voice asked.

"'Well, the rich woman's a widow, and there's a hint that she and Strether might get married. But that won't happen if Strether doesn't bring her son home.'

"'There were people talking behind the music'

"'Yes. A man and a woman.'

"'What were they discussing?'

"'They were supposed to meet at a restaurant for dinner, but the man arrived late, claiming last-minute responsibilities at his office. His wife believes he was with another woman.'

"'Continue reading,' the voice said."

Andrew remembered listening to his father explain how the test persisted for hours. In addition to the music, two and then three conversations took place simultaneously behind the songs. Periodically, the voice asked about each of them (a woman was fearful about an impending gall-bladder surgery; a man was angry about the cost of his daughter's wedding; a child was worried about a sick dog). The voice also wanted to know what was happening in the densely textured novel.

"Obviously, it was an exercise to determine how much I could be aware of at the same time, or whether the examiner could distract me and get under my skin," Andrew's father said. "It turned out that my political science teacher had recommended me to the Agency because of my ability to hold various thoughts at once without being distracted. I passed the test and was initially assigned to hotbed cities like Bonn, which in those days was the capital of West Germany. Pretending to be an attaché, I made chitchat at crowded embassy cocktail parties while monitoring the voices of foreign diplomats around me. No one expected state secrets to be revealed. Nonetheless, my superiors were surprised by the useful personal details I was able to gather at those diplomatic receptions: who was trying to seduce whom, for example, or who had money problems. Alcohol and the supposed safety of the chaos of voices in a crowded room made people careless. After that, I was promoted to junior analyst, where I rose through the ranks because I could balance the relative significance of various crises that erupted simultaneously around the globe."

The waves lapped stronger against the hull. The boat shifted. The memories made Andrew's father hesitate. Drawn into the past, he took a moment before glancing toward clouds moving across the sky.

"Finally, the wind's picking up. Grab the wheel, son. Check the compass. Take us southwest toward home. By the way, that James book, *The Ambassadors?* After all my effort, I was determined to finish it. In the end, it turned out that Strether's experience in Paris was so broadening that he felt he'd become smarter, aware of everything around him. But he was wrong. The rich woman's son gained his trust, only to make a fool of him. Despite all his awareness, Strether returned to America, where he assumed he'd lose everything."

•••

"Four days," Andrew promised the somber group in the high-security conference room. He was thirty-nine and spoke with the authoritative tone of his father.

"Is that a guarantee?"

"I can possibly get results sooner, but definitely no later than four days."

"There's a time element," a grim official warned, "the probability of smallpox dispersal in a subway system during peak hours. Ten days from now. But we don't know the exact time or which country, let alone which city. Our people apprehended the subject in Paris. His fellow conspirators were with him. One escaped, but the rest died in a gun battle. We have documents that indicate what they set in motion—but not the particulars. Just because they were in Paris, that doesn't rule out another city with a major subway system as the target."

"Four days after I start, you'll have the details," Andrew assured them. "Where's the subject being rendered?"

"Uzbekistan."

Andrew's beefy neck crinkled when he nodded. "They know how to be discreet."

"They ought to, given how much we pay them."

"But I don't want any foreign interrogator involved," Andrew emphasized. "Thugs have unreliable methods. A subject will confess to anything if tortured sufficiently. You want reliable information, not a hysterical confession that turns out to be baseless."

"Exactly. You're completely in charge."

"In fact, there's no reason why this needs to be an extraordinary rendition." Andrew's use of "rendition" referred to the practice of moving a prisoner from one jurisdiction to another, a common occurrence in the legal system. But when the rendition was "extraordinary," the prisoner was taken out of the legal system and placed where the normal rules no longer applied and accountability was no longer a factor. "The interview could just as easily take place in the United States."

"Unfortunately, not everyone appreciates the difference between torture and your methods, Andrew. A jet's waiting to fly you to Uzbekistan."

• • •

Andrew's father had been heavyset. Andrew was more so. A big man with a large chest, he resembled a heavyweight boxer, an impression that frequently made a detainee's eyes widen at first sight of him. With his deep, raspy voice, he exuded a sense of menace and power, causing his subjects to feel increasing dread, unaware that Andrew's true power came from numerous psychology courses taken at George Washington University, where he had earned a master's degree under a created identity.

A burly American civilian guard greeted him at a remote Uzbekistan airstrip next to a concrete-block building that was the rendering facility, the only structure in the boulder-dotted valley.

Andrew introduced himself as Mr. Baker.

The guard said he was Mr. Able. "I have the subject's documents ready for you. We know his name and those of his relatives, where they live and work, in case you want to make him talk by threatening to kill people he loves."

"That won't be necessary. I'll hardly ever speak to him." A cold wind tugged at Andrew's dark suit. When working, he always dressed formally, another way of expressing authority.

Escorted by Mr. Able, he passed through the security checkpoint, then entered the facility, which had harsh overhead lights and a row of doors with barred windows. The walls were made from unpainted cinder blocks. Everything felt damp.

"Your room's to the right," Mr. Able told him.

Andrew's travel bag contained four days of clothes, the maximum he would need. He set it on the concrete floor next to a cot. He barely looked at the stainless-steel sink and toilet. Instead he focused on a metal table upon which sat a laptop computer. "The other equipment should have arrived."

"It's been installed. But I don't know why we needed to bother. While we waited for you, my men and I could have put the fear of God into him."

"I can't imagine how that's possible when he's convinced God's on his side. Is the interpreter ready?"

"Yes."

"Reliable?"

"Very."

"Then let's get started."

•••

Andrew watched Mr. Able unlock a metal door. Holding a .45-caliber Glock pistol, the guard and two others armed with identical pistols entered the cell and aimed at the prisoner. Andrew and the interpreter stood in the open doorway. The compartment was windowless, except for the barred opening in the door. It felt damper than the corridor. The echo was sharp.

A short, gaunt Iraqi man was slumped on the concrete floor, his back against the wall, his wrists shackled to chains above his head. In his mid-thirties, he had a thin, dark face and short, black hair. His lips were scabbed. His cheeks were bruised. Dried blood grimed his black shirt and pants.

As if dazed, the subject stared straight ahead, not reacting to Andrew's entrance.

Andrew turned toward Mr. Able, his stark expression making clear that he'd sent explicit instructions not to abuse the prisoner.

"That happened when the team grabbed him in Paris," the guard explained. "He's lucky he didn't get killed in the gun battle."

"*He* doesn't think so. He wants to die for his cause."

"Yeah, well, if he doesn't talk, we can arrange for him to get his wish," Mr. Able said. "The thing is, as much as he'd like to be a martyr, I'm sure he didn't intend for any suffering to be involved." The guard faced the prisoner. "Isn't that right, chum? You figured you'd jump over the agony and get straight to the virgins in paradise. Well, you were wrong."

The prisoner showed no reaction, continuing to look straight ahead. As an experiment, Andrew raised his arm above his head and pointed toward the ceiling, but the prisoner's eyes didn't follow his broad gesture. They remained so resolutely fixed on the opposite wall that Andrew became convinced the subject wasn't as dazed as he appeared.

"Translate for me," Andrew told the interpreter, then concentrated on the prisoner. "You have information about a soon-to-occur attack on a subway system. This attack will probably involve smallpox. You will tell me exactly when and where this attack will take place. You'll tell me whether the attack does involve smallpox and how the smallpox was obtained. You'll tell me how the attack will be carried out. The next time you see me, you'll tell me all of these things and anything else I wish to know."

The prisoner kept staring straight ahead.

When the interpreter finished, Andrew pointed toward a narrow cot bolted to the floor along one wall. He told Mr. Able, "Remove it. Leave a thin blanket. Unshackle him. Lock the room. Cover the window in the door."

"Look, is all this really necessary?" the guard complained. "Just give me two hours with him and—"

Andrew left the cell.

•••

The way he avoids eye contact, Andrew thought. *He's been warned about some types of interrogation.*

Like most intelligence operatives, Andrew had received training in the ways humans processed information. According to one theory known as neuro-linguistic programming, most people were either sight-oriented, sound-oriented, or touch-oriented. A sight-oriented person tended to favor language that involved metaphors of sight, such as "I see what you mean." From an observer's point of view, that type of person tended to look up toward the left when creating a thought and to look up to the right when remembering something. In contrast, a sound-oriented person tended to use metaphors such as "I hear what you're getting at." When creating a thought, that type of person looked directly to the observer's left and, when remembering something, looked directly to the right. Finally a touch-oriented person favored metaphors such as "I feel that can work." When that type of person looked down to the left or the right, those movements, too, were revealing.

People were seldom exclusively one type, but through careful observation, a trained interrogator could determine the sense orientation an individual favored. The interrogator might ask, "What city will be attacked?" If a sound-oriented prisoner glanced directly to the left and said, "Washington," that statement was a created thought—an invention. But, if the prisoner glanced to the right and said the same thing, that statement was based on a memory. Of course, the prisoner might be remembering a lie he was instructed to tell. Nonetheless, through careful observation of eye movements, a skilled interrogator could reach reasonably certain conclusions about whether a prisoner was lying or telling the truth.

The trouble was, this particular prisoner obstinately refused to look Andrew in the eyes.

Hell, he knows about neuro-linguistic programming, Andrew thought. *He's been warned that his eye movements might tell me something about his mission.*

The sophistication made Andrew uneasy. To consider these fanatics as ignorant was a lethal mistake. They learned exponentially and seemed dangerously more complex every day.

He couldn't help thinking of the simplicity of an interrogation technique favored during his father's youth in the 1950s. Back then, a prisoner was injected with Sodium Pentothal or one of the other so-called truth serums. This relaxed a detainee to such a degree that his mental discipline was compromised, in theory making him vulnerable to questioning. But the process was often like trying to get information from a drunk. Fantasy, exaggeration, and fact became indistinguishable. Needing clarity and reliability, interrogators developed other methods.

•••

In his room, Andrew sat at his desk, activated the laptop computer, and watched an image appear. Transmitted from a hidden camera, it showed the prisoner in his cell. In keeping with Andrew's instructions, the cot had been removed. The barred opening in the door was covered. A thin blanket lay on the concrete floor. The subject's arms had been unshackled. He rubbed his chafed wrists. Now that he was alone, he confirmed Andrew's suspicions by looking around warily, no longer fixing his gaze toward a spot on a wall.

Andrew pressed a button on the laptop's keyboard and subtly increased the glare of the overhead lights in the cell. The change was so imperceptible that the subject couldn't notice. During the next four days, the intensity would continue to increase until the glare was blinding, but no moment in the gradually agonizing change would be perceptible.

Andrew pressed another button and reduced the cell's temperature a quarter of a degree. Again, the change was too small for the prisoner to notice, but during the next four days, the damp chill in the compartment would become extreme.

The subject sat in a corner with his back against the wall. In a moment, his eyes closed, perhaps in meditation.

Can't allow that, Andrew thought. He pressed a third button, which activated a siren in the prisoner's cell. On the screen, the prisoner jerked his eyes open. Startled, he looked up at the ceiling, where the siren was located. For now, the siren was at its lowest setting. It lasted only three seconds. But over the next four days, at unpredictable intervals, it would be repeated, each time louder and longer.

The prisoner would be given small amounts of bread and water to keep his strength at a sufficient level to prevent him from passing out. But the toilet in his cell would stop functioning, his wastes accumulating, their stench adding to his other sensory ordeals.

Andrew was reminded of the story his father had told him long ago on the sailboat. In his father's case, there had been various increasing challenges to his perceptions. In the prisoner's case, there would be increasing *assaults* to his perceptions. He would soon lose his sense of time. Minutes would feel like hours, and hours would feel like days. The intensifying barrage of painful stimuli would tear away his psychological defenses, leaving him so overwhelmed, disoriented, and worn down that he'd reveal any secret if only he could sleep.

•••

The prisoner lasted three and a half days. The sporadic faint siren eventually became a prolonged wail that forced him to put his hands over his ears and scream. Of course, his scream could not be heard amid the siren. Only the O of his mouth communicated the anguished noise escaping from him. The eventual searing glare of the lights changed to a pulsing light-dark, light-dark strobe effect that made the prisoner scrunch his eyes shut, straining to protect them. The thin blanket he'd been allowed was merely an attempt to give him false hope, for as the cold intensified, seeping up from the concrete floor and into his bones, the blanket gave him no protection. He huddled uselessly under it, unable to stop shivering.

•••

Again, Mr. Able and the other two guards entered the cell. Again, Andrew and the interpreter stood in the open doorway.

The prisoner twitched, this time definitely affected by Andrew's size.

"When and where will the attack occur?" Andrew asked. "Does the attack involve smallpox? If so, how did your group obtain it? How will the attack be carried out? Tell me, and this is what I'll do." Andrew took a remote control from his suit-coat pocket and pressed a button that lowered the lights to a pleasant glow.

"I'll also shut off the siren," Andrew said. "I'll make the room's temperature comfortable. I'll allow you to sleep. Wouldn't it be wonderful to sleep? Sleep is the greatest pleasure. Sleep will refresh you."

Hugging himself to keep from shaking, the prisoner confessed. Because he hadn't slept for almost four days, the information wasn't always clear. Andrew needed to rephrase questions and prompt him numerous times, on occasion reactivating the siren and the throbbing lights to jolt his nerves. In the end, Andrew learned all that he wanted, and the prisoner no longer avoided looking at him. With a beseeching gaze, the desperate man told him what he needed, and the movement of his red, swollen, sleep-deprived eyes told Andrew that he wasn't lying.

The target was New York City. The attack did involve smallpox. In four days, at five p.m. on numerous subway platforms, aerosol canisters that looked like hair-spray dispensers would be taken from backpacks. Their tops would be twisted, then returned to the backpacks. Their pressurized air would be vented through a tube in each backpack, dispersing the virus among the crowd. The victims wouldn't know about the attack until days later when symptoms of the disease began to appear, but by then, the victims would have spread the virus much farther.

As Andrew hurried toward a scrambler-equipped satellite radio to report what he'd learned, he heard muffled screams coming from another cell. Water splashed. Disturbed by the significance of the sounds, Andrew ran to an open doorway through which he saw a man strapped to a board. The board was tilted so that the man's head was lower than his feet. His head was in a brace so that he couldn't turn it from side to side. He was naked, except for his underwear. His features were covered by a cloth, but the brown color of his skin matched that of the prisoner Andrew had interrogated, making Andrew conclude that this man, too, was an Iraqi.

Mr. Able stood over this new prisoner, pouring water onto his covered face. The prisoner made a gagging sound. He squirmed desperately, barely able to move.

"Our team in Paris caught the guy who escaped," the guard told Andrew, then poured more water over the prisoner's face. "He arrived while you were questioning the other prisoner."

"Stop," Andrew said.

"You took almost four days. At the start, I told you I could get someone to confess in two hours. But the truth is, all I really need is ten minutes."

What Andrew watched helplessly was called waterboarding. The immobilized prisoner was subjected to a heavy stream of water over his face. The soggy cloth on his nose and mouth added to the weight of the water and made breathing even more difficult. The cloth covered his eyes and increased his terror because he couldn't see to anticipate when more water would strike him. The incline guaranteed that the water would rush into his nostrils.

Unable to expel the water, the prisoner kept gagging, relentlessly subjected to the sensation of drowning. Andrew knew of cases in which prisoners did in fact drown. Other times, panic broke their sanity. Intelligence operatives who allowed themselves to be waterboarded in an effort to understand the experience were seldom able to bear even a minute of it. Those prisoners who were eventually set free reported that the panic they endured created lifelong traumas that made it impossible for them to look at a rain shower or even at water flowing from a tap.

In this case, the prisoner thrashed with such force that Andrew was convinced he would dislocate his limbs.

"Okay, asshole," Mr. Able said through a translator. He yanked the drenched cloth from the victim's face.

Andrew was appalled to see a section of plastic wrap stretched over the prisoner's mouth. The only way the man could breathe was through his nose, from which water and snot erupted as he fought to clear his nostrils.

"Here's your chance not to drown." The guard yanked the plastic wrap from the prisoner's mouth. "Which subway system's going to be attacked?"

The prisoner spat water. He gasped for air, his chest heaving.

"Speak up, jerk-off. I haven't got all day."

The prisoner made a sound as if he might vomit.

"Fine." Mr. Able stretched the plastic wrap across the prisoner's mouth. He threw the dripping cloth over his face, picked up another container of water, and poured.

With his feet tilted above him, the prisoner squirmed and gagged insanely as water cascaded onto the smothering cloth and into his nostrils.

"One last time, pal." Again, the guard yanked the cloth and the plastic wrap from the prisoner's face. "Answer my question, or you'll drown. What subway system's going to be attacked?"

"Paris," the prisoner managed to say.

"You won't like it if I find out you're lying."

"Paris."

"Wait right there, chum. Don't go away" The guard left the prisoner strapped to the board and proceeded along the corridor to the man in the other cell.

"No," Andrew said. He hurried after the guard, and what he saw when he reached the cell filled him with dismay. Guards had stripped the first prisoner and strapped him to a board, tilting his head down. A cloth covered his face.

"Stop," Andrew said.

When he tried to intervene, two other guards grabbed him, dragging him back. Frantic, Andrew strained to pull free, but suddenly the barrel of a pistol was rammed painfully into his back, and he stopped resisting.

"I keep getting radio calls from nervous, important people," Mr. Able said. "They keep asking what the hell's taking so long. A lot of people will die soon if we don't get the right information. I tell those nervous, important people that you've got your special way of doing things, that you don't think *my* way's reliable, that you think a prisoner'll tell me anything just to make me stop."

"It's true," Andrew said. "Panic makes him so desperate he'll say anything he thinks you want to hear. The information isn't dependable. But *my* way strips away his defenses. He doesn't have any resistance by the time I finish with him. He doesn't have the strength to lie."

"Well, Mr. Baker, waterboarding makes them too terrified to lie." The guard began pouring water over the prisoner's face. It took less time than with the other man, because this prisoner was already exhausted from the sensory assaults that Andrew had subjected him to. He struggled. He gagged. As water poured over his downward-tilted face, rushing into his nostrils, he made choking sounds beneath the smothering cloth.

"What subway system's going to be attacked?" Mr. Able demanded.

"He already told me!" Andrew shouted.

"Well, let's hear what he answers *this* time." The guard ripped the cloth and a strip of plastic wrap from his mouth.

"Paris," the prisoner moaned.

Andrew gaped. "No. That's not the answer he gave me. He told me New York City."

"But now he says Paris, and so does the other guy. Paris is where they got captured. Why else would they be there if they weren't going to attack it? Enough time's been wasted. Our bosses are waiting for my report. We don't need you here. I'm the interrogator they should have hired."

"You're making a mistake."

"No, *you* made the mistake when you took so damned long. We can't waste any more time."

Andrew struggled to pull away from the guards who held his arms so tightly they made his hands numb, restricting the flow of blood. "Those people you want to impress—tell them the target's either New York *or* Paris. Tell them to increase surveillance at *all* the major subway systems but to emphasize New York and Paris. Four days from now. Thursday. Five p.m. local time. The attackers will wear backpacks. They'll have hair-spray canisters inside the backpacks. The canisters hold the smallpox."

"I haven't started questioning these maggots about the other details," Mr. Able said. "Right now, I just want to let everybody know the target area."

"When they confessed to you, they never looked at you!" Andrew shouted.

"How the hell could they look at me when their heads were braced?" Mr. Able demanded. "I was standing to the side."

"Their eyes. They should have angled their eyes toward you. They should have used their eyes to beg you to believe them. Instead they kept staring at the ceiling, the same way the first prisoner stared at the wall when I got here."

"You expect me to believe that NLP shit? If they look to the left, they're making things up. If they look to the right, they're remembering something. So they look at the ceiling to keep me from knowing if they're lying or not."

"That's the theory."

"Well, suppose what they're remembering is a lie they rehearsed? Left. Right. None of it means anything."

"The point is *they* think it means something. That's why they won't look at you. After three and a half days, when the man I interrogated was ready for questioning, he couldn't stop looking at me. His eyes wouldn't stop pleading for me to let him sleep. And he always looked to the right. Maybe he remembered a lie, but at least, his eyes didn't tell me he was inventing something. The men you waterboarded, though, when they confessed, they didn't give you a chance to learn *anything* from their eyes."

"But…" A sudden doubt made Mr. Able frown. "If you're right, the only way that would work…"

"…is if they were waterboarded other times. As part of their training," Andrew said. "Once they adjusted to it, their trainer could condition them to control their eyes."

"But the panic's overwhelming. No one would agree to be waterboarded repeatedly."

"Unless they welcome death."

The stark words made the guard cock his head, threatened by Andrew's logic.

Apparently the other guards reacted the same way. Confused, they released him. Feeling blood flow into his arms, Andrew stepped forward. "All these prisoners want is to die for their cause and go to paradise. They're not afraid of death. They welcome it. How can waterboarding make them panic?"

A long moment passed. Mr. Able lowered his gaze toward the water and scum on the floor. "Report whatever the hell you want."

"I will in a moment." Andrew turned toward the other guards. "Who stuck the pistol into my back?"

The man on the right said, "I did. No hard feelings."

"Wrong." Andrew rammed the palm of his hand against the man's face and shattered his nose.

•••

Four days later, shortly after five p.m. eastern standard time, Andrew received a radio message that five men with backpacks containing smallpox-dispersal cans had been arrested as they attempted to enter various sections of the New York City subway system. A weight seemed to fall from his chest. For the first time in a long while, he breathed freely. After the confidence with which he'd confronted Mr. Able, he'd begun to be troubled by doubts. So many lives depended on his skills. Given the sophistication of the prisoners, he'd been worried that, for once, he might have been fooled.

He was in Afghanistan now, conducting another sensory-assault interrogation. As before, the person usually in charge resented his intrusion and complained that he could get results much faster than Andrew did.

Andrew ignored him.

But on the eve of the third day of the interrogation, when Andrew was sure that his prisoner would soon lose all his psychological defenses and reveal what Andrew needed to know, he was again reminded of his father. He sat before the computer on his desk, watching the image of the prisoner, and he recalled that his father had sometimes been asked to go to the Agency's training facility at Camp Peary, Virginia, where he taught operatives to extend the limits of their perceptions.

"It's like most things. It involves practice," his father had explained to Andrew. "For old times' sake, I made my students read *The Ambassadors.* I tried to distract them with blaring music. I inserted conversations behind the music. A layer at a time. After a while, the students learned to be more aware, to perceive many things at once."

As Andrew studied the computer screen and pushed buttons that flashed the blinding lights in the prisoner's cell while at the same time causing a siren to wail, he thought about the lesson that his father had said he took from that Henry James novel.

"Lambert Strether becomes increasingly aware as the novel progresses," Andrew's father had told him. "Eventually, Strether notices all sorts of things that he normally would have missed. Undertones in conversations. Overtones in the way someone looks at someone else. All the details in the way people dress and what those details say about them. He becomes a master of consciousness. The sentences dramatize that point. They get longer and more complicated as the novel progresses, as if matching Strether's growing mind. I get the sense that James hoped those complicated sentences would make the reader's mind develop as Strether's does. But this is the novel's point, Andrew. Never forget this, especially if you enter the intelligence profession, as I hope you will. For all his awareness, Strether loses. In the end, he's outwitted. His confidence in his awareness destroys him. The day you become most sure of something, that's the day you need to start doubting it. The essence of the intelligence profession is that you can never be aware enough, never be conscious enough, because your opponent is determined to be even more aware."

Andrew kept watching the computer screen and the agony of his prisoner as lights flashed and sirens wailed. Abruptly he pressed buttons that turned off the lights and the siren. He wanted to create ten minutes of peace, ten minutes in which the prisoner would be unable to relax, dreading the further assault on his senses. It was a hell that the prisoner would soon do anything to end.

Except, Andrew thought.

The day you become most sure of something, that's the day you need to start doubting it. His father's words echoed in Andrew's memory as he thought about his conviction that the only sure method of interrogation was his own. But was it possible that…

A threatening idea wormed into Andrew's imagination. An operative could be trained to add one perception onto another and then another until he or she could monitor multiple conversations while reading a book and listening to brassy music.

Then why couldn't an operative of a different sort be trained to endure deepening cold, throbbing lights, and wailing sirens for three and a half days without sleep? The first time would be agony, but the agony of the second time would perhaps be less because it was familiar. The third time would be a learning experience, testing methods of self-hypnotism to make the onslaught less painful.

Watching the prisoner's supposed anguish, Andrew felt empty. Could an enemy become that sophisticated? If they learned NLP in order to defeat it, if they practiced being water-boarded in order to control their reactions to it, why couldn't they educate themselves in other methods of interrogation in order to defeat *those?* Any group whose members blew themselves up or infected themselves with smallpox to destroy their enemies and thus attain paradise was capable of anything.

Andrew pressed buttons on his computer keyboard and caused the strobe lights and siren to resume in the prisoner's cold cell. Imagining the blare, he watched the sleepless prisoner scream.

Or was the prisoner only pretending to have reached the limit of his endurance? Andrew had the troubling sense that the man on the screen was reacting predictably, almost on schedule, as if the prisoner had been trained to know what to anticipate and was behaving the way an interrogator would expect.

But how can I be sure? Andrew wondered. *How much further do I need to push him in order to be confident he isn't faking? Four and a half days? Five? Longer? Can anyone survive that and remain sane?*

Andrew recalled his father telling him about one of the most dramatic interrogations in American espionage. During the 1960s, a Soviet defector came to Washington and told the CIA that he knew about numerous Soviet moles in the U.S. intelligence system. His accusations resulted in investigations that came close to immobilizing the Agency.

Soon afterward, a second Soviet defector came to Washington and accused the first defector of being a double agent sent by the Soviets to paralyze the Agency by making false accusations about moles within it. In turn, the first defector claimed that the second defector was the true double agent and had been sent to discredit him.

These conflicting accusations finally brought American intelligence operations to a standstill. To break the stasis, the second defector, who'd been promised money, a new identity, and a consulting position with the Agency, was taken to a secret confinement facility where he was interrogated periodically for the next five years. Most of that time was spent in solitary confinement in a small cell with a narrow cot and a single lightbulb in the ceiling. He was given nothing to read. He couldn't speak to anyone. He was allowed to bathe only once a week. Except for the passage of the seasons, he had no idea what day or week, month or year it was. He tried making a calendar, using threads from a blanket, but each time he completed one, his guards destroyed it. His boarded window prevented him from ever breathing fresh air. In summer, his room felt like a sweatbox. For five hundred and sixty-two days of those five years, he was questioned intensely, sometimes around the clock. But despite his prolonged ordeal, he never recanted his accusation, nor did the first defector, even though their stories were mutually contradictory and one of them must have been lying. Nobody ever learned the truth.

Five years, Andrew thought. *Maybe I'm being too easy. Maybe I need more time.*

Suddenly wishing for the innocent era of Sodium Pentothal, he pressed another button and watched the prisoner wail.

It seemed the man would never stop.

As the father of the modern high-action thriller, and the creator of such universal icons as Rambo, **DAVID MORRELL**'s influence on the fiction and film of our time cannot be overestimated. Whether working in thrillers, suspense, horror or even the western, Morrell's indelible style and storytelling skills have been celebrated and honored by writers and critics around the world. Morrell is a co-founder of the International Thriller Writers organization. To research the aerial sequences in *The Shimmer,* he became a private pilot. Morrell is a three-time recipient of the distinguished Bram Stoker Award. Comic-Con International honored him with its Inkpot Award for his lifetime contributions to popular culture. The International Thriller Writers organization gave him its prestigious ThrillerMaster Award. With eighteen million copies of his work in print, his work has been translated into twenty-six languages. He is also a consummate short story writer and his "The Interrogator" gives us the title for this collection.

THE LIST

LOREN D. ESTLEMAN

THE SHOP WAS ONE OF DOZENS LIKE IT IN TIJUANA, WITH LOUIS Vuitton knockoffs hanging like Chinese lanterns from the ceiling, shelves of ceramic skulls wearing Nazi biker helmets, and cases of vanilla extract in quart bottles, the kind the Customs people seized at the border to prevent parasites from entering the U.S. A muumuu covered the female shopkeeper's tub-shaped body in strips of crinkly bright-colored cloth, and until she moved to swat a *cucaracha* the size of a field-mouse on the counter, Valentino thought she was a giant piñata.

"Buenos días, señora," he said.

"Buenos noches, señor," she corrected, scraping off the remains on the edge of a large can of refried beans.

It was, indeed, evening. He'd started out from L.A. early enough to get there by nightfall, but the rickety heap he was driving these days had blown a radiator hose in San Diego and it had taken the mechanic two hours to fashion a replacement because that model hadn't been made since Nixon.

"Buenos noches. Yo busto un hombre Americano se gusta—"

"I beg your pardon, sir, but are you trying to say you are looking for someone?"

"You speak English?"

"Everyone in Tijuana speaks English, but no one understands whatever language you were speaking. Whom do you seek?"

"An elderly gentleman named Ralph Stemp."

She smacked the swatter again, but this time there appeared to be nothing under it but the counter. "I do no favors for friends of Stemp. You must buy something or leave my store."

He decided not to argue with her scowl. He took a box of strike-anywhere matches off a stack and placed it before her. She took his money and made change from a computer register; the bronze baroque antique on the other end of the counter was just for show. He said, "I don't know Mr. Stemp. I'm here to do business with him."

"If it is money business, pay me. He died owing me rent."

He had the same sudden sinking sensation he'd felt when the radiator hose blew.

"I spoke to him on the phone day before yesterday. He was expecting me."

"Yesterday, in his sleep. He's buried already. He made all the arrangements beforehand, but he forgot about me."

Remote grief mingled with sharp frustration. Ralph Stemp was one of the last of the Warner Brothers lineup of supporting players who appeared in as many as ten films a year in the 1940s, more than double the number the stars made. He was always some guy named Muggs or Lefty and usually got shot in the last reel. Whatever insider stories he had had gone with him to his grave.

That was the grief part. The frustration part involved the unsigned contract in Valentino's pocket. A cable TV network that specialized in showing B movies was interested in a series of cheap heist pictures the ninety-year-old retired actor had directed in Mexico a generation ago, and Stemp had agreed to cut the UCLA Film Preservation Department in on the sale price if Valentino represented him in the negotiations. The films were trash, but they were in the university archives, and the department needed the money to secure more worthwhile properties. Without the old man's signature, the whole thing was off.

He excused himself to step out into the street and use his cell. Under a corner lamp a tipsy *norteamericano* couple in gaudy sombreros posed for a picture with a striped burro belonging to a native who charged for the photo op.

"Smith Oldfield here." There was always a whiff of riding leather and vintage port in that clipped British accent. The man who for all Valentino knew ate and slept in the offices of the UCLA Legal Department listened to the bad news, then said, "You should have faxed him the contract instead of going down there."

"He didn't trust facsimile signatures. It was his suspicion and resentment that swung the deal. He never forgave the country for branding him a Communist, or the industry for turning its back on him. He agreed to the split so he wouldn't have to deal directly with anyone in the entertainment business."

"I'm surprised he trusted you."

He took no offense at that. "I ran up a monstrous long-distance bill convincing him. I suppose now we'll have to start all over again with his estate."

"A U.S. citizen residing in Mexico? With two governments involved, you'd be quicker making peace in the Middle East. And the heirs might not share his distaste for Hollywood. In that likelihood they'd cut you out and make the deal themselves."

"He outlived all his relatives, and judging by his crankiness in general I doubt he had any close friends."

"Have you any idea what happened to his personal effects?"

"I can ask his landlady. Why?"

"It's a longshot, but if he left anything in writing that referred to the terms of your agreement, even a doodle, it might accelerate the process. The probate attorneys could take their fees out of his share in the sale."

Valentino thanked him and went back inside to talk to the human piñata. She said, "The room was furnished. Everything he owned fit in a suitcase. No cash, and not even a watch worth trying to sell. Some rags and papers. You can have it all for what he owed me. One hundred sixty dollars American."

"What kind of papers?"

She smirked. "A map to a gold mine in Guadalajara. Go down and dig up a fortune."

"Can I take a look?"

"This is a retail shop. The peep show's across the street."

He exhaled, signed three traveler's checks, and slid them across the counter. The woman held each up to the light, then locked them in the register and moved with the stately grace of a tramp steamer through a beaded curtain in back. She returned carrying an old-fashioned two-suiter and heaved it up onto the counter.

He frowned at the shabby piece of luggage, held together by a pair of threadbare straps. He'd be months wheedling reimbursement out of the department budget, if the bean-counters even signed off on it. He'd given up on disposable income the day he undertook the mortgage on a crumbling movie theater that resisted each step in the renovation the way a senile old man fought change. It was his home and his hobby and his curse.

"I'm closing," she said when he started to unbuckle one of the straps. "Open it someplace else."

Tijuana reminded him too much of *Touch of Evil* to stay there any longer than he had to, but he didn't want to risk taking the suitcase to the American side without knowing what it contained; an undeclared bottle of tequila, or perhaps an old movie man's taste for the local cannabis, would look bad on a job application under "Have you ever been convicted of a felony?" after UCLA let him go. He drove around until he spotted a motel belonging to an American chain and booked a room. He was free of anti-Mexican prejudice but border towns were affiliated with no country but Hell. Alone in a room with all the personality of a Styrofoam cup, he hoisted the suitcase onto the piece of furniture motel clerks regard as a queen-size bed and spread it open.

He sorted the contents into separate piles: a half-dozen white shirts with frayed collars and yellowed buttons, three pairs of elastically challenged sweatpants, a gray pinstripe suit with a Mexican label (fused at the seams rather than sewn), filthy sneakers, a pair of down-at-heels wingtips, socks and underwear in deplorable condition, an expired Diners Club card in a dilapidated wallet empty but for a picture of Deanna Durbin (just how long *had* it been since wallets came with pictures of movie stars?), a Boy Scout knife, two tablets of Tums in foil wrap—pocket stuff—a three-dollar digital watch, still keeping time after its owner had ceased to concern himself with such information, restaurant receipts (Stemp seemed to have gone out of his way to avoid Mexican cuisine, but his tastes and more likely his budget had run toward American fast food), dozens of folded scraps of paper that excited Valentino until they delivered only grocery lists of items that could be prepared on a hot plate or microwave; receipts for prescription drugs, which if he'd left any behind, his landlady had appropriated for sale on the black market. Other ordinarily useful things, pens and pencils and Band-Aids, had probably been seized by default for the service they offered.

A sad legacy, tins; that nine decades of living should yield so little of material value made a bachelor in his thirties wonder about his own place in the Grand Scheme. Well, he had hardly anticipated a complete print *of Metropolis,* but even the gossamer hope he'd been handed by Smith Oldfield, of some evidence to support the agreement he'd spent so many user minutes hammering out with the old man, had come to nothing.

Valentino lingered over the heaviest object in the case, a nine-by-twelve loose-leaf notebook bound in green cloth, faded, grubby, and worn shiny in patches by what appeared to have been many hands. The yellowed ruled sheets inside, dog-eared and thumb-blurred, reminded him of a dozen last days of school, when the detritus at the bottom of his locker served up the remains of the crisp stationery of the back-to-school sales of September. It seemed to contain a list, neatly typewritten in varying fonts as if it had been added to on different machines over time, and totally indecipherable. It appeared to be made up of random letters, suggesting no language he'd ever seen.

A code. Wonderful. From crossword puzzles to Rubik's Cube to Sudoku, there wasn't a conundrum or a cryptogram in existence that couldn't leave Valentino in the dust. He could track down a hundred feet of *London After Midnight* in a junk shop in Istanbul, but *Where's Waldo?* stumped him every time. If there wasn't an obvious motion-picture connection, he was useless.

There were a hundred pages at least, many of them torn loose of the rings and as yellow and tattered as ancient parchment, scattering crumbs like old bread when he turned them. He was a paleontologist of a very special sort, brushing the dust off the bones of obsolete civilizations; dead-end species (early 3-D, Sensurround, scenes hand-tinted frame by frame), but this was an artifact outside his area of expertise.

A prop, possibly, from one of Stemp's Mexican-movie atrocities; although from *prima facie* evidence the old man had saved nothing from his long career in movies, probably because of bitter memories.

He laid the notebook aside, exhaled again. Success and fame had always been a crapshoot, but a man's life ought to boil down to more than the contents of a suitcase in Tijuana.

•••

"You might have thought to bring me a bottle of mescal, with a real worm in the bottom," Kyle Broadhead said. "All you can get up here is a piece of licorice. Fine protégé you turned out to be."

They were sitting in the professor's Spartan office in the power center, unchanged since the campus had ceased to draw all its utilities from a single source. Only a smiling picture of the shaggy-haired academic's young love interest on the desk relieved the palette of gray cinder block and steel. Valentino smiled, opened his bulky briefcase, and set a bottle on the desk. "I had just enough cash left to pay the duty. Señora Butterworth took all my traveler's checks."

Broadhead beamed and stood the bottle in his file drawer, which rattled and clinked when he pushed it shut. "I talked to Smith Oldfield this morning. Any luck with Stemp's things?"

"I don't know how a man can live so long and leave so little behind. I'm one-third his age and I needed a tractor-trailer to move half a mile from my old apartment into the Oracle."

"That's because you're a pack rat. Your office looks like the Paramount prop department. You have to travel light in this life or your heirs will pick apart your carcass. What else is in the case? You didn't need it to run liquor across the hall."

"I was hoping you could tell me." He took out the heavy looseleaf notebook and laid it on the desk.

The professor's expression alarmed him, as blank and gray as the walls of the office, his eyes fixed on the object as if it were a dangerous animal. Valentino thought he was having a seizure.

"Kyle, what's wrong?"

"Where did you get that?"

"Stemp's suitcase. Do you know what it is?"

"Do *you* know what it is?"

Under other circumstances he'd have suspected his mentor of teasing, but the dead grimness on his face was something new in their long association. "I can't make head or tail of it. It seems to be written in code. I'm pretty sure it's a list of some kind."

"A list of some kind. You young fool. You carried that across the border? You should've thrown it into a volcano in Mexico."

"What is it, the formula for the atomic bomb?"

"As bad as. Sixty years ago it blew Hollywood to smithereens."

•••

Valentino kept the lid clamped on his curiosity while Broadhead fired up his ancient computer, a great steel-cased anachronism that was all one piece, monitor, keyboard, and tower; he practically expected the professor to start it by pulling a rope. It made various octogenarian noises under the whoosh of a built-in cooling fan while he worked the keys in a blur of index fingers.

"I'm looking up Stemp's biography," he said, his face bathed in the greenish glow from the screen. He looked like a mad scientist in a Hammer film. "There has to be some explanation for how he came by that thing."

"Right now I'd settle for an explanation of how you know what it is."

"The one and only time I saw it was in Darryl Zanuck's office at Fox. It isn't likely I'd forget it. He was in a power struggle with his son at the time, and preoccupied; he left the thing out while he went to see what became of his secretary. I was interviewing him for my book, and I wasn't about to give up the opportunity to snoop. I wish I had. It'd be easier to convince myself it was a myth."

"What *is* it?"

"You haven't guessed? I did, and I'd never even heard it described. Ah!" He sat back, still staring at the screen.

Valentino got up and went behind the desk to watch over his shoulder. A postcard-size photo of a young Ralph Stemp in padded shoulders and a snap brim hat accompanied a lengthy text and a sidebar listing his screen credits, beginning with a non-speaking bit in *Hot Town* in 1937 and ending with an unbilled cameo in *Clash of the Gladiators,* shot in three weeks in Mexico in 1962 on a shoestring budget. When the House Un-American Activities Committee interrogated him in 1950 about the presence of his name on a list of subscribers to *The Daily Worker,* he refused to answer, spent a month in jail for contempt of Congress, then went south to form an independent production company after U.S. studios turned their backs on him. He never returned to his native soil.

"No help," Broadhead said. "The rest is personal. Married, divorced, predeceased by a son. I saw the notebook in Zanuck's possession twenty years after Stemp expatriated."

"'Son' is highlighted. Try clicking on it."

He did so, and stuffed his pipe while waiting for the computer to respond. It wasn't geared to take advantage of the university's high-speed connection.

When at last the son's entry appeared, they looked at a grainy resume shot of a pasty-faced young man who bore scant resemblance to his father and two brief paragraphs on his life.

Broadhead laid aside the pipe. "Ralph Stemp, Junior. Had his name legally changed to Richard Stern, for obvious reasons, not that it did much for his career."

Valentino's eyes moved faster. "Keep reading."

"Huh."

Stern had been arrested for questioning after Darryl Zanuck's office at Twentieth Century Fox was broken into and vandalized in 1970. He'd been overheard making threats against the studio for dropping his contract after small parts in drive-in features, but the police released him when Zanuck declined to press charges. A month later, accidentally or on purpose, Stern died of an overdose of sleeping pills.

"Not before doing his old man a favor," Broadhead said. "I wonder if he sent him the notebook or delivered it in person."

"It doesn't say anything was reported missing."

"That would make it hard to deny it ever existed. A trial would have brought it out into the open, and the lawsuits would've bankrupted every studio in town. Zanuck was losing his grip or he'd have burned it. The witch hunts were over."

Valentino saw the dawn then, shining merciless light on the darkest chapter in Hollywood history. "You mean this list—"

Broadhead picked up his pipe and tamped the tobacco with his thumb, watching him over the bowl. "You didn't really think it was black, did you?"

•••

The film archivist returned to his seat. His legs felt rubbery. All his life he'd heard about the Hollywood Blacklist, compiled early in the Cold War when Washington had shifted its attention from Axis saboteurs to Communist infiltration of American society. Investigations into the alleged subversive influence of films had panicked the industry into expunging from its midst everyone who came under suspicion of harboring sentiments Congress considered unpatriotic. If your name appeared on the list, you were through in pictures.

"I always thought the list was symbolic," he said. "I thought it was just word-of-mouth."

"It was the only thing those old moguls ever shared with one another." Broadhead lit his pipe, violating university regulations and California law; he wasn't likely to be turned in by anyone who valued him as a pillar of the institution. "They were scared, sure, but it gave them a honey of an excuse to trim personnel and the budget with the Supreme Court pressuring them to sell off their theaters. A lot of innocent names wound up in that notebook."

"They were *all* innocent, Kyle. The Constitution protects every citizen's right to his beliefs, whatever his politics."

"You know nothing about that time. Your parents weren't even born when the Hollywood Ten stood trial."

Valentino was shocked by his friend's vehemence. He'd never seen him so worked up over events, current or otherwise. He said himself he hadn't voted in the last six presidential elections. A little levity seemed indicated. "I thought all you college professors were flaming liberals."

"Not quite all. Our employers are government-funded, so it's no surprise so many of my colleagues don't support conservatism and tax breaks. An old widower like me doesn't need much to live on, and I have an income from outside these hallowed halls." Which was no less than fact. *The Persistence of Vision,* his seminal work on the history and theory of film, had been in print for thirty years. Broadhead was the only film instructor in the country who hadn't made it a required text in his classes.

In any case, his feathers appeared to be smoothing out. He cut the power to his computer (he never bothered to shut down programs, and never complained about losing anything as a result); it made a whistling noise like a bomb falling in a war movie and went silent. "Do you know how the list got started?"

"It was based on names provided by witnesses friendly to the Congressional investigation."

"No. Those came later. The first forty or so were taken from a statement signed by a hundred and fifty American intellectuals in support of Stalin's purge of his political enemies in nineteen thirty-eight. Bud Schulberg and Dorothy Parker were among them, and they recruited as many of their show-business friends as possible. Bear in mind, the next time some neo-pinko squirt starts sniveling about all those poor souls who lost their jobs, that it all began with a petition that condoned mass murder by a man responsible for slaughtering twenty million of his own people."

"I didn't know that."

"To be fair, neither did they at the start. But I never heard of any of them coming forward later to set the record straight. Take the c out of 'activist' and what do you have?"

Valentino smiled. "'Atavist'; but only if you can't spell."

"That's why God made copy editors." Broadhead puffed smoke at the nicotine stain on the ceiling. "At least the studio chiefs suspected on some level that what they were doing was wrong, and that they might have to pay for it someday. That's the reason they put the list in code and kept the key."

"What *is* the key?"

"Who cares now? The men who shared the list are dead and so are most of the people on it. The damage to the rest can't be undone. Cracking it would be a waste of time."

"Kyle, you're the least curious academic I ever met."

"At my age I haven't time to be generous with my curiosity."

"Do you think Richard Stern's death is suspicious?"

"If it was arranged, it flopped, or they'd have gotten the list back. I never buy a suicide cocktail as a murder weapon. It's a Hollywood cliché. I'm more interested in what Stern's father had to gain by hanging on to the list."

"Blackmail?"

"Ransom, at first. But the men who built the movies would have been stubborn enough to tell him where to stick it, and try to reconstruct it from memory. Later, when the studio system tottered, he might've squeezed an income from them in return for not going public. By then, his Mexican film venture had failed. Then, when the last of the moguls died, he'd have been on his own again, living hand to mouth. That's why he died owing rent."

"Leaving the Film Preservation Department in the lurch."

"Wake up. What are a bunch of badly dubbed crime movies worth to a station broadcasting to insomniacs at four A.M.?"

"Hundred thousand, give or take; too much to sniff at, the state our treasury's in. And my ten-percent finder's fee would put me a step closer to finishing the Oracle before I'm too old to attend the grand opening."

The professor grimaced and knocked the smoldering plug out of his pipe into his empty wastebasket. He kept a paperless office, with his vast store of motion-picture history locked in his head. "Last year an advance poster for the original nineteen thirty-one *Frankenstein* went on the block at Christie's. It was the only one known to exist that advertised Bela Lugosi as the monster, before he dropped out of the production and Boris Karloff took his place. Do you remember what it went for?"

"I was in England at the time, chasing down *Charlie Chan Carries On*. It was predicted to go for a million."

"Seven hundred thousand. The second-highest bidder dropped out, believing that a duplicate poster might surface sometime and slash its value in half. There was no guarantee that only one was printed."

"I see where you're going."

"If you didn't, I'd resign as your mentor." Broadhead pointed at the notebook, but refrained from touching it; it was as if he thought it might spit venom. "This is a one-of-a-kind item, no warranties necessary. There are no copies, because that would have multiplied the risk of the studios' biggest secret falling into the wrong hands. It's more famous than *Citizen Kane, Gone With the Wind,* and the Jerry Lewis canon combined."

"Jerry Lewis?"

"He cracks me up; sue me. And don't get me wrong just because I played devil's advocate a minute ago: It's a symbol of tyranny. A screenwriter took his life because he happened to have the same name as a writer on the list and could no longer make a living. That's evil. Don't ask me why Hitler's autograph is worth ten times as much as Churchill's. There's no arguing with the market. Evil sells. The moment the word gets out that the Hollywood Blacklist—*the* Blacklist—is available, the offers will stream in from all over the world. UCLA will have the monopoly on every elusive foot of silver-nitrate stock in both hemispheres, and you'll be able to rebuild five theaters like the Oracle from your end."

•••

He took a cab to the Commerce Bank of Beverly Hills, holding the briefcase in his lap with both hands. His car was in the university parking garage, but he was afraid it would break down again, leaving him stranded with an armload of dynamite. The bank was the closest one to campus and he wasted no time in arranging for a safety deposit box and locking away the notebook. He hoped there wouldn't be an earthquake.

Work on the Oracle was progressing slowly. The man Valentino's contractor had engaged to apply the gold leaf to the auditorium ceiling, a Tuscan, moved like a snail, but left behind a trail that glittered, and the peacocks on the new Oriental carpet slumbered beneath a dropcloth. When the film archivist had gone house-hunting, he'd had no intention of rescuing a historic picture palace from destruction, but when the opportunity had presented itself he'd lacked the fortitude to ignore it. Now he was taking peanut butter sandwiches to work, sleeping on a sofa bed in the projection booth, and spending his weekends browsing for doorknobs in shops that sold fixtures reclaimed from demolished buildings.

Of which there were more in Los Angeles than Thai restaurants and Starbucks. Sometimes he felt he was the only resident who was building up instead of tearing down.

Whenever he had the energy, Valentino liked to recreate the movie-going experience of the first half of the twentieth century. He fired up the Bell & Howell projector he was still paying for, selected a film from his small personal library of classics on safety stock, and projected them onto the new polyester screen through the aperture in the booth. But tonight he was exhausted. Rather than spend a night in the cheap motel in Tijuana, he'd driven all the way back home, arriving in the gray light of day, and had caught only two hours' sleep before reporting to work. He poked a disc into the DVD player and settled himself in front of his forty-two-inch flat-panel TV.

He watched *The Front,* Woody Allen's tribute to the victims and survivors of the Hollywood witch hunt. He laughed during the funny parts and sat riveted when Zero Mostel's desperate funnyman was forced to suicide for the indiscretion of having attended a Communist Party rally to impress a girl ("I was just trying to get laid!"). At the end he read the long list of contributors to the movie who had spent time on the Blacklist, a virtual Memorial Wall of casualties of intolerance. He'd seen it before, of course, but until he'd actually held the list in his hand it had never seemed quite real.

Paranoia had done as much as anything else to destroy the Dream Factory. The old system of feudal bosses and contract players might have survived competition from television; when Anti-Trust forced the studios to break up the theater chains that had secured their monopoly for decades, they might have muddled through. But in the end it was the industry pioneers who shot themselves in the foot. The resentment they created led to the rise of the Screen Actors Guild. From that had come power to the proletariat: The on-screen talent seized the ability to choose the roles it wanted, reject the ones it didn't, and place the future of film in dozens of hands instead of only a few.

It had been a blow for individual freedom. But it had come at a cost.

As a movie buff, Valentino remembered that some of the greatest motion pictures of all time had been made in spite of the casts' unwillingness to appear in them (*Casablanca,* for one), and that some of the worst flops had stemmed from the vanity of actors and directors overcoming doubts about whether the vehicles were appropriate *(Ishtar; Robin Hood: Prince of Thieves; Heaven's Gate,* to name a few.) An L.B. Mayer or a Sam Goldwyn would have had the gut instinct to reject such projects or reassign them to someone more appropriate. The aftermath had made the case for autocracy, even as the event that had preceded it had made the case against.

That was the clinical view. Humanity said that the life of one disillusioned screenwriter was worth more than a couple of hours spent squirming through a bad movie.

When the banging came to the front door, Valentino shot bolt upright in the sofa bed, heart pounding like *The Guns of Navarone.* He'd dreamt he was a victim of the American version of Stalin's purge, and was certain they'd come for him.

He went downstairs in his robe and opened the door on Kyle Broadhead, wearing the corduroy coat and flat tweed cap that made him look like a refugee from the Iron Curtain. "Fanta says I should apologize for the hour, but I'm not responsible for the clock. Am I too late for the last show?"

"How *is* that child you kidnapped?" Valentino let him in.

"Past the age of consent." He followed his host up the steep unfinished stairs to the projection booth and looked at the DVD case Valentino had left open. "Research, I see. Watch *High Noon* again. Allegories make better box office than polemics."

"You're unpredictable. I expected you to make some comment about Woody Allen losing his sense of humor, followed by a paragraph on Chaplin."

"*The English Patient* was funnier than both of them put together. Here." Broadhead drew a stiff sheet of pasteboard out of a saddle pocket and held it out.

Valentino took it. It was soiled and tattered at the edges, and punched full of square holes in what appeared to be a random pattern. "It looks like an old-fashioned computer punch card."

"Yours is the last generation to make that comparison. Welcome to Old Fogeyhood. Mine would say it belongs in a player piano." Broadhead unbuttoned his coat and sat in a canvas director's chair with Anne Hathaway's name stenciled on the back. "I couldn't sleep. That exasperating young woman wrung a confession out of me and sent me over. I don't suppose you'd care to offer an old man a drink on a chilly November evening."

The thermometer had read seventy when Valentino went to bed, but he rummaged out a fifth of Jack Daniel's the professor had given him for his birthday. "I don't have any Coke."

"Really. A non sequitur, I hope. Anyone who would defile premium bourbon with sugar and syrup would slap a coat of Sherwin-Williams on top of the Sistine ceiling." He poured two fat fingers into the old fashioned glass Valentino put before him and set down the bottle. "I attended Darryl Zanuck's estate sale in 1980, purely out of scholarly curiosity. I didn't expect to buy anything. I'm no hoarder, as you know."

"You make Gandhi look like a compulsive collector."

"Zanuck was a big reader; most people don't know that, but he started out as a screenwriter, and you need to be literate to commit plagiary. His complete set of Shakespeare got no takers, generic thing that it was, so in the spirit of sportsmanship I bid fifty bucks, and damn if no one took up the challenge. That slid out of *Richard III* when I took it home." He pointed at the item in Valentino's hand. "I like to think he chose the hiding place out of guilt, but his bumps of greed and lechery were too big to leave room for any other human emotion."

"I'm not sure I know what you're getting at."

"I'm sure you do."

Valentino nodded. "It's the key, isn't it?"

"The simplest in the world, but without it, the code might slow down even Stephen Hawking. I'd never have guessed what it was if you hadn't plunked that notebook down on my desk. You have to understand it was ten years between the few minutes I had at Zanuck's and the moment that thing slid into my lap."

"I'm surprised you kept it."

"I was still curious then. I never made the connection until now. I might still be wrong." His eyes pleaded for a conclusion he seemed reluctant to suggest.

Valentino spoke carefully. "Fortunately, I can't do anything tonight because the notebook's in the bank and it's closed. Otherwise we'd be up all night. We'll go over it together in the morning when we're fresh."

"Sounds fair." Broadhead finished his drink and stood. "Don't expect any big names. Edward G. Robinson was washed up already, and if you think Larry Parks was any loss, go back and watch *The Jolson Story* again. Congress took a swipe at Lucille Ball and went down hard. It gave up on Hollywood because it couldn't win votes by running people no one had ever heard of."

"I won't peek, Kyle."

"Of course you will. I recommended you for your job because you're a bloodhound."

•••

The next morning, the professor lifted a stack of *Photoplay* magazines off the chair in Valentino's office, saw no place to put it down, and sat with it on his lap. "You look like you've been up all night with Harry Potter," he said.

"Just since the bank opened." Valentino planted an elbow on either side of the notebook on his desk and rested his chin on his fists. "That piece of cardboard fit right over the sheets. The names read diagonally, the letters showing through the holes. Some surprised me, especially on the last pages. The studio bosses got carried away near the end."

"Would you have recognized any if you weren't a film geek?"

"Never having been anything else, I can't be sure. Why didn't you tell me you were on it?"

"How could I know? I only had a minute with it and I didn't have the key then. I guessed what it was, because that's what I always thought it would look like."

"You don't seem surprised."

Broadhead chuckled. "You can label anyone you don't like a subversive. I worked on *The Persistence of Vision* for twenty years, reading excerpts to book clubs and film societies. I revealed that Jack Warner shut down the Warner Brothers animation studio when he found out he didn't own Mickey Mouse. I was the first to call Howard Hughes a nut publicly. I'd be disappointed if I *weren't* on the list."

"Why did they bother? It was discredited by then."

"They'd tinkered with it too long to quit. They'd lost most of their power; the Film School Generation was forcing them out. That notebook was the one thing they still had control over. Nowadays I suppose it would be called therapeutic. They say Nixon was still adding to his Enemies List in San Clemente." He took out his pipe, but to play with, not to smoke. "Have you decided how you're going to sell it?"

"Kyle, I can't. Some of these people are still around. Even if I withheld the key, someone would be bound to crack the code, causing a lot of embarrassment. Not for you, but I see nothing but legal action against the studios for ten years. They'd go bankrupt, which would affect the entire entertainment industry. What's it matter how many old films we can buy if no one will distribute them? They cost money to restore and preserve."

"You'd still profit personally."

Valentino smiled—ironically, he hoped. "I didn't apply for this job to get rich. If they stopped making movies, what would I spend it on?"

"You can always do what Zanuck should've done."

"I can't burn it either. Knowing I'd destroyed so large a part of Hollywood history would haunt me forever."

Broadhead got up, returned the magazines to the chair, and held out a hand.

Valentino didn't move. "It would be the same if I let you burn it."

"I won't burn it. I'll slip it onto a shelf at Universal, where anyone who finds it will just think it's a prop from a spy picture. Even if he suspects what it is, he couldn't prove it without your testimony or mine, and why would he even ask us? Can you think of a better place to hide an important historical artifact than in the land of make-believe?"

"Why do I keep thinking about the government warehouse scene in *Raiders of the Lost Ark?*"

"I knew you'd appreciate it. Just as I knew you would never sell the list."

Valentino picked up the notebook and held it out. Broadhead took it, touching it for the first time. He slid the riddled sheet of cardboard from between the pages where the other had left it and put it on the desk. "No sense making it easy."

The film archivist picked up the key to the code, opened a drawer, and took out the box of strike-anywhere matches he'd bought from the woman in Tijuana. "I knew these would come in handy sometime." He struck one.

LOREN D. ESTLEMAN has been called the most critically acclaimed author of his generation. The acclaim extends to every kind of Estleman book whether the private eye series involving Amos Walker, his numerous award-winning historical westerns or his Valentino or Peter Macklin books or the outstanding novels about historical Detroit, his home turf. Estleman has been acclaimed world-wide as the finest writer of private detective fiction working in the tradition of Raymond Chandler and he has certainly earned that acclaim over and over again; the Walker books just keep on getting better. In his story in this volume you get to see the range and power of the Estleman take on both storytelling and history. Sadly the theme of this story is more timely than ever. On the horizon are novels *Burning Midnight* and *Infernal Angel* as well as a collection titled *Valentino: Film Detective.*

THE SCENT OF LILACS

DOUG ALLYN

March 11, 1865
Reynolds County, Missouri

The horsemen drifted out of the dawn mist like wolves, strung out loosely across the hillside in a ragged line, their nostrils snorting steam in the morning chill. Two outriders on the flanks, five more in the main body. Polly guessed they'd already placed riflemen along the stone fence beyond her barn, ready to cut down anyone who tried to run.

Her son was sitting on the corner of the porch, whetting the scythe, daydreaming. "Jason," Polly said quietly. "Riders are coming. Get to the barn. And walk! All the way."

Without a word, the ten-year-old rose and sauntered across the yard as he'd been taught, toting a hay blade longer than he was tall. He disappeared inside. A moment later the loading door in the upper loft inched open a crack.

Picking up a besom broom, Polly casually swept her way across the porch to the front door of the farmhouse. She opened it to sweep off the sill, then left it ajar as she turned to face the riders coming across the stubbled fields to the house.

Federals. Of a sort. Only one rider was in full uniform, a Union cavalry captain—tall, hollow-eyed, and gaunt as a vulture, with a thin moustache and goatee. His men were irregulars, dressed in a mix of work clothes and uniform coats or pants. Farmers and tradesmen, from the look of them. Definitely Union, though. Their mounts were sleek and well fed. She'd heard Forrest's men were slaughtering their horses for food.

The riders sized her up as they filed into the yard. A farm wife, square as a stump in a man's flannel shirt, canvas trousers, and pebble-leg boots. Handsome once, perhaps, but careworn now, her auburn hair wild and awry in the chill March wind, her hands reddened and rough from field work.

Polly scanned their faces, desperately hoping to recognize someone—damn. Aaron Meachum was with them, slouch hat down over his eyes, grizzled cheek distorted by a plug of chaw. Trouble.

Casually, she sidled half a step closer to the doorway.

"Good day to you, ma'am," their leader said softly. "I am Captain Charles Gilliaume, of the Eighth Missouri. My men and I—"

"These men aren't Eighth Missouri," Polly said coldly. "They're Redleg militia. Hessians, most likely."

"Hessians?"

"It's what these Rebs call the kraut-heads," Meachum said. "Like them German mercenaries back in the Revolution? Most of Sigel's troops was Germans from St. Louis when they raided through here in 'sixty-two."

"I see." The captain nodded. "You're quite right, ma'am. My men are a militia unit from Jefferson City, and many of them are of German extraction. But they're as American as you or I now. May we step down?"

"Captain, there is a creek on the far side of my garden. You're welcome to water your animals. I have nothing more to offer you. We've been picked clean by both sides. Hospitality in southern Missouri is runnin' a little thin these days, hard to come by as seed corn."

"She'd find grain quick enough if we were wearin' butternut brown," Aaron Meachum said, spitting a stream of tobacco juice onto her porch. "The whole damn McKee family's secesh; everybody 'round here knows it."

"Is that true, ma'am?" the captain asked. "I see no men about. Are they with the rebels?"

"My husband is in Springfield trying to earn a few dollars. His eldest son is with Bedford Forrest up Tennessee way, his second boy's with the Union blockade at Charleston. The two youngest headed down to Arkansas to find Sterling Price after Yank militia run off our horses in 'sixty-one."

"Rebels," Meachum spat.

"Three Confederates," Polly corrected, "and one Federal. At least they're real soldiers, Captain."

"As we are, ma'am."

"Real soldiers don't ride with trash. This fella, Aaron Meachum, is a Jayhawker who was murdering and burning in Kansas long before the war. He runs easier with coyotes than with men."

"Mr. Meachum isn't actually a member of our unit, ma'am, he was retained as a guide."

"Well, he doubtless knows the trails through these hills. He's used most of them running from the law. If he's your guide, Captain, you're on the road to perdition."

"Armies are like families, ma'am, you can't choose your kin. We're seeking slaves and deserters, Miz McKee. I'm told you have slaves here."

"Who told you that? Meachum? Look around you, Captain, this ain't no plantation. We raise saddle horses and draft animals and we're only three days from the Illinois line. Even if we held with slavery, and we don't, it's tough enough to keep animals from runnin' off, to say nothin' of men. Our stock's been stolen, our crops burned. We had no slaves before the war and we've surely no need of them now. There's only me and my boy here, you have my word."

"In that case, a search won't take long," Gilliaume said. At his nod, the troopers and Meachum began to dismount.

"No!" Polly's voice cracked like a whip, freezing them as she snaked the scattergun from inside the open door, leveling it at Gilliaume, easing back both hammers.

"Madam, be reasonable, you can't possibly prevail against us."

"That won't matter to you, Captain. Or to Meachum. Or to one or two near you. My boy is covering you from the barn with a ten-gauge goose gun loaded with double-ought buckshot. If I fire, so will he."

"And you will surely die, ma'am. As will your son."

"No matter. We only have a little flour and some cornmeal. My boy's legs are bowing from the rickets 'cause Rebs butchered our milk cow. You soldier boys have taken all but the gleanings of the fields. For God's sake, sir, your animals are better fed than most folks around here. We have nothing for you. Unless Old Sam Curtis is paying bounty money for murdering women and boys."

Gilliaume stared coolly down at Polly, ignoring the shotgun muzzle, taking her measure. She knew that look. Death had shouldered him aside to kill his friends so often that he was weary of waiting for it, impatient for his turn.

But not today. "Gentlemen, the lady says she has no slaves and I believe her. And since there's clearly no forage for us here, we'll move on."

"You're lettin' her run us off?" Meachum said, outraged. "Our orders say deserters, slaves, and arms. She's armed, ain't she?"

"So she is," Gilliaume said wryly. "Personally, I interpret our orders to mean military arms, not rusty shotguns in the hands of farm wives, but you have my permission to disarm her if you wish, Mr. Meachum. But kindly give me a moment to back my mount away. This is my best cape and bloodstains are damned bothersome to remove."

Clucking to his gelding, Gilliaume backed his mount off a few steps, touched his hat brim to Polly, then turned away. The rest of the patrol fell in behind him, moving off at a walk. Leaving her to face Meachum alone. She shifted the shotgun, centering it on his chest.

"You got yourself an edge today, Polly McKee," Meachum spat. "But you ain't seen the last of me. I expect your britches must get mighty cold with your man gone. Maybe I'll swing by another time, get a little fire goin' in them pants of yours. I'll be back."

"But not by daylight, I'll wager, you Jayhawk son of a bitch! Come ahead on, anytime, I'll give you more fire than you can handle. If you ever so much as set foot on my land again, Aaron Meachum, I swear I will blow you out of your raggedy-ass boots! Now git off my place! *Git!*" she shouted into the face of his mount, spooking the beast. It shied away, kicking. Meachum sawed at the reins but the brute's manners were no better than its owner's. Bucking and snorting, it sprinted off to rejoin the patrol, with Meachum clinging to the saddle horn, cursing his animal and Polly all the way.

The laughter and catcalls that greeted him echoed off the hills. It wasn't much comfort, but it was something.

She waited on the porch, her old scattergun in the crook of her arm, watching the troop splash through the creek and vanish into the woods beyond. And then she waited a bit longer, until she was dead certain they were gone.

Stepping into the house, she carefully stood the shotgun in its customary place by the door. And then, in the sweet-scented silence of her parlor, she released a long, ragged breath. And hugged herself fiercely, trying to control her trembling.

•••

Gus McKee sensed the danger before he heard it. Huddled over his campfire, warming his hands, he felt a sudden tingle between his shoulder blades, sharp as a nudge from a spike bayonet. Something was moving outside the flickering halo of the firelight, inching closer in the dark.

Nerves, maybe? A ghost walking on his grave?

No. The horses sensed it too, shifting uneasily in their brush corral at the base of the ridge, raising their heads, tasting the wind. Someone was circling his camp. Definitely.

Gus hadn't survived three years in these mountains by ignoring his instincts.

His battered Jenks-Remington carbine was in a rock cleft with his bedroll but the primer tape was so old the gun only fired half the time. If the intruder meant to harm him, he'd probably be dead already. Best to wait him out and—a twig snapped in the shadows.

Gus rose slowly, keeping his hands in plain sight. "Come on in, and welcome," he said quietly. "I've got no weapon, and nothin' worth stealin', but I got stew on the fire—"

"Shut your mouth. Are you alone?"

"My son's up in the ridges, hunting. He'll be back in a while, I expect."

"When did he leave?"

"I…don't recall, around noon, I guess."

"You're lying, old man. I been watching your camp since morning. Nobody's come or gone." The youth stepped out of the shadows. Tall and gawky, he hadn't seen twenty yet, but his weapon was man-sized, a Colt horse pistol, the hammer reared back, the muzzle centered on Gus's belly.

His ragged uniform jacket was so faded and grimy Gus couldn't make out its original color. Union artillery blue? Or Arkansas gray? Didn't matter which side the boy was on anyway; he'd obviously been on the dodge awhile. Dirty face, scraggly beard, sunken eyes. His cheeks were hollow from hunger.

"My name's Gus McKee, son. I give you my word you got nothin' to fear from me. I'm hidin' in these mountains, waitin' out the fight, the same as you."

"Are you a soldier?" The boy's eyes flicked around the campsite, jumpy as a cricket on a cook stove.

"I was once," Gus acknowledged. "Went down to Mexico with Winfield Scott in 'forty-six. Killed folks I had nothin' against in places you never heard of. Hell, I never heard of 'em and I was there. Still carry a musket ball in my hip from those days. One war's enough for any man. I want no part of this one."

"If you ain't a deserter, why are you hidin' out up here?"

"Me and the wife got a little stock ranch west of Reynolds. Raise mostly draft animals, a few saddlebreds. But southern Missouri's sorry country for breedin' horses nowadays. Lyon and his Hessians raided my place on their way to Springfield in 'sixty-one—"

"Hessians?"

"Germans," Gus explained. "Immigrants fresh off the boat. Strong for the Union. After Lyon got killed at Wilson's Creek, both sides started raidin' stock, burnin' our crops. Between the sojer boys and runaway slaves headed north, we're about picked clean. I brung the last of our animals up into these hills so my boys will have somethin' to come home to when it's over."

"You got boys in the fight? Which side?"

"Both sides." Gus sighed. "Oldest run away to sea in 'fifty-seven, stayed with the Union navy when war broke out. Last I heard he was on the *Hartford,* off Mobile Bay. Second oldest is with Bedford Forrest, two younger boys went off with General Price in 'sixty-two."

"And which side do you favor, Mr. McKee?"

"I favor livin' through these troubled times, same as you. Can I put my hands down? Coffee's 'bout to boil over and it's damn hard to come by in these hills. I'm pleased to share my grub with you, son, but you might as well lower that pistol. You don't want to shoot nobody."

"Want's got nothin' to do with it, mister. I'll do what I have to, if you give me cause. Understand?" But the boy holstered his horse pistol as Gus knelt to retrieve the steaming pot from the coals. Pouring two cups of scalding brew, Gus passed one to the youth, who nodded his thanks.

"I didn't catch your name, son."

"It's Mitchell. Elias Mitchell. Eli will do. And I apologize for comin' down hard on you like this. I been on the run."

"You're a Federal. From up north." It wasn't a question.

Eli nodded, sipping the coffee. "How'd you know?"

"You never heard of Hessians, for one thing. Whereabouts you from?"

"Illinois. My folks farm eighty acres near Cairo. I enlisted for a year but my unit got busted up after Perryville and the new outfit they sent me to was drafted for the duration. I've served nearly four years, and seen more killin' than…Anyways, I got a letter that said my folks are farin' poorly. I've had enough. I joined up to save the Union and free the slaves but all we're doin' now is burnin' out farms and villages, leavin' poor folks to starve. I couldn't take it no more. Lit out from Vicksburg last month, been workin' my way home since."

"You're still a ways from Illinois."

"Not as far as I was. Had a horse for a while but she went lame on me, had to turn her loose."

"Near here?" Gus asked sharply, suddenly wary.

"No, down in Arkansas, two weeks back. Why?"

"These hills may look empty, but they ain't. Union patrols are out, foraging, huntin' stragglers from both sides. Got a bounty on Union deserters, boy, twenty dollars a head."

"Twenty dollars! Hell, that's more'n we been gettin' paid!"

"It's worse than that. The bounty's for dead or alive and they ain't fussy about which."

"Man, that's crazy," Eli said, shaking his head. "You're doin' the proper thing stayin' up here, Mr. McKee. There ain't no right side in this fight no more. If there ever was."

"Maybe not. You got any money, boy?"

"Money? No sir. A few Dixie singles for souvenirs, is all. I'm afraid I can't pay you for the coffee. Sorry."

"So am I, especially since I was hopin' to sell you a horse. Is your word any good?"

"Yes sir, I believe it is," Eli said, puzzled. "Why?"

"Because I believe I'm going to loan you a horse, young Mitchell. But I want your solemn word I'll get my animal back when this war is over."

"I don't understand."

"Boy, I been shiftin' my little herd around these hills, dodgin' Union and Reb patrols, Jayhawkers and outlaws, for damn near three years now. But I know every trail and pass in these mountains. You don't. If you keep on walkin' home through the Ozarks, you'll be taken sure as God made the green apples. Maybe they'll even track you back to me. The way I see it, the sooner you're long gone from here, the better for both of us. With a horse and a little luck you can be home in a week."

"You're taking a hell of a gamble for somebody you just met, Mr. McKee. To be honest, I staked you out because I planned to steal a horse off'n you. At gunpoint if I had to."

"You're a terrible fella, young Eli, I seen that right off. Care for some more coffee?"

"I'm dead serious."

"I expect you are. But you didn't back-shoot me or try to rustle my stock, and nowadays that'll pass for righteous. Help yourself to some stew, son, before it gets cold. Come moonrise, I'll put you on an old Jayhawk trail. You can cover eight, maybe ten miles yet tonight."

"I—surely do thank you, Mr. McKee. Only it ain't quite that simple."

"Why not?"

"The past few days, I been layin' up with a wounded Reb at a spring about a mile south of here. I told him I'd fetch him some help."

"A creek with cedars around it, end of a long valley?"

"You know it?"

"I know every waterhole for sixty mile around, boy. But I ain't the only one who knows it. Yank patrols scout that valley regular."

"I didn't see no soldiers."

"Then you was lucky. How long's the Reb been there?"

"I don't know. A week, maybe. He's hurt bad. Gutshot."

"Is he a local boy?" Gus asked, swallowing.

"No sir, I believe he's from Arkansas. He's ravin' out of his head half the time. Near as I could tell, he was a lieutenant with General Price. He won't last much longer without help."

"Gutshot, he won't last long, period. Your home lies in the other direction, young Mitchell. Goin' back for that Reb will only bring trouble down on yourself, maybe on him, too."

"But I gave him my promise."

"You can't be held to that! Forgodsake, son, there's a war on. He's probably dead already. Tell you what, I'll try to look in on him in a day or two. Will that satisfy you?"

"I—guess it will have to. Thank you."

"No need for thanks. Bein' a damned fool comes natural to me. Here, get your ribs around some of this stew." Dumping a steaming mix of rabbit, wild corn, and slivered yams onto a metal plate, Gus passed it to Eli. "I don't get much news up here. How goes the war?"

"Don't know much myself," Eli mumbled around a mouthful. "Nobody tells the infantry nothin'. But from what we've been hearin', it might be over come spring."

"I've heard that joke once or twice already."

"This time it might be true. Sherman took Atlanta last fall, then burned it before he moved on to Savannah. They're burnin' everything in a sixty-mile swath. Richmond's surrounded. General Hood's still in the field, though, maybe headed for Nashville to make a stand."

"And General Sterling Price?"

"He got whipped bad at Westport in the fall, retreated back into Arkansas. I hear his men have fallen on hard times, eatin' their horses, livin' on grass…Sorry, you said your sons…?"

"Two of my boys are with Price," Gus spat. "Damned nonsense. I never owned a slave in my life, don't hold with it. But after them Yanks raided our place, there was no keepin' my boys back. Went off to fight for the Glorious Cause."

"For slavery?"

"Hell no, for independence, by our lights. To live free without Yanks or Hessians runnin' off our stock. The only slaves I've seen since the Emancipation were runaways, ragged and starvin'. Rootin' in my fields like animals. Think they're better off than before?"

"Sir, I don't believe this war's made anybody better off, black or white. The slaves we set free had nowhere to go, no food, no land. Like I said, there don't seem to be no right side to it no more. I just want to go home."

"I know the feelin'," Gus agreed. "Know it real well."

Later on, in the final faint sliver of moonlight, Gus saddled his own mare with a serviceable working rig, put Elias Mitchell aboard her, and sent him north along an old Jayhawk trace. Watching the boy move off into the shadows, Gus felt surprisingly content, considering he'd just given away a sweet-natured animal he'd raised from a foal.

But later that night, Gus woke in the darkness, tense and edgy, his hand clamped on the carbine at his side. Listening. To nothing. The keening of the wind. Foxes yapping at the stars. He'd been in these hills so long he was half wild himself. Jumpy as a mole in an anthill. But he knew something was wrong. Knew it down to his boots. He just couldn't put a name to it. So he let the fire die out, and settled himself between two boulders away from the glowing embers, keeping his carbine cocked under his threadbare blankets.

He drowsed lightly through the night, at rest, but coming instantly alert at the slightest sound. Then easing back to rest again, all the while staring slit-eyed out into the darkness.

Knowing something was wrong.

•••

At noon the next day, Polly was mucking out the barn when she heard the *tlot-tlot* of approaching hoofbeats. Meachum? Not likely, not openly. Picking up a pitchfork, she peeked out through a crack in the sagging door.

A single-seat Stanhope buggy was coming up the road from the west, a lone woman at the reins. Turning the rig in at the gate, she guided her animal down the long lane, slowing it to a walk as she approached the farmhouse.

Still holding the fork, Polly stepped out, shading her eyes, waiting. Her visitor was dressed warmly for travel, a fine seal plush cape over a tailored woolen suit, the first new clothes Polly'd seen since… she couldn't remember how long.

"Afternoon, ma'am. Can I help you?"

"Pleasse, I'm becomp lost," the woman replied, her accent harsh. Hessian. Polly's eyes narrowed. "I left Corridon this mornink—"

"Just wheel that buggy around and head out the gate, miss. A mile further on, the road splits. The north fork will take you to Centerville."

"I'm not going to Centerville."

"Look, ma'am, I haven't got all day—"

"Pleasse, I'm seeking the McKee place," the Hessian woman said desperately. "Is it far from here?"

Polly stepped closer to the buggy, frowning up at the woman. Younger than she thought, her face as pale as buttermilk, with nearly invisible eyelashes. A bruise and some swelling along her jaw. Still, all in all, a handsome girl, Hessian or not.

"What do you want with the McKees? Who are you?"

"My name iss Birgit Randolph. My husband is Tyler Randolph. He iss a cousin to Angus McKee. He—"

"I'm Polly McKee, Gus's wife. I've known Tyler since he was a sprout, but I still don't know who the hell you are. Tyler ain't married."

"We married a few months ago. We met when he was with the state militia in St. Louis. He was very…dashing. After the riots he joined General Price. We wrote back and fort' when he was in Arkansas. This past August he came for me and we were married."

"What do you mean he came for you? Came where?"

"To St. Louis. Tyler iss not a soldier anymore. He was wounded at Pea Ridge. He is discharged now."

"Wounded? How bad?"

"His leg…was shot. It is mostly healed now, but he limps. It causes him a lot of pain, I think. He never says. He's very…stubborn about it."

"That sounds like Tyler. Where have y'all been stayin'?"

"At his farm near Mountain Grove."

"I'll be damned," Polly said, shaking her head. It was too much, first Meachum and his Jayhawks, now a half-daft Hessian woman claiming to be kin. The damned war was making the world a madhouse.

"Well, you might as well step in out of the wind, miss—I mean—Mrs. Randolph. I'm afraid we're out of coffee—"

"I haff tea and some sugar," Birgit said, offering Polly a three-pound sack. "Tyler said the plundering hass been bad here."

"We get hit by both sides," Polly conceded grimly, leading the way. "Come into the kitchen, I'll make us some tea."

Birgit hesitated just inside the door. Though the walls hadn't seen paint in years, the small farmhouse was immaculate.

"You keep a fine home. Very clean. Even it smells nice."

"What did you expect? A pigpen?"

"No, I—please. I know I don't always say things right but I don't mean to make you angry. I think I've come at a bad time."

"There aren't any good times nowadays. And exactly why have you come, ma'am? What do you want here?"

"Tyler—told me to come to you. He hoped you can drive me to St. Louis then bring the buggy back here. He will send for it later."

"Send for the buggy? But not for you? Why? Is farm life too rough for your taste, missus?"

"No, I grew up on farm in Bavaria. I'm not afraid of work."

"What then? Ah, the lame dirt farmer isn't a dashing rebel lieutenant anymore? So you go runnin' home to Mama. Sweet Jesus, it serves Tyler right for marryin' a Hessian in the first place."

"I'm not Hessian."

"Don't lie to me, anybody with ears can tell what you are!"

"But I'm not!" Birgit flared, her throat and cheeks flushing, but not backing off an inch. "My family is German, but we are come from Freystadt in Bavaria! Hessians come from Hesse. I'm not Hessian! And I didn't leaf Tyler, neither. He drove me out!"

"What are you talking about?"

"It's true! I tell him our child is growing in me and he got terrible angry. He says I must go home to my family. And I say I won't. And he says I must obey him. Still I say no. And he…struck me!" Her hand strayed to her bruised mouth, her eyes brimming. "And now I am come here, and you are angry with me too—I don't know why—but I don't anymore know what to do. I don't know what to do!"

Polly knew. Wordlessly, she wrapped the younger woman in her massive arms, holding her while she sobbed like a lost child. Which she was, in a way. Good Lord, the girl couldn't be more than seventeen or eighteen. Polly was barely forty, but Birgit's age seemed like a fever dream to her, only dimly remembered now.

The low moan of the blue enameled teapot broke the spell.

"I'm sorry," Birgit said, pulling away. "This is my own trouble. I shouldn't burden you with it."

"Don't talk foolishness," Polly said, lifting the kettle off the stove lid, filling two vitreous china mugs. God help you, girl, we're family now. Sit yourself down at the kitchen table, we'll work something out."

"But how?" Birgit asked numbly, sipping the steaming brew. "Tyler doesn't want me. He doesn't want our child."

"That can't be true. He had to snake through half the damned Union army to marry you. Discharge papers or no, he could have been lynched or thrown in a Yankee prison any step of the way. Tyler's a stubborn boy; all the Randolphs are, and the McKees, too. But there's no quit in any of 'em. If Tyler was willing to risk dyin' to marry you in August, he hasn't changed his mind. There must be more to this. How are things between you two? Has he hit you before?"

"No! Never, never. It's been good with us. The best. But this last month, he's…his mood is very dark. Far off. He stays up nights, watching. There are fires in the hills near the farm. Deserters, he says. Or Jayhawkers. Then a few days ago, men took our plow horse. Five of them. Came up on Tyler in the field and just took our animal. He doesn't speak to me since. I thought telling him of the baby would cheer him but…" She swallowed, shaking her head.

Polly sipped her tea, mulling it over. "He's afraid," she said simply.

"Afraid? Tyler?"

"Oh, not of dyin'. After all the fightin' that boy's seen, death's less troublesome than a drunken uncle. No, it's you he's afraid for. Afraid he can't protect you. Or your child. That's a terrible fear for a man to face, especially a soldier like Tyler. He's seen slaughter, he knows how wrong things can go. And in his heart, he's afraid of failing you, though I doubt he realizes it."

"So he drives me away?"

"Looks like it."

"What should I do?"

"That depends. Maybe he's right, girl. God knows there's trouble in the wind around here."

"But you stay."

"I got no choice, this place is all we have. You'll be safer in St. Louis, Birgit. Maybe you should go home to your family awhile."

"No. Tyler is my family now."

"You sure about that? You seem awful young to me."

"It's true, I am, maybe. But I know. When I met Tyler, St. Louis is full of young soldiers. Thousands. And I am at a cotillion, and Tyler is laughing with his friends when he sees me. And he walks over and we talk a minute. No more. And we danced. Once. But I already know."

"Know what?"

Birgit eyed Polly's wind-weathered face warily, then shrugged. "Laugh if you want, but I look in Tyler's eyes and I see…my life. With him. I see our children. I know it sounds crazy, but…I saw all this, in that one moment. But maybe you're right, maybe I am just…Hessian."

"No. I was wrong about that. And about you. I apologize for taking that tone with you earlier. And Tyler shouldn't have treated you like he done neither, though I can't fault his reasons."

"I don't care about his reasons. He's wrong to push me away. And I was wrong to leaf. I have to go back."

"It's not that simple, girl. These are dangerous times, he's got good cause to fear for you."

"I know that. I am afraid, too. But I'm more afraid to lose him, to lose what we have together."

"Havin' a stout heart's all well and good, darlin', but it ain't hardly enough. There are men in these hills who'd kill you for your horse or a dollar. Or no reason at all. And the truth is, Tyler can't always be there to protect you. You'll have to protect one another. Do you know about guns?"

"A little. Tyler bought me a pocket pistol. He tried to teach me but I'm no good with it."

"Just like a man," Polly said drily. "Give the little lady a little gun. Know the trouble with pistols? Men don't believe a woman will shoot. Or hit anything if she does. You have to kill 'em to prove it. Or die tryin'. Over there, that's a real woman's gun," she said, indicating a coach shotgun beside the back door. "No skill required, only sand enough to touch it off. You still have to watch out for border trash, but they'd better watch out, too. I can teach all you need to know in twenty minutes. If you'd like."

"Yes, I would. Thank you."

"We'll finish our tea first, and talk a little. I seldom see other women these days. I work like a man, dress like one. Sometimes I think I'm turning into one."

"I think you are very much woman, Mrs. McKee. And your home—now don't be angry with me—it's very clean. It even smells clean. What is that wonderful scent?"

"*Eau de lilac.* Lilac water. Before the war, with the boys home and their clothes and boots and such, sometimes it'd get to smellin' like a horse barn in here. Lilac water helps. I'm surprised you can smell it at all, I've watered it down somethin' fierce tryin' to make it last. The boys each promised to bring me a fresh bottle when they went off soldierin'."

"You say boys. How many?"

"Angus had the four older boys by his first wife, Sarah. She died of the consumption, quite young. It wasn't like you and Tyler with Gus and me. We didn't meet at no dance. I was orphaned, livin' with kin and Angus needed a mother for his boys. I was only fifteen when we married. We've got a boy of our own now, Jason. And I lost a girl in childbirth. It ain't been easy for us but we've built ourselves a life here. It was a good place before the war. We'll make it so again."

"But you do…care for him? Your husband?"

"Oh, surely. He's a good man, with a good heart, and I'm…fond of him, I suppose. But it's not always easy between us. Gus is older than me, set in his ways. When I took to his bed, all I knew about love and…such things, was seeing horses or hogs breedin' in the fields. Angus was gentle with me, and mostly we pull together like a yoked team. But I can't say I've ever had a moment like you talked about, no…special feeling like that. We work hard, try to make the best we can of whatever comes. To be honest, Gus has been gone so long I wonder sometimes if things will be the same with us…afterward."

"Gone where?"

"To the hills. I tell folks he's in Springfield, but he ain't. After Price's troops got drove down to Arkansas, both sides were raidin' the border, runnin' off our stock. So Angus took the last of our horses up into the hills. He's been movin' around with 'em since, hidin' 'em away so us and the boys can start over when the war ends. If it ever does. When he left we thought it'd be for a few months.

"But it's been more than two years now. Closer to three. He slips back once a month for a few hours. Seems like it's going to go on like this forever."

"Maybe not much longer. Tyler says it will end soon."

"Darlin', I've been hearin' that ole sweet song since 'sixty-one."

"No, it is true. Tyler sees the St. Louis paper almost every month. The Federals have all the Shenandoah Valley now. Price's men are scattered. Hood is retreating from Atlanta and the city is burning."

"Atlanta burning? But why? Who fired it?"

"Union, I think, but…" Birgit shrugged helplessly. Even in faultless English, no words could explain the madness on the land.

"Dear God," Polly said, slumping back in her chair. "This war may stop someday, but it won't never be finished. Not for a hundred years. No wonder the hills are fillin' with deserters and the Jayhawkers are back on the prowl. Both sides smell blood. You need to get home, girl, if that's what you mean to do. But first I'm gonna teach you a bit about killin'. In a ladylike fashion, of course."

In a scant half-hour, Polly instructed Birgit in the basics of the short-barreled coach gun. Pointed and fired at close range, the stunted scattergun would erase anything in its path from a poplar stump to three men standing abreast.

The girl took to the gun as a practical matter, learning to deal out death in defense of herself and her own with no more compunction than killing a coyote raiding after chickens. Or a child.

Neither woman derived the pleasure men seem to take from slaughter. It was a chore to be done, perhaps more dangerous than some, but also more necessary.

At the lesson's end Birgit could manage the coach gun competently. And as she seated herself in the buggy to leave, Polly placed the stubby weapon on her lap. "You take this with you; I've got another. And if there's trouble on the road, you don't hesitate. These boys been killin' each other regular for a long time, they're damned quick about it. Surprise and that gun are all you have."

"I'm not afraid. I'll manage. If nothing else, I think Tyler will hear me out when I explain how things will be with us now."

"I expect he will at that," Polly grinned. "You can make Corridon before dusk. Stay the night there, move on in the morning. You'll be home before supper tomorrow."

"And in summer, when my time comes for the baby, can I send for you?"

"You surely can, darlin'. I'll come runnin' and we'll haul that child into this world together. I'll see you in the summer, Mrs. Randolph, maybe sooner if this madness ends and our boys come home. Meantime, you take care, hear?"

•••

Ordinarily Gus was up at first light, but his late-night sending off of Eli Mitchell and his restlessness afterward made him wake later than usual, with the darkness still dogging his spirit as the pale sun chased the timber shadows across his camp. After carefully stowing his rifle and blankets in a rock cleft, Gus used his last dab of coffee to brew a single cup, all the while troubled by the nagging sense of something amiss. Some warning sign he'd overlooked.

His supplies were down to nothing but it would be dark of the moon tonight. He could slink out of the hills to his farm. Somehow Polly always managed to scrape together a few necessaries for him; sugar, coffee. Local news and rumors of war. Enough to see him through another month of hiding out in these hills.

But before he could risk a visit home, he'd have to resolve this nettlesome worry, lest the faceless danger follow him home. Huddled in his blanket beside the embers of his campfire, Gus sipped the bitter dregs of his coffee, trying to put a face or a name to the trouble.

Had there been anything suspicious about Eli Mitchell? Something he'd said or done? Didn't seem likely. Gus had given the deserter his mare freely and had no regrets about that decision. What else could he do? Kill the boy? Drive him off?

True, he scarcely knew the lad, but Gus was a lifelong stockman. He could rank a horse at forty paces and he considered himself a fair judge of people as well. Young Eli Mitchell struck him as an honest young man. He'd promised to return the mare later on and Gus believed he would try to do so…

And that was it! That was the burr under his saddle, the itch that was rankling him.

Eli's promise.

He would try to return the mare because he'd given Gus his word of honor and he was an honest lad. But he'd also given his promise to help that wounded Reb lieutenant. And now he had a fresh horse under him and some food to share…*Damn it to hell!*

Cursing his own stupidity, Gus fetched his rifle from the cache and headed down the trail at a trot. The mare's tracks were easy to follow in the morning dew. The boy had ridden north just long enough to get out of Gus's sight, then he'd turned south, working his way back to the spring to help his wounded friend.

But Gus knew these hills far better than young Mitchell. Leaving the trail, he trotted uphill through the aspens at a mile-eating lope. A horse would have difficulty threading through the brush up to the mountain crest, but a man could manage it, and it cut the journey in half. With luck, he'd make the water hole by noon.

But Gus was running low on luck. And Eli Mitchell's was gone altogether.

As Gus crested the ridge overlooking the valley, he heard a shout, then the thunder of hoof beats. Walking the mare through the trees at the edge of the valley, Eli Mitchell had been spotted by a Union patrol. Though he was clearly trapped, the boy never hesitated. Scrambling into the saddle, Eli wheeled his mount and he raced down the valley toward the mouth, leading them away from the spring. The patrol fanned out to intercept him, cutting him off easily, encircling him before he'd covered half a mile.

Dropping to his belly on the ridge, Gus fumbled in his pouch for the brass-cased Mexican field glass, his only trophy from that long-ago war. Snapping it open, he hastily homed in on the meadow below, bringing it into focus. It was already over. The Union patrol had Eli surrounded. The boy dropped his reins and held both hands high in the air as the troopers closed in, weapons at the ready.

Gus was too far away to make out faces clearly. Didn't recognize the officer in charge. A captain, tall, gaunt, with a Van Dyke goatee, a cape, and a French-style kepi forage cap. Judging from their mismatched uniforms, the troopers were militia. Probably Hessians from St. Lou or Jefferson City. But their civilian scout…

Damn! Gus recognized the slouch hat and stooped shoulders even before he zeroed in on the scout's face. Aaron Meachum, a Jayhawker renegade who'd been raiding and robbing in Kansas years before the war came, camouflaging thievery and murder with a smokescreen of abolitionist bushwa.

As a Hessian sergeant questioned Eli, Meachum casually circled his mount around behind the boy, looking Eli's horse over carefully.

Would he recognize the animal? Gus searched his memory, trying to recall if Meachum had ever seen his mare. Once, maybe, at the Reynolds County fair. Meachum had tried to goad Gus's youngest son into a fight, but backed off when Gus and two of his boys stepped in. Meachum might have seen the horse then, but that was before the war and—

With a casual, fluid motion, Meachum drew his pistol and shot Eli Mitchell in the head! His hands still raised to the sky, the boy collapsed like a broken puppet, toppling from the saddle to the grass of the valley floor.

"No!" Gus leapt to his feet, stunned, staring. But too far away to be heard. The other troopers seemed just as surprised. Red-faced, the sergeant was yelling at Meachum, his voice carrying across the valley. Ignoring him, the Jayhawker scout dismounted and ran his hands over Eli's horse, stepping across the boy's crumpled body without so much as a downward glance.

Satisfied, Meachum unsaddled Eli's borrowed mare. Tossing Gus's battered rig aside, Meachum transferred his own McClellan saddle to the mare's back, kicking the wind out of her belly as he yanked the cinch taut.

The troopers watched in silence as Meachum swung into the saddle, then the sergeant muttered something and two men dismounted. Hoisting Eli's body onto Meachum's rank gelding, they tied him across its back. Meachum said something to them, a joke, apparently, since Gus could read his grin clear across the meadow. None of the others smiled.

Wheeling his horse, the captain led the troop out of the valley by twos with Eli's body bouncing like a saddlebag on the gelding, blood from his fatal wound dripping down its flanks.

Crouched in the brush, Gus watched them vanish into the distance, then waited another half-hour to be certain.

When he was sure they were gone, he began working his way across the ridge crest toward the spring Eli had described, the one he'd led the patrol away from before they rode him down. Keeping its secret with his death.

Gus was hoping the lieutenant would be dead as well. It would be simpler that way. He could get back to his camp to think, clear his head of the vision of Eli, falling with his hands still raised…

He heard a soft click. A pistol hammer being reared back.

"Stop where you are. Raise your…" The voice faded away. Gus stayed put.

"Lieutenant? My name's McKee. Elias Mitchell sent me to you." No answer, only a muffled cough. Gus could see him now, concealed in a copse of cedars beside the brook that trickled into the basin. An officer all right, cadet-gray tunic, gilt buttons, yellow cavalry stripe on his trousers. And a .36 Paterson Colt in his fist.

But the gun wasn't aimed directly at Gus. Only in his general direction. And even at that distance Gus caught the sour stench of mortification. Of blood festering, turning rank.

Kneeling beside the boy, who was even younger than Eli, Gus gently took the gun from his hand. He doubted the Reb even knew it.

Mitchell had been mistaken, the boy wasn't gutshot. Not that it made much difference. His lung wound was low enough in his chest to let the blood leak out slowly, draining his life away with every heartbeat.

He'd propped himself up against a cedar bole to keep his lungs from filling. Fighting for every breath. But his war was nearly over now. A lost cause. Like the gray he wore. And the medals on his blouse.

The lieutenant's eyes were open, but he was gazing into some impossible distance, his face chalk-white, arterial blood bubbling in the corners of his mouth, coloring his lips a livid crimson, scarlet as a painted lady.

After a time the boy slowly returned to his senses, staring up at Gus, faintly puzzled.

"I'm sorry," he said, licking his crimsoned lips. "I was talking with my mother…Do I know you?"

"No, Lieutenant. My name's Angus McKee. Elias Mitchell sent me."

"Who?"

"Elias Mitchell. A boy who stayed with you a few days back?"

"Mitchell, yes. The Yankee boy. He's well, I hope?"

"He's…just fine, Lieutenant. He's gone on home. To be with his people."

"I'm glad. He was very kind to me…" The young soldier swallowed. "I haven't much time, sir. I am Lieutenant James Oliver Neeland, of the First Arkansas. I have family in the White River valley. My father is Phineas Neeland, of Clarendon." The boy coughed, spewing red froth down his shirt front.

"Lieutenant Neeland, I have two sons serving in Arkansas with Sterling Price. Jared and Levon McKee. Have you heard anything of them…?" But the coughing had sapped the last of Neeland's strength. The boy had drifted off again, his lips moving in soundless conversation.

Gus waited for what seemed an age. And realized Neeland was staring up at him, frowning.

"I'm sorry. I…seem to have forgotten your name."

"It's McKee, Lieutenant. Angus McKee."

"Mr. McKee. Of course. And you were asking me about…? Was your son Jared McKee? A sergeant with the Missourians?"

"Yes! He and his brother were both—"

"Sir, Sergeant Jared McKee was among the fallen at Westport, badly wounded. I saw him carried to the surgeons. I doubt he survived. Not many do. I shall ask my mother when I see…" He broke off, coughing again. "I'm very sorry. I knew your son in passing. He seemed a fine soldier. I don't recall hearing about his brother. I hope he is well."

Gus looked away, his eyes stinging. It was too much. Eli's death. And now Jared too. Dear God.

"Mr. McKee, I'm sorry to trouble you at such a time but I find myself in a…quandary, sir. I am dying. And in truth, I don't mind so much anymore. The pain's not as bad now. And my mother is…very near. May I ask, sir, where your loyalties lie? North or South?"

Gus didn't answer. Couldn't. He saw Eli falling, his hands upraised in surrender…and then Jared. Falling.

Gus shook his head to clear it. "I have sons in gray, Lieutenant," he said hoarsely. "I stand with my sons."

"Good." Neeland closed his eyes. "There's a letter in my tunic. It is to my father but it contains…details of our troubles that might be useful to the Yanks. I would count it a great favor if you could place my medals in the letter and pass it to someone sympathetic to our cause. Would you do that for me, Mr. McKee?"

"Lieutenant—"

"Please!" Neeland grasped Gus's forearm desperately, pulling himself up. "For your sons, sir. For the South!"

"All right, boy, take it easy. I'll see to it."

"Thank you." Neeland fell back, spent. "The letter is in my vest pocket. Take it, please."

Gently, Gus reached inside the lieutenant's coat, found the envelope, then hesitated. He felt no heartbeat. He glanced at Neeland. His eyes were empty. He was gone. Just like that. Dead and…gone.

Rising stiffly, Gus looked over the envelope. It was probably as the lad said, only a letter home. But nowadays, passing along such a note, or even possessing it, would be considered conveying dispatches to the enemy.

Treason.

A hanging offense, or a firing squad. On the spot.

No judge, no jury. No mercy.

Swallowing his distaste, Gus quickly searched the boy's body, but the only thing of use was the dress dagger at Neeland's belt, fifteen inches of Damascus steel, double edged with a needle point. A style some called the Arkansas toothpick.

The knife had bright brass pommels and a carved ivory hilt with silver insets, beautifully engraved. *1st Arkansas* on one side, *Lt. J.O. Neeland* on the other. The hilt and the Damascus steel were darkly stained with the lad's blood. He could soak the blood off later, but he'd broken his camp bowie the week before and Neeland had no more need of the dagger. His war was over.

Gus slid the Arkansas blade into his boot, the Paterson Colt in his belt at the small of his back.

After carefully removing the lieutenant's medals, Gus placed them in the envelope and slipped it under his shirt. Then he buried Lieutenant James Oliver Neeland in a sheltered clearing not far from the creek.

He buried the boy deep, covering him over with rocks at the last, carefully camouflaging the grave afterward so no animal could dig him up. Nor any man. There'd be no blood money paid for this Rebel.

Good Lord. He'd spent the better part of two years hiding like a stray dog, waiting out the madness, and now that it was nearly over, he'd finally been forced into making a choice. Eli Mitchell said there wasn't any right side to this but he was mistaken. His own death proved it. And Jared's. And this poor bastard who'd kept himself alive long enough to pass along a last letter to his people. Gus hoped some part of their damned *cause* was worth dying for. And killing for. Because he was done running and hiding. Right or wrong, he'd just volunteered. Again.

Maybe he couldn't cure the outlawry in these Missouri hills, but he could rectify one small portion of it. Aaron Meachum was Jayhawker scum. He'd murdered Eli Mitchell as casually as a field hand stomping a vole. Killed him for his horse and a share of a twenty-dollar bounty. And there would, by God, be a reckoning for that.

After a final look around the clearing, Gus set off at a steady lope, heading back to his camp. To pack up.

Leaving the herd untended would be risky, but the horses had forage enough for a week or so in this blind valley and they were well concealed. A straggler might stumble across them as Eli had done, and steal one, or run off the lot, but there was no helping that. He'd just have to chance it.

He chose his own mount with care, a swaybacked gray plow horse named Nell. Six years old, she had a canted jaw, broken by a kick when she was a filly. Her crooked mouth kept her gaunt and her disposition was on the surly side of rabies. But most importantly, her injury made her nearly mute. She seldom whickered or whinnied. An admirable trait in a companion of the trail, horse or human.

After rubbing soot between the mare's ribs to accent her bones, Gus smeared small lumps of bloody suet on her legs to simulate open sores. It wasn't perfect, but only an expert would spot it. Most stockmen's tricks were intended to disguise a nag's shortcomings, not make them look worse.

Finished, Gus stepped back to admire his handiwork and nodded.

"Nell, old girl, you are just about the sorriest looking piece of horseflesh I've ever laid eyes on, too swaybacked to work and too scrawny to eat. And definitely not worth stealing."

Nell didn't reply, but her glare was so ferocious Gus couldn't help smiling. The last time he'd gone to war he'd been wearing a proud new uniform with brass buttons. This time, his best hope for survival was to pass for a ragamuffin, pride be damned.

Saddling Nell with his shabbiest work rig, he lashed his worn bedroll to the cantle, tossed a few hardtack biscuits and some jerky in a sack, and climbed aboard. He took a long last look over his camp, making sure he'd erased all traces, campfire buried, gear stowed in the rock cleft. He had a half-dozen hideouts like this one scattered through the mountains, moving from one to the other as the horses cropped down the grass or army patrols got too close.

Hadn't been much of a life these past two years, living like a bandit, seeing his wife and youngest boy one night a month during the dark of the moon when he could slink out of the hills without being spotted.

It was a sorry-ass way to live, but it was his only chance to save what little they had. Now he was risking it all for two dead boys he'd hardly known, boys who'd fought on opposite sides. As his own sons were doing.

Sweet Jesus. It was utter lunacy and he knew it, yet he'd seen murder done, in cold blood, and there was no backing away from that. Not if he was ever going to face himself in a shaving mirror again.

But being swept up in the madness of this fight didn't give him leave to be careless. It meant the exact opposite. He understood the odds he was facing. A stockman going up against a half-dozen seasoned fighters? His chances were slim to none. It would take every shred of skill he owned and all the luck in the world.

And even with that, it likely wouldn't be enough.

•••

He had no trouble picking up the trail of the Yank patrol.

Meachum was riding Gus's mare and he could read her prints like a bill of sale. The patrol had headed northeast, angling from the valley into the forested foothills of the Ozarks. Probably still on the prowl, hunting more bounties. More lost, desperate boys like Eli.

Nell's bony back and plodding gait made for a damned uncomfortable ride and since she tended to balk in the face of rough cover, he was often forced to lead her through it on foot, walking much of the way.

And with every step he saw Eli fall again, his hands raised in surrender, or the blood bubbling at the corners of young Neeland's mouth. Or he'd think back to Jared as a boy, a towheaded kid with a gap between his front teeth.

Jared's brothers often joshed him, claiming Jared missed every other row on a corncob. Jared grinning, saying lunch lasted longer that way…

Dead now. Probably thrown into a mass grave with a dozen others and covered over. Slain in the final throes of a lost war, both sides savaging each other, mindless as wolves in a sheep pen, blood-crazed, lost in the red madness of slaughter.

A contagious disease, apparently.

By early afternoon, Gus was fairly sure he was gaining ground on the patrol. Their tracks were cleaner, more sharply defined. Fresher. He guessed they'd likely lay up for a meal soon, rest their animals, make coffee.

He guessed wrong.

He was threading Nell through a tangle of sumac when he spotted the horsemen ahead. Four—no, five troopers, blocking the trail.

Yanks. And his heart sank as he recognized them. Militia. The same bunch who'd murdered Eli, the Hessians, with Aaron Meachum as their scout. No officer with them this time. One of them was leading Meachum's gelding, with Eli's corpse draped over its back.

The others were already angling in toward him. No point in hightailing it. Nell couldn't outrun a three-legged stool. He had only a few seconds to act.

As he passed through the sumac bushes, he let his Jenks carbine slide out of his grasp. Dumped the Colt as well, heard it tumble into the brush, hoped to Christ they landed out of sight. Thought about the Arkansas blade in his boot, but it was too late to toss it. They'd see him reach down for sure. So he left it. As Nell plodded slowly up to the patrol, Gus could feel the sweat trickling down his back—

God! The letter! It was still concealed beneath his shirt!

"Who are you, mister? What you doin' way out here?" the sergeant asked. His Hessian accent was strong as sauerkraut. Red-faced, stocky. His blue wool uniform coat looked homemade and probably was, but his gray eyes were wary. And dangerous.

"My name's McKee. Got a place over in Reynolds County. I'm headed east to visit a cousin."

"What cousin would that be?" Aaron Meachum asked. "Robert E. Lee?" The Jayhawker sat lazy in his saddle, shoulders slumped, eyeing Gus from beneath the brim of his sagging slouch hat.

"Keith Stewart, at Buckhorn."

"Didn't know the Stewarts were kin to you, McKee."

"You know this man?" the sergeant asked Meachum.

"I know who he is. That farm woman that gave the captain mouth yesterday? This is her man. A Reb sympathizer, got boys in gray. Ain't that right, McKee?"

"Well, he's too old to be a sojer boy so he ain't worth no bounty," the sergeant said. "Let's move on."

"Not so fast," Meachum drawled. "He might be carryin' contraband. Step down, McKee."

Gus hesitated.

"Best do like he says, mister," the sergeant sighed. "He likes to kill people, this one." Forcing his fear back, Gus swung down.

"Step away from that nag and raise your hands. Search him, Dutch."

"Come on, Meachum, this bummer ain't got two pennies to rub together. Let's go."

"The captain left me in charge and I say we search him, Dutch. Now do it! Check his horse, then pat him down."

Muttering to himself in German, the sergeant swung down, stalked over to Nell…and hesitated. Eyeing the oil spots on the strap that had held the Jenks. He gave Gus a look, then glanced back down the trail. But if he spotted the rifle, he didn't say anything. He cast a critical eye on Nell instead, then nodded.

"You got her lookin' pretty sorry, mister," he said quietly in his harsh accent. "Them suet lumps you stuck on her legs? They look worse if you wet 'em with berry juice. It dries black like blood. Keeps the flies down, too."

"You know horses?" Gus asked.

"I had me a stock ranch outside Jeff City, till the Rebs burnt us out. Now I sell dead men."

"This ain't no Sunday social," Meachum growled. "Search him, Dutch."

Sighing, the Hessian quickly ran his hands over Gus's torso. And felt the letter! No question, Gus heard the rustle as the German's hands passed over it. Their eyes met for a split second, then the sergeant stepped away.

"Nothing," the Hessian said. "I told you."

"Looked like a pretty careless search to me, Dutch. We'd best make sure. Take off your clothes, McKee."

"What?"

"You heard me, old man. Strip down. Get them duds off. Let's see what you been givin' that ole woman of yours that makes her so sassy."

Gus swallowed, hard, wanting to rush at Meachum, drag him from his saddle or die trying. But he couldn't. Meachum would kill him, sure as sunup. He was just itching for an excuse. Gus could see it in his eyes. But if they saw the letter, or the Arkansas blade, he'd probably die anyway. No explanation would satisfy this bunch. He'd be a Rebel under arms, worth a twenty-dollar bounty at St. Lou. And he'd already seen how they transported prisoners.

"No," he said. "I won't do it."

"No?" Meachum echoed. "Strip him down, Dutch. If he gives you any trouble, kill him. Or I will."

The sergeant turned to Gus, his face a mask. "Don't give me no trouble, mister. He means it."

"Go to hell!" Gus heard a quaver in his voice and hated it. "You want my clothes, Meachum, step down. Come get 'em yourself."

Grabbing Gus by his collar, the sergeant spun him around, pulling him close, ripping at his shirt. Gus struggled against him but could feel the power in the Hessian's arms, knew he hadn't a chance in hell—then suddenly he was free.

Thrusting him away, the Hessian stalked back to his horse. He said something in German and the troopers roared with laughter.

"What the hell do you think you're doing?" Meachum demanded furiously. "What did you say?"

"I said now we know why women got no use for you, Meachum. You get hard lookin' at bare-ass old men." The sergeant reached for his pommel to mount and found himself staring down the muzzle of Meachum's navy Colt.

"I told you to strip him, Dutch."

"And I say there's no bounty on him and no contraband. Look at him, look at his crow-bait horse. You waste our time here." He said something else in German, but this time there was no laughter. The others were eyeing Meachum warily now.

"What did you tell them?"

"You keep that pistol pointed my way, you'll find out." Swinging into the saddle, the Hessian wheeled his mount around to face Meachum.

"I don't like you much, Jayhawker," the sergeant spat. "You're brave, back-shooting a boy, but that farm woman ran you off like a dog. And when this old man says step down, you stay mounted. The captain says you know the land, so in the field, we follow you. But from now on, if you see me in town? You don't talk to me. You cross the street. *Verstehen Sie?* You-cross-the-gott-dampt street."

Jerking his mount around, the sergeant clucked her to a trot. He glanced down at Gus as he passed, but his face was unreadable. The others fell into line behind him by twos, with Eli's corpse bouncing along on the last horse.

But Meachum didn't move. The Jayhawker scout considered Gus a moment, the cocked pistol still in his fist, death in his eyes, then shook his head.

"You ain't worth my powder today, old man. But we'll have us another day, McKee. Count on that." Holstering the Colt, he swept off his hat and charged his horse at Nell with a *whoop!* Driving her off. The old plow horse took off at a stiff-legged trot, as fast as she could manage, running toward the hills, her empty stirrups flapping as she fled.

Cackling, Meachum swung his mare in a wide circle and galloped off after the troop.

Gus could have lunged at him as he passed. Dragged him off his animal, stomped his brains in for Eli, for Jared—but again, he didn't.

Couldn't.

Even if he won, the Hessians would kill him, and no part of Aaron Meachum was worth dying for. Not if it meant leaving his family to starve. Or so Gus told himself.

Or maybe, it was just plain yellow-dog cowardice. Getting old and slow, losing heart, making excuses. That was the worst of it for Gus. Not knowing the truth of his own courage. Or the lack of it.

Still shaking, Gus McKee waited till Meachum was well out of sight, then he doubled back down his own trail to collect his Jenks carbine and the Colt. No point in trying to catch Nell, she'd be halfway to the horse camp by now. If he had half a brain he'd follow her back to the hills.

But he didn't. Instead he checked his weapons, shoved the Colt in his belt, then set out after the patrol again. On foot this time.

Which made their tracks all the easier to read.

•••

After sending Birgit on her way, Polly spent part of the afternoon cleaning the house, absurdly pleased that Birgit noted how well she kept it. In such matters, only women's opinions carry weight. Men wouldn't notice a slaughtered hog on the sofa unless they had to shift its carcass to sit.

With her home immaculate, she had Jason bring in a load of kindling wood, then sent him down the valley to stay over with a cousin, as was customary during the nights of the dark moon. Every time Gus came out of the hills, there was a risk that he'd be followed, or braced by a patrol. If there was trouble, better if the boy was clear of it.

Hauling the copper bathtub into the kitchen, Polly lit the stove, getting it ready to boil water. And for a moment, she glimpsed herself in the hall mirror. And couldn't help thinking how fresh and young Birgit looked. Her own face was growing leathery, weathered by the wind and the work. She wondered if Angus still saw her as a woman at all, and wondered if she'd ever truly feel like one again—

Gunshot! A single blast, echoing down the valley like distant thunder. Polly froze, listening for another. But only silence followed.

Which might be good. Because she was sure she'd recognized the bark of a coach gun. And not many used them. Banking the fire in the kitchen stove, she took up her own gun, checked the primer, then eased out onto the shaded porch. To watch. And wait.

An hour crept by. Half of another. Dusk settled softly over the hills like a dark drape and still she waited, standing in the shadows. The last of the light was fading out through the tree line when she heard the distant drum of racing hoof-beats, growing louder as they came, then the clatter of a wagon as the Stanhope buggy burst over the crest of a hill, hurtling madly down the road toward the farm.

Polly was up and running as the buggy skidded through the gate into the yard. Birgit sawed on the reins, yanking her lathered, gasping animal to a halt. Her face and clothing were mud-smeared and filthy, hair awry, eyes wild.

"What happened?"

"A man came out of the woods, grabbed the horse. I warned him off but he won't let go. I struck him with the buggy whip and he rushed at me, grabbed me, tried to drag me down and—" she swallowed hard—"and I shot him!

"He pulled me from the buggy as he fell and I ran into the woods. Lost. Couldn't find my way. After a while I came out on the road. And I see the buggy. The man is lying by it."

"Dead?"

"I—think so," Birgit said, gulping down a sob. "I'm pretty sure. His head—oh God. Yes, he's dead. He must be."

"It's all right, girl. You did right. But we're not out of this. Is the body in the road?"

"By the side, yes."

"And the gun? Where is it?"

"I—don't know. I lost it when I fell. I don't know what happened to it."

"All right, now you listen to me," Polly said, seizing the girl's shoulders. "We have to go back. Right now."

"I *can't!*"

"*You have to!* It don't matter if he was Federal or a Reb, if his friends find him kilt they'll come after us, 'specially if they find that gun nearby. Too many people know it. I'd go alone, but I might miss him in the dark. Can you find that place again?"

Birgit nodded mutely.

"Good. Then gather yourself together, girl. I'll fetch a shovel."

•••

Gus figured the patrol would likely make camp at dusk, and he only knew of one creek within easy riding distance. He knew a shorter route, and considered pushing hard to get there first. Take them by surprise from the high ground.

But the risk was too great. If they didn't know about the waterhole, he could lose them altogether. And if he fired on them from ambush, they'd scatter and take cover. Or just ride him down.

No. Better to trail them, come up on them quiet in the dark after they'd made camp and settled in.

Gus kept thinking of the Hessian sergeant. The man had definitely felt the letter. Probably spotted the carbine in the brush as well. Gus saw it in his eyes. Yet he deliberately misled Meachum about it. All the Germans were strong for the Union, why had he let it pass?

The best Gus could come up with was that the sergeant had seen enough dead men in the road for one day. Amen to that.

The twilight was coming on when Gus spotted the orange glow of a fire ahead in the distance, shadows dancing above it, reflected on the pale bark of the aspens. The patrol had camped at the head of the creek, exactly where he expected them to be.

He felt a surge of energy, fired by his rage. Slowing his pace, he shifted from shadow to shadow like a ghost as he approached the camp. He could see the men clearly now, clustered about the campfire, washing down salt pork and sourdough biscuits with raw chicory coffee.

Relaxed. Easy targets, less than two hundred yards off, most of them starkly outlined against the firelight. But if the patrol was in range, so was Gus. Most of them appeared to be kraut-head farmers or townsmen, but he'd underestimated them once, and barely escaped with his life. If they caught him out here now, they'd run him down like dogs on a possum, and sell his carcass in Springfield or St. Lou for the bounty money. Two dollars and change apiece. The price of a life.

Circling south to put a low rise between himself and the camp, Gus picked up his pace, trotting crouched through purple shadows, feeling the land rising beneath his boots as full dark settled over the hills.

Slowing to a walk short of the summit, he circled the hilltop to avoid being skylined. Then he dropped to his belly, snaking over the ridgeline in the shadow of a rotted poplar log. Edging into a cluster of gorse, he waited a bit for his heart to slow, then gently parted the branches.

The Yank camp was spread out below him like a target range, every man clearly visible in the firelight. A somber camp, none of the joshing and laughter he remembered from the Mexican War. God, that seemed so long ago, before his first wife, before their boys—he swallowed hard, remembering his boys. Remembering Jared, with his gap-toothed grin. And Eli, pitching from the saddle with his hands still raised in surrender…

Settle down, Angus McKee. Get this done. Pulling his Mexican field glasses from his jacket, Gus carefully scanned the camp. The Hessians were already bedding down for the night, weary from a long day in the saddle, rolling up in their blankets near the fire. Gus made a quick count, one, two—

Shit! There were only five men in view. But there'd been eight this afternoon. Slow down. Count again.

He spotted one immediately. A picket was on guard near the horses, sitting with his back against a tree, wrapped in a blanket, his rifle across his knees.

Scanning along the river, Gus stiffened. A second man was bedded down away from the others. Aaron Meachum. His slouch hat down over his eyes, his head resting on the McClellan saddle. Either he was unsociable, or the kraut-heads disliked him as much as his Missouri neighbors.

Still a man short. And as he scanned the camp again, Gus had the uneasy feeling he knew who was missing. The Hessian sergeant. The only seasoned soldier in the lot. And knowing his man, Gus surmised where he'd be found…

There! Halfway up the far hillside, well above the camp, with a clear view of the narrow glen and the approaches to it. A perfect spot for an experienced sharpshooter. And the Hessian had the gun for it. Even at this distance, Gus recognized the odd outlines of the .451 Whitworth with its slender telescopic sight. Deadly out to five hundred yards.

Sweet Jesus. Gus had planned a hit-and-run attack. Pot Meachum, maybe one more, then slink away in the confusion. But the sergeant's position changed all that. He had the high ground, and a long-range gun that gave him the advantage. Resting away from the camp, his eyes wouldn't be dazzled by firelight. Killing Meachum wouldn't disconcert him, it would only bring him to full alert.

And he could shoot farther than Gus could run, even in the dark.

If he potted Meachum from here, the Hessian would kill him sure as Christmas. Hell, he might not get clear of this even if he didn't pot Meachum. Depending on how alert the sergeant was.

He didn't seem to be alert at the moment. Gus couldn't see him clearly at that distance, but he looked relaxed. Probably dozing. So Gus's plan might still work.

But only if he shot the sergeant first.

How far away? Two hundred yards, maybe two-twenty. Gus had taken deer in the hills with his Jenks-Remington at greater distances. The poor light made it tricky, but Gus was fairly sure he could make the shot. Kill the Kraut, or leave him in no shape to return fire.

The problem was, he had no wish to kill the Hessian. The man had probably saved his life. And if he shot the sergeant first, Meachum would scurry to cover before Gus could reload and fire again anyway.

Damn it!

The smart thing would be to back the hell away from this. Survive this night. Try for Meachum another time.

But Gus was weary of waiting. And border-Scot stubborn. He'd come far, and his enemy was in sight. Scanning the camp again, he looked for some other way to—

And there it was.

Maybe.

The horse herd was picketed at the far end of the draw. The campfire was midway along the creek, with men rolled in their blankets near it. Meachum was bedded down alone between the fire and the picket line.

From his hillside perch, the Hessian sergeant could see the approaches to the valley, but the slopes were wooded with poplar and ash. Gus doubted the sergeant could see the horses clearly…

No time to chew on it. The sky was clearing to the west, stars showing through. If he was going to move, it would have to be now. Gus carefully stashed his carbine under the rotted log. If he lived, he'd come back for it later. If not…?

Dropping to his belly, he began snaking down the hillside toward the picket line, using every clump of brush, every woodland skill he'd learned in his years in the hills.

Nearing the creek, he was able to rise a little, moving along in a crouch. The brush grew a bit thicker close to water, and there was a well-worn deer trail along the bank. On the far side, he could see the lone sentry, wrapped in his blanket, his head resting on his arms. Asleep? Maybe. No way to be certain.

The horses heard him coming, of course, but they were as spent as the troopers and accustomed to the sounds and scent of men. Gus posed no threat.

Drawing Neeland's Arkansas toothpick from his boot, he slid along the picket rope, cutting the horses loose, one at a time. Last in line was the mare Meachum had taken from Eli. But as he reached for her, he stumbled over something and went down, landing hard. The horse beside him spooked, shying away with a snort. Gus whispered to her softly, calming her, and she halted, still eyeing him uneasily. Ready to bolt.

Groping around at his feet, Gus brushed against a human arm! He nearly slashed at it with the blade before he realized he'd tripped over a corpse.

Sweet Jesus. It was Eli. They'd dumped the boy's body downwind of the camp, near the herd, to save trouble loading him again in the morning. Leaving him out here in the dark like trash. Like nothing…God damn their eyes!

Rising slowly, Gus stroked the neck of the nervous mare, peering over her rump, scanning the camp as he waited for her to settle down. Across the creek, the sentry stirred once in his sleep. No one else was moving.

Except Meachum. Grunting, the Jayhawker rolled over on his side, turning away from the fire. Facing Gus.

But not seeing him. Meachum's eyes were closed, or nearly so. He was either asleep or drowsing…and no more than twenty paces away. Gus was already edging around the mare toward the creek before he'd given it conscious thought.

Easing into the water, he waded quietly across, heading directly at the sleeping gunman with Neeland's Arkansas blade in his fist, ready to…

What? As he stepped warily out of the water Gus realized his misjudgment. Jesus, he'd crossed the creek right into the middle of the damned camp. Sleeping Yanks were all around him, a sentry between him and the horses and a sharpshooter on the hillside above. The slightest noise, a sneeze, a bad dream? If anyone woke in the camp, he was a dead man.

And yet, Aaron Meachum was only a few steps away, now. Within easy reach. A thrust to his black heart, a slashed jugular...but no.

He couldn't risk it. No man dies silently. Butchering Meachum here would be suicide, pure and simple.

But he was so close...he damned well had to do something.

Moving a step closer, he carefully slid the bloodstained Arkansas blade into the ground, an inch from Aaron Meachum's nose. A remembrance. From Lieutenant James Oliver Neeland, of the First Arkansas. And his friend Eli Mitchell. Of Cairo, Illinois.

"Hey." A trooper near the campfire sat up slowly, blinking, only half awake.

"What...?"

But Gus simply waved at the man as he turned away, walking easily along the creek bank as though he belonged in the camp. As he passed the dozing picket sentry, he casually lifted the rifle off his lap, then slammed the butt into his head! Sending him sprawling into the brush!

Then Gus was off! Plunging into the creek, he waded across in three long strides. Vaulting up onto Eli's mare, he fired the sentry's musket in the air and cut loose a shrill Rebel yell, stampeding the horses down the glen away from the camp.

Throwing the empty musket aside, Gus crouched low on the mare's neck, clinging to her mane for dear life. As she ran flat out over the uneven ground it took every ounce of skill and tenacity Gus owned to stay on her back. A few shots rang out in the camp, but he wasn't worried about them. With smoothbore muskets, the patrol couldn't hit a barn at twenty paces. Nor was pursuit a problem; they'd be chasing down their scattered mounts for a week. A minié ball whistled past his head, close enough to feel the hot wind of its passing. The echo of its report came a second later. Damn it, the sharpshooter! No man could hit a horseman running at full gallop, not by starlight at this distance—

But Gus was already counting down the seconds it would take the Hessian to reload, trying to time the next shot. At the last instant, he leaned sharply over the mare's neck, trying to swing her with his weight—too late!

He felt the blow of a heavy slug hammer into his left shoulder, knocking him off the mare, spinning him into the darkness.

He slammed down hard, rolling to break his fall, crashing to a halt against a cluster of brush. He lay there stunned a moment, gasping, his wind driven out. Then he was crawling, scrambling up the hillside on his hands and knees into the cover of the aspens, out of sight, out of range.

He crouched there awhile, panting like a dog, gathering his addled wits. In the distance behind him, he could still see gun flashes, hear the reports as the panicked patrol fired blindly into the dark, blasting away at shadows.

Rising slowly, Gus looked back, trying to gauge the distance to the camp. At least five hundred yards, maybe six. That Kraut bastard was one hell of a shot. Gus gingerly touched his wounded shoulder with his fingertips. It burned like a brand, but there didn't seem to be much blood. A graze, no more. Still, a very near thing. Another inch, he'd be visiting with Eli and Jared.

But so far, he was still breathing. He might make it through this after all.

He'd have nothing to fear from the patrol for a while. They wouldn't venture out after their horses until full daylight, and they'd never recover them all in these hills.

A few lost boys would come upon stray mounts for the ride home. And some of the Hessians would have one hell of a long hike back to Springfield. Meachum too, most likely. Gus doubted the Kraut sergeant would loan him a mount.

Meachum. His only regret for this night's work was not seeing the Jayhawker's face when he woke to find a bloody Reb dagger an inch from his nose.

He was a yellow cur at heart. Knowing how close death had come would keep him sweating until it came for him again. And it would. Somewhere down the line, Gus would make sure of that.

Easing out of the trees, he looked to the hills, orienting himself. He was a good five miles from his horse camp, and nearly that far from the farm.

He read the stars, estimating the hours of darkness remaining. Knew he should circle back to the horse camp and his herd. It wouldn't be the first time he'd missed his supply run. Polly and the farm would keep another month—

But he wouldn't. On this night, Gus needed to see his farm, his land, his woman. To be sure they were real, and not part of some blood-crazed fever dream.

He knew he'd crossed a line tonight, risking everything to make a pointless gesture. Only a fool would do that. Or a man losing his grip.

He needed a few moments of peace amidst the madness of this life. Just a few.

So he collected his wits, then set off down the hillside at a brisk pace, marching toward the farm in the dark. Headed home.

•••

In that same moonless dark, Polly nearly missed the corpse. Dappled with faint, starlit silhouettes, the road was a slender gray ribbon threading through the shadowed hills. Birgit wasn't sure how far she'd traveled or how long she'd been lost. The women could easily have driven past the corpse without seeing it. But the horse recognized the spot. She snorted, tossing her head, shying away from the crumpled form lying beside the road.

"You wait here," Polly hissed, stepping down from the buggy, her shotgun leveled at the body. But there was no need. The blast had shredded his upper torso. She could smell the reek of death from ten feet away. Not just the stench of blood and voided bowels, but the sickly sweet odor of gangrene as well.

Couldn't tell if he was Reb or Federal. Linsey-woolsey shirt drenched with blood, canvas pants, broken-down boots.

"Is he…?" Birgit whispered.

"Oh my, yes. He's dead as a beaver hat, girl. He was near to dyin' anyways. Got a bandaged wound on his thigh and it was mortifyin'. The gangrene would have took him soon. You probably did the poor bastard a favor. Come on, let's get him underground."

Straining and stumbling, the two women tried to drag the reeking body off the road into the trees, but the corpse kept snagging on the underbrush. In the end, Polly put her gun aside and lifted him by the shoulders while Birgit took his legs, and they carried him into the forest.

Spotting a natural trench at the base of a fallen sycamore, Polly widened it with her shovel, then they rolled the corpse in and covered it over with dirt and forest debris.

"The wind will do the rest," Polly panted, straightening. "A day or two, it'll be like we was never here."

"We should say words for him," Birgit said.

"You mean pray? For a damned road agent?"

"We can't just leave him like this. It's wrong." Birgit's voice was shaking, very near to tears.

"All right, girl, all right. Do you know what to say?"

"Not—in English."

"Then say it in Hessian. Or whatever that place is you're from."

"Bavaria. But the language is the same."

"Well, I expect the good Lord understands 'em all, and this poor devil's beyond caring. You go ahead."

Kneeling silently in the moist forest mold, the two women bowed their heads while Birgit prayed. Polly didn't understand a word of it. Yet somehow she felt a bit better for it as they made their way back to the road.

The girl was right. A proper prayer was a righteous thing to do, even for no-account border trash.

They found the coach gun in the brush beside the road where Birgit had dropped it. After reloading it, Polly handed it up to the girl in the buggy.

"You drive on now. Corridon's less than an hour away and you'll be safer travelin' this time of night than by daylight. You shouldn't have no more trouble, but if you do, well, God help 'em. You blast away and don't stop for nothin'."

"But what will you do?"

"I'll walk home. I been in these hills my whole life, starlight's as bright as a lantern. Don't fret none about me. You just take care of yourself and that baby. I'll see you come summer, girl. I promise."

Polly watched until the buggy disappeared, then set off for her farm, a long, weary march. It was well past midnight when she finally trudged up the lane to her home.

She'd hoped Angus might be waiting. But he wasn't here. Or at least, not yet.

Exhausted, Polly relit the kitchen woodstove to warm the water, then stumbled into her bedroom. By the light of a lone candle, she filled the basin from the pitcher on the washstand, then stripped off her shirt, hanging it carefully on the doorknob to avoid getting bloodstains on the bedspread.

But as she plunged her arms in the basin to rinse off the gore, the scent of it came roiling up, suffusing the air, a powerful sweet-sour blend of gangrene and…

Lilacs.

Stunned, Polly stared down at the basin, already reddening with blood from her hands. Leaning down, her face just above the water, she drew a long, ragged breath. Dear God. It was *eau de lilac.* Full strength, undiluted.

Her throat closed so tightly she could hardly breathe. Still, she forced herself to take her shirt from the doorknob to sniff a blood-stained sleeve. It was drenched with lilac water.

No doubt about it.

The—man—Birgit had killed must have been carrying the bottle in his shirt pocket. The shotgun blast splattered it all over his chest. With a low moan, Polly sank to the floor beside the bed, burying her face in her hands, rocking. No tears came, her agony was soundless and soul-deep, a pain so savage she thought she might die. And wished to God she could.

Which boy had they buried out there? She'd never looked into his face, hadn't wanted to. He was just another lost scarecrow of war, another starving, walking corpse, looking for a place to die.

Or to kill. Why in God's name had he attacked Birgit on the road? Was he too sick to walk any further? Or had the war bled away his soul and his honor? Made him into another Meachum?

She wasn't sure how long she knelt there. Perhaps she fell asleep.

Because suddenly she woke with a start! Someone was moving in the kitchen. And for a wild moment she thought she'd been mistaken, that the boy hadn't been quite dead. That he'd clawed his way out of the earth somehow, to find his way home…But no.

In the kitchen Angus was fumbling with a lantern.

"Don't light that," Polly said quietly, carrying her candle to the rough wooden table. "Cavalry patrol was here yesterday. They might be watching the house."

"Whose cavalry?"

"Federals, out of Jefferson City."

"Oh." In the flickering shadows, her husband's seamed face was hewn from granite, his beard unkempt, his graying hair wild. She wanted to hold him, to feel his strength. But it wasn't their custom. And she wanted no questions.

"You're late," she said, her voice quiet, controlled. "It's nearly three."

"I had to walk in. Took longer than I figured."

"You walked? Why?"

He avoided her eyes. "I run into a branch in the dark. Took a fall. Lost my horse."

"Your mare? Why did she run off? She comes to your whistle."

"I don't know, somethin' spooked her, maybe. She run off, damn it. I wanted to get home so I walked on in. She'll likely find her own way back to the herd. If not, I'll hunt her up tomorrow. Let it be, Pol. What's the news? What do the neighbors say?"

"The war might be over soon, truly. I had a visitor today, Tyler Randolph's new wife. She said the Federals burned Atlanta. Hood's retreating."

"I heard that, too. Met a deserter, a Yankee boy."

"Did he give you trouble?"

"No, I...put him on a Jayhawk trail, sent him on his way. I've been seein' a lot of strays in the hills lately, mostly Rebs but some Union, too. Federal patrols are shootin' deserters now. Got a bounty on 'em. Huntin' them boys down like coyotes. Is that why the cavalry came?"

"For that, and to steal anything that wasn't nailed down. Aaron Meachum was with them. Gave me some mouth, nothing I couldn't handle."

"Meachum," Angus rasped, his eyes narrowing. "That blood-suckin' scum's ridin' high now. Got the Hessians around him, thinks he's safe. But when this is over and the boys are home, we'll be payin' a moonlight visit to that Jayhawker sonofabitch—"

Polly slapped him, hard! Snapping his head around! He stared at her in stunned disbelief.

"No! By God, Angus, when this is over, it's truly gonna be over for us. We've given enough, bled enough. Let the dead bury the dead. No more killing, no more burning, not for justice nor revenge nor any other goddamn thing!"

"What the hell's got into you, Pol?"

"I met Tyler Randolph's wife! And she's a Hessian, except she's not, she's from—some other place in Germany. But she's a fine girl! And God willing, she and Tyler will have children. I can midwife for her, and they can come visit of a Sunday, stay a few days over Christmas, maybe.

"But so help me God, Angus, if you ever talk about any more killin' or use that word Hessian to me again, I'll leave you! I'll take our boy and go! Do you understand me?"

Hot tears were streaming now. She couldn't stop them and she didn't care. Angus stared at her like a stranger, utterly baffled. He touched his lip and his fingertip came away bloody.

"No," he said slowly, "I don't understand, Pol. But I think it's a damn sight more than we can talk through this night. I'd best go. I need to get back to the hills before sunup anyhow."

"No! Not yet! You came in for some hot food and a bath and you're damned well gonna have 'em!"

"I came in for a kind word, too. But I guess I'll have to settle for a bath."

"Good! You soak yourself and I'll fry up some eggs. Go on, shuck your duds. You smell like a damned horse camp." Polly carried the steaming buckets from the woodstove to the tub, filling it with practiced ease as Angus unbuttoned his shirt, eyeing her warily all the while.

"What happened to your arm, Gus?"

"Must've banged it up when I fell."

"Give me that!" Snatching the shirt out of his hands, she examined the tear.

"That's a bullet hole, Angus. And you never fell off a horse in your damn life! What really happened up there?"

"Nothing, Pol. Let it go."

"Don't lie to me! What—"

"I said nothin' happened and that's an end to it! If it needed tellin', I'd say so. It don't. Not tonight, not ever. Let it be, Polly. Just give me some peace! Please. I fell. That's it."

That wasn't it. Gus was lying to her face and she damned well knew it. But he was right about one thing, it was more than they could talk through this night.

When the tub was full, he turned his back and so did she, giving him his privacy, as was their custom.

But not tonight. Instead, Polly turned and watched Gus strip off his frayed shirt and the tattered union suit beneath. Saw his pale, scrawny frame, the bloody gash on his shoulder from his so-called fall. Next to an older scar where a horse had broken his collarbone years ago. He let his drawers drop, revealing his flat butt and skinny legs, the hipbones showing through.

My God. He'd been up in those hills more than two years, living with their animals, living *like* an animal. Freezing and going hungry. For her. For their boys. With no complaints.

As he turned to climb in the bath, he saw her watching and colored with embarrassment. But he said nothing. He just eased his aching bones down into the steaming water with a muffled groan.

But in that briefest of moments, when their eyes met, she'd seen her life. With him.

And nothing else mattered. Nothing.

Not the hunger, not the war, not even the lost boy in the forest. Somehow they'd get through this. They would.

Ordinarily she left him alone to bathe. Instead she knelt behind the tub, and after a moment's hesitation, she undid her muslin under-blouse and slipped out of it, freeing her breasts.

Wrapping her arms around his gaunt shoulders, she gathered Gus to her bosom, enveloping him in her warmth. Closing his eyes, he leaned back, resting his head against her shoulder. Feeling her heart beating with his own, breathing in her scent.

"I'm sorry," she said, after a time.

"No, it's my fault. Up in those hills I forget how hard it must be for you down here, toughing it out all alone. Coming home feels so good to me that…well, I forget, that's all. Are you all right?"

"I'm fine, this minute. With you. I'll be better when all this is over."

"Soon, maybe. And you're right, Pol. When it's finished we'll get back to some kind of a life. Make up for these sorry times. All of us. I miss you, Polly, I miss our boys, our home. God, I even miss the way it always smells…so clean. So sweet. Like now. What is that scent you favor?"

"*Eau de lilac,*" she murmured. "Lilac water."

Award winning author **DOUG ALLYN** is a Michigan writer with an international following. The author of eight novels and over a hundred short stories, Doug hit the ground running in 1985 when his first short story won the Robert L. Fish Award from Mystery Writers of America. As a writer, he is a rarity who has literally sold everything he's ever written.

Critical response has continued to be remarkable. He has won the coveted Edgar Allen Poe Award twice (plus six nominations), the International Crime Readers' Award, four Derringer Awards for novellas, and the Ellery Queen Readers' Award an unprecedented nine times.

Published internationally in English, German, French and Japanese, more than two dozen tales have also been optioned for development as feature films and for television. Mr. Allyn's background includes Chinese language studies at Indiana University, and extended duty in southeast Asia during the Vietnam War.

Returning to school on the G.I. Bill, Doug studied creative writing and criminal psychology at the University of Michigan while moonlighting as a songwriter/guitarist in the rock group Devil's Triangle and reviewing books for the *Flint Journal.*

Doug and his wife Eve reside in chaotic bliss in Montrose, Michigan. Career highlights: drinking champagne with Mickey Spillane and waltzing with Mary Higgins Clark.

SECTION 7(A) OPERATIONAL

LEE CHILD

THE TEAM FIRST CAME TOGETHER LATE ONE TUESDAY EVENING IN my apartment. There was none of the usual gradualism about the process; I had none of them, and then I had all of them. Their sudden appearance as a complete unit was certainly gratifying, but also unexpected, and therefore I was less immediately grateful than perhaps I could have been, or should have been, because I was immediately on guard for negative implications. Was I being rolled? Had they come with an established agenda? I had begun the process days before, in the normal way, which was to make tentative approaches to the key players, or at least to let it be known that I was in the market for certain *types* of key players, and normally the process would have continued over a number of weeks, in an accretional way, a commitment secured here, a second commitment there, with an accompanying daisy chain of personal recommendations and suggestions, followed by patient recruitment of specialist operators, until all was finally in place.

But they all came at once. I was reluctant to let myself believe such an event was a response to my reputation; after all, my reputation has neither increased nor decreased in value for many years, and I never met a response like that before. Nor, I felt, could it be a response to my years of experience; the truth was I had long ago transitioned to the status of an old hand, and generally I felt my appeal had been dulled by overfamiliarity. Which was why I looked the gift horse in the mouth: as I said, I was suspicious. But I observed that they seemed not to know one another, which was reassuring, and which removed my fears of a prior conspiracy against me, and they were certainly appropriately attentive to me: I got no feeling that I was to be a passenger on my own ship. But I remained suspicious nonetheless, which slowed things down; and I think I might even have offended them a little, with my slightly tepid response. But: better safe than sorry, which I felt was a sentiment I could rely on them to understand.

My living room is not small—it was two rooms before I removed a wall—but even so, it was somewhat crowded. I was on the sofa that gets the view, smoking, and they were facing me in a rough semicircle, three of them shoulder to shoulder on the sofa that faces mine, and the others on furniture brought in from other rooms, except for two men I had never met before, who stood side by side close behind the others. They were both tall and solid and dark, and they were both looking at me with poor-bloody-infantry expressions on their faces, partly resigned and stoic, and partly appealing, as if they were pleading with me not to get them killed too soon. They were clearly foot soldiers—which, obviously, I needed—but they weren't the hapless, runty, conscripted kind: indeed, how could they be? They had volunteered, like everyone else. And they were fine physical specimens, no doubt trained and deadly in all the ways I would need them to be. They wore suit coats, of excellent quality in terms of cut and cloth, but rubbed and greasy where they were tight over ledges of hard muscle.

There were two women. They had dragged the counter stools in from the kitchen, and they were perched on them, behind and to the right of the three men on the sofa—a kind of mezzanine seating arrangement. I admit I was disappointed that there were only two of them: a mix of two women and eight men was borderline unacceptable by the current standards of our trade, and I was reluctant to open myself to criticism that could have been avoided at the start. Not public criticism, of course—the public was generally almost completely unaware of what we did—but insider criticism, from the kind of professional gatekeepers who could influence future assignments. And I wasn't impressed by the way the women had positioned themselves slightly behind the men: I felt it spoke of the kind of subservience I would normally seek to avoid. They were very nice to look at, though, which delighted me at the time, but only reinforced my anticipation of later carping. Both wore skirts, neither one excessively short, but their perching on high stools showed me more thigh than I felt they intended. They were both wearing dark nylons, which I readily admit is my favorite mode of dress for shapely legs, and I was truly distracted for a moment. But then I persuaded myself—on a provisional basis only, always subject to confirmation—that they were serious professionals, and would indeed be seen as such, and so for the time being I let my worries go, and I moved on.

The man on the right of the group had brought in the Eames lounge chair from the foyer, but not the ottoman. He was sitting in the chair, leaning back in its contour with his legs crossed at the knee, and he made an elegant impression. He was wearing a gray suit. I assumed from the start that he was my government liaison man, and I was proved right. I had worked with many similar men, and I felt I could take his habits and abilities on trust. Mistakes are made that way, of course, but I was confident I wasn't making one that night. The only thing that unsettled me was that he had positioned his chair an inch further away from the main group than was strictly necessary As I said, my living room is not small, but neither is it infinitely spacious: that extra inch had been hard won. Clearly it spoke of a need or an attitude, and I was aware from the start that I should pay attention to it.

My dining chairs are the Tulip design by the Finnish designer Eero Saarinen; both now flanked the sofa opposite me and were occupied by men I assumed were my transport coordinator and my communications expert. Initially I paid little attention to the men, because the chairs themselves had put me in a minor fugue: Saarinen had, of course, also designed the TWA Flight Center at John F. Kennedy Airport—or Idlewild, as it was called at the time—a building which had quite rightly become an icon, and an absolute symbol of its era. It recalled the days when the simple word jet meant much more than merely a propulsive engine. Jet plane, jet set, jet travel… the new Boeing 707, impossibly fast and sleek, the glamour, the larger horizons, the bigger world. In my trade we all know we are competing with the legends whose best work—while not necessarily *performed* in—was indisputably *rooted* in that never-to-be-repeated age. Periodically I feel completely inadequate to the challenge, and indeed for several minutes that particular evening I felt like sending everyone away and giving up before I had even started.

But I reassured myself by reminding myself that the new world is challenging, too, and that those old-timers might well run screaming if faced with the kind of things we have to deal with now—like male-to-female ratios, for instance, and their mutual interactions. So I stopped looking at the chairs and started looking at the men, and I found nothing to worry about. Frankly, transport is an easy job—merely a matter of budget, and I had no practical constraint on what I was about to spend. Communications get more complex every year, but generally a conscientious engineer can handle what is thrown at him. The popular myth that computers can be operated only by pierced youths whose keyboards are buried under old pizza boxes and skateboards is nonsense, of course. I have always used exactly what had arrived: a serious technician with a measured and cautious manner.

On my left on the sofa opposite me was what I took to be our mole. I was both pleased with and worried by him. Pleased, in the sense that it was obvious he had been born in-country, almost certainly in Tehran or one of its closer suburbs. That was indisputable. His DNA was absolutely correct; I was sure it was absolutely authentic. It was what lay over his DNA that worried me. I was sure that when I investigated further I would find he had left Iran at a young age and come to America. Which generally makes for the best moles: unquestioned ethnic authenticity, and unquestioned loyalty to our side. But—and perhaps I am more sensitive to this issue than my colleagues—those formative years in America leave physical traces as well as mental ones. The vitamin-enriched cereals, the milk, the cheeseburgers—they make a difference. If, for instance, due to some bizarre circumstance, this young man had a twin brother who had been left behind, and I now compared them side by side, I had no doubt our mole would be at least an inch taller and five pounds heavier than his sibling. No big deal, you might say, in the vernacular, and I might agree—except that the *kind* of inch and the *kind* of pound does matter. A big, self-confident, straight-backed *American* inch matters a great deal. Five *American* pounds—in the chest and the shoulders, not the gut—matter enormously. Whether I had time to make him lose the weight and correct the posture remained to be seen. If not, in my opinion, we would be going into action with a major source of uncertainty at the very heart of our operation. But then, when in our business have we ever not?

At the other end of the sofa opposite me was our traitor. He was a little older than middle-aged, unshaven, a little fat, a little gray, dressed in a rumpled suit that was clearly the product of foreign tailoring. His shirt was creased and buttoned at the neck and worn without a tie. Like all traitors he would be motivated by either ideology, or money, or blackmail. I hoped it would prove to be money. I'm suspicious of ideology. Of course it gives me a warm feeling when a man risks everything because he thinks my country is better than his; but such a conviction carries with it the smack of fanaticism, and fanaticism is inherently unstable, even readily changeable: in the white heat of a fanatic's mind, even an imagined slight of the most trivial kind can produce mulish results. Blackmail is inherently changeable too: what is an embarrassment one day might not always be. Think back to those jet-set days: homosexuality and honey-trap infidelities produced riches beyond measure. Would we get a tenth of the response today? I think not. But money always works. Money is addictive. Recipients get a taste for it, and they can't quit. Our boy's inside information would clearly be absolutely crucial, so I hoped he was bought and paid for, otherwise we would be adding a second layer of uncertainty into the mix. Not, as I said, that there isn't always uncertainty at the heart of what we do: but too much is too much. It's as simple as that.

Between the mole and the traitor was the man clearly destined to lead the operation. He was what I think we would all want in that position. Privately I believe that a cross-referenced graph of the rise and fall of mental versus physical capabilities in men would show a clear composite peak at about the age of thirty-five. Previously—when I have had a choice, that is—I have worked with men not younger than that and not older than forty. I estimated that the man facing me fell neatly in that range. He was compact, neither light nor heavy, clearly comfortable in his mind and body, and clearly comfortable with his range of competencies. Like a Major League second baseman, perhaps. He knew what he was doing, and he could keep on doing it all day if he had to. He was not handsome, but not ugly either; again, the athletic comparison was, I felt, apt.

He said, “I’m guessing this is my show.”

I said, “You’re wrong. It’s mine.”

I wasn’t sure exactly how to characterize the way he had spoken: was he a humble man pretending not to be? Or was he an arrogant man pretending to be humble pretending not to be?

Obviously it was a question I needed to settle, so I didn’t speak again. I just waited for his response.

It came in the form of an initial physical gesture: he patted the air in front of him, right-handed, his wrist bent and his palm toward me. It was a motion clearly intended to calm me, but it was also a gesture of submission, rooted in ancient habits: he was showing me he wasn’t armed.

“Of course,” he said.

I mirrored his gesture: I patted the air, wrist bent, palm open. I felt the repetition extended the meaning; I intended the gesture to say, Okay no harm, no foul, let’s replay the point. It interested me that I was again unconsciously thinking in terms of sports metaphors. But this was a team, after all.

I said out loud, “You’re the leader *in the field*. You’re my eyes and ears. You have to be, really. I can’t know what you don’t know. But let’s be clear. No independent action. You might be the eyes and the ears, but I’m the brain.”

I probably sounded too defensive, and unnecessarily so: casting modesty aside, as one must from time to time, I was, after all, reasonably well known among a narrow slice of interested parties for my many successful operations in charge of a notably headstrong individual. I was competent in my role, no question. I should have trusted myself a little more. But it was late, and I was tired.

The government liaison man rescued me. He said, “We need to talk about exactly what it is we’re going to do.”

Which surprised me for a moment: why had I assembled a team before the mission was defined? But he was right: beyond the fact that we would be going to Iran—and let’s face it, today all of us go to Iran—no details had yet been settled.

The traitor said, “It has to be about nuclear capability.”

One of the women said, “Of course—what else is there, really?”

I noted that she had a charming voice. Warm and a little intimate. In the back of my mind I wondered if I could use her in a seduction role. Or would that get me in even more trouble, with the powers that be?

The communications man said, "There's the issue of regional influence. Isn't that important? But hey, what do I know?"

The government man said, "Their regional influence depends entirely on their nuclear threat."

I let them talk like that for a spell. I was happy to listen and observe. I saw that the two bruisers at the back were getting bored. They had above-my-pay-grade looks on their faces. One of them asked me, "Can we go? You know the kind of thing we can do. You can give us the details later. Would that be okay?"

I nodded. It was fine with me. One of them looked back from the door with his earlier expression: Don't get us killed too soon.

The poor bloody infantry. Silently I promised him not to. I liked him. The others were still deep in discussion. They were twisting and turning and addressing this point and that. The way the Eames chair was so low to the ground, it put the government man's face right next to the right-hand woman's legs. I envied him. But he wasn't impressed. He was more interested in filtering everything that was said through the narrow lens of his own concerns. At one point he looked up at me and asked me directly: "How much State Department trouble do you want exactly?"

Which wasn't as dumb a question as it sounded. It was an eternal truth that very little of substance could be achieved without upsetting the State Department to some degree. And we worked with liaison men for that very reason: they quelled the storm long enough to let us conclude whatever operation was then in play. I thought his question implied an offer: he would do what it took. Which I thought was both generous and brave.

I said, "Look, all of you. Obviously I'll try to make the whole thing as smooth and trouble-free as possible. But we're all grown-ups. We know how it goes. I'll ask for the extra mile if I have to."

Whereupon the transport coordinator asked a related but more mundane question: "How long are we signing up for?"

"Eighty days," I said. "Ninety maximum. But you know how it is. We won't be in play every day. I want you all to map out a six-month window. I think that's realistic."

A statement which quieted things down a little. But in the end they all nodded and agreed. Which, again, I thought was brave. To use another sports metaphor, they knew the rules of the game. An operation that lasted six months, overseas in hostile territory, was certain to produce casualties. I knew that, and they knew that. Some of them wouldn't be coming home. But none of them flinched.

There was another hour or so of talk, and then another. I felt I got to know them all as well as I needed to. They didn't leave until well into the morning. I called my editor as soon as they were through the door. She asked me how I was, which when questioned from an editor really means, "What have you got for me?"

I told her I was back on track with something pretty good, and that a six-month deadline should see it through. She asked what it was, and I told her it was something that had come to me while I was high. I used the tone of voice I always use with her. It leaves her unsure whether I am kidding or not. So she asked again. I said I had the characters down, and that the plot would evolve as it went along. Iran, basically. As a private joke I couched the whole thing in the kind of language we might see in the trade reviews, if we got any: I said it wouldn't transcend the genre, but it would be a solid example of its type.

LEE CHILD was born in 1954 in Coventry, England, but spent his formative years in the nearby city of Birmingham. By coincidence he won a scholarship to the same high school that JRR Tolkien had attended. He went to law school in Sheffield, England, and after part-time work in the theater he joined Granada Television in Manchester for what turned out to be an eighteen-year career as a presentation director during British TV's "golden age." During his tenure his company made *Brideshead Revisited, The Jewel in the Crown, Prime Suspect,* and *Cracker*. But he was fired in 1995 at the age of 40 as a result of corporate restructuring. Always a voracious reader, he decided to see an opportunity where others might have seen a crisis and bought six dollars' worth of paper and pencils and sat down to write a book, *Killing Floor,* the first in the Jack Reacher series. He is the author of sixteen Jack Reacher thrillers, including *The Affair*, the #1 New York Times bestsellers *Worth Dying For, 61 Hours, Gone Tomorrow, Nothing to Lose*, and *Bad Luck and Trouble*. His debut, *Killing Floor*, won both the Anthony and the Barry awards for Best First Mystery, and *The Enemy* won both the Barry and the Nero awards for Best Novel. Foreign rights in the Jack Reacher series have sold in more than fifty territories. All titles have been optioned for major motion pictures. Child, a native of England, lives in New York City.

THE LAMB WAS SURE TO GO

GAR ANTHONY HAYWOOD

Ollie Brown finally got tired of chasing Jetta Brown's tail. Jetta was Ollie's wife, a fine and tart little thing who liked to wear dresses that made her teardrop body look like a shrink-wrapped party invite, and her man-mountain husband had been trying to force the idea of monogamy upon her ever since I'd known the pair, which was going on eleven years.

The night I heard the news, I was off my stool and headed for the door of the Deuce, passing Howard Gaines just as he was dropping a cold thirty on my cousin Del, winning another game of dominoes from a man who was both younger and far less inebriated than he. In an effort to blunt Del's humiliation with casual conversation, Howard mentioned offhandedly that Ollie had jumped in front of a Metro Rail train three days before on Flower and Eleventh, leaving Jetta a widow with little in the way of a body to center a funeral around.

I stopped in my tracks. "He killed himself?"

Howard's gray head bobbed up and down. "He left a note. Said he couldn't take Jetta's games no more, and he loved her too much to leave her. And we all know the fool sure as hell couldn't kill her, so..."

"Kill her? That man couldn't touch a hair on that woman's head, didn't matter how bad she treated him," Del said.

And that was the God's honest truth. Anyone who made a habit of drinking at the Deuce became familiar with the pair's routine eventually: Jetta sniffing every pants leg in the house until she found something stiff and willing inside, and Ollie losing his mind and temper in response, pitting his rage and giant hands against all but Jetta herself. That was the one line he could never bring himself to cross.

I shook my head at the shame of it all and sat back down at the bar.

"Hell of a thing, ain't it? Lovin' a woman that much?" Howard said. "Me, I couldn't do it. Throw myself in front of a damn train just 'cause my wife don't know how to keep her drawers on."

"Shoot, you don't know what you could do," Lilly Tennell sneered. The barkeep had ambled over to our end of the bar to regale us with the magnificence of her opinion, and none of us was going to tell her it wasn't appreciated. Lilly was bigger than any two male patrons in the house combined, and she had less patience for disagreement than a black bear with its foot in a trap. "Let the right girl come along and open your nose, see if you ain't turnin' flips and doin' cartwheels at the snap of her little finger!"

The big woman snapped two of her own meaty fingers and laughed, eyes rolling up toward the ceiling.

"Hate to say it, but girlfriend's right," Del said. "I've been there myself. We all have."

"So what?" Howard asked, unconvinced. "Just 'cause a man's crazy in love don't mean he's gotta let a woman treat 'im like a damn dog. She don't wanna do you right, show you the proper respect—"

"Walk away," Del said.

"That's right. Walk the hell off. Shoot, you ain't a man if you can't do that."

Lilly chuckled, grandly amused by Howard and Del's unified front of imperial maleness, and turned—as I knew she inevitably would—in my direction. "You're awful quiet there, hotshot. What do you got to say about it?"

"Me?" I produced a casual shrug. "I guess I say it all depends upon the woman. A man feels one deep enough, there isn't anything she can do to make him leave."

"Oh." Del nodded his head with recognition, a small smile growing larger on his face. "I bet I know who you're talking about."

"Who?" Howard asked.

"A client G had once. She said this fool—"

I silenced him with a shake of my head, but Lilly caught the gesture and jumped on it like a cat pawing a mouse.

"Uh-uh. To hell with that. Finish what you was sayin'," she told Del.

"It's a private matter, Lilly," I said, "and it's not worth talking about."

"You let me an' Howard be the judges of that." The big woman behind the flaming red mouth and dirty apron slapped a fresh glass down in front of me, set a bottle of Wild Turkey alongside it, and said, "Let's hear it."

It's not a story I care much to reflect upon, let alone regale friends with, but confession is supposed to be good for the soul, so I told it.

My soul has always needed all the help it can get.

•••

I remember that it happened during one of those extended lulls in my business that turn my every waking thought to loan sharks and debt consolidation. A stranger and I were sitting out front at the barbershop, watching Mickey Moore shave the stubble from Hobie London's jawline as we all played the dozens at the expense of Condoleezza Rice, when a sister I'd never seen before stepped through the door and sheepishly asked for me.

"I'm lookin' for Aaron Gunner?"

She was a reed-thin, middle-aged black woman who hadn't been the knockout she was dressed up to be for a long time, and like most of my would-be clients, she couldn't believe she hadn't come to the wrong address.

"That's him right there," Mickey said, pointing his scissors in my direction before I could identify myself.

"Aaron Gunner, the private investigator?" She glanced around the barbershop as if it were an apparition that had suddenly sprung up all around her.

"My office is in the back," I said, rising to my feet. "Come on in, Ms....?"

She didn't give me her name, but she followed my lead through the beaded curtain filling an open doorway that separates Mickey's workspace from mine. The sight of my office confused her even further because there's nothing more to it than a desk, two chairs, and a couch, but I took little offense. The sight of it often sets my own head reeling.

I coaxed her into a chair and took my own seat behind the desk, then asked for her name again.

"Innes. Deirdre Innes," she said.

"What can I do for you, Ms. Innes?"

"I thought you'd have a real office. This is nice, but—"

I could have told her it was the best a brother in my profession working out of his own Central Los Angeles neighborhood could do, but I exchanged that explanation for the shorter, less cynical version. "The rent's cheap, and Mickey does my head twice a month for free. How I can help you, Ms. Innes?"

She hugged her purse close to her stomach, gathering nerve, and said, "I need a bodyguard. A man I know's gonna kill me." Her eyes were starting to tear up.

"What man is this?"

"His name's Samuel Stills. I seen 'im kill a man outside a bar eight years ago, and I had to say so in court. He told me then, they ever let 'im out, I was good as dead."

"And he's out now?"

"Girl I know in Corrections says he's scheduled for release this Wednesday."

I started jotting down some notes. "This man he killed. He was a friend of yours?"

"A friend?" Innes shook her head. "He was just somebody asked me to dance that night." Her eyes lit up with anger as she added, "So Samuel followed 'im out back and shot 'im dead afterwards."

"Samuel was your boyfriend?"

"Hell no. That's what he always liked to *think* he was, but it wasn't never like that between us."

I continued my note taking, examining my prospective client more closely as I did so. She was afraid of Stills, to be sure, yet her contempt for him seemed strangely dismissive, as if he wasn't worth all the trouble she was going through to seek protection from him. The contradiction bothered me enough to make me wonder how badly I wanted her business, even as desperate as my circumstances were.

"Eight years is a long time," I said. "How do you know Stills even remembers you?"

"Because I know Samuel Stills." My questions were frustrating her now. "Look, Mr. Gunner, I went to the police, and they said they couldn't help me. They said Samuel had to threaten me over the phone or somethin' 'fore they could even bring 'im in for questionin'. So I come to you, 'cause somebody told me personal security is part of your business. Now if that ain't right—"

"It's right, sure. But—"

"All I want you to do is follow me around for a while. Keep an eye out for Samuel, and let me know if you see 'im. You can do that, can't you?"

"Yes, and I'd be happy to. But it's not going to be cheap. The kind of surveillance you're talking about involves a lot of man hours, and can get rather expensive. How much money were you thinking about spending?"

"I got two hundred dollars."

She said it with a straight face because it wasn't meant to be a joke, but I found myself wanting to laugh out loud nonetheless.

"What?" she asked, keen enough to have sensed that my mood had suddenly changed for the worse.

"I'm afraid there's nothing I can do for you, Ms. Innes. But thanks for stopping by."

"Excuse me?"

"I can't help you. I'm sorry."

"You're *sorry?* I'm tellin' you the man's gonna kill me!"

"I'm sure you're mistaken. After eight years inside, you're probably the last thing on Stills's mind. If I were you, I'd go home and forget about him, just as he's almost certainly forgotten about you."

"No! I need your help, and I ain't got nobody else I can turn to!"

I stood up to encourage her to do likewise, said, "I wish I could do more for you, but I can't. For two hundred dollars, the most I could do is roll by the crib once, maybe twice a day for a week, just to make sure you're okay."

"That ain't enough!"

She was pushing me now, and I was in no mood to be forgiving about it. "Look. You come in here talking about Stills like he's a homicidal maniac, then offer me two lousy bills to stand between him and you. I may be crazy, sister, but I'm not that crazy. Now, I can walk you to the door, or you can find your own way out, but either way, you're leaving, 'cause this conversation is over."

She finally leapt to her own feet, quaking with rage, and stormed out, throwing a full-bodied epithet behind her in farewell.

As soon as she was gone, I sat down again, feeling like a prize ass, yet cheered by the almost certain knowledge that I would not be left to wallow in my self-deprecation for long.

"That was kinda cold, wasn't it?" Mickey asked, dropping in on me right on cue.

"Nobody asked you back here, old man. And I believe you've still got somebody in your chair."

He kept right on coming as if I hadn't spoken, clippers still in his hand, said, "Lady's in trouble. Ain't her fault she ain't got a dime to get herself out of it."

"I'm all done, Mick, working for the next thing closest to free. It's bull."

"It is what it is. What you gonna do, move the business out to Brentwood?"

"There is no business. That's the problem in a nutshell."

"You run into a cold spell, that's all. We all do, don't matter what line we're in. You just gotta wait it out."

He made it sound so simple. Wait it out. Keep my shingle up in the heart of the 'hood, where few people have a dollar to spend on something other than the barest of necessities, and hope somebody one day would walk through my door and offer me something to do with my time that both paid well and would be worth talking about afterward, without any soul-crushing embarrassment.

Sure.

I fixed my eyes on my landlord until he, too, fled the room, and then I resigned myself to taking his advice and doing what I always do when I arrive at this pathetically redundant crossroads in my "career"—Nothing.

•••

Jolly Mokes and his late wife Grace had once been the polar opposites of Ollie and Jetta Brown. The only playing around on Jolly Grace ever did was all in her husband's head, and unlike Ollie, Jolly had no problem directing his jealous rages at the woman he loved, rather than the men he imagined she was sleeping with. A convenient excuse for his abuse was the nightmare we both had endured over a nineteen-month span in the jungles of Long Binh, as Jolly took the carnage we witnessed there harder than most, but the truth was that Jolly didn't need any excuse to be a bully; he'd been a big, insecure little boy when he arrived in Vietnam, and that was what he was when he got out.

He killed Grace two years after we came home. Her death was unintentional. He meant only to slap her around to the point of tears as usual, but ever since he beat her to death instead, he's had to live with the crime as if he'd put a gun to her head and pulled the trigger all the same. On the surface, it wouldn't appear that he deserved anybody's sympathy, and I never thought he'd get an ounce of mine. Then he came to see me at Mickey's one day after they let him out of Corcoran State Prison, begging for some kind of work, and the guilt-wracked shell of the giant I remembered demanded my pity in spite of my best efforts to withhold it. He had found God in prison, and part of the deal he had made with his Savior was to carry his wife's murder around on his back like a ton of iron chain mail, for every minute of every day he had left to live.

It's a hard penance to watch, and an even harder one to ignore.

So I found a way to give him a job, and I've been doing the same as my workload and finances allow ever since. It's no great sacrifice. I only assign him things I have no wish to do myself, and I pay him next to nothing for the privilege.

When neither my own conscience nor Mickey's needling would allow me to forget Deirdre Innes after three days of trying, I finally got the idea to let Jolly watch her back for me. It was a task tailor-made for him.

"All you have to do is watch her crib for a while, let me know if you see this boy Stills anywhere," I told him.

"And if I do?"

"You call me immediately. He sounds like a real piece of work, I don't want you trying to deal with him alone. You got that?"

Jolly said he did. But Deirdre Innes wasn't exactly grateful when I took him over to her place to introduce them.

"Uh-uh, Mr. Gunner. I want *you* to look after me, not him. I need a professional."

"Jolly is a professional," I said.

"Has he got a gun?"

"He doesn't need a gun. What, you can't see how big this man is?"

"Samuel don't give a damn about big. If he comes over here lookin' for me, only thing gonna stop 'im from killin' me is a bullet. I told you that."

I gave her an easy choice to make: Jolly or nothing.

She took Jolly.

•••

The next day, I finally picked up some work of my own. A well-to-do sister in the technical writing trade named Seneca Latimore was about to marry David Fields, her fiancé of ten months, and before she went down the aisle with him, she wanted me to do a thorough background check on him, just in case he'd left any embarrassing details out of the life story he'd offered her. She was a careful woman, Ms. Latimore, and it was a good thing she was because over the course of the next two weeks, I would discover that "David Fields" was only the latest of many false identities her betrothed had seen fit to invent in recent years. Fields was actually an ex-con out of Louisiana whose real surname was Spencer, and if the treatment he'd given the three women he'd married previously was any indication, the post-honeymoon plans he had for Seneca Latimore were not going to be of the happily-ever-after variety. I had seen armed bank robbers hit and run without leaving as much emotional carnage behind.

I was only two days into the task of documenting the full breadth of the David Fields iceberg when Jolly called me away.

"I seen Samuel Stills," he said.

He was calling from a ramshackle eyesore known as the Red Owl Motel, ten shoebox rooms slathered in crumbling white stucco that made the blight of Van Ness and Gage complete. He met me across the street where I parked my car and we walked back over together.

"He still here?"

"Yeah. Room 4. I followed him over from Ms. Innes's place. She was out when he came around. I figured you might wanna know where he's stayin'."

"You figured right. What'd he do over at Ms. Innes's place?"

"He didn't do anything. Just walked past the house a couple times, like he was tryin' to make up his mind 'bout goin' to the door. But he never did."

We were moving past the motel office now, no one visible behind the dust-caked screen door, and I could see Room 4 waiting for us less than fifteen yards away.

"What're we gonna do?" Jolly asked.

"I'm not sure yet. Let's just see how it goes."

"Okay. But we better watch this boy close, G. He looks like the wrong end of trouble to me."

I knocked on the door and waited as Jolly loomed behind me, both of us aware that we were taking a chance that Stills wouldn't make any assumptions about who was calling and put a few bullet holes in the door before opening it. It was the risk you always took when you dropped in on bad people unexpectedly.

But Stills just flung the door open without a word and snapped, "What you want?" No more concerned about us being a danger to him than the line of red ants snaking across the dusty motel porch at our feet.

"Samuel Stills?" I asked.

California cons don't have access to weight rooms anymore, but Stills had been doing some kind of heavy lifting while he'd been inside. Shirtless and barefoot, his arms were massive slabs of chiseled muscle and his waist was narrow and hard, abs rippling beneath his gleaming black skin like a tightly coiled serpent.

"Who the hell are you?"

"My name's Gunner, his is Mokes. We're friends of Deirdre's. May we come in?"

"No. Deirdre who?"

"Deirdre Innes. You were just by her place. She's asked us to come by and find out what you want with her. Do we really have to do this out here?"

He didn't say anything, just let a long spell go by while deciding what move to make. In the space of that moment, I came to understand why Innes was so terrified of him. Even motionless, he exuded the threat of sudden violence. Jolly was right: Stills *was* the wrong end of trouble.

"Come on in," he said at last, and stepped away from the door so we could enter.

He sat on a corner of his bed and interlocked the fingers of both hands between his legs, a grin appearing out of nowhere on his face. I scanned the room quickly for a weapon within his reach but saw nothing of the kind, a warning that he was confident enough of his chances against us without one.

"So. Deirdre sent you over here, huh?"

"That's right. She wants to be left alone," I said.

"Alone? She tol' you that?"

"Yeah. And she wanted us to tell you."

"That's bull. I love Dee."

"Apparently, that's not the impression you left her with back at your trial. Or don't you remember threatening to kill her?"

He laughed. "Now I *know* this is bull," he said.

And then he came off the bed.

He plowed into me first and the two of us together drove Jolly to the floor. The big man went down beneath us like a pole-axed buffalo and struck the back of his head on a dresser against the wall, damn near knocking the face-board off one of its drawers. From the sound the air made leaving his lungs, I could tell he wasn't going to be of much help to me for a while.

I'd brought my Ruger 9 into the room with me along with Jolly, but Stills was keeping me too busy fending off blows to find it. He had a knee in my chest as he threw punches at my face, working like hell to put my lights out before Jolly could shake the cobwebs off. One of his right hands connected solidly with the bridge of my nose and I heard bone snap, felt my nostrils cloud with warm blood. Something shrill kept ringing in my ear, and I finally realized Stills had yet to stop laughing.

I reared up and bucked him off, but somewhere in the process my Ruger slipped its holster and slid under the table behind me, well out of reach. Meanwhile, Stills was demanding my ongoing attention. He was faster and stronger than I, and the punches I threw at him kept meeting thin air. I caught him once with a good left under the right eye, but he took it like a bitch-slap from an old woman with rheumatism. All it did was stop the laughter; it didn't stop him.

Our fight had been a fair one up to now, and that was the problem with it. I was overmatched. I reached out for an equalizer and found one in the only chair in the room, an armless, straight-backed piece of old kindling no homeless person would have brought back to the shanty. I swung it in a sideways arc Stills couldn't duck and broke it across his left shoulder, legs and seat flying in all directions. He charged me in response, enraged and hurt now, and I used the chair back still in my hand to counter. My blow caught him flush on the left side of his lowered head and sent him sprawling to the floor, grasping for me in vain. He was climbing back to his feet in seconds, going for the gun under the table, but his time had run out: Jolly was back in action. The big man kicked him under the jaw with the size fourteen on his right foot and Stills went down for good, blinking at the ceiling and gasping for breath.

I retrieved my sidearm and moved in close so Stills would have no choice but to hear me clearly.

"Leave the lady be, Sammy. You scare her, and she doesn't like being scared. If my boy and I have to come back here again, it won't be to ask for the same favor with sugar on top."

Stills propped himself up on his elbows, teeth painted crimson. "Go to hell, punk! Me an' Dee got mad love for each other! Ain't nothin'—or nobody—gonna keep us apart!"

He was laughing again, spitting blood, too tickled by the weightlessness of my threat to contain himself.

"You know he ain't gonna listen, right?" Jolly asked me later, when we had returned to my car across the street.

"I know. That's why you're gonna forget all about Ms. Innes for now and start following him. And the first step he takes in her direction—"

"I call you. Got it. But—"

"I don't know what we'll do after that, Jolly. Guess we'll just have to cross that bridge when we come to it."

It wasn't much of an answer, but it was the only one I had to offer.

•••

Late the next day, a man came to see me at Mickey's. I didn't know him, but I knew the type. Shaved-head white men in short-sleeved dress shirts and eyesore neckties aren't always agents of the law, but a foul mood thrown into the mix makes it all but an absolute certainty.

He flashed the badge as soon as Mickey showed him to my desk and I'd nodded at the sound of my name. "Larry Milton, Mr. Gunner. Department of Corrections. I understand you've been harassing one of my parolees."

I didn't follow fast enough to suit him.

"Samuel Stills. You and a friend went by his place yesterday and roughed him up. Maybe you'd like to tell me why."

"Sure. But first, a salient correction: Stills was the one who started the heavy horseplay, not us. My associate and I only went there to talk."

"About what?"

"My client, Deirdre Innes. She's worried Stills intends to do her harm, and hired me to make sure that he doesn't."

"Deirdre Innes?" Milton scrunched his face up in what appeared to be minor confusion. "Why would Stills want to hurt Deirdre Innes?"

"You don't know? She's the reason he *is* a parolee. It was her testimony that put him away eight years ago. What, you didn't read the man's file?"

"I *wrote* the man's file. What the hell are you talking about?"

I began to feel uneasy. "The guy Stills shot at the bar. She testified at his trial she saw it happen. Are you trying to say she didn't?"

He smirked and shook his head, as if I'd just finished telling a bad joke he'd heard a million times before. "Christ, you make-believe policemen. How stupid can you get? Innes never testified against Stills and neither did anyone else. The man made a full confession, his case never even went to trial."

My mouth inched open and something came out, but it wasn't anything either of us could understand.

I asked Milton politely to have a seat and set myself for the jarring impact of a long, humiliating fall from grace.

•••

The downside to having a man like Jolly Mokes do your dirty work is how rarely you can reach him when you desperately need to. It's all Jolly can do to keep peanut butter on his bread, so a telephone, even one of those pay-as-you-go cellular numbers, is well beyond his reach. That means the only time I ever talk to him during a case is when he sees fit to either call me from a pay phone or visit me in the office. Our lines of communication are entirely one sided.

I waited three hours after Larry Milton left me for Jolly to make contact, then went out to find him. I drove to the Red Owl Motel first, hoping both Jolly and Samuel Stills would be there, but neither man was in evidence. I tried to sit in the car and wait for one or the other to show up, not wanting to give in to the dread that was trying its damnedest to take hold of me, but fifteen minutes was all the waiting I could do. My calls to Deirdre Innes's home were still going unanswered and my mind was working overtime inventing reasons for her absence. It was just after 7 P.M. now, and night had set its full weight down upon the city of black angels.

A single light burned in the front window of my client's little tool shack of a house on Third Avenue when I pulled up at the curb. The place was quiet, too, like a prison cell just before the bulls slam the door on you for the first time. No one answered the door when I knocked or called out Innes's name. None of this added up to anything more ominous than an empty house, but my nerves were on edge just the same.

I slid around the side of the house and knocked on the back door with the same result. Every window at the rear was dark. I tried the knob and the door came open in my hand like a well-oiled stage prop. I called Innes's name one more time, received no answer, then drew my gun and started in. Slowly.

Somebody grabbed my shoulder from behind, and I spun around on my heels, put the gun in a big man's face, and damn near pulled the trigger.

"Dammit, Jolly! Where the hell's Stills?"

"I'm sorry, G. I lost 'im. He went up in this mall and…There were so many people. I looked and I looked, but—"

"Forget it. Come on."

I led the way into the house. We crept down a narrow hallway past three open doors—a bedroom, bathroom, and kitchen—only to be greeted by shadows and more silence. The burning light in the living room beckoned. With Jolly's breathing booming like thunder in my ears, we finally reached the front of the house, and that was where we found them: Innes sitting motionless on the edge of a sofa, Samuel Stills laying on one side of his face at her feet, the carpet beneath his torso drenched in blood.

"Damn," Jolly said.

The gun she had used was still in Innes's left hand. Her eyes were fixed on a meaningless spot on the floor, unblinking, and it looked like they had been for a while now. I slipped the revolver from her grasp, then checked Stills's body for a pulse, just to make sure.

"Call 911," I told Jolly, before bearing down on Innes, my voice quavering with rage.

"What the hell happened?"

She didn't answer, oblivious to the question. I hunkered down to make direct eye contact and tried again, a little more forcefully.

"What the hell happened!"

This time my voice registered. Her eyes fluttered to life and refocused. Her mouth changed shape, she gave out a small moan. "Where were you?" she asked. She looked over at Jolly, who was hanging up the phone. "Where the hell was *he*?"

"Never mind that. There's a dead man on the floor and the Man's on his way over here to ask us both how he got there."

"How he got there?" Her eyes flared as white as a camera flash. "How the hell you think he got there? He broke into my crib an' I shot 'im, that's how!"

"That you shot him is obvious. What isn't is why. And don't give me any more of that crap about Stills wanting revenge for your having testified at his trial eight years ago because we both know that's a lie."

"What?"

"You heard me. I had a little talk with his parole officer today. Stills gave the cops a full confession, Deirdre, his case never even went to trial."

Now her eyes went cold again, the telltale sign of a liar being forced without warning to regroup. "So? I still had to tell the cops what I seen! What difference does it make that there wasn't no trial?"

"It doesn't make any difference. Unless Stills wasn't the one who actually pulled the trigger that night."

It was just a hunch, but that was the scenario I'd kept coming around to, ever since Larry Milton left my office. Innes tried hard not to give me anything back in the way of a response, but her silence alone was response enough.

"His P.O. says he took the rap on a charge he might've beaten if he'd only cared to try. Two brothers wrestling over a gun in a dark parking lot, only one witness there to see the gun go off. People walk in cases like that all the time. Only Stills showed no interest in walking. The only thing he seemed to have any interest in was *you*."

"You're crazy. I saw 'im—"

"He was in love with you, the poor bastard, and he wanted to protect you. When that gun went off, he wasn't the one holding it, you were. But he did the time for the crime so you wouldn't have to. Didn't he?"

"Nobody asked him to!" She leapt to her feet, suddenly teary eyed and livid. "Nobody ever asked that fool for nothin'!" She glared down at Stills's body, her contempt for him too far gone to conceal a moment longer. "But he was always hangin' around, buyin' me stuff and treatin' me special, like I was his damn woman or somethin'." She looked at me and Jolly, smiled as if we were both as great a fool as Stills. "But I wasn't never his woman! His or nobody else's, and I ain't ever gonna be!"

She started to chuckle, but it died in her throat. Jolly and I said nothing, just stared at her in awe, and a siren building in the distance became the only sound in the room.

"I was only tryin' to help 'im that night," Innes said, winding down again. "They dropped the gun and I picked it up. If I hadn't shot that man…"

She waited for one of us to say something, but neither of us did.

"Why the hell're you lookin' at me like that?" Jolly and I kept our thoughts to ourselves.

•••

"So Stills never did mean the girl no harm?" Howard Gaines asked, putting the last of his dominoes back in their box. He and I, Del and Lilly were the only ones left standing at the Deuce.

"Until that night? No. I don't think he ever did," I said.

"Damn. Then why'd she tell you—"

"She was hopin' G would kill the fool for her," Lilly said, further demonstrating her own capacity for detection. "That's why she was always tellin' 'im how dangerous Stills was, and how only somebody with a gun could stop 'im from hurtin' her, and all that." She turned to me. "Ain't that right?"

I nodded.

"She wanted to be rid of the boy that bad?" Howard asked.

"She would have made the argument she had no choice. She eventually produced letters he'd written her from prison, expressing his undiminished love for her, and his intent to be with her again the minute he was released. It's for sure he still felt that way the day Jolly and I went to see him at his motel."

"He was whipped," Del said. "Just like Ollie. It didn't matter that she didn't want him. The man was in love."

"Or at least he was until the night he died," I said.

"How do you mean?" Howard asked.

"The story Innes told the police was that Stills broke into her place in a rage. He was furious that's she'd hired Jolly and me to scare him off, and if she hadn't put those three bullets in him, he would have done something very similar to her."

"And you all believed that?" Lilly asked.

"The district attorney did. Me?" I shrugged and slid off my stool, my enthusiasm for the tale wearing thin. "I'm not so sure."

"Come on, cuz," Del said. "Don't leave 'em hangin' like that. Tell 'em the rest of it."

"The rest of it?" Howard asked.

I looked around the empty room, caught in a trap of my own making, and said, "Stills's P.O. came to see me again a few days after he died. He said the letters Stills wrote Innes from prison didn't contain a single threat against her, and the cops never found any signs of forced entry at her crib. To him, that could only mean two things: She let Stills in herself that night and shot him in cold blood."

"And?" Howard asked.

"And she finally hit the man she was really aiming at eight years before."

I went to the Deuce's door and drove my tired ass home.

GAR ANTHONY HAYWOOD is the Shamus and Anthony Award-winning author of twelve crime novels. Haywood's first of six mysteries featuring African-American private investigator Aaron Gunner, *Fear of the Dark* (1989), won the Private Eye Writers of America's Shamus award for Best First Novel of 1989, and his first Aaron Gunner short story, "And Pray Nobody Sees You" (1995), won both the PWA's Shamus and World Mystery Convention's Anthony awards for Best Short Story of 1995. His most recently published short story, "The First Rule Is" (2010), was featured in the 2010 edition of *Best American Mystery Short Stories*. Haywood has written for both the *New York Times* and *Los Angeles Times*, such television dramas as *New York Undercover* and *The District*, and he has co-authored two Movies of the Week for the ABC Television Network. His latest novel is the noir thriller *Assume Nothing* (2011).

LUCK

T. JEFFERSON PARKER

PAXTON WATCHES THE RIVER THROUGH A LODGE WINDOW. LATE spring, the water high and fast. He is thirty years old, the only son of a roaming father and a mother who doted, drank, and sobbed. Thus Paxton understands opportunity and need. He is handsome and often referred to as charming. When instructing skiers and seducing neglected Aspen trophy wives grew dicey, Paxton stole off to Sun Valley and taught himself to fly-fish, and when the fishing bored him he took up guiding fly-anglers, and when guiding bored him he took over management of Rolling Thunder Lodge on the East Walker in Nevada. Rolling Thunder is of, by, and for the rich. Paxton sees it as a land of milk and honey and himself as a pretender trying to find a way in, but he presents as the man in charge. He perceives in himself the need for putting down roots.

He watches more of the new guests arrive, collected at the Reno airport by Don in one of the Rolling Thunder Escalades. Paxton has asked Don to make this run for him, paid him nicely for the favor. Now Don swings out a rear passenger door and offers his hand, which goes untaken for a long beat.

Then Paxton sees her hand appear in Don's, then the flash of her blouse and the unfurling of denim and the black bounce of her hair as she steps out and lands with a light little hop and of course she's smiling. Lourdes. Lourdes of Austin. Married since their Aspen days, new last name. From around the vehicle comes the husband—hawk-faced, silver-haired, no taller than she is. He surveys her with pride of ownership. A Denver entrepreneur, Paxton knows—private security, fat on Iraq contracts. And a onetime regular at the Jerome Hotel where Lourdes once tended bar.

Paxton takes a deep breath and strides through the door to meet his new guests.

"Welcome to Rolling Thunder, Lourdes."

"John? Johnny! Honey, John Paxton, the best ski coach in all Aspen! John, this is my husband, Cole Trainer."

"Cole."

"I remember you," says Trainer.

She waits for the men to shake hands before offering her own, checking over Paxton with that generous smile. "It's good to see you again."

•••

At cocktail hour in the dining room Paxton rises and pings a knife against his beer bottle to quiet down the spirited conversation. Elk-horn chandeliers high in the beam ceiling cast their glow over the redwood walls and redwood bar and redwood floor, all taken, according to Rolling Thunder lore, from a single Coast Redwood downed by a storm on Cape Mendocino a century ago.

"I just want to say welcome to all of you. Some of you know each other and some have just met. What we've got here is twenty great people, twenty fine anglers..." At this, words of protest rise toward the chandeliers, mostly a few of the women demurring, though Paxton hears Cole Trainer crack something about being lucky to catch one damned fish..."And of course, that means ten good teams who have paid up some good money to see who can land the biggest fish on a fly. Trout, that is. The carp in the pools don't count. Now, before we get to all the measuring and photographing and release rules, let's get the dollars straight: the teams are already good on the ante for the first five days—that's ten grand per team per day. Then it's going to double to twenty thousand per team per day for the last two days, kinda like the flip in hold 'em, which will give us a pot of nine hundred thousand dollars. You wanted winner take all so that's what you've got. It's a nice pot if everyone stays in for the whole week. It's not going to make or break anybody in this room, but it certainly ramps up the fun level on the river!"

Laughter. Paxton thinks that nine hundred grand would go a long way toward making *him* but he has spent a lifetime masking such thoughts. People like these, he knows, will hardly notice that their wagers would be his fortune. Paxton has learned that their own hale and hearty voices are all these people really hear or have ever heard. The common man is just that. Privilege has its privileges.

Paxton smiles and lifts his beer, then runs down more of the rules: ten beats on five miles of river, beats assigned by random drawing each night after dinner, beats may be traded or sold between consenting teams; barbless artificial flies fished no more than two at a time, no scents or additives of any kind; all fish to be digitally photographed while hung upon IGA certified Boga grips that will be issued tomorrow, the scale and the fish must *both* be in the picture and the poundage clearly visible; each grip will be marked with unique designs and numbers to discourage scale substitution and other trickery; all fish caught dawn to dusk; all fish revived and released.

"But basically it's an honor system," says Paxton. "It's either that or an auditor watching over every shoulder. We're not the IRS!"

•••

The first morning Paxton watches the Trainers on beat one, just west of the lodge. Breakfast is done, the beats have been drawn by lottery the night before, the Boga grips have been issued.

The morning is cool and breezeless and jays bicker in the stand of lodgepole pines that line this part of the river. The water is high and fast with runoff, near-record snow pack in the Eastern Sierras last season, the East Walker rushing at eight hundred cubic feet per second, the tremendous volume disguised by a smooth surface and straight runs. Where the river bends, the pools are trenched deep by time and water, and in the pools and in the heads of pools and in the tailouts lie the big fish.

The Trainers move slowly along the bank, close to each other, and Paxton, back in the trees, catches bits of their conversation. They stop at the first pool and rig up dry-droppers. Wrong choice, Paxton knows. Their voices have the eager tone of anglers getting ready. Cole holds up his terminal fly to Lourdes and she looks at it and nods and of course smiles. She pulls a dispenser of split shot from her vest and tips out some weight and drops it into his outstretched hand. Until now he had no idea she fished. In Aspen she was one of the best beginning adult skiers he'd ever taught, a tall, raven-haired, fair-skinned beauty who had glided her way into his heart with the same effortlessness with which she had learned to ski. She was single then and Paxton had used every trick in his book to interest her, but she'd seen him for what he was and found him wanting.

Cole Trainer kisses her lightly then heads upstream. He picks his way along, arms out for balance, the metal studs of his boots chirping against the rocks. He's short but wiry and athletic, and a beginner at this, Paxton sees. There is something endearing about them, he thinks: the way they can kiss eye to eye, the way he's willing to take up her sport, their expensive matching waders and boots, rods and reels. Something puzzling, too: he's twice her age, not much to look at, exhibits only moderate personality. Money? Maybe not. Paxton remembers Lourdes in Aspen tending bar at the Jerome, working hard for the tips and not wasting them on anything he could see. Guys stacked up five deep with offers for her of everything on God's earth. One of them Cole Trainer, of course. She rented a little condo year-round down in Basalt. She cooked at home most meals, drove an aging Subaru, bought her skis and boots one-year-used from a local outfitter. She was maddeningly sensible. He couldn't shake her loose with fine wines, expensive restaurants, or good blow. She'd just smile them off and turn in early so she could hit the mountain when the lifts started up the next morning.

Trainer sizes up the next pool. One of the best on the whole five miles, Paxton thinks. You can fish up through the tail-out then about midway there's a string of big boulders that reach halfway across. Only the first three are visible from shore now, with the runoff raging down the Sierras in this unseasonably hot spring. The last rock is just underwater, a great, declined, moss-greased tabletop nicknamed Monster Rock and the saying here at Rolling Thunder is that there are only two kinds of anglers, those who have fallen off Monster Rock and those who are about to. Further guidelines: don't even try this pool without good studded boots and a staff and a wading belt worn tight; the bottom is stacked with boulders and sharp branches so if you go in, keep your feet in front of you and use your arms and hands to protect your head; let the current take you down and across; you'll hit the tail-out eventually; stay out of the big tangle of boulders and root balls along the west bank because it's superdeep and fast; Bill Overby got caught in there two years back, no belt, waders filled and he drowned. Nice guy, a good man.

Trainer wobbles out onto the first boulder, then the second, then he makes the third. He pokes his wading staff into the East Walker and it nearly rips it from his hand. He's only ankle deep on the rock but Paxton watches his balance come and go. He's surrounded by depth. Trainer has his arms out again for stability. His knees are bent and his weight is forward like a new skier and Paxton knows that just a little surge in the current or a little slip on the mossy rocks is all it will take to dunk the man.

Somewhat surprisingly, Trainer makes it to Monster Rock. He collapses the staff and worries it back into the sheath on his belt. Then he slowly stands up straight and brings the rod closer and unhooks the terminal fly from the line guide. He sways. Paxton thinks that he looks like a child's toy, one of those bottom-weighted dummies that always springs back upright after being kicked or hit. Trainer casts upstream but with far too much power, and the flies and split-shot bolo into a gruesome tangle that lands on the swift water and streaks downriver past him.

Then, with a sharp yelp, he falls.

Paxton makes the bank and times the current and wades into the same murderous flow. He's in sandals and shorts and a light windbreaker and years ago he lifeguarded down at the Wedge in Newport and even the mighty East Walker can't touch the Wedge. Can't touch it. It is very damned cold though. He intercepts and steers Trainer downstream and sees the fear in his eyes, but he eases the little man to the bank and drags him up on the smaller boulders of the tail-out. Trainer climbs over the rocks on all fours, breathing fast and whinnying quietly. Paxton turns to see Lourdes crunching across the rocks toward them.

"Where's my rod? I lost my fuckin' rod."

•••

After dinner Trainer finds Paxton at the bonfire. The flames throw shadows on the private security man's face, sharply divided by a curt mustache. He wears a golf shirt with his company logo on it. He has a tumbler of ice and booze of some kind. Paxton hears the boom and trill of laughter on the other side of the big fire. It's been a good day for the Swedes—Lars and Ursula Lagervist, owners of a commercial fishing fleet plying the Baltic Sea—who landed a five-pound, seven-ounce brown trout on beat nine, besting Sean and Cassy Robertson of Jackson, Wyoming. Lars's laughter booms again.

"I owe you thanks," says Trainer. "So, thanks. And I do mean it."

"You bet. I've seen it happen there before. Monster Rock. I'm glad I was close by."

"Took me an hour to thaw out."

"Water was fifty degrees this morning."

Trainer eyes the lodge manager. "Just happened by at the right time, didn't you?"

"Good luck for both of us, for sure."

"You've had some practice, happening by at the right time."

"What do you mean by that?"

"I remember you from Aspen. One of the gigolos."

Paxton and Trainer lock stares as men do.

"Every other man's a gigolo when you hit fifty," says Paxton.

"There was Jan Firestone and Deb Morse and Jennifer Donovan."

"Yes, there were. Good people. I didn't realize you were keeping such a close eye on me. Or was it on them?"

"Security. It's what I do. I know their husbands. You wouldn't last a half hour in my world."

"You barely made it five minutes in mine."

"I never make the same mistake twice."

"Good luck in the contest."

"I've got luck. But I caught squat. And Lourdes's little two-pounders won't cut it."

"You had enough luck to get the best beat today, Trainer. That's where the biggest fish are. If you draw it again in the lottery, you better make it pay. If you don't draw it, you can always buy it from a willing seller. Shitcan that stimulator fly. Put a size-sixteen Green Copper John on top and an eighteen Red Tiger Midge on bottom. Get some of those articulating midge flies made by that guide over in Mammoth. We sell 'em here in the shop. If you don't get grabs, switch colors. Go deep, sink-tip line, three-X fluorocarbon tippet. You've got six more days to fish."

Trainer clinks his ice and drinks. "Why the advice?"

Paxton isn't entirely sure why. Something to do with a genuine desire to offer a thing of value, something of his father's notions of romance and his mother's need to please her husband against all odds. "A wedding present to you and Lourdes."

"I know about you and her."

"There isn't much to know about me and Lourdes."

"Keep it that way."

"Take care of your wife," says Paxton. "And I'll take care of the lodge."

Trainer drinks and clinks and studies Paxton. "Thanks again. For the tips."

"Nymphs don't always work on the East Walker. Sometimes the only way to get the big pigs is with a streamer—low light, mornings and evenings when the sun is off the water. If you're not in the lead by Friday, it's time to switch out. Tell Don in the shop we talked."

"I've never fished a streamer," says Trainer.

"It can get technical," says Paxton, thinking: any idiot can fish a streamer.

"Hey, gigolo, if I win this contest on your setup, we'll split the money."

"Deal."

"You just keep the good advice coming in. And keep it between us."

•••

Early the next morning Paxton stands before one of the lodge windows and watches the Trainer cabin. Their matching waders hang side by side from the lacquered log wall, their matching boots wait below them, their matching rods and reels are slotted into the rod holders. Only their vests are different—olive for Lourdes and tan for Cole.

Paxton views this tableau, this outdoorsy fantasy of doing what you love with a person you love, and he knows it's partially a marketing illusion but he buys into it anyway. Completely. It just takes money and a person you love, he thinks. He would buy in if he could. He sips his coffee and indulges ideas of what he could do with his half of the Trainers' $900,000. Big Sky, maybe—not the high-end stuff but something small and warm, maybe an acre or two. He could find a woman to love in Bozeman. Or Mammoth, maybe—neat little condo, slopes to ski. Women all over. Or screw the cold altogether—rent back in Newport Beach again, out on the peninsula, lifeguard part time, no worries, man, and wall-to-wall women.

He watches Lourdes and Cole come out to the cabin deck and gear up. Of course their coffee mugs match. They sit in big rough-hewn rockers to yank on their boots. They talk unhurriedly, like old friends, though Paxton can't hear the words. Cole hands Lourdes two small boxes and a small opaque tub that Paxton recognizes as the fly containers used by the lodge shop. Lourdes cocks her head in interest. So, Paxton thinks: sometime between last night and now Trainer has prevailed on Don to supply him with sink-tip line, backing, Copper Johns, and articulating midge flies. Trainer is serious about this. From his vest he produces a spare spool and hands it to Lourdes. She begins to tie on the backing.

After the Trainers set off for beat eight, Paxton waits a few minutes and follows. Again he watches them unseen, Lourdes landing small fish and Cole landing nothing, hooking nothing, his small body emanating an almost visible frustration. He shouts profanities. He sets the hook on an already vanished trout, or perhaps a twig or rock, and the line jumps into the air above him in a hurricane of tangles. More profanities. The private security man has around him an aura of razor wire.

•••

In the early afternoon housecleaning is in the Trainer cabin. The front door is propped open by a wheeled red bucket from which a mop leans against the doorjamb. Under the guise of keeping an eye on the help Paxton enters the cabin and gives the woman a nod. He sees the still-unmade bed. He imagines the smooth beauty of Lourdes and the gristly reality of Cole and wonders that they share the same bed. This is a mystery he tries to solve but cannot. It strikes him that he will never have enough for Lourdes or any woman like Lourdes, enough of anything they need, and the money is just the beginning of what he'll never have enough of. On his way out he sees the rustic hat rack in the corner, Trainer's big Stetson on an upper stump and Lourdes's lavender lace nightie hanging by a thin strap, off center and somehow occupied.

•••

The Swedes best their own record with a six-pound, five-ounce rainbow measuring twenty-four inches. They gloat through cocktail hour and dinner, big-toothed and blue-eyed and clearly addled by the Maker's Mark. The Robertsons of Jackson have managed a five-pound brown; the Keelers of San Diego landed one slightly heavier; a father-son team out of Michigan landed a four-pound, nine-ounce fish. But none of them matter. Lars and Ursula Lagervist pour bourbons all around and Lars tells a long joke about the agonizing humorlessness of Norwegians.

Late that night Paxton walks to the river and watches the moonlight wobble upon the currents of beat two. He senses something nearby, then he sees a shape in the darkness. A bear, he thinks. He watches and backs off a few steps, but the shape becomes Lourdes sliding down from a boulder.

"I'm glad you're not a bear," he says.

"So am I."

"Cole here?"

"Sleeping. He told me about your deal—the winning strategy for half the money."

"Is that okay with you?"

"Why wouldn't it be?"

"It's your money too."

"I'd love to see us all win. It's all in good fun."

Nine hundred thousand dollars is not good fun, thinks Paxton. He says nothing as his awareness of their present differences cascade down on him. He feels like a tiny man staring up at a towering cliff whereupon giants enact great scripts.

"Why'd you offer to help him?" she asks.

"Looked like he could use some help."

"You wouldn't believe how lucky he is."

"I might, Lourdes."

"At things he has no talent for."

"He'll need more than luck to catch some fish on this water. Spring is the toughest when the runoff is like this. You should have done the contest in November."

A moment goes by.

"How do you like running the lodge here, as opposed to giving ski lessons?"

"Steadier work. You know."

"Haven't met anyone yet?"

"Just playing. Thirty's the new twenty."

"It's not anysuch. You'd jump at the right one and you know it."

"You were the right one. I told you so."

"Not like you meant it!"

"I was quietly planning some self-improvement on your behalf."

"Maybe you shouldn't have been so darned quiet about it."

"Why him?" asks Paxton, genuinely interested and genuinely perplexed.

"It's all in the heart, Johnny. He was the last one I would have predicted, really. He's got good morals. Stubborn as a goat. He's the toughest softie there is. Never had an advantage and made himself into what he wanted to be. He'd do anything on earth for me. I don't seem to be doing him justice by talking about him. It's hard to explain. I don't really have to, do I?"

"You don't."

Paxton looks at Lourdes in the moonlight and he feels all his old affections and desires. There was a time when *he* would have done anything on earth for her, and that time had submerged years ago then breached into the present, but what was the point of doing anything on earth for someone if they didn't know you would? Why had he been so darned quiet about it? Why had he believed that she might be more drawn to his athletic grace, his charm, his looks, his fine wine and fun drugs, than to the larger fact that he loved her with all of his imperfect heart and really *would* do anything in the world for her? Except tell her.

"I always liked you, Johnny."

"I didn't know that. I liked you so much I missed it."

"I was pretty darned quiet about it myself. People like us, we hold out, you know? We wait. See, with Cole, it's a whole different thing, he forces you to react to him, one way or another. Just barges right in. He does that to the whole world. But we're okay, you and me. We're good. It's never too late to make a friend, is it?"

"It's a good thing to make a friend, Lourdes."

•••

On the sixth day of competition, Paxton watches again through the lodge window as Lourdes and Cole emerge from their cottage with a lantern and cups of coffee, pull on their waders and boots, and fiddle with their leaders and flies. The weather has turned cold overnight and smoke faintly issues from the cabin chimney. The Trainers have a rosy glow that angers Paxton.

After they leave he wends his way to beat seven, stopping to watch and talk with the teams along the way. At beat five he watches Ursula Lagervist land—and with the help of her husband—weigh, photograph, and measure a seven-pound, eight-ounce, twenty-five-inch rainbow.

"This fish cannot be defeated," Lars insists. "We have won the competition."

"Two more days, Lars," notes Paxton.

"We will catch one still bigger," says Ursula.

"You crafty Swedes will be tough to beat!" says Paxton.

At beat seven he kneels unseen amidst the boulders behind Cole and watches the man flail away with his casts, tangle his line, curse, hook nothing. Even from this distance Paxton can see that Cole will not fool a single fish with his drifts. The line is tight, the drag pronounced, the East Walker fish far too wary to fall for a fly that bullets downstream then slows to a wake-inducing crawl for another twenty feet while it angles sharply across the current. Cole may as well be grabbing at the fish with his hands. Paxton intuits that his $450,000 has all but slipped away.

Downstream Paxton finds Lourdes and again he crouches among the rocks at the tree line and observes. She fishes like she skied—without strain. He watches her high-stick the hole, ride out the drift and lower the rod tip, let the flies rise up through the water column as the line tightens, and pop the flies once in case a trout likes a rising bug. Then she water-hauls, letting the river load the rod before she arches a roll cast that morphs into a reach cast that nicely turns over the flies and weight upstream. And again, and again, each cast finding a new slice of river.

•••

At dusk Paxton is down in the lodge basement, working on the drag system of a failing reel. He likes this semi-hidden lair, likes the workbench and the tools and the scent of pine pitch and earth, likes the whiskey he's already had two of, likes this time of evening. It is hot outside again but cool down here in the eternal half-light.

He stands at the workbench and looks out one of the ground-level windows. And he sees first Cole then Lourdes Trainer loping up the trail from the river toward the lodge. They are running hard and purposefully and Lourdes is smiling, of course she's smiling, and she's so beautiful it hurts. They're whooping and yipping like war party braves. Cole stumbles and rights himself and now he's smiling too.

Out on the lodge veranda the Trainers present the pictures of their fish and of the certified grip from which the fish hangs, and one nonrequired photo of the fish laid out on the bank beside a tape measure held taut in Lourdes's lovely hands.

A brown trout, deep black and honey yellow and fired through with red dots. Bulky, kype-jawed, magnificent.

Nine pounds, seven ounces.

Twenty-eight inches long.

Paxton takes his turn on the camera. His first reaction is he respects this fish. His second reaction is that he respects the person who caught it. His third reaction is that he's just made $450,000 and this slab of cold muscle has changed his life.

"It was pure luck," says Cole. "It just happened about half hour ago. I was reeling in the line for another cast and I was cussing my fool head off because I hadn't even had a grab all day and then the damned lure gets caught on a rock and I cuss even louder and yank the damned pole and guess what? The rock swims away! It goddamned swims away! And you'll like this, Johnny—I caught him on my own setup. I got sick of all that sinking fly-line and put my floatin' stuff back on. And I got rid of all those hooks and weights you had me on, and I tied on my lucky fly, it's a Royal Coachwhip or something like that, and guess what? It gets the job done. It nails that fish.

"What do you think of that, Gigolo John?"

•••

Later that night around the bonfire Cole Trainer cuts Paxton off from the herd and states his case: "I thank you for all your help, Paxton. I do. But I caught that fish on my own stuff with my own methods and therefore I will not split the money with you. Doesn't mean a nice tip won't be in order. If I end up winning, I mean."

"I understand, Cole."

"I won it fair and square. On my own."

"Yes, you did. But it's not over. The Robertsons have beat one tomorrow and there are bigger fish than yours in that hole. I've seen them. I've caught them."

"Don't worry about beat one. I already bought it off the Robertsons. Cost me twenty grand but it was worth it."

"You're cagey, Cole. But let me tell you something. Don't call me what you called me tonight in front of the other guests. Do not do that again."

Trainer pauses a beat. "Naw, I won't. I'm sorry. I shouldn't have said that. Nobody likes the truth thrown in their face at cocktail hour."

•••

But for Paxton it's too late for apologies. By midnight he's downed the rest of the whiskey and opened a new bottle. He walks to the river. He walks through the woods. He stands in the now empty dining room with the tables already set for the pre-dawn anglers' breakfast. He feels clear, heightened, acutely sober. It isn't the money that makes his fury. It isn't that Cole Trainer has luck. It isn't that Paxton had had a grab from Lourdes in Aspen but was too busy trying to impress her to even know it and so had failed to act, opening the way for Cole Trainer to deploy his blunt forces upon her. No. What makes his fury is Trainer's rudeness, his enormous rudeness. In front of Paxton. In front of his guests. In front of Lourdes.

He takes another swallow. He can see their cabin from here, still in the night. *I always liked you, Johnny.* Paxton hears the sudden roaring in his ears, the sound of the Wedge waves breaking around him on a September south swell, the sound of dashed hope, the sound of continuing fury. It is growing. He drinks again. He can bear the thousand injuries of Cole Trainer, but his insults? These must be avenged. He must act now, for the past and present and the future, for Lourdes and for himself.

•••

Half an hour later he stands at the basement workbench, one of Cole Trainer's wading boots clamped firmly in the vise before him, sole up, studs twinkling in minor moonlight coming through the ground-level windows. Paxton tests the firmness of the boot in the vise. The boot is firm. It moves very little as he vees the blades of the bolt cutter up against the tiny carbide cleat and clips it off. He hears it ping to the floor behind him. Then the next, and the next. Then the second boot, then the steel file and some elbow grease, get those stumps smooth, get them ready for Monster Rock. He stalks back to the Trainers' cabin under cover of the night, drunk as a pirate but quiet as a cat as he holds his breath and sets the boots back where they belong.

•••

Paxton dreams terrible dreams, rises well before the sun, breakfasts with his guests, and later watches the Trainers head off for beat one. They walk side by side down the trail on this last day, Cole with one arm around Lourdes's waist. He angles his head toward hers to hear her better. He looks every inch the man to beat, a man with a nine-plus-pound, kype-jawed, nine-hundred-thousand-dollar fish to his credit. A man with luck. Luck enough for Monster Rock in late spring. Strands of Lourdes's black hair wobble free from her hat and catch the first unfettered sunlight coming through the trees.

Paxton fusses around the dining room, watches the cable news turned down low. A slaughter of tourists in a luxury hotel. More nuclear exhibitions by a rogue state. A deadly flu pandemic brewing. Drought and flood. War and famine. Genocide and celebrity babies.

At evening Paxton sits and waits in the shade of the veranda. He feels like a man awaiting a verdict. He can see the East Walker rolling silently by, its great tonnage disguised by its glassy surface. He leans his head back against the logs of the lodge and falls into a dream in which Lourdes sits beside him, right here on the Rolling Thunder deck, and the years have grayed her hair but her beauty is still intact. In the dream Paxton has aged too, and there is an understanding in their silence, a knowing complicity in all it has taken to get them here. They hold hands. From within the dream he hears Cole Trainer cry out and Paxton awakens.

A minute later Trainer comes slowly walking up the trail through the trees. In his arms is Lourdes, dripping river water, her legs jack-knifed over one of his forearms, her shoulders supported by the crook of his other arm, her arms dangling and her hair swaying in rhythm with his steps. Cole stumbles but catches himself. He stops amidst the trees and rears back his head and roars.

They lay Lourdes out on one of the veranda picnic tables and Paxton prepares to begin CPR, but Cole Trainer throws him against the lodge wall. "Don't touch her. I did that. I did that already."

"I'll do it again."

"You won't touch her."

"She can come back."

"Go to hell, John. Don't touch her."

Then some of the early-returned anglers are there, and one of them is a doctor from Santa Fe, and he takes over in a bluster of activity: he orders a call to 911, orders Don to fetch blankets; he checks her eyes and pulse and commences chest compressions and orders Cole to do the interval breathing for Lourdes and this goes on for five minutes and then ten. But Lourdes is utterly without sign of life. Paxton stands and watches in dull horror. The Rolling Thunder housekeeper appears at the far end of the big deck, big-eyed, crossing herself. After another five minutes the doctor stops his compressions and sets a hand on Lourdes Trainer's forehead.

"It's okay Cole," he says softly. "We've done what we can."

Cole Trainer rises from her mouth and roars again. Paxton leans over the table, looking into Lourdes's face, one hand placed on her arm as if trying to awaken her and the other brushing across the sole of her wading boot, feeling for the studs but finding only the smooth stumps on which he had staked the beginning of his new life.

T. JEFFERSON PARKER is a native of the Southern California suburbs that are the backdrops to his bestselling crime dramas. He is an alumnus of the University of California, Irvine, which honored him in 1992 as a Distinguished Alumnus. His writing career began in 1978 as a cub reporter on the weekly newspaper, *The Newport Ensign*. After covering police, city hall and cultural stories for the *Ensign*, Parker moved on to the *Daily Pilot* newspaper, where he won three Orange County Press Club awards for his articles. While working by day as a technical writer for an Orange County aerospace company, he worked on drafts of a novel at night and on weekends, resulting in *Laguna Heat*, published to rave reviews and made into an HBO movie starring Harry

Hamlin, Jason Robards and Rip Torn. His novels and stories are noted for their realism, their page-turning suspense and their sharp-eyed look at contemporary Southern California.

THE STORY OF THE STABBING

JOYCE CAROL OATES

Four years old she'd begun to hear in fragments and patches like handfuls of torn clouds the story of the stabbing in Manhattan that was initially her mother's story.

That morning in March 1980 when Mrs. Karr drove to New York City alone. Took the New Jersey Turnpike to the Holland Tunnel exit, entered lower Manhattan and crossed Hudson and Greenwich Streets and at West Street turned north, her usual route when she visited an aunt who lived in a fortresslike building resembling a granite pueblo dwelling on West Twenty-seventh Street, but just below Fourteenth Street traffic began abruptly to slow—the right lane was blocked by construction—a din of air hammers assailed her ears—vehicles were moving in spasmodic jerks—Madeleine braked her 1974 Volvo narrowly avoiding rear-ending a van braking to a stop directly in front of her—a tin-colored vehicle with a corroded rear bumper and a New York license plate whose raised numerals and letters were just barely discernible through layers of dried mud like a palimpsest. Overhead were clouds like wadded tissues, a sepia glaze to the late-winter urban air and a stink of diesel exhaust and Madeleine Karr whose claim it was that she loved Manhattan felt now a distinct unease in stalled traffic amid a cacophony of horns, the masculine aggressiveness of horns, for several blocks she'd been aware of the tin-colored van jolting ahead of her on West Street, passing on the right, switching lanes, braking at the construction blockade but at once lurching forward as if the driver had carelessly—or deliberately—lifted his foot from the brake pedal and in so doing caused his right front fender to brush against a pedestrian in a windbreaker crossing West Street—crossing at the intersection though at a red light, since traffic was stalled—unwisely then in a fit of temper the pedestrian in the windbreaker struck the fender with the flat of his hand—he was a burly man of above average height—Madeleine heard him shouting but not the words, distinctly—might've been *Fuck you!* or even *Fuck you asshole!*—immediately then the van driver leapt out of the van and rushed at the pedestrian—Madeleine blinked in astonishment at this display of masculine contention—Madeleine was expecting to see the men fight together clumsily—aghast then to see the van driver wielding what appeared to be a knife with a considerable blade, maybe six—eight—inches long—so quickly this was happening, Madeleine's brain could not have identified *Knife!*—trapped behind the steering wheel of the Volvo like a child trapped in a nightmare Madeleine witnessed an event, an action, to which her dazzled brain could not readily have identified as *Stabbing! Murder!*—in a rage the man with the knife lashed at the now stunned pedestrian in the windbreaker, who hadn't time to turn away—striking the man on his uplifted arms, striking and tearing the sleeves of the windbreaker, swiping against the man's face, then in a wicked and seemingly practiced pendulum motion slashing the man's throat just below his jaw, right to left, left to right causing blood to spring instantaneously into the air—*A six-foot arc of blood at least* as Madeleine would describe it afterward, horrified—for never had Madeleine Karr witnessed anything so horrible—never would Madeleine Karr forget this savage attack in the unsparing clarity of a morning in late March—the spectacle of a living man *attacked, struck down, stabbed, throat slashed* before her eyes. The victim wore what appeared to be work clothes—work boots—he was at least a decade older than his assailant—late thirties, early forties—bareheaded, with steely-gray hair in a crew cut—only seconds before the attack the victim had been seething with indignation—he'd been empowered by rage—the sort of individual with whom, alone in the city in such circumstances on West Street just below Fourteenth Street, Madeleine Karr would never have dared to lock eyes. Yet now the burly man in the windbreaker was rendered harmless—stricken—sinking to his knees as his assailant leapt back from him—very quick, lithe on his feet—though not quick enough to avoid being splattered by his victim's blood. Making no attempt to hide the bloody knife he held—he seemed to be visibly brandishing the knife—the van driver ran back to his vehicle, deftly climbed inside and slammed shut the door and in virtually the same instant propelled the van forward head-on and lurching—with a squeal of tires against pavement—aiming the van into a narrow space between another vehicle and the torn-up roadway where construction workers in safety helmets were staring—knocking aside a sawhorse, a series of orange traffic cones scattering in the street and bouncing off other vehicles as in a luridly colorful and comic simulation of bowling pins scattered by an immense bowling ball; by this time the stricken man was kneeling on the pavement desperately pressing both hands—these were bare hands, big-knuckled, Madeleine could see from a distance of no more than twelve feet—against his ravaged throat in a gesture of childlike poignancy and futility as blood continued to spurt from him *Like water from a hose—horrible!*

As if paralyzed Madeleine stared at the stricken man now writhing on the pavement in a bright neon-red pool—still clutching desperately at his throat—amid a frantic din of horns—traffic backed up for blocks on northbound West Street as in a nightmare of mangled and thwarted movement like snarled film. Nothing so mattered to Madeleine as escaping from this nightmare—in a panic of thudding heart, clammy skin and dry mouth thinking not of the stricken man a short distance from the front bumper of the Volvo but of herself—yearning only to turn her car around—reverse her course on accursed West Street back to the Holland Tunnel—the Jersey Turnpike—and so to Princeton from which scarcely ninety minutes before Madeleine had left with such exhilaration, childish anticipation and defiance *Manhattan is so alive!—Princeton is so embalmed. Nothing ever feels real to me there, this life in disguise as a wife and a mother of no more durability than a figure in papier-mâché. I don't need any of you!*

So strangely Madeleine had seemed to be watching the spectacle a few yards away through a kind of tunnel—through the wrong end of a telescope—curiously drained of light and color; now she could see other people—fellow pedestrians approaching the fallen man—workmen from the construction site—on the run a police officer—and a second police officer.

Soon then there came a deafening siren—several sirens—emergency vehicles could come no closer than a side street peripheral to Madeleine's vision—Madeleine saw figures bent over the fallen man—a stretcher was lifted, carried away—nothing to see finally but a pool of something brightly red like old-fashioned Technicolor glistening on the pavement in cold March sunshine. *And the nightmare didn't end. The police questioned all the witnesses they could find. They came for me, they took me to the police precinct. For forty minutes they kept me. I had to beg them to let me use the women's room—I couldn't stop crying—I am not a hysterical person but I couldn't stop crying—of course I wanted to help the police but I couldn't seem to remember what anything had looked like—what the men had looked like—even the "skin color" of the man with the knife—even of the man who'd been stabbed. I told them that I thought the van driver had been dark-skinned—maybe—he was "young"—in his twenties possibly—or maybe older—but not much older—he was wearing a satin kind of jacket like a sports jacket like high school boys wear—I think that's what I saw—I couldn't remember the color of the jacket—maybe it was dark—dark purple?—a kind of shiny material—a cheap shiny material—maybe there was some sort of design on the back of the jacket—Oh I couldn't even remember the color of the van—it was as if my eyes had gone blind—the colors of things had drained from them—I'd seen everything through a tunnel—I thought that the van driver with the knife was dark-skinned but not "black" exactly—but not white—I mean not "Caucasian"—because his hair was—wasn't—his hair didn't seem to be—"Negroid hair"—if that is a way of describing it. And how tall he was, how heavy, the police were asking, I had no idea, I wasn't myself, I was very upset, trying to speak calmly and not hysterically, I have never been hysterical in my life. Because I wanted to help the police find the man with the knife. But I could not describe the van, either. I could not identify the van by its make or by the year. Of course I could not remember anything of the license plate—I wasn't sure that I'd even seen a license plate—or if I did, it was covered with dirt. The police kept asking me what the men had said to each other, what the pedestrian had said, they kept asking me to describe how he'd hit the fender of the van,* *and the van driver—the man with the knife—what had he said?—but I couldn't hear—my car windows were up, tight—I couldn't hear. They asked me how long the "altercation" had lasted before the pedestrian was stabbed and I said that the stabbing began right away—then I said maybe it had begun right away—I couldn't be sure—I couldn't be sure of anything—I was hesitant to give a statement—sign my name to a statement—it was as if part of my brain had been extinguished—trying to think of it now, I can't—not clearly—I was trying to explain—apologize—*I *told them that I was sorry I couldn't help them better, I hoped that other witnesses could help them better and finally they released me—they were disgusted with me, I think—I didn't blame them—I was feeling weak and sick but all I wanted to do was get back to Princeton, didn't even telephone anyone just returned to the Holland Tunnel thinking I would never use that tunnel again, never drive on West Street not ever again.*

•••

In that late winter of 1980 when Rhonda was four years old the story of the stabbing began to be told in the Karr household on Broadmead Road, Princeton, New Jersey. Many times the story was told and retold but never in the presence of the Karrs' daughter, who was too young and too sensitive for such a terrifying and ugly story and what was worse, a story that seemed to be missing an ending. *Did the stabbed man die?—he must have died. Was the killer caught?—he must have been caught.* Rhonda could not ask because Rhonda was supposed not to know what had happened, or almost happened, to Mommy on that day in Manhattan when she'd driven in alone as Daddy did not like Mommy to do. Nothing is more evident to a child of even ordinary curiosity and canniness than a family secret, a "taboo" subject—and Rhonda was not an ordinary child. There she stood barefoot in her nightie in the hall outside her parents' bedroom where the door was shut against her daring to listen to her parents' lowered, urgent voices inside; silently she came up behind her distraught-sounding mother as Madeleine sat on the edge of a chair in the kitchen speaking on the phone as so frequently Madeleine spoke on the phone with her wide circle of friends. *The most horrible thing! A nightmare! It happened so quickly and there was nothing anyone could do and afterward...*Glancing around to see Rhonda in the doorway, startled and murmuring *Sorry! No more right now, my daughter is listening.*

Futile to inquire what Mommy was talking about, Rhonda knew. What had happened that was so upsetting and so ugly that when Rhonda pouted wanting to know she was told *Mommy wasn't hurt, Mommy is all right—that's all that matters.*

And *Not fit for the ears of a sweet little girl like you. No no!*

Very soon after Mrs. Karr began to tell the story of the stabbing on a Manhattan street, Mr. Karr began to tell the story too. Except in Mr. Karr's excitable voice the story of the stabbing was considerably altered for Rhonda's father was not faltering or hesitant like Rhonda's mother but a professor of American Studies at the University, a man for whom speech was a sort of instrument, or weapon, to be boldly and not meekly brandished; and so when Mr. Karr appropriated his wife's story it was in a zestful storytelling voice like a TV voice—in fact, Professor Gerald Karr was frequently seen on TV—PBS, Channel 13 in New York City—discussing political issues—bewhiskered, with glinting wire-rimmed glasses and a ruddy flushed face. *Crude racial justice! Counter lynching!*

Not the horror of the incident was emphasized, in Mr. Karr's telling, but the irony. For the victim, in Mr. Karr's version of the stabbing, was a *Caucasian male* and the delivery-van assailant was a *black male*—or, variously, a *person of color.* Rhonda seemed to know that *Caucasian* meant *white,* though she had no idea why, she had not heard her mother identify *Caucasian, person of color* in her accounts of the stabbing, for Mrs. Karr dwelt almost exclusively on her own feelings—her fear, her shock, her dismay and disgust—how eager she'd been to return home to Princeton—she'd said very little about either of the men as if she hadn't seen them really but only just the stabbing *It happened so fast—it was just so awful—that poor man bleeding like that!—and no one could help him. And the man with the knife just—drove away...*But Mr. Karr who was Rhonda's daddy and an important professor at the University knew exactly what the story meant for the young black man with the knife—the young *person of color*—was clearly one of *an exploited and disenfranchised class of urban ghetto dwellers rising up against his oppressors crudely striking as he could, class vengeance, an instinctive "lynching," the white victim is collateral damage in the undeclared and unacknowledged but ongoing class war.* The fact that the delivery-van driver had stabbed—killed?—a pedestrian was unfortunate of course, Mr. Karr conceded—a tragedy of course—but who could blame the assailant who'd been provoked, challenged—hadn't the pedestrian struck his vehicle and threatened him—shouted obscenities at him—a good defense attorney could argue a case for self-defense—the van driver was protecting himself from imminent harm, as anyone in his situation might do. For there is such a phenomenon as *racial instinct, self-protectiveness. Kill that you will not be killed.*

As Mr. Karr was not nearly so hesitant as Mrs. Karr about interpreting the story of the stabbing, in ever more elaborate and persuasive theoretical variants with the passing of time, so Mr. Karr was not nearly so careful as Mrs. Karr about shielding their daughter from the story itself. Of course—Mr. Karr never told Rhonda the story of the stabbing, directly. Rhonda's Daddy would not have done such a thing for though Gerald Karr was what he called *ultra liberal* he did not truly believe—all the evidence of his intimate personal experience suggested otherwise!—that girls and women should not be protected from as much of life's ugliness as possible, and who was there to protect them but men?—fathers, husbands. Against his conviction that marriage is a bourgeois convention, ludicrous, unenforceable, yet Gerald Karr had entered into such a (legal, moral) relationship with a woman, and he meant to honor that vow. And he would honor that vow, in all the ways he could. So it was, Rhonda's father would not have told her the story of the stabbing and yet by degrees Rhonda came to absorb it for the story of the stabbing was told and retold by Mr. Karr at varying lengths depending upon Mr. Karr's mood and/or the mood of his listeners, who were likely to be university colleagues, or visiting colleagues from other universities. *Let me tell you—this incident that happened to Madeleine—like a fable out of Aesop.* Rhonda was sometimes a bit confused—her father's story of the stabbing shifted in minor ways—West Street became West Broadway, or West Houston—West Twelfth Street at Seventh Avenue—the late-winter season became midsummer—in Mr. Karr's descriptive words *the fetid heat of Manhattan in August.* In a later variant of the story which began to be told sometime after Rhonda's seventh birthday when her father seemed to be no longer living in the large stucco and timber house on Broadmead with Rhonda and her mother but elsewhere—for a while in a minimally furnished university-owned faculty residence overlooking Lake Carnegie, later a condominium on Canal Pointe Road, Princeton, still later a stone and timber Tudor house on a tree-lined street in Cambridge, Massachusetts—it happened that the story of the stabbing became totally appropriated by Mr. Karr as an experience he'd had himself and had witnessed with his own eyes from his vehicle—not the Volvo but the Toyota station wagon—stalled in traffic less than ten feet from the incident: The delivery van braking to a halt, the pedestrian who'd been crossing against the light—*Caucasian, male, arrogant, in a Burberry trench coat, carrying a briefcase—doomed*—had dared to strike a fender of the van, shout threats and obscenities at the driver and so out of the van the driver had leapt, as Mr. Karr observed with the eyes of a frontline war correspondent—*Dark-skinned young guy with dreadlocks like Medusa, must've been Rastafarian—swift and deadly as a panther*—the knife, the slashing of the pedestrian's throat—a ritual, a ritual killing—sacrifice—in Mr. Karr's version just a single powerful swipe of the knife and again as in a nightmare cinematic replay which Rhonda had seen countless times and had dreamt yet more times there erupted *the incredible six-foot jet of blood* which was at the very heart of the story—the revelation toward which all else led.

What other meaning was there? What other meaning was possible?

Rhonda's father shaking his head marveling *Like nothing you could imagine, nothing you'd ever forget. Jesus!*

•••

That fetid-hot day in Manhattan. Rhonda had been with Daddy in the station wagon. He'd buckled her into the seat beside him for she was a big enough girl now to sit in the front seat and not in the silly baby seat in the back. And Daddy had braked the station wagon, and Daddy's arm had shot out to protect Rhonda from being thrown forward, and Daddy had protected Rhonda from what was out there on the street, beyond the windshield. Daddy had said *Shut your eyes, Rhonda! Crouch down and hide your face darling* and so Rhonda had.

•••

By the time Rhonda was ten years old and in fifth grade at Princeton Day School Madeleine Karr wasn't any longer quite so cautious about telling the story of the stabbing—or, more frequently, merely alluding to it, since the story of the stabbing had been told numerous times, and most acquaintances of the Karrs knew it, to a degree—within her daughter's presence. Nor did Madeleine recount it in her earlier breathless appalled voice but now more calmly, sadly *This awful thing that happened, that I witnessed, you know—the stabbing? In New York? The other day on the news there was something just like it, or almost*...Or *I still dream about it sometimes. My God! At least Rhonda wasn't with me.*

It seemed now that Madeleine's new friend Drexel Hay—"Drex"—was frequently in their house, and in their lives; soon then, when they were living with Drex in a new house on Winant Drive, on the other side of town, it began to seem to Rhonda that Drex who adored Madeleine had come to believe—almost—that he'd been in the car with her on that March morning; daring to interrupt Madeleine in a pleading voice *But wait, darling!—you've left out the part about*...or *Tell them how he looked at you through your windshield, the man with the knife*—or *Now tell them how you've never gone back—never drive into the city except with me. And I drive.*

Sometime around Christmas 1984 Rhonda's mother was at last divorced from Rhonda's father—it was said to be an *amicable parting* though Rhonda was not so sure of that—and then in May 1985 Rhonda's mother became Mrs. Hay—which made Rhonda giggle for *Mrs. Hay* was a comical name somehow. Strange to her, startling and disconcerting, how Drex himself began to tell the story of the stabbing to aghast listeners *This terrible thing happened to my wife a few years ago—before we'd met—*

In Drex's excited narration Madeleine had witnessed a street mugging—a savage senseless murder—a white male pedestrian attacked by a gang of black boys with switchblades—his throat so deeply slashed he'd nearly been decapitated. (In subsequent accounts of the stabbing, gradually it happened that the victim had in fact been decapitated.) The attack had taken place *in broad daylight in front of dozens of witnesses and no one intervened—somewhere downtown, below Houston*—unless *over by the river, in the meatpacking district*—or *by the entrance to the Holland Tunnel*—or (maybe) it had been *by the entrance to the Lincoln Tunnel, one of those wide ugly avenues like Eleventh? Twelfth?—not late but after dark.* The victim had tried to fight off his assailants—valiantly, foolishly—as Drex said *The kind of crazy thing I might do myself, if muggers tried to take my wallet from me*—but of course he hadn't a chance—he'd been outnumbered by his assailants—before Madeleine's horrified eyes he'd bled out on the street. *Dozens of witnesses and no one wanted to get involved—not even a license plate number or a description of the killers—just they were "black"—"carried knives"—Poor Madeleine was in such shock, these savages had gotten a good look at her through her windshield—she thought they were "high on drugs"—only a few yards from Madeleine my God if they hadn't been in a rush to escape they'd have killed her for sure—so she couldn't identify them—who the hell would've stopped them? Not the New York cops—they took their good time arriving.*

Drex spoke with assurance and authority and yet—Rhonda didn't think that the stabbing had happened quite like this. So confusing!—for it was so very hard to retain the facts of the story—if they were "facts"—from one time to the next. Each adult was so persuasive—hearing adults speak you couldn't resist nodding your head in agreement or in a wish to agree or to be liked or loved, for agreeing—and so—how was it possible to know what was *real?* Of all the stories of the stabbing Rhonda had heard it was Drex's account that was scariest—Rhonda shivered thinking of her mother being killed—trapped in her car and angry black boys smashing her car windows, dragging her out onto the street stab-stab-stabbing… Rhonda felt dazed and dizzy to think that if Mommy had been killed then Rhonda would never have a mother again.

And so Rhonda would not be Drex Hay's *sweet little stepdaughter* he had to speak sharply to, at times; Rhonda would not be living in the brick colonial on Winant Drive but somewhere else—she didn't want to think where.

Never would Rhonda have met elderly Mrs. Hay with the soft-wrinkled face and eager eyes who was Drex's mother and who came often to the house on Winant Drive with presents for Rhonda—crocheted sweater sets, hand-knit caps with tassels, fluffy-rabbit bedroom slippers which quickly became too small for Rhonda's growing feet. Rhonda was uneasy visiting Grandma Hay in her big old granite house on Hodge Road with its medicinal odors and sharp-barking little black pug Samson; especially Rhonda was uneasy if the elderly woman became excitable and disapproving as often she did when (for instance) the subject of the stabbing in Manhattan came up, as occasionally it did in conversation about other, related matters—urban life, the rising crime rate, deteriorating morals in the last decades of the twentieth century. By this time in all their lives of course everyone had heard the story of the stabbing many times in its many forms, the words had grown smooth like stones fondled by many hands. Rhonda's stepfather Drex had only to run his hands through his thinning rust-colored hair and sigh loudly to signal a shift in the conversation *Remember that time Madeleine was almost murdered in New York City*...and Grandma Hay would shiver thrilled and appalled *New York is a cesspool, don't tell me it's been "cleaned up"—you can't clean up filth—those people are animals—you know who I mean—they are all on welfare—they are "crack babies"—society has no idea what to do with them and you dare not talk about it, some fool will call you "racist"—Oh you'd never catch* me *driving into the city in just a car by myself—even when I was younger—what it needs is for a strong mayor—to crack down on these animals—you would wish for God to swipe such animals away with his thumb—would that be a mercy!*

When Grandma Hay hugged her, Rhonda tried not to shudder crinkling her nose against the elderly woman's special odor. For Rhonda's mother warned *Don't offend your new "grandma"—just be a good, sweet girl.*

Mr. Karr was living now in Cambridge, Mass. for Mr. Karr was now a professor at Harvard. Rhonda didn't like her father's new house or her father's new young wife nor did Rhonda like Cambridge, Mass. anywhere near as much as Rhonda liked Princeton where she had friends at Princeton Day School and so she sulked and cried when she had to visit with Daddy though she loved Daddy and she liked—tried to like—Daddy's new young wife Brooke who squinted and smiled at Rhonda so hard it looked as if Brooke's face must hurt. Once, it could not have been more than the second or third time she'd met Brooke, Rhonda happened to overhear her father's new young wife telling friends who'd dropped by their house for drinks *This terrible thing that happened to my husband before we were married—on the street in New York City in broad daylight he witnessed a man stabbed to death—the man's throat was slashed, blood sprayed out like for six feet Gerald says it was the most amazing—horrible—thing he'd ever seen—he tried to stop the stabbing—he shouted out his car window—there was more than one of them—the attackers—Gerald never likes to identify them as* black—persons of color—*and the victim was a white man—I don't think the attackers were ever caught—Gerald was risking his life interfering—the way he describes it, it's like I was there—I dream of it sometimes—how close we came to never meeting, never falling in love and our entire lives changed like a miracle…*

You'd have thought that Mr. Karr would try to stop his silly young wife saying such things that weren't wrong entirely—but certainly weren't right—and Rhonda knew they weren't right—and Rhonda was a witness staring coldly at the chattering woman who was technically speaking her *stepmother* but Mr. Karr seemed scarcely to be listening in another part of the room pouring wine into long-stemmed crystal glasses for his guests and drinking with them savoring the precious red burgundy which appeared to be the center of interest on this occasion for Mr. Karr had been showing his guests the label on the wine bottle which must have been an impressive label judging from their reactions as the wine itself must have been exquisite for all marveled at it. Rhonda saw that her father's whiskers were bristly gray like metal filings, his face was ruddy and puffy about the eyes as if he'd just wakened from a nap—when "entertaining" in his home often Mr. Karr removed his glasses, as he had now—his stone-colored eyes looked strangely naked and lashless—still he exuded an air of well-being, a yeasty heat of satisfaction lifted from his skin. There on a nearby table was Gerald Karr's new book *Democracy in America Imperiled* and beside the book as if it had been casually tossed down was a copy of *The New York Review of Books* in which there was said to be—Rhonda had not seen it—a "highly positive" review of the book. And there, in another corner of the room, the beautiful blond silly young wife exclaiming with widened eyes to a circle of rapt listeners *Ohhh when I think of it my blood runs cold, how foolishly brave Gerald was—how close it was, the two of us would never meet and where would I be right now? This very moment, in all of the universe?*

Rhonda laughed. Rhonda's mouth was a sneer. Rhonda knew better than to draw attention to herself, however—though Daddy loved his *sweet little pretty girl* Daddy could be harsh and hurtful if Daddy was displeased with his *sweet little pretty girl* so Rhonda fixed for herself a very thick sandwich of Swedish rye crisp crackers and French goat cheese to devour in a corner of the room looking out onto a bleak rain-streaked street not wanting to think how Daddy knew, yes Daddy knew but did not care. That was the terrible fact about Daddy—he knew, and did not care. A nasty fat worm had burrowed up inside Daddy making him proud of silly Brooke speaking of him in such a tender voice, and so falsely; the *stepmother* who was so much younger and more beautiful than Rhonda's mother.

•••

Here was the strangest thing: when Rhonda was living away from them all, and vastly relieved to be away, but homesick too especially for the drafty old house on Broadmead Road where she'd been a little girl and Mommy and Daddy had loved her so. When Rhonda was a freshman at Stanford hoping to major in molecular biology and she'd returned home for the first time since leaving home—for Thanksgiving—to the house on Winant Drive. And there was a family Thanksgiving a mile away at the Hodge Road house of elderly Mrs. Hay to which numerous people came of whom Rhonda knew only a few—and cared to know only a few—mainly Madeleine and Drex of course—there was the disconcerting appearance of Drex's brother Edgar from Chevy Chase, Maryland—identified as an *identical twin* though the men more resembled just brothers than twins. Edgar Hay was said to be a much wealthier man than Drex—his business was pharmaceuticals, in the D.C. area; Drex's business was something in *investments,* his office was on Route One, West Windsor. The Hay twin brothers were in their late sixties with similar chalky scalps visible through quills of wetted hair and bulbous noses tinged with red like perpetual embarrassment but Edgar was heavier than Drex by ten or fifteen pounds, Edgar's eyebrows were white-tufted like a satyr's in an old silly painting and maddeningly he laughed approaching Rhonda with extended arms—*Hel-lo My sweet li'l stepniece happy Turkey-Day!*—brushing his lips dangerously close to Rhonda's startled mouth, a rubbery-damp sensation Rhonda thought like being kissed by a large squirmy worm. *(Call me Ed-gie* he whispered wetly in Rhonda's ear *That's what the pretty girls call me.)* And Madeleine who might have observed this chose to ignore it for Madeleine was already mildly drunk—long before dinner—and poor Drex—sunken-chested, sickly pale and thinner since his heart attack in August in high-altitude Aspen, Colorado, clearly in some way resentful of his "twin" brother—reduced to lame jokes and stammered asides in Edgar's presence. And there was Rhonda restless and miserable wishing she hadn't come back home for Thanksgiving—for she'd have to return again within just a few weeks, for Christmas—yet more dreading the long holiday break—wishing she had something useful to do in this house—she'd volunteered to help in the kitchen but Mrs. Hay's cook and servers clearly did not want her—she'd have liked to hide away somewhere and call her roommate Jessica in Portland, Oregon, but was fearful she might break down on the phone and give away more of her feelings for Jessica than Jessica had seemed to wish to receive from Rhonda just yet… And there was Rhonda avoiding the living room where Hay relatives were crowded together jovial and overloud—laughing, drinking and devouring appetizers—as bratty young children related to Rhonda purely through the accident of a marital connection whose names she made no attempt to recall ran giggling through a forest of adult legs. Quickly Rhonda shrank back before her mother sighted her, or the elderly white-haired woman who insisted that Rhonda call her "Grandma"—sulkily making her way along a hall, into the glassed-in room at the rear of the house where Mrs. Hay kept potted plants—orchids, African violets, ferns. Outside, the November air was suffused with moisture. The overcast sky looked like a tin ceiling. A few leaves remained on deciduous trees, scarlet bright, golden yellow, riffled by wind and falling and sucked away even as you stared. To Rhonda's dismay there was her stepfather's brother—Drex's twin—wormy-lipped Edgar—engaged in telling a story to a Hay relative, a middle-aged woman with a plump cat face to whom Drex had introduced Rhonda more than once but whose name Rhonda couldn't recall. Edgar was sprawled on a white wicker sofa with his stocky legs outspread, the woman in a lavender silk pantsuit was seated in a matching chair—both were drinking—to her disgust and dismay Rhonda couldn't help but overhear what was unmistakably some crude variant of the story of the stabbing of long ago—narrated in Edgar's voice that managed to suggest a lewd repugnance laced with bemusement, as the cat-faced woman blinked and stared open-mouthed as in a mimicry of exaggerated feminine concern *My brother's crazy wife she'd driven into Manhattan Christ knows why Maddie'd been some kind of hippie fem-ist my brother says those days she'd been married to one of the Commie profs at the university here and so, sure enough Maddie runs into trouble, this was before Giuliani cleaned up the city, just what you'd predict the stupid woman runs into something dangerous a gang of Nigra kids jumping a white man right out on the street—in fact it was Fifth Avenue down below the garment district—it was actual Fifth Avenue and it was daylight crazy "Made-*

line" she calls herself like some snooty dame in a movie came close to getting her throat cut—which was what happened to the poor bastard out on the street—in the paper it said he'd been decapitated, too—and the Nigra kids see our Made-line gawking at them through the windshield of her car you'd think the dumb-ass would've known to get the hell out or crouch down and hide at least—as Rhonda drew nearer her young heart beating in indignation waiting for her stepfather's brother to take notice of her. It was like a clumsy TV scene! It was a scene improbable and distasteful yet a scene from which Rhonda did not mean to flee, just yet. For she'd come here, to Princeton. For she could have gone to her father's house in Cambridge, Mass.—of course she'd been invited, Brooke herself had called to invite her, with such forced enthusiasm, such cheery family feeling, Rhonda had felt a stab of pure loneliness, dread. *There is no one who loves me or wants me. If I cut my throat on the street who would care. Or bleed out in a bathtub or in the shower with the hot water running…*

So she'd had a vision of her life, Rhonda thought. Or maybe it was a vision of life itself.

Not that Rhonda would ever cut her throat—of course! Never. That was a vow.

Not trying to disguise her disgust for what she'd heard in the doorway and for Edgar Hay sprawling fatuous drunk. The ridiculous multicourse Thanksgiving dinner hadn't yet been brought to the dining room table, scarcely five thirty P.M. and already Edgar Hay was drunk. Rhonda stood just inside the doorway waiting for Edgar's stabbing story to come to an end. For maybe this would be the end?—maybe the story of the stabbing would never again be told, in Rhonda's hearing? Rhonda would confront Edgar Hay who'd then gleefully report back to Drex and Madeleine how rude their daughter was—how unattractive, how *ungracious*—for Rhonda was staring, unsmiling—bravely she approached the wormy-lipped old man keeping her voice cool, calm, disdainful *Okay then—what happened to the stabbed man? Did he die? Do you know for a fact he died? And what happened to the killer—the killers—the killer with the knife—was anyone ever caught? Was anyone ever punished, is anyone in prison right now?* And Edgar Hay—"Ed-gie"—looked at Rhonda crinkling his pink-flushed face in a lewd wink *How the hell would I know, sweetheart? I wasn't there.*

In the early 1980s, **JOYCE CAROL OATES** surprised critics and readers with a series of novels, beginning with *Bellefluer,* in which she reinvented the conventions of Gothic fiction, using them to reimagine whole stretches of American history. Just as suddenly, she returned, at the end of the decade, to her familiar realistic ground with a series of ambitious family chronicles, including *You Must Remember This,* and *Because It Is Bitter, and Because It Is My Heart.* The novels *Solstice* and *Marya: A Life* also date from this period, and use the materials of her family and childhood to create moving studies of the female experience. In addition to her literary fiction, she has written a series of experimental suspense novels under the pseudonym Rosamond Smith.
As of this writing, Joyce Carol Oates has written 56 novels, over 30 collections of short stories, eight volumes of poetry, plays, innumerable essays and book reviews, as well as longer nonfiction works on literary subjects ranging from the poetry of Emily Dickinson and the fiction of Dostoyevsky and James Joyce, to studies of the gothic and horror genres, and on such non-literary subjects as the painter George Bellows and the boxer Mike Tyson. In 1996, Oates received the PEN/Malamud Award for "a lifetime of literary achievement."

TRADE SECRET

BILL PRONZINI

I WAS SITTING ON ONE OF THE CANVAS CHAIRS ON THE BACK DECK, adjusting the drag on my Daiwa fishing reel, when I heard the car grinding uphill through the woods.

My cabin is on a backcountry lake, pretty far off the beaten track, and the gate across the private road has a No Trespassing sign. The only visitors I get are occasional tradespeople from the little town a dozen miles away, by invitation only, and I wasn't expecting anybody today. I got up, slow—now that the cool early fall weather had set in, my arthritis was acting up—and shuffled inside for my .30-06. Then I went out front to find out who it was. The car that rolled out of the pines was a shiny new silver Lincoln I'd never seen before. Illinois plates—that told me something right there. The driver was a man and he was alone; the angle of the sun let me see that much. But I didn't get a good look at his face until the Lincoln swung to a stop alongside my Jeep and he opened the door. Surprise. Easy Ed Malachi.

He hadn't changed much. A little less of the dyed black hair, a few extra wrinkles in his jowly face and another ten pounds or so bulging his waistline. Dressed same as in the old days, like an Armani ad in a magazine—silk shirt, Bronzini tie, a suit that must've set him back at least three grand. But the outfit was all wrong for a trip into this wilderness country. That told me something, too.

Malachi was smiling when he got out, one of those ear to ear smiles of his that had always made me think of a shark. I leaned the rifle against the wall next to the stacked firewood, moved over to meet him when he came up onto the porch.

"Hey, Griff," he said, and grabbed my hand and pumped it a couple of times. Sunlight glinted off his gold baguette diamond ring, the platinum Patek Philippe watch on his left wrist. "Hope you don't mind me just showing up like this, but you're a hard man to get hold of. Long time, huh? Must be, what, six years?"

"More like seven and a half."

"Some place you got here. Middle of nowhere, not easy to find."

"That's the way I like it."

"Sure, you always were your own man. But I never figured you'd turn into a hermit."

"People change."

"Sure they do. Sure. You're looking good, though, fit as ever. Retirement agrees with you."

"You didn't come all the way up here to make small talk," I said. "What do you want, Ed?"

"How about a drink for starters? I been on the road five hours, I can use one. You still drinking Irish?"

"Now and then."

"Spare a double shot for an old friend?"

We'd never been friends, but there was no point in making an issue of it. I led him inside, poured his drink and a dollop for myself while he looked around at the knotty pine walls, the furniture and bookcases I'd built myself, the big native stone fireplace. "Some place," he said again.

"Suits me."

"I see you got a phone, but I couldn't find a number."

"It's unlisted. I don't use it much."

"Where's your television? Bedroom?"

"I don't have a TV. Or want one. Can't get reception up here anyway."

"Yeah? So what do you do nights, winters?"

"Read, mostly. Work puzzles, listen to CB radio. Fall asleep in front of the fire."

"The quiet life." Malachi's expression said what he meant was boring life. He couldn't imagine himself living the way I did, without luxuries and all the glitz he was used to. "What about women?"

"What about them?"

"You always had one around in the old days."

"That was the old days. Now I like living alone."

"But you don't always sleep alone, right? I mean, you're not even seventy yet."

"One more year."

"Hell, sixty-nine's not old. I'm sixty-five and I still get my share." His laugh sounded forced. "Good old Viagra."

"Let's take our drinks out on the deck," I said.

We went out there. Malachi carried his glass over to the railing, stood looking down at the short wooden dock with my skiff tied up at the end, then out over the mile and a half of glass-smooth lake, the pine woods that hemmed it on three sides, the forested mountains in the near distance.

"Some view," he said. "Anybody else live on this lake?"

"No. Nearest neighbors are two miles from here and they're only around in the summer."

"You do a lot of fishing?"

"Fair amount. Mostly catch and release."

"No fun in that. What about deer? Catch and release them too?"

"I don't hunt as much as I used to."

"How come? Still got your eye, right?"

"My eye's fine. Arthritis is the problem."

"But you can still shoot? Your hand's still steady?"

"Steady enough. Why don't you get to the point, Ed, save us both some time?"

He took a swallow of his Irish, coughed, drank again. He was still smiling, but it looked as forced now as his laugh had been. "I got a problem," he said. "A big problem."

"You wouldn't be here if you didn't. And you wouldn't've come alone."

"I don't know who to trust anymore, that's the thing. I'm not even sure of my bodyguards, for Christ's sake. Things've gotten dicey in the business, Griff. Real dicey."

"Is that right?"

"Might as well tell you straight out. Me and Frank Carbone, we're on the outs. Big time."

"What happened?"

"Power struggle," Malachi said, "and it's none of my doing. Frank's gotten greedy in his old age, wants to expand operations, wants full control."

"Why come to me about it?"

"Why do you think? Do I have to spell it out?"

"Contract offer? After all these years?"

"Sure, a contract. Best one you ever had."

"I'm an old man. Why not bring in some young shooter from out of town? Detroit, Miami, LA."

"I got to have somebody I know, somebody I can trust. I could always trust you, Griff. You never took sides, never rocked the boat. Just took the contracts we gave you and carried them out."

"That was a long time ago," I said. "I've been out of the business almost eight years."

"Not such a long time. I'm betting you're as good as you ever were. The best. Not one screw-up, not one miss. And you always had an angle nobody else thought of. Like the time the cops stashed that fink Jimmy Conlin in the safe house with half a dozen guards, and still you found a way to make the hit. How'd you manage it, anyway? I always wondered."

"Trade secret," I said.

Another forced laugh. He gulped the rest of his drink before he said, "Fifty K was the most you ever got in the old days, right? For Jimmy Conlin? I'll pay you seventy-five to hit Frank Carbone."

"I'm not interested."

"What? Why the hell not? Seventy-five's a lot of money."

"Sure it is. But I don't need it."

"Everybody needs money. Sooner or later."

Well, he was right about that. I was down to only a few thousand stashed in the strongbox under the bedroom floor, and the cabin could use a new roof, a new hot water heater. I could use a bigger skiff, too, with a more reliable outboard. But money and the things it could buy weren't important to me anymore. I could make do with what I had, make it last as many years as I had left.

"No sale, Ed."

"Come on, don't play hard to get. Seventy-five's all I can afford. Think what that much green'll buy you. Round the world cruise. Trips to Europe, South America, anywhere you want to go."

"There's no place I want to go," I said. "Everything I want is right here. I haven't been away from this wilderness in five years, not even for one day, and I don't intend to leave again for any reason or any amount of money. I'm staying put for the rest of my life."

"Bullshit, Griff. Can't you see how desperate I am?"

"I see it, but the answer is still no."

Malachi's fat face was a splotchy red now—anger, fear, the whiskey. "Goddamn you, I done plenty for you in the old days. Plenty. You owe me."

"No, I don't. I don't owe you or anybody else. I paid all my debts before I retired."

"You better take this contract," he said. He pointed an index finger at me, cocked his thumb over it. "You hear me? You know what's good for you, you take it and you do it right."

"You threatening me, Ed? I don't like to be threatened."

"I don't care what you like. You got to do this for me, you got to hit Frank, that's all there is to it. If you don't and I have to take a chance on somebody else—"

"Then that somebody hits me too. That what you're saying?"

"Don't make me do this the hard way, that's what I'm saying. I like you, Griff, I always have, you know that. But you got to take this contract."

I gave him a long look. His words had been hard, but his eyes were pleading and he was sweating into the collar of his expensive silk shirt. I said, "I guess I don't have much choice."

"Neither of us has. So you'll take it?"

"Yeah. I'll take it."

"Good! Good man! I knew you'd come around." Malachi's big smile was back, crooked with relief. He used a monogrammed handkerchief to wipe off his sweat, then clapped me on the arm. "How about we have another drink," he said, "seal the bargain?"

I said that was fine with me and went inside to refill our glasses. Before I took them out to the deck, I made a quick detour into the bedroom.

"What's that you got there?" Malachi asked when I handed him his drink. He was looking at the wicker creel I'd slung over my shoulder.

"Creel. I'm going fishing after you leave. Let's take our drinks down to the dock."

"The dock? What for?"

"Nice by the water this time of day, good place to talk. There're a few things I'll need to know about Frank and his habits. Besides, there's something I want to show off, something I pulled out of the lake."

"Sure, okay, what the hell."

We went down the back steps, across to the dock, out along it to where the skiff was tied at the end.

Malachi said, "So what's this thing you want to show me?"

"Down there, in the skiff."

When he turned and bent to look, I took the silenced .38 out of the creel and shot him twice point blank. He fell over into the skiff's stern, just as I'd intended him to. Neat and clean like in the old days.

I climbed down and made sure he was dead. Then I stripped off his diamond ring and the Patek Philippe watch, put them in my pocket, and covered him up with the tarp. Later I'd run the body out to the middle of the lake and weight it and drop it overboard. I'd have to get rid of the Lincoln, too, but in mountain country like this it wouldn't be too much of a chore, even for an old guy like me.

Back in the cabin, I put in a long distance call that got picked up right away. "I changed my mind," I said. "I'll take you up on that contract offer after all. But it'll cost you seventy-five."

"For you I don't argue," Frank Carbone said. "Seventy-five it is. But how come you changed your mind? You told me before you're never leaving that retirement place of yours."

I didn't have to, now. Didn't have to worry about having enough money to last me the rest of my life, either. But all I said was, "Send somebody up with the cash in a couple of days. I'll have proof the job's done in exchange."

"A couple of days? How you going to do it that quick?"

"That's my business."

"Sure, sure. Same old Griff. Trade secret, huh?"

"That's right," I said. "Trade secret."

In a career spanning nearly half a century, **BILL PRONZINI** has published 75 novels, four nonfiction books, and 350 short stories, articles, and essays. His awards include a Mystery Writers of America Grand Master, the organization's highest honor, presented in 2008; three Shamuses, two for best novel, and the Lifetime Achievement Award from the Private Eye Writers of America; and France's Grand Prix de la Litterature Policiere for *Snowbound* (1988). Two other suspense novels, *A Wasteland of Strangers* and *The Crimes of Jordan Wise,* were nominated for the Hammett Prize in 1997 and 2006 respectively by the International Crime Writers Association. His most recent novel is *Hellbox* (Forge 2012), the 36th in his "Nameless Detective" series.

THE PLOT

JEFFERY DEAVER

When J. B. Prescott, the hugely popular crime novelist, died, millions of readers around the world were stunned and saddened.

But only one fan thought that there was something more to his death than what was revealed in the press reports.

Rumpled, round, middle-aged Jimmy Malloy was an NYPD detective sergeant. He had three passions other than police work: his family, his boat, and reading. Malloy read anything, but preferred crime novels. He liked the clever plots and the fast-moving stories. That's what books should be, he felt. He'd been at a party once and people were talking about how long they should give a book before they put it down. Some people had said they'd endure fifty pages, some said a hundred.

Malloy had laughed. "No, no, no. it's not dental work like you're waiting for the anesthetic to kick in. You should enjoy the book from page one."

Prescott's books were that way. They entertained you from the get-go. They took you away from your job, they took you away from the problems with your wife or daughter, your mortgage company.

They took you away from everything. And in this life, Malloy reflected, there was a lot to be taken away from.

"What're you moping around about?" his partner, Ralph DeLeon, asked, walking into the shabby office they shared in the Midtown South Precinct, after half a weekend off. "I'm the only one round here got reason to be upset. Thanks to the Mets yesterday. Oh, wait. You don't even know who the Mets are, son, do you?"

"Sure, I love basketball," Malloy joked. But it was a distracted joke.

"So?" DeLeon asked. He was tall, slim, muscular, black—the opposite of Malloy, detail for detail.

"Got one of those feelings."

"Shit. Last one of those *feelings* earned us a sit-down with the Dep Com."

Plate glass and Corvettes are extremely expensive. Especially when owned by people with lawyers.

But Malloy wasn't paying much attention to their past collars. Or to DeLeon. He once more read the obit that had appeared in the *Times* a month ago.

> J.B. Prescott, 68, author of thirty-two best-selling crime novels, died yesterday while on a hike in a remote section of Vermont, where he had a summer home. The cause of death was a heart attack. "We're terribly saddened by the death of one of our most prolific and important writers," said Dolores Kemper, CEO of Hutton-Fielding, Inc., which had been his publisher for many years. "In these days of lower book sales and fewer people reading, J.B.'s books still flew off the shelves. It's a terrible loss for everyone."

Prescott's best known creation was Jacob Sharpe, a down-and-dirty counterintelligence agent, who traveled the world, fighting terrorists and criminals. Sharpe was frequently compared to James Bond and Jason Bourne.

Prescott was not a critical darling. Reviewers called his books, "airport time-passers," "beach reads," and "junk food for the mind—superior junk food, but empty calories nonetheless."

Still, he was immensely popular with his fans. Each of his books sold millions of copies.

His success brought him fame and fortune, but Prescott shunned the public life, rarely going on book tour or giving interviews. Though a multimillionaire, he had no interest in the celebrity lifestyle. He and his second wife, the former Jane Spenser, 38, owned an apartment in Manhattan, where she is a part-time photo editor for *Styles,* the popular fashion magazine. Prescott himself, however, spent most of his time in Vermont or in the countryside of Spain, where he could write in peace.

Born in Kansas, John Balin Prescott studied English literature at the University of Iowa and was an advertising copywriter and teacher for some years while trying to publish literary fiction and poetry. He had little success and ultimately switched to writing thrillers. His first, *The Trinity Connection,* became a runaway hit in 1991. The book was on *The New York Times* bestseller list for more than one hundred weeks.

Demand for his books became so great that ten years ago he took on a co-writer, Aaron Reilly, 39, with whom he wrote sixteen bestsellers. This increased his output to two novels a year, sometimes more.

"We're just devastated," said Reilly, who described himself as a friend as well as a colleague. "John hadn't been feeling well lately. But we couldn't get him back to the city to see his doctor, he was so intent on finishing our latest manuscript. That's the way he was. Type A in the extreme."

Last week, Prescott traveled to Vermont alone to work on his next novel. Taking a break from the writing, he went for a hike, as he often did, in a deserted area near the Green Mountains. It was there that he suffered the coronary.

"John's personal physician described the heart attack as massive," co-author Reilly added. "Even if he hadn't been alone, the odds of saving him were slim to nonexistent."

Mr. Prescott is survived by his wife and two children from a prior marriage.

"So what's this feeling you're talking about?" DeLeon asked, reading over his partner's shoulder.

"I'm not sure. Something."

"Now, *there* is some evidence to get straight to the crime lab. 'Something.' Come on, there's some real cases on our plate, son. Put your mopey hat away. We gotta meet our snitch."

"Mopey hat? Did you actually say mopey hat?"

A half hour later, Malloy and DeLeon were sitting in a disgusting dive of a coffee shop near the Hudson River docks, talking to a scummy little guy of indeterminate race and age.

Lucius was eating chili in a sloppy way and saying, "So what happened was Bark, remember I was telling you about Bark."

"Who's Bark?" Malloy asked.

"I told you."

DeLeon said, "He told us."

"What Bark did was he was going to mark the bag, only he's a nimrod, so he forgot which one it was. I figured it out and got it marked. That worked out okay. It's marked, it's on the truck. Nobody saw me. They had, I'd be capped." A big mouthful of chili. And a grin. "So."

"Good job," DeLeon said. And kicked Malloy under the table. Meaning: Tell him he did a good job, because if you don't the man'll start to feel bad and, yeah, he's a little shit nimrod, whatever that is, but we need him.

But Malloy was remembering something. He rose abruptly. "I gotta go."

"I didn't do a good job?" Lucius called, hurt.

But he was speaking to Jimmy Malloy's back.

•••

Jane Prescott opened the door of the townhouse in Greenwich Village. Close to five-eleven, she could look directly into Malloy's eyes.

The widow wore a black dress, closely fitted, and her eyes were red like she'd been crying. Her hair was swept back and faint gray roots showed, though Malloy recalled that she was only in her late thirties. Three decades younger than her late husband, he also recalled.

"Detective." Hesitant, of course, looking over his ID. A policeman. She was thinking this was odd—not necessarily reason to panic but odd.

"I recognize you," Malloy said.

She blinked. "Have we met?"

"In *Sharpe Edge.* You were Monica."

She gave a hollow laugh. "People say that, because an older man falls in love with a younger woman in the book. But I'm not a spy and I can't rappel off cliffs."

They were both beautiful, however, if Malloy remembered the Prescott novel correctly. But he said nothing about this, she being a new widow. What he said was, "I'm sorry for your loss."

"Thank you. Oh, please come inside."

The apartment was small, typical of the Village, but luxurious as diamonds. Rich antiques, original art. Even statues. Nobody Malloy knew owned statues. A peek into the kitchen revealed intimidating brushed-metal appliances with names Malloy couldn't pronounce.

They sat and she looked at him with her red-rimmed eyes. An uneasy moment later he asked, "You're wondering what a cop's doing here."

"Yes, I am."

"Other than just being a fan, wishing to pay condolences."

"You could've written a letter."

"The fact is, this is sort of personal. I didn't want to come sooner, out of respect. But there's something I'd like to ask. Some of us in the department were thinking 'bout putting together a memorial evening in honor of your husband. He wrote about New York a lot and he didn't make us cops out to be flunkies. One of them, I can't remember which one, he had this great plot line here in the city. Same NYPD rookie helps out Jacob Sharpe. It was about terrorists going after the train stations."

"Hallowed Ground."

"That's right. That was a good book."

More silence.

Malloy glanced at a photograph on the desk. It showed a half dozen people, in somber clothing, standing around a grave site. Jane was in the foreground.

She saw him looking at it. "The funeral."

"Who're the other people there?"

"His daughters from his first marriage. That's Aaron, his co-writer." She indicated a man standing next to her. Then, in the background another, older man in an ill-fitting suit. She said, "Frank Lester, John's former agent."

She said nothing more. Malloy continued, "Well, some folks in the department know I'm one of your husband's biggest fans, so I got elected to come talk to you, ask if you'd come to the memorial. An appreciation night, you could call it. Maybe say a few words.

Wait. 'Elected' makes it sound like I didn't want to come. But I did. I loved his books."

"I sense you did," she said, looking at the detective with piercing gray eyes.

"So?"

"I appreciate the offer. I'll just have to see."

"Sure. Whatever you'd feel comfortable with."

•••

"You made him feel bad. He nearly got capped on that assignment."

Malloy said to his partner, "I'll send him a balloon basket. 'Sorry I was rude to my favorite snitch.' But right now I'm on to something."

"Give me particulars."

"Okay. Well, she's hot, Prescott's wife."

"That's not a helpful particular."

"I think it is. Hot…and thirty years younger than her husband."

"So she took her bra off and gave him a heart attack. Murder-by-boob isn't in the penal code."

"You know what I mean."

"You mean she wanted somebody younger. So do I. So does everybody. Well, not you, 'cause nobody younger would give you the time of day."

"And there was this feeling I got at the house. She wasn't really in mourning. She was in a black dress, yeah, but it was tighter than anything I'd ever let my daughter wear, and her red eyes? It was like she'd been rubbing them. I didn't buy the grieving widow thing."

"You ain't marshalling *Boston Legal* evidence here, son."

"There's more." Malloy pulled the limp copy of Prescott's obit out of his pocket. He tapped a portion. "I realized where my feeling came from. See this part about the personal physician?"

"Yeah. So?"

"You read books, DeLeon?"

"Yeah, I can read. I can tie my shoes. I can fieldstrip a Glock in one minute sixteen seconds. Oh, and put it back together, too, without any missing parts. What's your point?"

"You know how if you read a book and you like it and it's a good book, it stays with you? Parts of it do? Well, I read a book a few years ago. In it this guy has to kill a terrorist, but if the terrorist is murdered there'd be an international incident, so it has to look like a natural death."

"How'd they set it up?"

"It was really smart. They shot him in the head three times with a Bushmaster."

"That's fairly unnatural."

"It's natural because that's how the victim's 'personal physician'"—Malloy did the quote things with his fingers "—signed the death certificate: cerebral hemorrhage following a stroke. Your doctor does that, the death doesn't have to go to the coroner. The police weren't involved. The body was cremated. The whole thing went away."

"Hmm. Not bad. All you need is a gun, a shitload of money, and a crooked doctor. I'm starting to like these particular particulars."

"And what's *particularly* interesting is that it was one of Prescott's books that Aaron Reilly co-wrote. *And* the wife remembered it. *That* was why I went to see her."

"Check out the doctor."

"I tried. He's Spanish."

"So's half the city, in case you didn't know. We got translators, *hijo*."

"Not Latino. *Spanish.* From Spain. He's back home and I can't track him down."

The department secretary stuck her head in the doorway. "Jimmy, you got a call from a Frank Lester."

"Who'd be?..."

"A book agent. Worked with that guy Prescott you were talking about."

The former agent. "How'd he get my number?"

"I don't know. He said he heard you were planning some memorial service and he wanted to get together with you to talk about it."

DeLeon frowned. "Memorial?"

"I had to make up something to get to see the wife." Malloy took the number, a Manhattan cell-phone area code, he noticed. Called. It went to voice mail. He didn't leave a message.

Malloy turned back to his partner. "There's more. An hour ago I talked with some deputies up in Vermont. They told me that it was a private ambulance took the body away. Not one of the local outfits. The sheriff bought into the heart-attack thing but he still sent a few people to the place where Prescott was hiking just to take some statements. After the ambulance left, one of the deputies saw somebody leaving the area. Male, he thinks. No description other than that, except he was carrying what looked like a briefcase or small suitcase."

"Breakdown rifle?"

"What I was thinking. And when this guy saw the cop car, he vanished fast."

"A pro?"

"Maybe. I was thinking that co-author might've come across some connected guys in doing his research. Maybe it was this Aaron Reilly."

"You got any ideas on how to find out?"

"As a matter of fact, I do."

•••

Standing in the dim frosted-glass corridor of a luxurious SoHo condo, Jimmy Malloy made sure his gun was unobstructed and rang the buzzer.

The large door swung open.

"Aaron Reilly?" Even though he recognized the co-author from the picture at Prescott's funeral.

"Yes, that's right." The man gave a cautious grin.

Which remained in place, though it grew a wrinkle of surprise when the shield appeared. Malloy tried to figure out if the man had been expecting him—because Jane Prescott had called ahead of time—but couldn't tell.

"Come on inside, detective."

Reilly, in his late thirties, Malloy remembered, was the opposite of Jane Prescott. He was in faded jeans and a work shirt, sleeves rolled up. A Japanese product, not a Swiss, told him the time and there was no gold dangling on him anywhere. His shoes were scuffed. He was good-looking, with thick longish hair and no wedding ring.

The condo—in chic SoHo—had every right to be opulent, but, though large, it was modest and lived-in.

Not an original piece of art in the place.

Zero sculpture.

And unlike the Widow Prescott's abode, Reilly's was chock-a-block with books.

He gestured the cop to sit. Malloy picked a leather chair that lowered him six inches toward the ground as it wheezed contentedly.

On the wall nearby was a shelf of the books. Malloy noted one: *The Paris Deception.* "J.B. Prescott with Aaron Reilly" was on the spine.

Malloy was struck by the word, "with." He wondered if Reilly felt bad, defensive maybe, that his contribution to the literary world was embodied in that preposition.

And if so, did he feel bad enough to kill the man who'd bestowed it and relegated him to second-class status?

"That's one of my favorites."

"So you're a fan, too."

"Yep. That's why I volunteered to come talk to you. First, I have to say I really admire your work."

"Thank you."

Malloy kept scanning the bookshelves. And found what he'd been looking for: two entire shelves were filled with books about guns and shooting. There had to be something in one of them about rifles that could be broken down and hidden in small suitcases. They were, Malloy knew, easy to find.

"What exactly can I do for you, detective?"

Malloy looked back. "Just a routine matter mostly. Now, technically John Prescott was a resident of the city, so his death falls partly under our jurisdiction."

"Yes, I suppose." Reilly still looked perplexed.

"Whenever there's a large estate, we're sometimes asked to look into the death, even if it's ruled accidental or illness related."

"Why would you look into it?" Reilly asked, frowning.

"Tax revenue mostly."

"Really? That's funny. It was my understanding that only department of revenue agents had jurisdiction to make inquiries like that. In fact, I researched a similar issue for one of our books. We had Jacob Sharpe following the money—you know, to find the ultimate bad guy. The police department couldn't help him. He had to go to revenue."

It was an oops moment, and Malloy realized he should have known better. Of course, the co-author would know all about police and law enforcement procedures.

"Unless what you're really saying is that you—or somebody—think that John's death might not have been an illness at all. That it was intentional...But how *could* it be?"

Malloy didn't want to give away his theory about the crooked doctor. He said, "Let's say I know you're a diabetic and if you don't get your insulin you'll die. I keep you from getting your injection, there's an argument that I'm guilty of murder."

"And you think somebody was with him at the time he had the heart attack and didn't call for help?"

"Just speculating. Probably how you write books."

"We're a little more organized than that. We come up with a detailed plot, all the twists and turns. Then we execute it. We know exactly how the story will end."

"So that's how it works."

"Yes."

"I wondered."

"But, see, the problem with what you're suggesting is that it would be a coincidence for this 'somebody,' who wanted him dead, to be up there in Vermont at just the moment he had the attack…We could never get away with that."

Malloy blinked. "You—?"

Reilly lifted an eyebrow. "If we put that into a book, our editor wouldn't let us get away with it."

"Still. Did he have any enemies?"

"No, none that I knew about. He was a good boss and a nice man. I can't imagine anybody'd want him dead."

"Well, I think that's about it," Malloy said. "I appreciate your time."

Reilly rose and walked the detective to the door. "Didn't you forget the most important question?"

"What's that?"

"The question our editor would insist we add at the end of an interrogation in one of the books: Where was I at the time he died."

"I'm not accusing you of anything."

"I didn't say you were. I'm just saying that a cop in a Jacob Sharpe novel would've asked the question."

"Okay. Where were you?"

"I was here in New York. And the next question?"

Malloy knew what that was: "Can anyone verify that?"

"No. I was alone all day. Writing. Sorry, but reality's a lot tougher than fiction, isn't it, detective?"

•••

"Yo, listen up," the scrawny little man said, "This is interesting."

"I'm listening." Malloy tried to look pleasant as he sat across from Lucius the snitch. Before they'd met, Ralph DeLeon reminded him how Malloy had dissed the man earlier. So he was struggling to be nice.

"I followed Reilly to a Starbucks. And she was there, Prescott's wife."

"Good job," DeLeon said.

Malloy nodded. The whole reason to talk to the co-author had been to push the man into action, not to get facts. When people are forced to act, they often get careless. While Malloy had been at Reilly's apartment, DeLeon was arranging with a magistrate for a pen register—a record of phone calls to and from the co-author's phones. A register won't give you the substance of the conversation, but it will tell you whom a subject calls and who's calling him.

The instant Malloy left the condo, Reilly had dialed a number.

It was Jane Prescott's. Ten minutes after that, Reilly slipped out the front door and headed down, moving quickly.

And tailed by Lucius, who had accompanied Malloy to Reilly's apartment and waited outside.

The scrawny snitch was now reporting on that surveillance.

"Now that Mrs. Prescott, she's pretty—"

Malloy broke in with "Hot, yeah, I know. Keep going."

"What I was *going* to say," the snitch offered snippily, "before I was interrupted, is that she's pretty tough. Kind of scary, you ask me."

"True," Malloy conceded.

"Reilly starts out talking about you being there." Lucius poked a bony finger at Malloy, which seemed like a dig, but he let it go—as DeLeon's lifted eyebrow was instructing. "And you were suspecting something. And making up shit about some police procedures and estate tax or something. He thought it was pretty stupid."

Lucius seemed to enjoy adding that. DeLeon, too, apparently.

"And the wife said, yeah, you were making up something at her place, too. About a memorial service or something. Which she didn't believe. And then she said—get this. Are you ready?"

Malloy refrained from glaring at Lucius, whose psyche apparently was as fragile as fine porcelain. He smiled. "I'm ready."

"The wife says that this whole problem was Reilly's fucking fault for coming up with the same idea he'd used in a book—bribing a doctor to fake a death certificate."

He and DeLeon exchanged glances.

Lucius continued; "And then she said, 'Now we're fucked. What're you going to do about it?' Meaning Reilly. Not *you*." Another finger at Malloy. He sat back, smugly satisfied.

"Anything else?"

"No, that was it."

"Good job," Malloy said with a sarcastic flourish that only DeLeon noted. He slipped an envelope to the snitch.

After Lucius left, happy at last, Malloy said, "Pretty good case."

"Pretty good, but not great," the partner replied slowly. "There's the motive issue."

"Okay, *she* wants to kill her husband for the insurance or the estate and a younger man. But what's Reilly's motive? Killing Prescott's killing his golden goose."

"Oh, I got that covered." Malloy pulled out his Blackberry and scrolled down to find something he'd discovered earlier.

He showed it to DeLeon.

> ***Book News.***
> The estate of the late J.B. Prescott has announced that his co-author, Aaron Reilly, has been selected to continue the author's series featuring the popular Jacob Sharpe character. Prescott's widow is presently negotiating a five-book contract with the author's long-time publisher, Hutton-Fielding. Neither party is talking about money at this point but insiders believe the deal will involve an eight-figure advance.

Ralph DeLeon said, "Looks like we got ourselves a coupla perps."

•••

But not quite yet.

At 11:00 P.M. Jimmy Malloy was walking from the subway stop in Queens to his house six blocks away. He was thinking of how he was going to put the case together. There were still loose ends. The big problem was the cremation thing. Burning is a bitch, one instructor at the academy had told Malloy's class. Fire gets rid of nearly all important evidence. Like bullet holes in the head.

What he'd have to do is get wiretaps, line up witnesses, track down the ambulance drivers, the doctor in Spain.

It was discouraging, but it was also just part of the job. He laughed to himself. It was like Jacob Sharpe and his "tradecraft," he called it. Working your ass off to do your duty.

Just then he saw some motion a hundred feet head, a person. Something about the man's mannerisms, his body language set off Malloy's cop radar.

A man had emerged from a car and was walking along the same street that Malloy was now on. After he'd happened to glance back at the detective, he'd stiffened and changed direction fast. Malloy was reminded of the killer in Vermont, disappearing quickly after spotting the deputy.

Who was this? The pro? Aaron Reilly?

And did he have the break-down rifle or another weapon with him? Malloy had to assume he did.

The detective crossed the street and tried to guess where the man was. Somewhere in front of him, but where? Then he heard a dog bark, and another, and he understood the guy was cutting through people's yards, back on the *other* side of the street.

The detective pressed ahead, scanning the area, looking for a logical place where the man had vanished. He decided it had to be an alleyway that led to the right, between two commercial buildings, both of them empty and dark at this time of night.

As he came to the alley, Malloy pulled up. He didn't immediately look around the corner. He'd been moving fast and breathing hard, probably scuffling his feet, too. The killer would have heard him approach.

Be smart, he told himself.

Don't be a hero.

He pulled out his phone and began to dial 9-1-1.

Which is when he heard a snap behind him. A foot on a small branch or bit of crisp leaf.

And felt the muzzle of the gun prod his back as a gloved hand reached out and lifted the phone away.

We're a little more organized than that. We come up with a detailed plot, all the twists and turns. Then we execute it. We know exactly how the story will end.

Well, Prescott's wife and co-author had done just that: come up with a perfect plot. Maybe the man on the street a moment ago was Reilly, acting as bait. And it was the professional killer who'd come up behind him.

Maybe even Jane Prescptt herself.

She's pretty tough…

The detective had another thought. Maybe it was none of his suspects. Maybe the former agent, Frank Lester, had been bitter about being fired by his client and killed Prescott for revenge. Malloy had never followed up on that lead.

Hell, dying because he'd been careless…

Then the hand tugged on his shoulder slightly, indicating he should turn around.

Malloy did, slowly.

He blinked as he looked up into the eyes of the man who'd snuck up behind him.

They'd never met, but the detective knew exactly what J.B. Prescott looked like. His face was on the back jackets of a dozen books in Malloy's living room.

•••

"Sorry for the scare," Prescott explained, putting away the pen he'd used as a gun muzzle—an ironic touch that Malloy noted as his heart continued to slam in his chest.

The author continued, "I wanted to intercept you before you got home. But I didn't think you'd get here so soon. I had to come up behind you and make you think I had a weapon so you didn't call in a ten-thirteen. That would have been a disaster."

"Intercept?" Malloy asked. "Why?"

They were sitting in the alleyway, on the stairs of a loading dock.

"I needed to talk to you," Prescott said. The man had a large mane of gray hair and a matching moustache that bisected his lengthy face. He looked like an author ought to look.

"You could've called," Malloy snapped.

"No, I couldn't, if somebody had overheard or if you'd told anyone I was alive, my whole plot would've been ruined."

"Okay, what the hell is going on?"

Prescott lowered his head to his hands and didn't speak for a moment. Then he said, "For the past eighteen months I've been planning my own death. It took that long to find a doctor, an ambulance crew, a funeral director I could bribe. And find some remote land in Spain where we could buy a place and nobody would disturb me."

"So you were the one the police saw walking away from where you'd supposedly had the heart attack in Vermont."

He nodded.

"What were you carrying? A suitcase?"

"Oh, my laptop. I'm never without it. I write all the time."

"Then who was in the ambulance?"

"Nobody. It was just for show."

"And at the cemetery, an empty urn in the plot?"

"That's right."

"But why on earth would you do this? Debts? Was the mob after you?"

A laugh. "I'm worth fifty million dollars. And I may write about the mob and spies and government agents, but I've never actually met one…No, I'm doing this because I've decided to give up writing the Jacob Sharpe books."

"Why?"

"Because it's time for me to try something different: publish what I first started writing, years ago, poetry and literary stories."

Malloy remembered this from the obit.

Prescott explained quickly: "Oh, don't get me wrong. I don't think literature's any *better* than commercial fiction, not at all. People who say that are fools. But when I tried my hand at literature when I was young, I didn't have any skill. I was self-indulgent, digressive… boring. Now I know how to write. The Jacob Sharpe books taught me how. I learned how to think about the audience's needs, how to structure my stories, how to communicate clearly."

"Tradecraft," Malloy said.

The author gave a laugh. "Yes, tradecraft. I'm not a young man. I decided I wasn't going to die without seeing if I could make a success of it."

"Well, why fake your death? Why not just write what you wanted to?"

"For one thing, I'd get my poems published *because* I was J.B. Prescott. My publishers around the world would pat me on the head and say, 'Anything you want, J.B.' No, I want my work accepted or rejected on its own merits: But more important, if I just stopped writing the Sharpe series my fans would never forgive me. Look what happened to Sherlock Holmes."

Malloy shook his head.

"Conan Doyle killed off Holmes…But the fans were furious. He was hounded into bringing back the hero they loved. I'd be hounded in the same way. And my publisher wouldn't let me rest in peace either." He shook his head. "I knew there'd be various reactions, but I never thought anybody'd question my death."

"Something didn't sit right."

He smiled sadly. "Maybe I'm better at making plots for fiction than making them in real life." Then his long face grew somber. Desperate, too. "I know what I did was wrong, detective, but please, can you just let it go?"

"A crime's been committed."

"Only falsifying a death certificate. But Luis, the doctor, *is* out of the jurisdiction. You're not going to extradite somebody for that. Jane and Aaron and I didn't actually sign anything. There's no insurance fraud because I cashed out the policy last year for surrender value. And Jane'll pay every penny of estate tax that's due…Look, I'm not doing this to hurt or cheat anybody."

"But your fans…"

"I love them dearly. I'll always love them and I'm grateful for every minute they've spent reading my books. But it's time for me to pass the baton. Aaron will keep them happy. He's a fine writer… Detective, I'm asking you to help me out here. You have the power to save me or destroy me."

"I've never walked away from a case in my life." Malloy looked away from the author's eyes, staring at the cracked asphalt in front of them.

Prescott touched his arm. "Please?"

•••

Nearly a year later Detective Jimmy Malloy received a package from England. It was addressed to him, care of the NYPD.

He'd never gotten any mail from Europe and he was mostly fascinated with the postage stamps. Only when he'd had enough of looking at a tiny Queen Elizabeth did Malloy rip the envelope open and take out the contents: a book of poems written by somebody he'd never heard of.

Not that he'd heard of many poets, of course. Robert Frost. Carl Sandburg. Dr. Seuss.

On the cover were some quotations from reviewers praising the author's writing. He'd apparently won awards in England, Italy, and Spain.

Malloy opened the thin book and read the first poem, which was dedicated to the poet's wife.

> ***Walking on Air***
> Oblique sunlight fell in perfect crimson on your face
> that winter afternoon last year.
> Your departure approached and, compelled to seize
> your hand, I led you from sidewalk to trees
> and beyond into a field of snow—
> flakes of sky that had fallen to earth days ago.
> We climbed onto the hardened crust, which held
> our weight, and, suspended above the earth,
> we walked in strides as angular as the light,
> spending the last hour of our time together
> walking on air.

Malloy gave a brief laugh, surprised. He hadn't read a poem since school, but he actually thought this one was pretty good. He liked that idea: Walking on the snow, which had come from the sky—literally walking on air with somebody you loved.

He pictured John Prescott, sad that his wife had to return to New York, spending a little time with her in a snowy Vermont field before the drive to the train station.

Just then Ralph DeLeon stepped into the office and before Malloy could hide the book, the partner scooped it up. "Poetry." His tone suggested that his partner was even more of a loss than he'd thought. Though he then read a few of them himself and said, "Doesn't suck." Then, flipping to the front, DeLeon gave a fast laugh.

"What?" Malloy asked.

"Weird. Whoever it's dedicated to has your initials."

"No."

DeLeon held the book open.

With eternal thanks to J. M.

"But I *know* it can't be you. Nobody'd thank you for shit, son. And if they did, it sure as hell wouldn't be eternal."

The partner dropped the book on Malloy's desk and sat down in his chair, pulled out his phone, and called one of their snitches.

Malloy read a few more of the poems and then tossed the volume on the dusty bookshelf behind his desk.

Then he, too, grabbed his phone and placed a call to the forensic lab to ask about some test results. As he waited on hold he reflected that, true, Prescott's poems weren't bad at all. The man did have some skill.

But, deep down, Jimmy Malloy had to admit to himself that, given his choice? He'd rather read a Jacob Sharpe novel any day.

The author of twenty-two novels, **JEFFREY DEAVER** has been nominated for six Edgar Awards from the Mystery Writers of America, an Anthony award, a Gumshoe Award, and is a three-time recipient of the Ellery Queen Reader's Award for Best Short Story of the Year. In 2001, he won the W.H. Smith Thumping Good Read Award for his Lincoln Rhyme novel *The Empty Chair.* In 2004, he was awarded the Crime Writers Association of Great Britain's Ian Fleming Steel Dagger Award for *Garden Of Beasts* and the Short Story Dagger for "The Weekender." Translated into 35 languages, his novels have appeared on a number of bestseller lists around the world, including the *New York Times,* the *London Times* and the *Los Angeles Times. The Bone Collector* was a feature release from Universal Pictures, starring Denzel Washington as Lincoln Rhyme. *A Maiden's Grave* was made into an HBO film retitled *Dead Silence,* starring James Garner and Marlee Matlin.

He has also released two collections of his short stories, called *Twisted* and *More Twisted.*

THE VENGEANCE OF KALI

DAVID DEAN

Kieran sat on his bike at the edge of the wood line and watched the new people transfer their furnishings from the van to the house. He had been doing so for nearly half an hour and not been noticed. This did not surprise him. It was in his character, in fact integral to his lifestyle, that he not be seen or remarked upon. Living in his older brother's long shadow, and dwelling at the lower tier of his neighborhood age group, had taught him the art of near invisibility. Even his red hair failed to excite notice so practiced was he at living in the shadows.

The people that he watched from astride his travel-worn, stripped-down bike, however, could expect nothing but scrutiny. The strange reddish hue of their dark skins and the exotic chirping of their outlandish language guaranteed it in Kieran's neighborhood, and he found it difficult to take his eyes from them. In fact, he could not have been more astounded at their manifestation had they been deposited there by a space craft, as opposed to the Mercedes SUVs and other expensive cars they had arrived in just minutes before the moving van.

Moments before their remarkable landfall, Kieran had been coursing along on the narrow bike paths that bisected the few remaining woods of his neighborhood, traveling unseen from one street to the next as he studied the back yards of the houses within a several block radius. It was from these observations that he would sometimes schedule return visits under cover of darkness to select and remove objects that he coveted—his bike being an example, hence its stripped-down conversion to avoid identification.

Other thefts lacked such obvious value, but spoke to some inarticulate need, such as his surprising and difficult appropriation of a backyard soccer net. The actual removal of this unwieldy object had been extremely difficult and fraught with the peril of discovery, yet he had accomplished it in the dark of night and somehow dragged it the two blocks to his home, without arousing victim or witness.

Sadly, as Kieran had failed to secure a soccer ball and did not know how the game was played in any case, the net was left to collect only leaves and debris as it began its slow decline from neglect in his back yard—a monument, perhaps, to something he could not yet articulate. But on this long Sunday afternoon in early autumn no such thoughts occupied his mind, for he had chanced upon the interlopers just as they began their disembarkation.

With cries like strange birds they greeted one another as their caravan of luxury cars disgorged them onto the newly asphalted drive. The men were all quite thin and small, sporting thick mustaches; their clothing running the gamut from somber suits to brightly colored and zippered warm-up togs. The women were even more arresting, with long, black hair that glistened in the warm sun, while their bodies, draped in diaphanous materials dyed outlandish pinks, purples and greens, glimmered beneath the soft September sky.

Each person stopped short of embracing the other, instead bringing their hands together as if in prayer and momentarily bowing their heads. Once this had been accomplished, it appeared they were free to hug, shake hands or kiss. Kieran watched entranced; thinking of the dragonflies he sometimes observed over the lichen-covered bird bath in his back yard, hovering and circling close to one another before dipping slightly in the humid air and racing off.

Suddenly, one of the older men pointed in Kieran's direction and without any unnecessary movement, the boy withdrew several feet further into the shadows beneath the canopy of dry, coloring leaves. It was as if he had simply faded out of the picture—a minute, but possibly distracting figure in the landscape removed with cloth and turpentine.

Yet, he needn't have feared, for the gaze of all rose to the tree tops and halted, the faces of the men closing in consternation, even as the women's pursed in distaste and their large, dark eyes widened in barely suppressed horror. There followed a silence that was, in turn, replaced by a hubbub in the foreign tongue of the newcomers. Several more of them began pointing at the tree tops and exclaiming in alarmed tones.

Kieran had no need of a translator to divine the cause of their clamor; he was very familiar with the troop of undertakers that roosted opposite their home site and even now, flapped their ragged wings and sidled uneasily on their branches under the hostile gaze of their newest neighbors. Kieran could not recall a time when they had not dwelt there.

As a small boy, he could remember lying on his back in the adjoining field, now long given over to lots for upscale homes, and watching the great birds rustle and flap amongst the branches of the largest trees. On such mornings, clear and dappled with sun, they emerged from the boreal gloom as dark, shapeless shadows perched singly or in discontented, peevish clusters, shoving and pecking their fellow tribe members.

As the sun's rays began to pierce their enclave, wings would be thrown wide to absorb the warmth and dry the damp from their feathers; these violent, inconsiderate actions often dislodging a fellow vulture and forcing him to flap wildly as he sought to obtain the next available perch and avoid crashing into the earth.

After a period of this, at what always appeared to be an agreed upon moment, though Kieran had never heard the carrion eaters utter a single sound, first one, followed by another, then another, would fall forth from the limbs they had been so unwilling to leave but moments before, throw wide their great wings and begin their ungainly climb into the morning sky.

At these moments, Kieran thought there could not be a clumsier, less flight-worthy bird, yet once they clambered onto that first thermal that would raise them into the heavens on its column of superheated air; they attained the grace of angels. They were no longer the clown princes of the bird world, but an aerial ballet troupe silently wheeling across the heavens in follow-the-leader acrobatics. It seemed to Kieran that they could glide for hours without a single beat of the wing; without the least effort at staying aloft. It was only when they returned to their roost each evening that he was reminded again of what ugly creatures they really were, with their ragged cloaks of dusty wings and their raw, blood-dipped heads—their forlornly comic return heralded by the crash of branches, the scattering of leaves and a rain of sad, dirty feathers.

Kieran watched as the oldest of the men, the same one who had first noticed the turkey vultures, hurried over to the rear door of one of the Mercedes. Even from across the street, Kieran could recognize the body language of deference, as the man opened the door, made the obligatory prayer gesture, and offered his arm to whomever was within.

Kieran stared in wonder as the tiny figure, wrapped in gold and white cloth, was deposited onto the smooth, oily-looking drive and the entire company went silent, brought their hands together as one, and bowed. The ancient woman, who appeared no larger than a child to the eleven-year-old Kieran, returned the gesture, then spoke; her tiny voice carried away in the light breeze. The newcomers smiled without showing their teeth; their heads still slightly inclined. Kieran sensed that they were uncomfortable about something—that they were awaiting the old woman's judgment.

The older gentleman who stood clutching her elbow (Kieran couldn't help but think of him as a gentleman due to his age and the fact that he wore a suit) spoke then, and pointed again to the trees; though this time it appeared to be for the old woman's benefit. His gesture was at once reluctant and dismissive. Then he and the rest returned once more to silence.

Kieran had already guessed that this ancient woman was the matriarch of the clan and the rest her children, grandchildren and possibly great-grandchildren. He awaited her judgment with interest—if she disapproved of the vultures, would they simply return to their cars and leave?

She stood within the circle of her large family and tilted her head up to the tree tops; shading her eyes with one hand as she steadied herself on her eldest son's arm with the other. Her hair, uncovered like the younger women, fell down her back as a great rope of gray, bound by gold ribbon.

All eyes, including Kieran's, followed her gaze to settle on the unattractive birds who shuffled uneasily on their whitened limbs. Several, apparently unable to bear the tension, launched themselves in muffled explosions of discomfort to cant awkwardly this way and that between the trees as they sought the anonymity of the deeper forest. The old woman continued to study them.

Kieran's interest returned to her and there he found her eldest regarding her with concern and it suddenly dawned on the boy that this gentleman had failed to notice the birds prior to this day, and that this failure might have actual consequences—it was up to the old lady to pronounce judgment.

Suddenly, she brought her palms together and held them aloft as if greeting the vultures and smiled. She spoke several words to the assembled family and laughed merrily; then pointed quite openly to the great birds and spoke once more. Now everyone joined in on the joke, if that was what it was, and Kieran could see, even at a distance, relief flood the features of the eldest son; the lines of consternation smoothed out by hilarity and laughter. This time when they smiled, the entire family revealed brilliant teeth and uplifted faces. They would stay—and with that, the eldest escorted her toward the front door and possession, as the older sons and all the women followed in train, leaving only the younger men to resume the job of unpacking the van.

As the front door closed behind the procession, Kieran was left in the shadow of the wood, his curiosity replaced by a strange longing that felt like a fragile egg within his bony chest. And after several long moments of watching for something more, though he could not say what, he lifted the bike between his legs and walked it in a semi-circle to face the way he had come, suddenly aware of the cheap quality of his stolen prize and the dull, faded colors of his jeans and black T-shirt gone nearly gray with washings. Then, like his feathered companions, the boy flew back into the woods, bumping and careening his way into the greater darkness.

•••

When Kieran arrived home, his mother stood at the kitchen sink, still wrapped in her house coat, coffee in one hand and first cigarette of the day in the other, watching the sun sink beneath the western tree line. Her mass of springy red hair floated about her shoulders in an unkempt nimbus highlighted by the fading light from the window. Though she looked tired and dark beneath the eyes, her smile upon seeing him lent her face a plucky, good-natured attractiveness that might be confused with beauty in a younger woman. Kieran sometimes thought that she was beautiful.

She reached out expertly with the hand holding her smoke, and without so much as spilling her ash, caught his long hair as he tried to slip by, leant over and planted a large, moist kiss on his reluctant cheek. In that brief instance, Kieran was treated to an unwanted glimpse of her ample cleavage, barely contained within the loose confines of her gown.

As she straightened up and caught the focus of his gaze, she popped the cigarette back into her mouth and ran a finger down his short, straight nose. "Boys," she said wistfully and smiled, "always grow up to be men and men can never get over..." She caught herself and stopped. "All girls have these, you know," she arched an eyebrow at her son. "They're no big deal, believe me."

"I *know* that," Kieran mumbled as he tried to slip by once more.

"I've got to work tonight...you *know* that too, right," she continued, turning to place her cup in the sink, still smiling.

"Yessss," he hissed in exasperation and embarrassment. Kieran's mom worked rotating twelve hour shifts as a dispatcher at the police department; and he was well acquainted with her schedule—it was while she was on night shifts that he was able to do *his* best work. Kevin, his sixteen year old brother, was supposed to watch him during these absences, but seldom actually did and made little pretence of the matter.

"You smell like pine," his mom said thoughtfully. "Where've you been?"

"Nowhere," he replied automatically. "Did you know some foreigners are moving in on Palomino Drive?"

"Foreigners," she repeated. "What makes you say that?"

"You should see them," he answered.

"There are some barbeque ribs from that take-out you like in the fridge," she pronounced, suddenly aware of the time; then stubbed out her smoke and sailed down the short corridor to the bathroom and her shower. "I also got that coleslaw and potato salad you love so much," she called back to him as she was closing the door, "and don't wait for your brother…believe it or not, he called and said he'd be a little late."

"Good," Kieran replied; snatching up the remote for the television and the video games controls. "I hope he never comes home."

"What's that?" His mother's muffled voice reached him through the door and over the running water.

"Nothing," Kieran assured her. "I said *okay*."

•••

It was after one o'clock in the morning when Kevin finally arrived home for his babysitting duties. He awoke Kieran as he stumbled down the hallway searching for his own bedroom; then suddenly retraced his steps back to his little brother's room and threw open the door. There was a pause as he hung silhouetted in the door frame, reeking of booze and an odd, chemical odor. Kieran tried to pretend he was still asleep by keeping his breathing steady; then, Kevin switched the light on.

"Just wanted to make sure the boogeyman hadn't gotten you," he slurred, his long, dark hair framing a lean face that might someday be handsome. His heavy-lidded blue eyes slid over Kieran with amusement.

"There's no such thing," Kieran responded automatically, the barbeque sauce now sour in his stomach.

"You better hope not, as much time as mom leaves you alone."

"*You're* supposed to watch me," Kieran blazed hotly in defense of their mother and much against his own best judgment.

"Is that right?" Kevin asked. "Wouldn't that be the job of your daddy?"

Kieran winced at the allusion to their separate fathers.

"I'm not your daddy," his brother concluded flatly. "But, at least I look in on you to make sure you're alive. Who else would?"

This was a question that Kieran had no wish to dwell on and it hurt his pride that he was, in fact, very glad to see his brother. "Get out of my room, Kevin, I'm trying to sleep," was all he could think to say.

Kevin chuckled tolerantly and said, "You're such a tool," then turned and began to close the door. Halfway out he stopped and asked, "Hey, what's for supper, little man?"

"Ribs," Kieran answered, turning his face to the wall. "They're in the fridge."

Kevin closed the door without turning off the light.

"Turn off the light," Kieran shouted.

"Switch is on the wall," his brother shouted happily back as he made his uncertain way to the kitchen.

•••

The following morning being a Monday, Kieran dressed himself in his usual jeans and T-shirt, ate a bowl of cereal heavily glazed with sugar and drowned in milk, and left for school in plenty of time to allow for wandering. His mother, having arrived home just after six AM, was sleeping the first of what she called her 'shifts', having long ago discovered what most night workers learn—that it is almost impossible to sleep through the daylight hours; no matter how dark the room, or silent the house—it's just unnatural to the human condition. Therefore, she would arise sometime in the early afternoon, putter about the house; then return to her bed once more as the day wore on. In any event, Kieran typically made his own way on such mornings.

As to Kevin, he remained behind the closed door of his bedroom, snoring, snorting, and occasionally shouting incoherently while in the grips of his alcohol and drug-induced unconsciousness. The hour of the day was of no matter to him and that it was a school day was of even less import. Kieran knew that his brother would deal with the consequences of his actions in his typical laconic, amused fashion, because, he had, as he confided to Kieran, "an ace up his sleeve"—he did not *care* if he was thrown out of school. Surprisingly to Kieran, who never brought attention to himself and asked for nothing, the administration went out of their way to keep his brother in school, offering accommodations such as specialized schedules and classes that the average student could only dream of in stupefied envy.

Kieran made a point of kicking Kevin's door on the way out but was rewarded with only silence for his effort.

Kieran's ride to school would not normally have taken him through the woods, but this day he bumped along the narrow path, veined with exposed roots, until he popped out at his vantage point of the previous day and braked to a dusty halt. The two-story, yellow and green house appeared just as anonymous as its neighbors—only two of the cars from the previous day remained and all the blinds were drawn. There was nothing whatsoever to distinguish it from its bland, modern counterparts and Kieran felt a pang of disappointment.

He allowed himself to roll down the slight incline and into the street; turning as he reached it to pedal slowly past the front of the house. He had almost completed this pass when he glimpsed something in the shadows between the front door and the wall of the garage. Almost hidden amongst the fronds of a voluminous, green plant with long, slender leaves, pointed and sharp-edged, a carved figure peeked out at him, and even at a distance, Kieran's young eyes easily took in the unmistakable curves and voluptuous proportions of a tiny naked woman. He looked away and then back again in astonishment—did they have a naked dancing woman on their front porch? And did she have four arms?—his front tire scrubbed the curb and wobbled dangerously before he was able to regain control of his bike.

At the nearby bus stop, an overweight, pimply kid, two years his senior, laughed and shouted something obscene at him, but Kieran paid no mind so enthralled was he at his extraordinary discovery. Turning for another pass, he saw a slat in one of the blinds near the statue lift to reveal a triangle of darkness; then fall once more into place, and sensing a trap he reversed himself—further reconnaissance would have to wait; though he knew it could not wait long, for the desire to possess was hard upon him.

•••

Kieran's school day was interminable and his distraction so great that he was twice called to account for it. Worse still, his English teacher caught him in the midst of a feverish attempt to recreate with pencil and paper what he had only glimpsed that morning. Her sudden intake of breath at the generous proportions he had endowed his sketch with had been his only warning, and as this was a young teacher, whom he found especially attractive and nice, he was particularly mortified. Though clearly shocked at his depiction, she had nonetheless simply ripped the page from his notebook, wadded it up, and without word or comment consigned it to the trash basket. Even so, her gasp and his own blazing face told his class mates all they needed to know, and for the rest of the day he was treated to the nickname, "Perv".

But, with the ringing of the final bell, all of these trials were forgotten and left behind, as he rocketed out of the school yard ahead of the rush. So great was his hurry that he stood on his pedals, pumping madly down the streets until he made the turn onto Palomino Drive, and even then he drove on, desire replacing reason and stealth with boldness and inspiration.

Still riding at break-neck speed, Kieran aimed at the curb he had collided with earlier in the day; then, at the last possible moment, jerked the bike into the air and leaped the barrier to resume his juggernaut across the soft green of the strangers' new lawn. The façade of the house remained unchanged, its windows still blinded to the outside world. The figurine that had danced in his mind all day hove into view as he turned to parallel the veranda, and her naked exuberance instantly burned away his earlier imaginings. She was like nothing he had ever seen before!

She did, indeed, have four arms and was as black as the space between the stars of a winter's night. One of the arms wielded a scimitar, its blade curved and cruel as a shark's mouth, while another brandished the head of someone, or something; Kieran had not drawn close enough yet to determine which. The remaining arms appeared to have been captured in graceful motion; in keeping with the thick, shapely leg seemingly raised in the act of a merry pirouette. Kieran applied the brakes just short of the porch and twisted the handlebars to execute a sudden, sliding stop, intending to launch himself onto the veranda and test the weight of the prize he must surely possess, and if it were possible, make away with it at that very moment. That was when his front tire flew off.

His collision with the soft, new fill of the lawn drove the wind from his lungs, but saved him from breaking any bones, and he rolled once before coming to a stop, splayed out on his back with his head at the feet of the sword-wielding goddess. From this vantage he could see that her enormous, blood-red tongue protruded at him in derision and that she sported a necklace of grinning skulls; whilst round her waist were strung a belt of human hands. Perhaps more ominously, she did not dance, but stood atop the body of a prostrate male. As his vision grew dark with the lack of oxygen, her form appeared to loom ever larger over him in triumph and he could see now that her allurements included a third eye on her forehead.

Suddenly, his lungs inflated, and his sight cleared like the passing of a squall line. He leapt to his feet, all action and resolve once more, and clambered onto the porch to seize his prize. He did not recognize himself in this new-found boldness and hurried to complete his task before his current incarnation abandoned him.

Even as he took hold of the slick, cold stone of the statue, he could sense its solidity. Whatever it had been carved from was incredibly dense and heavy, and it only took one attempt at lifting it to convince him that he would require assistance for this task. The old woman appeared at his elbow as if for just that purpose.

Kieran cried out, he was so surprised at her appearance. How had he not seen her? The front door stood wide open; she had obviously made no attempt at stealth. He stood slack-jawed in her presence, both due to her extraordinary appearance and the fact that he had never, in all his thieving, been caught in the act before now. He simply did not know what to do. Would her sons rush out; seize him and call the police?

She shuffled toward Kieran, her hands raised in what was now a familiar gesture, even as he began to back away towards the edge of the porch. She was once again garbed in vibrant colors, though this time of gold and green. Up close, Kieran could see that her arms, face, and exposed midriff were networked in wrinkles; her dark countenance sunken and dried-looking; any resemblance to the abundant and curvaceous statue long since sloughed off with great age. She continued to advance on Kieran, gently shaking her pressed hands as if in supplication and speaking all the while in her lilting birdsong language. Kieran stumbled backwards off the veranda and only just managed to keep his footing. He glanced nervously at the open door. The old woman stopped at the edge of the porch and pointed to the statue of the goddess. "Kali," she whispered happily; "Kali."

Kieran looked to the statue as well. "Kali," he repeated.

The old woman smiled broadly, revealing surprisingly good and numerous teeth, then laughed. "Chop, chop," she said, "chop, chop."

• • •

Kieran sat in the blue glow of the computer screen in the silent house and read the words he had conjured up from the ether, "Kali, the Dark Mother, is the fierce and fearful form of the mother goddess and is adorned with awesome symbols," it began. "She was born from the brow of the Goddess Durga during a great battle with evil forces and became so enraged that she began to kill not just the enemies of Durga, but all things. In order to stop her, Shiva threw himself under her feet. So shocked was she at this, that she stuck out her tongue in astonishment and ceased her homicidal rampage."

"Shiva," Kieran said softly, trying the word on for size. He made a note to look him up as well; then read the article through. It explained that Kali's black complexion symbolized her transcendental nature, whatever that meant, and her nudity showed that she was beyond false consciousness, while the garland of human heads stood for the letters in the Sanskrit alphabet and symbolized infinite knowledge; the severed hands liberation from karma, her sword the destroyer of the eight bonds that bind man, her three eyes, the past, present and future—the sum total of which meant very little to Kieran other than to endow the object that he desired with yet greater power and allure. Hadn't his bike been knocked to pieces by merely approaching?

He turned away from the screen and looked across the dim, empty living room. From somewhere in the walls, a pipe knocked several times as the water within it cooled; then all went silent once more. His mother was still on night shift and he could count on Kevin to be either absent or disinterested in his whereabouts. Slipping on a black, vinyl jacket with a ripped seam at the cuff, he searched through Kevin's room until he located his woolen navy watch cap and pulled it down to his eyebrows. Then he took several towels from the bathroom closet and went out to the aluminum shed in the backyard.

The shed leaned drunkenly against the chain link fencing and it took him several attempts to force the warped door and locate the beach wagon he had stolen the summer before from the Richardsons. Several minutes of frantic effort followed, as he struggled to free it from the towering accumulation of eclectic, rusting property he had appropriated over the past several years. When he was finished, he didn't bother to try and restore the items he had strewn onto the patchy lawn, but left them as they lay, exposed and newly worthless.

He lined the bottom of the wagon with the towels, and as soon as he felt it was dark enough, began to tow it toward the street, passing his crippled bicycle as he did so. His "new" bike stood propped against the back wall of the house; out of sight of the neighbors. The chubby kid at the bus stop, who had laughed at his near mishap the day prior was the unwitting "donor", as this had seemed just. Kieran entered the woods before moonrise and made his certain way to Palomino Drive.

Though it was not yet ten o'clock, the neighborhood appeared empty and lifeless; the work-a-day world had locked itself in for the night and the street belonged to the stealthy and feral. Kieran crossed the silent street pulling his fat-wheeled wagon behind him. He did not hesitate or think any more on what he was doing, as it was only through calm focus and deliberate action that he achieved the cloak of invisibility he required. This was a skill he had taught himself long before, and it had been his mistake to have abandoned this the day before in his excitement—this was how he had been caught by the old woman. He quietly pulled the wagon onto the lawn and made directly for the darkened corner of the porch where Kali dwelt.

As he neared the alcove, the moon began to peek over the tree tops and its first pale light glistened on the statue's black skin, revealing her raging, three-eyed face and sword-wielding upraised arm. Kieran paused, his concentration momentarily derailed by the vision; then brought his hands together in front of his face and bowed his head—he hoped that this might placate any resistance over her transference to his keeping. After several moments, he stepped up onto the porch, seized the statue and began to walk it, by ever so carefully rocking it on its base, to the edge of the porch. Other than his breathing, it was accomplished in remarkable silence. Leaving her at the edge he stepped down to the lawn and centered the wagon beneath her—this was the dicey part.

Kieran took hold of her two upraised arms and tipped her forward; gravity did the rest. With an audible thump, she landed amongst the towels and the night was still. Yet, all had not gone well. The tiny hand clasping the grisly head remained clutched within his own, even as the dispossessed glared at Kieran in frozen rage from the bottom of the wagon, the scimitar still within her possession and poised to strike. He shivered and stuck the broken hand into his jacket pocket. "Superglue," he whispered nervously.

Even with this setback, no lights had come on within the house, and it only remained for him to make away with his prize. He began to tow the wagon to the street and the safety of the woods beyond and did not see the boy waiting at the head of the path that was to be his escape route.

The punch to his chest knocked Kieran to the ground, and for the second time in as many days, he suffered the sensation of having the air driven from his lungs. The half moon, which had now climbed well above the trees, threw his assailant's face into shadow as he leaned over his victim, yet Kieran recognized him—it was the boy from the bus stop.

"You little loser," he chortled, "Did you honestly think I wouldn't know it was you that stole my bike? Everybody in town knows you're the biggest thief there is. You must be retarded to think I wouldn't—you sure look it."

Kieran gasped a lungful of air at last.

"And sound it," the boy added. He reached down and placed all his weight on Kieran's narrow shoulders and breathed a stench of meat and gravy into his face. "Does your mom do retards, too? She does everybody else, my dad says."

Kieran struggled to rise, but it was useless. "Screw you, fatty," he hissed.

The fat boy abruptly sat on his victim; then calmly and lightly punched Kieran in the right eye; just enough to cause sparks of pain to dance in his occluded vision. "You shut up. I'm gonna take this statue…thing," he waved his hand carelessly at the wagon, "and you're gonna bring my bike back first thing in the morning…get it? And it better be in one piece, moron. Do…you…understand…me?" he asked brightly. "I sure hope so…for your sake." He stood up and took the handle of the wagon in his pudgy hand and began to saunter down the moonlit street with Kieran's prize in tow. "If my bike's okay, I might…just might, I said, give this statue of your mother back to you." He never bothered to look back.

Kieran hauled himself painfully up from the dewy weeds and dirt, tears of shame, more than hurt, running over his sallow cheeks. "Chop, chop," he sobbed at his assailant's broad back, "chop, chop."

•••

The sirens wailing through the neighborhood awoke Kieran even earlier than usual, and he hastened to the window—a dark, oily column of smoke rose in the near distance. It was not yet fully light outside, and so he knew his mother wouldn't be home yet. In fact, it was probably she that had dispatched the police and fire departments to the scene, he thought with some pride, even as he gingerly probed the swollen, abraded flesh around his right eye.

He didn't dare take the bike and so had to run the three blocks to the scene of the fire. He arrived panting and out of breath, and felt his knees go wobbly and his vision swim as he recognized what was left of the fat boy's house.

Only the lower floor remained, its blue vinyl siding drooping sadly as melted icing on a cake; the windows now gaping, scorched eyes sporting schizophrenic mascara. Charred and broken timbers commemorated the memory of the second floor bedrooms, while the odor of liquefied plastic almost masked the greasy, sweet tang of what could only be—must be—burned pork.

Kieran glanced about in near panic at all the neighbors that had gathered at the awful spectacle, sick with an unreasonable feeling of complicity, and fearful that others might sense it as well.

A fireman that Kieran thought his mother might have dated at some time, spotted him and called out, "Get back from there, kid… don't make me tell you again!"

Kieran did as he was told and scurried off to the far end of the property line and nearer the separate garage. There, he came upon two young men in blue jump suits, almost hidden behind a screen of ambulances, struggling with someone, or something, on the ground and cursing between gasps of held breath. As Kieran shifted closer, without leaving the sharply edged shadows of early morning, the scene revealed itself in unwelcome clarity—they were struggling to sheath the charred and uncooperatively contorted figures of what must once have been people into black, zippered bags. One of the corpses awaiting their ministrations was not much larger than Kieran and he felt the blood drain from his face and wondered if he were about to faint; then forced himself to look away. It was then he spotted his wagon next to the back door of the garage; a tiny scimitar raised in triumph from its depths.

Without thinking, he walked directly to it, took it by the handle; turned and began to haul it behind him down the street. In spite of his fears, no one took any notice of him, and he walked slowly home without challenge.

•••

"Where in the hell did you get that thing?" Kevin asked breathlessly. "It's wicked!"

Kieran had been so engrossed in gluing on the broken hand that he had failed to hear his brother approach. He jumped to his feet, placing himself protectively between the statue of Kali and

Kevin, all his plans to keep her hidden amongst the clutter of their tottering, one-car garage instantly dashed by his brother's unexpected appearance.

"She's mine!" was all he could think to say.

"Easy, my little psycho…who said any differently, huh?" He advanced on Kieran's prize, unable to take his eyes from it. "Oh yeah, my man, you have scored big with this. She's Hindu, right? Goddess of something, right?"

Kieran held his ground, suddenly uneasy. Kevin did not sound right—the rapid fire speech and questions were unlike him. If he didn't know something, he would usually act as if it were unimportant or trivial; it was out of character for him to show enthusiasm or undue interest.

"Don't touch her," Kieran warned.

Kevin was standing over both boy and carving now, scrutinizing the amazing figure; his face a rapacious mask, his eyes all dark pupil. "What does somebody pay for something like this?" he asked aloud. "That's what I'd love to know. A few thousand wouldn't surprise me…maybe more."

Not once did he actually address his little brother. Kieran felt as if Kevin did not see him at all, and he didn't like the odor that seemed to pulse from his brother's sweat-sheened skin. It reminded him of hospitals and industrial disinfectant. He took a step back involuntarily and collided with the statue of Kali. Even as he spun about he could hear it totter on the loose wooden planks of the garage floor, and only just caught it in time. The newly reattached appendage flew off with his clumsy embrace and skittered beneath a bench.

He turned and shouted into his brother's face, "Get out of here, Kevin! And don't touch her, you stupid crankhead, she's mine."

Kevin took a surprised step back, his face pale and blank. "No one said different…I hear you. Whoa…what has gotten into little brother? You gone all schizoid, or something? Just came in to check on you—Mom's a little worried, that's all…what with the black eye and all, and you being more of a psycho than usual, that kind of thing. I couldn't give a rat's ass myself."

He took another step back and his face grew crafty and bold. "But if I did want…that," he pointed at the voluptuous warrior, "I'd take it…hear me?" He stuck his tongue out in unconscious imitation of the object of their dispute; then withdrew it again.

"No you won't," Kieran blazed back.

"You've got to sleep sometime," Kevin teased. "Not me, though. I can stay awake for *days*." The next step back took him out the door and Kieran was left with only the medical stench that trailed his brother like a following ghost.

For the next three nights, Kieran slept on a pallet in the garage at the foot of Kali.

•••

The morning of the third night, Kieran was unexpectedly greeted by his mother when he came into the kitchen from the garage. He knew instantly that something was wrong; she stood between him and the cereal boxes in the cabinet, still in her house coat and smoking nervously.

"I need to know what's going on," she began, "why you are sleeping in the garage, for God's sake, and where is your brother?" Her words were rapid and urgent; and her anxiety frightened Kieran.

"It's stuffy in my room because that window still sticks…"

"Stop that," she demanded. "I don't have time to listen to that nonsense just now. Where is Kevin? Did you know he hasn't been here…or at school in three days? When is the last time you saw your brother?"

Kieran was stunned into silence by his mother's vehemence, even as he struggled to understand the situation—Kevin was missing? Her fear entered him like the wet, charred smell that still hung over the neighborhood. Tears stood in her eyes.

"I don't know…" Kieran began weakly; fearing that somehow he might be held responsible; that somehow he might *be* responsible, though for what, he wasn't certain. "Three nights ago," he whispered. "I'm pretty sure."

"Three nights ago," his mother repeated in a near wail. "Oh God," she cried. "Then it's true, he *has* been gone that long! When the school called, I thought he had just been playing hooky; it never occurred to me that he wasn't coming home at night. I just thought I was missing him 'cause of the shift work.

"Why didn't you tell me, Kieran? And why are you sleeping in the garage? What's been happening around here…can you please tell me?"

Her pleas cracked that fragile thing that he carried about in his chest, and tears began to leak from his eyes, as well. "I didn't notice he wasn't here," he confessed; feeling suddenly very ashamed. "I'm sorry, Mom, I'm sorry. We had an argument and..." he trailed off, uncertain how to proceed without revealing his secrets.

"An argument about what," she asked, sensing a clue, a thread that might lead her to her eldest son. "Tell me."

"Over something of mine," he hedged. "Something he wanted, but I said no, that's all. I don't think I should have to..."

Suddenly, he recalled his bike flying apart on his first attempt at possession of Kali and the words of the old woman, followed by his pummeling at the hands of the fat boy on the night of the actual theft and the inferno that followed, and lastly, he remembered Kevin approaching his hard-won prize, greed and avarice etched into his features, and it was suddenly clear to Kieran what must happen next.

His mother's words finally pierced his thoughts and he looked up to find her crying openly. "I want you to go out, right now, and talk to everybody you know and find out if they've seen Kevin. Are you listening, Kieran? I mean everybody." She clearly gave little weight to his story of the argument and this relieved him of having to lie about its object.

"Yes ma'am...okay," he agreed; already turning for the door.

"I'm gonna get on the phone to the department," she continued, sniffling. "I know Kevin's been a handful and maybe some people think he's delinquent or something, but he's my boy and I'm gonna..."

"Wait," Kieran demanded, alarmed at the thought of the police entering into the matter. Once they arrived, his freedom of movement would be severely curtailed. "Just let me try and find out something," he pleaded. "Once the cops get involved no one will say anything."

His mother said nothing, but studied him warily.

•••

Now that his mind was made up, Kieran could not return the ominous, black carving quickly enough, though he did exercise caution upon lowering her once more into the wagon. His repair of the broken hand was barely visible and it was his desire to return the Dark Mother without further damage.

Kieran didn't bother to wait until night, as he felt certain the old woman knew quite well who had stolen her property in any case. He paused only at the foot of her driveway in order to gather his courage for the last leg of his penitent journey. The house awaited him with the same blank countenance of his previous visits.

As he hauled the heavy wagon up the smooth drive, the front door silently opened and the old woman, dressed this day in scarlet, and accompanied by her eldest son in his gray suit, stepped out onto the porch. Kieran thought they appeared to be expecting him.

Swallowing the knot of fear that threatened to choke him, he completed the final few steps and brought the wagon to a halt at their feet; stopped, brought his hands together and bowed. They responded in kind. Then the old woman laughed delightedly and pointed with some excitement at the contents of the wagon; even as her son stepped down and carefully lifted the statue of Kali from within and returned it to the spot from which Kieran had taken it. They appeared well pleased altogether.

The son extracted several bills of large denomination from his wallet and offered them to Kieran, who stared at them in bafflement. He backed away, dragging his now-empty wagon with him. "Thank you," the man said in heavily accented English. "Thank you very much."

"I just want my brother back," Kieran said softly; still backing away.

The man appeared puzzled, as if he were having trouble interpreting Kieran's words. "Your brother?" he repeated. "Yes, I hope so. Good luck with that, my young friend."

"We need him back," Kieran said once more, as the vultures across the street began to launch themselves into the air in their clumsy morning ritual, and the old woman placed newly picked flowers at the feet of Kali.

•••

When Kieran returned home, the police had already arrived—his mother had not been able to wait—Kevin was still missing and there was no light he could shed on his brother's disappearance. His mother did not go in to work that day and allowed Kieran to remain at home as well, and after the officers had departed, they spent the entire day together watching old movies on TV wrapped in a comforter on the couch. The phone never rang.

That evening Kieran heated up canned soup and prepared tuna fish sandwiches for their supper, but his mother barely tasted hers, and at some point he must have fallen asleep. The sound of his door knob rattling brought him instantly to wakefulness and he sat up in bed, puzzled as to how he had gotten there, and switched on his bedside lamp.

Kevin, looking drawn, haggard and years older than he should, peered at him through fingers raised to shield his tender eyes against the light. "Hey loser," he said, his voice sounding dry and unused, "why's mom asleep on the couch? I miss somethin' around here?"

Kieran vaulted out of his bed and threw his arms around his bewildered brother, causing him to stagger. "Kevin," he said hoarsely into the folds of his jacket. "Kevin."

Kevin pushed him away to arms length and stared blearily at his younger sibling. "I must have," he rasped, "I must have missed something alright, for all…this." He grinned at Kieran. "Hugging me and all."

"Where have you been? Mom's worried sick about you. Where have you been?" Kieran whispered urgently.

"Been?" Kevin repeated, as if really trying to remember. "Out," he concluded.

"For three days?" Kieran asked.

"Three days," he stupidly repeated Kieran's words once more. "You sure it's been three days, Lil' Bro'?" He could see from Kieran's expression that he was. "Oh, huh. How 'bout that? Do you know I have no earthly idea?"

"I thought *she* had you," Kieran suddenly sobbed.

"*She*…who?" Kevin asked, puzzled and alarmed at his little brother's unusual display of emotion. But Kieran remained silent.

Kevin knelt down and took his hands. "No, K-man, there's no 'she'…not that I remember, anyway," he joshed. "But I'll tell you something, freaky boy, wherever I was, it wasn't good, that much I do know, and I'm not ever gonna go back there again. I mean that, little brother…I'm turned inside out."

"Me too," Kieran agreed, dragging a sleeve across his running nose.

From the darkness of the living room they could hear their mother stir and call out in rising tones, "Kev', is that you, Kevin, honey?"

"Is she gonna rip me a new one?" Kevin asked with a lopsided grin.

"Oh yeah," Kieran assured him. "She loves you, Kevin…me too," he added quietly.

"I know that," his brother replied; then turned to face their mother as she thundered down upon them, screaming his name.

DAVID DEAN's short stories have appeared regularly in *Ellery Queen Mystery Magazine,* as well as a number of anthologies, since 1990. His stories have been nominated for the Shamus, Barry, and Derringer Awards and "Ibrahim's Eyes" won the *EQMM* Readers Award for 2007. His story, "Tomorrow's Dead," was a finalist for the Edgar for best short story of 2011. He is a retired Chief of Police in New Jersey and once served as a paratrooper with the 82nd Airborne Division.

SOMETIMES YOU CAN'T RETIRE

MARCIA MULLER

SOME MORNINGS I FEEL EVERY ONE OF MY 102 YEARS. ACTUALLY I'm only seventy-two, but my life, it's been rough.

Thing is, you never know what to expect. Comes up, blindsides you. Of course, I should've realized that. But I didn't, oh, no.

I wanted to be of help. Wanted to ease them out of their pain. Ease out the others who were causing their pain. Damn, though, it wasn't pleasant work. It took too much out of me. I decided to stop, and I did. You can't save everybody no matter how much you want to.

There are some things you just can't retire from.

BOSTON, MASSACHUSETTS—A LONG TIME AGO.

Woman on Charles Street. Furs wrapped around her neck like they were clinging there for their lives—only they were dead, stone dead. She had a fat, smug face, too much makeup for somebody her age. Sixty, seventy—does it matter? Little yappy dog on a leash—shit-zoo, one of those silly breeds. Its little legs were working hard, but not fast enough to keep up with her. She jerked on its lead till it near choked.

The sidewalk was crowded with people stopped at a crosswalk. When the light was about to change, the woman lurched forward in front of a bus. After her body was removed, the ASPCA came for the dog.

Houston, suffocating heat and humidity.

The brown Labrador—dragged by an impatient, Spandex-clad male jogger—was breathing hard, heaving. They paused at an intersection near Rice University, the jogger bouncing from foot to foot and making the dog's head bob. Then the jogger stumbled out into traffic. Brakes screeched and there was the sound of something being smashed like a Halloween pumpkin.

Venice Beach, California.

The standard poodle was being run too hard by the guy on Rollerblades. Drool dripping off its jowls and a dazed, coated look in its eyes. The guy didn't notice, just kept zipping along, dodging pedestrians, other skaters, and tourists. As dusk was setting in, he veered off into a video store, came out with a plastic bag, and tugged the animal toward an alleyway.

Venice Beach is not a very safe place at night. Gang violence claims many.

•••

So now you're wondering what happened to the canine victims. Well, they're safe now. I made sure of that.

The shit-zoo got adopted before I had time to go to the animal shelter. A good thing, too, I can't stand that yapping. My work as a structural engineer took me from Boston to Houston, where I acquired Sam the Labrador. It was a few years later, after I'd moved to LA, That I rescued the spaniel, Delia, from a pet adoption agency.

Now I'm retired, live in Los Alegres, California, a small town in the Sonoma County wine country. I've had other pets along the way: An abused German Shepherd. Three cats whose owner was caught dropping them off in a Dumpster just hours after their birth on a 102-degree day. A parrot that was clinging to the inside of a screen door of a house in West LA, screaming "Help me, help me!" More dogs, more cats, even a rabbit—all of them needing good homes.

Mr. Bleeding Heart they call me.

Life here in Los Alegres is pleasant. People are friendly, but pretty much mind their own business. The streets are tree-lined, the homes well kept, the gardens tended. There're a couple of good dog parks, and my vet gives me a discount because I've got nearly a dozen animals—mostly cats, a couple of dogs, the parrot, two white rats, and Ambrose the Snake. Ambrose is gentle, but the mailman sure gets shook up when he slithers up the window screen and looks out. I even have a girlfriend, Marilyn, who works at the animal shelter and alerts me when a promising adoptee comes in.

One day in September Marilyn came over as she often does after work. She looked troubled.

"Charley, you hear what Supervisor Lambruschi is up to now?"

"No good, I assume."

Marilyn unwound her scarf and dropped it, then her coat, on my couch. Scout, the yellow cat, immediately went and sat on them. Marilyn is a hefty woman, with long gray-blonde hair, plain but goodhearted. She bent down to pat Godwin, a terrier, and her sweat pants strained at the seams. Doesn't matter; I like them with some meat on their bones.

"Charley," she said, "Lambruschi is trying to enforce the three-pets-per-home ordinance."

Leo Lambruschi. My next-door neighbor. New to the city council this year. He'd also—so far unsuccessfully—tried to get the council to approve a ruling changing the animal shelter's policy from no-kill to euthanizing after thirty days.

This latest action was aimed directly at me.

"If he's successful, you'll have to move out of the city," Marilyn added.

I considered that. A place in the unincorporated country outside of town sounded good to me, but no way could I afford the inflated prices, even with what my paid-for 1930s bungalow would bring. I could buy in one of the less expensive and less populated northern California counties but, dammit, Los Alegres was home. I'd moved around enough in my time. No more.

Leo Lambruschi...

He was a mean, petty little man who wore his city council membership like the mantle of some king. He hadn't tried to poison my pets or trash my yard or beat me up. In fact, he struck me as a physical coward. But I hadn't counted on him burning the midnight oil while poring over obscure city statutes.

Leo had a handsome collie, Jewel, and took her everywhere with him. I mean, everywhere. Work, shopping, jogging, the post office; in cold weather he even sat in the outdoor section of our local pub, where dogs are allowed. But there was a downside to the owner-pet relationship: Leo drank, and he was an angry drinker. Sometimes in the night I would hear Jewel crying as if afraid.

Leo and Jewel would set out for his insurance agency at eight o'clock sharp every morning. By that time I'd let my golden retriever, Bella, into the yard, and when they went past she'd go off barking, leaping at the fence, snarling. Bella's normally a docile animal, but there was something about that collie. Or Leo.

Jewel would cringe and cower, and Leo would stare, first at Bella and then at my house, his dark eyes burning with little pinpricks of rage. He started leaving notes on my gate.

"Curb your dog." Ridiculous; she was in her own yard.

"Keep that damn dog in the house!" Well, no, I wasn't about to do that. She's a big dog, needs room to stretch her legs.

"If you don't shut that dog up, I'll call the cops about the noise." Yes, our city does have an ordinance about barking dogs, but apart from when Leo and Jewel walked by, Bella hardly uttered a sound.

Did I say people mind their own business here? Well, most of them do, but one day I'd come home from the grocery store and found Leo snooping around my front porch, peering through the living room window. I kind of sneaked up on him, but that wasn't what made him rear back. No, it was Ambrose. He was sunning himself on the window seat along with two of my cats and when Leo peered inside, Ambrose slithered up against the glass to see who this might be.

Leo kept backpedaling and smacked into me. I dropped my grocery bag, it split, and cat- and dog-food cans, fish flakes, and bird seed spilled onto the porch. Leo whirled, stared at me, then looked down at his feet. When he raised his eyes to mine, they were knowing and accusing.

"Charley," he said, "how many damn animals you got in there?"

I didn't answer. Tell the truth, I was trying to calculate.

"That snake. Fish, apparently. Those cats. That dog."

"Two dogs," I corrected.

"Anything else?"

"A parrot and—"

At that moment Miles the Parrot started yelling "Help me, help me!"

"I'll help you," Leo muttered. "I'll help you all right out of here."

•••

Los Alegres is a former farming community. Still plenty of agriculture on the flatlands to the east, although a lot of acreage has been developed into shopping centers and tract houses. Every year some silly bastard who bought a home overlooking a plowed field writes a letter to the editor complaining about the "awful" fertilizer smell and asking why the city "doesn't tell them not to do that." Like people who buy a house directly under the flight path of the local airport and then want the planes to stop flying over.

I live on the west side, but animals are plentiful here—and welcome. A neighbor up the hill from me keeps two fat sheep. He's partially disabled and can't cut his lawn, but they do a fine job. Another neighbor keeps chickens and hand delivers a basket of fresh eggs every week or so. At the top of the hill, horses graze, and I can hear cows bellow and goats bleat not far away.

So why, in 1980, did the city council enact a dumb-ass law about allowing only three pets per household?

Well, with all the new development, they were trying to go upscale, like the cities down in Marin. Reaching for a new image. But the sheep and chickens and horses and cows and goats were grandfathered in—meaning you can't kick 'em out if they're already there. And if a sheep dies and you replace it with another, who can tell the difference? We've got some of the oldest livestock in the world here in Los Alegres.

Leo's challenge to my owning all these animals was as petty and mean as he himself.

A week after Marilyn told me what Leo was up to, an order came from the city to find new homes for all of my animals except three. But they were my family—the only one I'd ever really had. Sweetheart the Rat was old and arthritic; nobody would want her, and the shelter would euthanize her. Leo'd see to that. The cats—people favor kittens over adult cats. Miles was too loud and sometimes crapped on the floor when outside the confines of his cage. Ambrose was... well, creepy to most people.

There was a hearing. Leo self-assured and condemnatory. Me nervous, trying to plead my case in stammering sentences. The judge took pity on me, gave me ninety days to find new homes—for my animals or all of us together.

The day the ultimatum came down, Marilyn provided a solution. "I've got an idea, Charley—you and I could move to my ranch."

Marilyn had inherited a small dairy ranch in the countryside to the west of town from her father. The cows had been sold, and the property was just sitting there, vacant. It would be an ideal place for pets, but…

"I don't know," I said. "I've always lived alone, except for my animals."

"It's a big house, and I work long hours. You'd be alone as much as you want."

It sounded like a plan, so I told Marilyn to start packing, and I put some things in boxes myself. But before I went anywhere, I had to do something about Jewel, the handsome collie who had her special table at the pub. Jewel, who went to work every day. Jewel, who cried at night while Leo drank and raged.

•••

I was waiting at the light at Main and D Street—center of town—all newly redeveloped and shiny, a reflection of what Los Alegres would become, no stopping progress. Cars, trucks, buses speeding by, going too fast as usual.

In front of me Leo, with Jewel on her lead, bounced on the curb, impatient to get on with his run. I'd staked out this intersection for two weeks, I knew the traffic patterns.

And soon it happened: the red Corvette, its driver seeing the amber light and speeding up to get through before it turned.

A shove, so slight that no one in the knot of pedestrians noticed it.

Leo stumbled forward in front of the Corvette.

I grasped Jewel's leash to prevent her from running off. She shivered and leaned into me as we moved through the excited crowd. But she'd be all right once she joined my other liberated animals.

Like I said before, some things you just can't retire from.

A native of the Detroit area, **MARCIA MULLER** grew up in a house full of books and self-published three copies of her first novel at age twelve, a tale about her dog complete with primitive illustrations. The "reviews" were generally positive.

Since the early 1970s Muller has authored over 35 novels—three of them in collaboration with husband Bill Pronzini—seven short-story collections, and numerous nonfiction articles. Together she and Pronzini have edited a dozen anthologies and a nonfiction book on the mystery genre. In 2005 Muller was named a Grand Master by Mystery Writers of America, the organization's highest award. Pronzini was named Grand Master in 2008, making them the only living couple to share the award (the other being Margaret Millar and Ross Macdonald). The Mulzinis, as friends call them, live in Sonoma County, California, in yet another house full of books.

CLUTTER

MARTIN EDWARDS

"You will be aware that your grandfather died in, ah, rather unusual circumstances?"

I bowed my head. "We can only hope his last thoughts were pleasurable."

Beazell raised bushy eyebrows. "At least his, um, companion, did her best by calling an ambulance. And she tried to administer the kiss of life herself. To no avail, sadly."

"I gather there was no suspicion of…foul play?"

"Goodness me, no. The doctor was emphatic, and of course a second opinion is required for a sudden death. There is no doubt the poor fellow died of a heart attack, brought on by excessive exertion. Your grandfather was seventy and unfit, he'd led a sedentary life, and frankly, cavorting with a nineteen-year old foreign woman was the height of folly. I recall advising him…" Beazell cleared his throat. "Well, that wasn't why I asked you here this afternoon. The important question concerns his last will and testament."

Beazell was a lawyer with a shiny suit and a glass eye with an inbuilt accusatory stare, as if it suspected me of concealing a dark secret. His offices occupied a single floor above a kebab house in a back street in Manchester, and the posters in the waiting room spoke of legal aid, visas for migrant workers, and compensation for accidents. I was unsure why Rafe (as my grandfather liked me to call him) had entrusted his legal affairs to such a firm. Beazell's services must come cheap, but Rafe was by no means short of money. Certainly, though, the two men had one thing in common. Beazell's floor was stacked high with buff folders bulging with official documents, and fat briefs to counsel tied up in pink string. He'd needed to clear a pile of invoices from my chair before I could sit down. Rafe too gloried in detritus; perhaps he regarded Beazell as a kindred spirit.

"I don't suppose wills are ever read out nowadays?" I said. "And presumably there's nobody apart from me to read it to?"

"My understanding is that you were his only close relative."

I nodded. My grandparents divorced a couple of years after my grandmother gave birth to their only child, my father. She had a stroke a month before my parents married, and they, in turn, succumbed to cancer and coronary disease respectively shortly after I left school and took a job as a snapper for a local newspaper. My mother was an only child, and her parents had died young. I was alone in the world—except for Hong Li.

"I saw very little of him, I'm afraid, even before I moved overseas. But we got on well enough. He had artistic inclinations, as you must know, and he encouraged my interest in photography"

Beazell exhaled; his breath reeked of garlic. "Artistic? Candidly, I never thought much of his sculpture. However, he told me that, in his opinion, you were a man after his own heart."

"That was kind of him," I said, although Beazell had not made it sound like a compliment.

"The will is straightforward." The lawyer could not keep a note of professional disapproval out of his voice. "He left you the whole of his estate."

My eyes widened: I had not known what to expect. "Very generous."

"There is, however, one condition."

"Which is?"

"The will stipulates that you must live in Brook House for a period of five years after his death, and undertake not to dispose of any items of his property whatsoever during that time. You are, of course, at liberty to enjoy full use of your own possessions, upon the proviso that you retain all of your grandfather's."

The glass eye glared. Presumably Beazell thought my own possessions wouldn't amount to much, and he was right. Since coming back to England six months earlier, I'd rented a one bedroom flat in Stoke-on-Trent and although I was by nature a voracious hoarder, I'd had little opportunity to accumulate belongings on my travels. Even so, the flat resembled a bomb site. My chronic reluctance to throw anything away was the one thing which provoked Hong Li to outbursts of temper.

"But I would lose the whole caboodle if I didn't agree to live there and keep his things?"

"In the event that the condition of the bequest fails to be satisfied," Beazell said, refusing to recognize *caboodle* as a legal term, "the estate passes to charities supporting the homeless."

I'd never thought of Rafe as a charitable donor. He must have expected me to toe the line. "Is that legal? To force someone to live somewhere, I mean?"

"There is no compulsion, the choice is yours." Beazell swiveled in his chair. "I may not specialize in the drafting of wills, but I can assure you that challenging your grandfather's testamentary provisions would be a costly exercise, and litigation is always fraught with uncertainty."

"What field do you specialize in, may I ask?"

"Criminal law." As if to remind me that his time was money, Beazell consulted his watch. A fake Rolex, I suspected, possibly supplied by one of his clients. "Indeed, I am due to appear at the magistrates' court in half an hour. Perhaps you would advise me by the end of the week whether or not you will undertake to accept the condition of the bequest?"

"No need to wait," I said. "My grandmother was right. I once heard her say that whatever Rafe wanted, he got. I'll take the house, and all his clutter."

•••

"This is an adventure," Hong Li said, as we turned off the motorway.

"I hope you'll like the place…"

She fiddled with the silver bracelet I'd given her after our first night together. "I'm sure I shall love it. Life in the English countryside! I can't believe this is happening to me. Six weeks ago, I was working shifts in a chip shop in Stafford for half the minimum wage, now…my only worry is, how will the people in the village take to me?"

"Rafe never worried about other people, and you shouldn't, either. Besides, the village is little more than a shabby pub and half a dozen cottages a mile's walk from Brook House."

"Sounds idyllic." Her voice became dreamy. "So tell me more about Rafe."

"My grandmother never had a good word to say about him. According to her, he didn't really want a wife, but a servant at his beck and call. He and I didn't even meet until after my parents died. What I'd heard about him made me curious."

"He sounds rather sexist."

"I prefer to think he was just a product of his time. Neither Grandma nor my father talked much about him. They blamed him for the marriage breakdown, though I never found out precisely what caused it. It was as if they wanted to air-brush him out of our lives. I could understand their bitterness. Even so, the degree of their hostility seemed unfair."

"You like to see the good in people."

"Why not? I wanted to find out what he was really like."

"And did you?"

"Sort of. He was a small man, bald with dark gleaming eyes, rather charismatic. Yet I found him almost…scary. When we talked, he always seemed to be enjoying a private joke. He inherited the farm from a bachelor uncle when he was in his twenties, but he had no interest in farming. He sold off the bulk of the land and lived on the proceeds for the rest of his life."

"After your grandmother left him, he never married again?"

"No, but he cohabited with various women he called housekeepers. He had a rather old-fashioned attitude towards what he liked to call the fair sex."

Hong Li raised her eyebrows. "Actually, you're not exactly a new man yourself."

I chose to ignore this. "The first time I visited him, someone called Ramona was looking after him. Paraguayan and voluptuous, with a low-cut top and a spangly brooch on her bosom."

"So he didn't recruit her simply for her housekeeping skills?"

"Even he described her as sluttish, though he made it sound like high praise. The house was such a mess that it would send anyone who was remotely house-proud into a tail-spin. He never believed in putting things away—he used to say he liked to have everything handy. Every cupboard and every drawer overflowed. Shelves buckled under the weight of books, ornaments and knick-knacks. The floors were covered with his things. I suppose it's no real wonder that his marriage fell apart."

Hong Li frowned. She'd come from Canton to England three years ago, and she wasn't supposed to have stayed here so long. The immigration laws are draconian; they don't give such people a hope of staying if they play by the rules. So they lurk in the twilight, taking work where they can to make ends meet. We met when I called in her shop for a bag of chips, and was smitten at first sight. Hong was not only a perfect model for any photographer, she also spoke better English than most people born and bred here. I felt a yearning for a passionate woman, and my only complaint was that her passion extended to tidiness. She was worse than my grandmother, whose mantra was *a place for everything, and everything in its place.* Hong enthused about *feng shui*, and tried to persuade me there was more to it than an aesthetic approach to interior design. Given half a chance, she would chatter for hours about discovering correlations between human life and the universe, and energizing your life through positive *qi*. For her, clutter was a metaphor for negative life circumstances. She wouldn't have suited Rafe, that was for sure.

"When did you last visit Brook House?"

"Four years ago, before I left for France. Ramona had moved on, and he'd installed a Thai girl he'd met through the internet. She wore thick spectacles and seemed very earnest, but he hinted that when she let her hair down..."

"I really don't think I would have liked Rafe," Hong said.

"But he was generous to a fault. He paid to bring these women to England on extended holidays, and looked after them well. He was just...idiosyncratic, that's all."

"It did him no good in the long run," she said. "What about the girl he was with when he died?"

"From Turkey by way of Berlin, according to Beazell. Poor kid, she called the emergency services when Rafe keeled over, and her reward was to be put on the first plane out of Britain."

Hong murmured, "You won't tell anyone about my situation, will you? I know I must get things sorted. I want to have the right to live in England, but it takes time to tick all the boxes."

"No need to worry," I said in a soothing tone, hoping she wasn't about to drop another hint about marriage. I might have promised to live in Brook House, but there's a limit to how many commitments a man can take on. Hong Li was the most accommodating model I'd worked with in ages, and I understood why, after the long and difficult journey from Canton, she felt a need to create order out of the chaos of a life in the shadows. But sometimes chaos is impossible to avoid. "There's no way the authorities will come looking for you here."

•••

"This is such a weird place," she said that evening, as we lay together on the sofa, in front of a roaring fire.

"I was afraid you'd loathe it," I murmured.

"Because of all the rubbish?"

There was no escaping Rafe's clutter. Since my last visit, he had spent another four years accumulating stuff. You could barely move in any of the downstairs room for junk. It wasn't only the discarded lumps of stone, the incomplete bits of sculpture that he'd abandoned whenever he chiselled off one chunk too many. He collected indiscriminately. Stacked next to the sofa was an early run of copies of *Playboy* from the 1950s, side-by-side with a pile of P.G. Wodehouse paperbacks and a dozen bulging postcard albums. He'd indulged in philately for years, but seemed to have become bored with the hobby in recent years, since countless unopened packets of gaudily colored stamps from all four corners of the world were stashed away in cupboards and in between the elderly encyclopedias crammed on groaning shelves.

"I know you can't bear mess."

"Come on, sweetheart. Mess is too mild a word, you must admit. There's so much negative energy here. We really have to start clearing up tomorrow."

"It won't be easy. It's a big house, but there isn't much room left to put all this stuff away."

"We drove past a waste disposal site on the way here."

"You can't be serious," I protested. "Remember the terms of his will?"

Hong shifted on the sofa, edging away from me. "You don't have to take everything so literally."

"It's a legal requirement. You wouldn't want me to lose my inheritance, would you?"

"Nobody would notice if you carried out a bit of…what's the right word? Rationalisation?"

"Don't you believe it. Councils hide cameras on wheelie-bins these days, they spy on folk who put electrical goods in containers meant for cardboard, it's scandalous."

"Out here in the middle of nowhere? You're making feeble excuses."

"Not in the least. It's a nightmare to dispose of anything. So easy to infringe some by-law or environmental regulation."

"That evening we first met, when I told you my story, you said laws were made to be broken."

"It was a figure of speech."

"Look!" She ran her finger along the arm of the sofa, showing me the dust. "Dirt interrupts the flow of natural energies. And the springs in the sofa have gone, it's so uncomfortable, we really must replace it."

"But it's flammable. Even if I wasn't bound to comply with Rafe's will, it would be impossible to chuck it out without a fistful of licenses and bureaucratic permissions."

She sighed. "This house needs some positive *chi*."

I put my arms around her, not bothering to argue. Better prove that I had all the positive *chi* she needed.

•••

Brook House stood on a winding lane in a quiet corner of Lancashire, surrounded by tumbledown sheds packed with mis-shapen sculptures and rusting cars that Rafe had driven into the ground and then abandoned. A preliminary reconnaissance indicated that he'd never got rid of a single thing. There wasn't another house in sight, which suited Rafe, who was not gregarious by nature. It suited me, too. The land that once belonged to the farm was now occupied by a business that hired out plant and machinery. A row of huge skips lined the horizon, but as I'd made clear to Hong, it would be unthinkable to use them as a dumping ground for Rafe's possessions. It wasn't simply about complying with legal niceties; to flout his wishes would be a betrayal.

I've never cared for an excess of noise and chatter, but it was bound to take Hong longer to adjust to a new life. She came from a large family, and loved to socialize. Unlike me. During my years in Europe, I'd had a number of relationships, but none of them worked out. At least I'd got the wanderlust out of my system. When I admitted I was an old-fashioned chap at heart, and felt it was time to settle down, Hong took it as a precursor to tying the knot. Which was not what I meant at all.

"Lucky that girl was with him when he had his heart attack," she hissed, glaring at a tower of boxes full of Rafe's correspondence from the past thirty years. "If he'd died alone, it might have been weeks before his body was discovered. Imagine being buried under a load of magazines, broken toasters and old shirts. Do you have any idea how many ancient sinks are outside the kitchen? Not one, but two!"

"Let's recycle them," I suggested, in a spirit of compromise. "They make ideal planters."

"And this whole house smells," she complained, throwing open the windows in the living room. "Musty books, old pairs of underpants. It's unhealthy."

"Hey, we'll freeze if you're not careful," I said. "Let me build up the fire."

"With some of those old yellow newspapers in the scullery?"

"No way. They go back twenty years. Some of them might be valuable."

"You must be joking. And what about this?" With a flourish, Hong produced a tin box and fiddled with a small key to open it.

"You found the key!" Extraordinary. Two whole drawers in the sideboard were packed with keys of all shapes and sizes, none bearing any tag to indicate to which lock they belonged.

"It took an hour and a half of trial and error, and now I've broken in…well, see for yourself."

She lifted the lid of the box to reveal half a dozen locks of hair. Red, fair, and black, wavy and straight.

"Who do you think they belonged to?"

"Old girlfriends, some of the housekeepers, who knows? Rafe must have had a sentimental streak, hence not wanting me to dispose of his clutter. I guess he kept snippets of their hair long after they'd moved on."

"They spook me." She pulled a face. "For pity's sake, be reasonable, sweetheart. We have to clear this crap out, it makes me ill just to look at it all."

I picked up one of the dark strands of hair. "I bet this was cut from Ramona's head. It's precisely her shade."

Hong shivered. "Creepy."

"You don't understand. They are keep-sakes. It's touching that they meant so much to him."

As I spoke the words, I knew instinctively how Rafe had felt about his souvenirs. Our possessions define us. Throw them out, and you throw away your history, your personality, the very life that you have lived. When we are gone, our possessions remain; they give our loved ones something to remember us by.

"You're right," she muttered, "I don't understand."

•••

The next day I continued to sift through the endless clutter. Hong set out for a long walk, much to my relief. I'd been afraid that she might embark on a clear-out when I wasn't looking. I dropped in on the pub for a snack lunch, and found myself chatting to the Russian barmaid. Anya was a pretty student, on a gap year. Something prompted me to ask for her phone number, and she wrote it down for me with a coquettish smile.

When Hong returned late in the afternoon, she was sneezing and out of humor. I pointed out that opening windows on a damp winter's day had been unwise, and she stomped off to bed with a glass of whisky and a paperback of *Zuleika Dobson* that she'd found under a pile of coffee filters in a kitchen cupboard. She was a voracious reader of English fiction, one of the reasons why she had mastered the language, and I said she ought to be thrilled to live in a house containing as many novels as a public library. She sniffed and headed upstairs without another word.

As the bedroom door slammed, I picked up the phone, and dialed Beazell's office.

"How did you come to meet my grandfather?"

The solicitor hesitated. "Why do you ask?"

"You're a criminal lawyer. Did Rafe do something wrong?"

"Certainly not." Beazell sounded as if I'd impugned his integrity. "Innocent until proven guilty, that's the law of the land."

"But he was accused of something?"

"He was a man of certain…tastes, shall we say? His lifestyle was by no means risk-free, his untimely demise is evidence for that."

"What happened?"

Beazell sighed. "He is dead now, so I am not breaching a confidence. A young Filipina accused him of whipping her black and blue, she claimed he was a sadist. He insisted that the, um, acts in question were consensual."

"Was he prosecuted?"

"A summons was issued, but the complainant dropped the charges and refused to testify. The case collapsed."

"A change of mind? Or did he buy the girl off?"

"I will not dignify that question with an answer." I pictured Beazell puffing out his sallow cheeks. "Suffice to say that I gave my client certain advice as to his future conduct. He went to his grave without a stain on his character."

I put the phone down and stared at the contents of the casket I'd discovered under Rafe's bed after returning from the pub. It wasn't covered in as much dust as the rest of his possessions, and I suspected that he regularly inspected its contents. When I grew frustrated after trying a couple of dozen keys in the lock, I took a hammer he'd kept in the dining room and smashed open the lid. Inside the casket were photographs, some of which I recognized. A portrait of Ramona was among them, another showed the girl from Thailand in the nude.

But it wasn't the photographs that made me catch my breath, it was the spangly brooch that once adorned Ramona's prominent chest, the little round spectacles worn by the Thai girl, the heart-shaped locket containing a picture of a Slavic woman. Hooped earrings which I recognized from another woman who posed for one of Rafe's photographs. And a whip streaked with dark blotches.

In my head, I heard my grandfather's silky tones. A conversation I'd forgotten until this very moment.

"You may consider it strange that I surround myself with so much ephemera, but the most precious of my possessions make me feel more *real.* Tangible reminders of the life I've lived, and those with whom I've shared it. Memories of the highs and the lows, the ups and downs. These are things to be cherished, not tossed away as if they never mattered."

"I think I understand," I'd said, although until now, I had not.

He'd smiled and said, "Well, well, my boy. I believe you do."

•••

When Hong came downstairs, she was in a mood to conciliate. The whisky had brightened her eyes, and made her voice rather loud.

"We don't need to clear out much," she announced. "Just the bare minimum. Enough to enable us to turn this place into a decent home."

"You know," I said, almost to myself, "I think I've finally found somewhere I can be myself."

As she squeezed my hand, her bracelet brushed my wrist. "We don't need to clear out everything."

"Tell you the truth," I said. "I really don't want to clear out anything at all."

Her pleasant face hardened. The smile vanished, and for an instant I saw her face as it might look in forty years' time.

"We have a perfectly good incinerator outside the back door," she hissed. "Why not use it?"

I gave a long, low sigh, as I surrendered to the inevitable. Rafe was right, I was a man after his own heart. I patted the mobile in my pocket. Anya's number was safely stored.

"All right." I ran my fingertips along her silver bracelet. I must no longer think of it as a present, but as a souvenir. "Tomorrow, I will."

MARTIN EDWARDS is an award-winning crime writer whose fifth Lake District Mystery is *The Hanging Wood*, long-listed for two awards at Crimefest 2012. The series includes *The Coffin Trail* (short-listed for the Theakston's prize for best British crime novel of 2006), *The Arsenic Labyrinth* (short-listed for the Lakeland Book of the Year award in 2008) and *The Serpent Pool.* He has written eight novels about Liverpool lawyer Harry Devlin, which are now available again as e-books, and two stand-alone novels, including *Dancing for the Hangman*. He won the CWA Short Story Dagger for "The Bookbinder's Apprentice" in 2008, has edited 20 anthologies and published eight non-fiction books.

He can be found online at www.martinedwardsbooks.com and his blog is located at www.doyouwriteunderyourownname.blogspot.com

A GRAVE MATTER: A MIKE HAMMER STORY

MAX ALLEN COLLINS
AND MICKEY SPILLANE

AUTHOR'S NOTE: In the early 1990s, Mickey Spillane and I created a science-fiction variation on his Mike Danger character for comic books. (The Danger character had been developed for comics by Mickey just before World War Two, and he attempted to market it after the war, as well, without success. In 1947, he decided to change "Danger" to "Hammer" and *I, the Jury* was the result.) At some point, the comic book company asked Mickey and me to develop a prose short story for a market that fell through. Mickey approved this story and gave me notes but did not do any of the writing, which explains the unusual byline above (with me getting top billing). Later, I recycled this idea for a third-person short story that used a different lead character, but this represents the first appearance of the story in its original, intended form… although for various reasons, I have changed "Danger" back to "Hammer." The tale takes place in the early 1950s.

IF I HADN'T BEEN ANGRY, I WOULDN'T HAVE BEEN DRIVING SO DAMN fast, and if I hadn't been driving so damn fast, in a lashing rain, on a night so dark closing your eyes made no difference, my high beams a pitiful pair of flashlights trying to guide the way in the vast cavern of the night, illuminating only slashes of storm, I would have had time to brake properly when I came down over the hill and saw, in a sudden white strobe of electricity, that the bridge was gone, or anyway out of sight, somewhere down there under the rush of rain-raised river. When the brakes didn't take, I yanked the wheel around, and my heap was sideways in a flooded ditch, wheels spinning. Like my head.

I got out on the driver's side, because otherwise I would have had to swim underwater. From my sideways-tipped car, I leapt to the slick highway as rain pelted me mercilessly, and did a fancy slip-slide dance, keeping my footing. Then I snugged the wings of the trench coat collar up around my face and began to walk back the way I'd come. If rain was God's tears, the Old Boy sure was bawling about something tonight.

I knew how he felt. I'd spent the afternoon in the upstate burg of Hopeful, only there was nothing hopeful about the sorry little hamlet. All I'd wanted was a few answers to a few questions. Like how a guy who won a Silver Star charging up a beachhead could wind up a crushed corpse in a public park, a crumpled piece of discarded human refuse.

Bill Reynolds had had his problems. Before the war he'd been an auto mechanic in Hopeful. A good-looking, dark-haired bruiser who'd have landed a football scholarship if the war hadn't gotten in the way, Bill married his high school sweetheart before he shipped out, only when he came back missing an arm and a leg, he found his girl wasn't interested in what was left of him. Even though he was good with his prosthetic arm and leg, he couldn't get his job back at the garage, either.

But the last time I'd spoken to Bill, when he came in to New York to catch Marciano and Jersey Joe at Madison Square Garden, he'd said things were looking up. He said he had a handyman job lined up, and that it was going to pay better than his old job at the garage.

"Besides which," he said, between rounds, "you oughta see my boss. You'd do overtime yourself."

"You mean you're working for a woman?"

"And what a woman. She's got more curves than the Mohonk Mountain road."

"Easy you don't drive off a cliff."

That's all we'd said about the subject, because Marciano had come out swinging at that point, and the next I heard from Bill—well not from him, *about* him—he was dead.

The only family he had left in Hopeful was a maiden aunt; she called me collect and told me tearfully that Bill's body had been found in the city park. His spine had been snapped.

•••

"How does a thing like that happen, Chief?"

Chief Thadeous Dolbert was one of Hopeful's four full-time cops. Despite his high office, he wore a blue uniform indistinguishable from his underlings, and his desk was out in the open of the little bullpen in Hopeful City Hall. A two-cell lockup was against one wall, and spring sunshine streaming in the windows through the bars sent slanting stripes of shadow across his desk and his fat, florid face. He was leaning back in his swivel chair, eyes hooded; he looked like a fat iguana—I expected his tongue to flick out and capture a fly any second now.

Dolbert said, "We figure he got hit by a car."

"Body was found in the city park, wasn't it?"

"Way he was banged up, figure he must've got whopped a good one, really sent him flyin'."

"Was that the finding at the inquest?"

Dolbert fished a pack of cigarettes out of his breast pocket, right behind his tarnished badge, lighted himself up a smoke. Soon it was dangling from a thick, slobber-flecked lower lip. "We don't stand much on ceremony around here, mister. County coroner called it accidental death at the scene."

"That's all the investigation Bill's death got?"

Dolbert shrugged, blew a smoke circle. "All that was warranted."

I sat forward. "All that was warranted. A local boy, who gave an arm and a leg to his country, wins a damn Silver Star doin' it, and you figure him getting his spine snapped like a twig and damn near every bone in his body broken, well, that's just pretty much business as usual here in Hopeful."

Under the heavy lids, fire flared in the fat chief's eyes. "You think you knew Bill Reynolds? You knew the old Bill. You didn't know the drunken stumblebum he turned into. Prime candidate for stepping out in front of a car."

"I never knew Bill to drink to excess—"

"How much time did you spend with him lately?"

A hot rush of shame crawled up my neck. I'd seen Bill from time to time, in the city, when he came in to see me, but I'd never come up to Hopeful. Never really gone out of my way for him, since the war…Till now.

"You make any effort to find the hit-and-run driver that did this?"

The chief shrugged. "Nobody saw it happen."

"You don't even know for sure a car did it."

"How the hell else could it have happened?"

I stood up, pushed back, the legs of my wooden chair scraping the hard floor like fingernails on a blackboard. "That's what I'm going to find out."

A finger as thick as a pool cue waggled at me. "You got no business stickin' your damn nose in around here, Hammer—"

"I'm a licensed investigator in the state of New York, pops. And I'm working for Bill Reynolds's aunt."

He snorted a laugh. "Working for that senile old biddy? She's out at the county hospital. She's broke! Couldn't even afford a damn funeral…we had to bury the boy in potter's field…"

That was one of Hopeful's claims to fame: the state buried its unknown, unclaimed, impoverished dead in the potter's field here.

"Why didn't you tell Uncle Sam?" I demanded. "Bill was a war hero—they'd've put him in Arlington…"

Dolbert shrugged. "Not my job."

"What the hell *is* your job?"

"Watch your mouth, city boy." He nodded toward the holding cells, and the cigarette quivered as the fat mouth sneered. "Don't forget you're in *my* world…"

Maybe Bill Reynolds didn't get a funeral or a gravestone, but he was going to get a memorial by way of an investigation.

•••

Only nobody in Hopeful wanted to talk to me. The supposed "accident" had occurred in the middle of the night, and my only chance for a possible witness was in the all-night diner across from the Civil War cannon in the park.

The diner's manager, a skinny character with a horsey face darkened by perpetual five o'clock shadow, wore a grease-stained apron over his grease-stained T-shirt. Like the chief, he had a cigarette drooping from slack lips. The ash narrowly missed falling into the cup of coffee he'd served me as I sat at the counter with half a dozen locals.

"We got a jukebox, mister," the manager said. "Lots of kids end up here, tail end of a Saturday night. That was a Saturday night, when Bill got it, ya know? That loud music, joint jumpin', there coulda been a train wreck out there, and nobody'da heard it."

"Nobody would have seen an accident out your windows?"

The manager shrugged. "Maybe ol' Bill got hit on the other side of the park."

But it was just a little square of grass and benches and such; the "other side of the park" was easily visible from the windows lining the diner booths—even factoring in the grease and lettering.

I talked to a couple of waitresses who claimed not to have been working that night. One of them, Gladys her name tag said, a heavyset bleached blonde who must have been pretty cute twenty years ago, served me a slice of apple pie and cheese and a piece of information.

"Bill said he was going to work as a handyman," I said, "for some good-lookin' gal. You know who that would've been?"

"Sure," Gladys said. She had sky-blue eyes and nicotine-yellow teeth. "He was working out at the mansion."

"The what?"

"The mansion. The old Riddle place. You must've passed it on the highway, comin' into town."

"I saw a gate and a drive, and got a glimpse of a big old gothic brick barn..."

She nodded, refilled my coffee. "That's the one. The Riddles, they owned this town forever. Ain't a building downtown that the Riddles ain't owned since the dawn of time. But Mr. Riddle, he was the last of the line, and he and his wife died in that plane crash, oh, ten years ago. The only one left now is the daughter, Victoria."

"What was Bill doing out at the Riddle place?"

She shrugged. "Who knows? Who cares? Maybe Miz Riddle just wanted some company. Bill was still a handsome so-and-so, even minus a limb or two. He coulda put his shoe under my bed anytime."

"Victoria Riddle isn't married? She lives alone?"

"Alone except for that hairless ape."

"What?"

"She's got a sort of butler, you know, a servant? He was her father's chauffeur. Big guy. Mute. Comes into town, does the grocery shopping and such. We hardly ever see Miz Riddle, less she's meeting with her lawyer, or going to the bank to visit all her money."

"What does she do out there?"

"Who knows? She's not interested in business. Her daddy, he had his finger in every pie around here. Miz Riddle, she lets her lawyer run things, and I guess the family money, uh, under-what's-it? Underwrites, is that the word?"

"I guess."

"Underwrites her research."

"Research?"

"Oh, yeah. Miz Riddle's a doctor."

"Medical doctor."

"Yes, but not the kind that hangs out a shingle. She's some kind of scientific genius."

"So she's doing medical research out there?"

"I guess." She shook her head. "Pity about Bill. Such a nice fella."

"Had he been drinking heavy?"

"Bill? Naw. Oh, he liked a drink. I suppose he shut his share of bars down on a Saturday night, but he wasn't no alcoholic. Not like that other guy."

"What other guy?"

Her expression turned distant. "Funny."

"What's funny? What other guy?"

"Not funny ha-ha. Funny weird. That other guy, don't remember his name, just some tramp who come through, he was a crip, too."

"A crip?"

"Yeah. He had one arm. Guess he lost his in the war, too. He was working out at the Riddle mansion as a handyman—one-handed handyman. That guy, he really was a drunk."

"What became of him?"

"That's what's funny weird. Three, four months ago, he wound up like Bill. They found him in the gutter on Main Street, all banged up, deader than a bad battery. Hit-and-run victim—just like Bill."

•••

The wrought-iron gate in the gray-brick wall stood open, and I tooled the heap up a winding red-brick drive across a gentle, treeless slope where the sprawling gabled tan-brick gothic mansion crouched like a lion about to pounce. The golf course of a lawn had its own rough behind the house, a virtual forest preserve that seemed at once to shelter and encroach upon the stark lines of the house.

Steps led to an open cement pedestal of a porch with a massive slab of a wooden door where I had a choice between an ornate iron knocker and a simple doorbell. I rang the bell.

I stood there, listening to birds chirping and enjoying the cool breeze that seemed to whisper rain was on its way, despite the golden sunshine reflecting off the lawn. I rang the bell again.

I was about to go around back, to see if there was another door I could try, when that massive slab of wood creaked open like the start of the *Inner Sanctum* radio program; the 350-pound apparition who stood suddenly before me would have been at home on a spook show himself.

He was six-four, easy, towering over my six-one; he wore the black uniform of a chauffeur, but no cap, his tie a loose black string thing. He looked like an upended Buick with a person painted on it. His head was the shape of a grape and just as hairless though considerably larger; he had no eyebrows, either; wide, bulging eyes; a lump of a nose; and an open mouth.

"Unnggh," he said.

"I'd like to see Miss Riddle," I said.

"Unnggh," he said.

"It's about Bill Reynolds. I represent his family. I'm here to ask some questions."

His brow furrowed in something approaching thought.

Then he slammed the door in my face.

Normally, I don't put up with crap like that. I'd been polite. He'd been rude. Kicking the door in, and his teeth, seemed called for. Only this boy was a walking side of beef that gave even Mike Hammer pause.

And I was, in fact, pausing, wondering whether to ring the bell again, go around back, or just climb in my heap and drive the hell away, when the door opened again, and the human Buick was replaced by a human goddess.

She was tall, standing eye-to-eye with me, and though she wore a loose-fitting white lab jacket that hung low over a simple black skirt, nylons, and flat shoes, those mountain-road curves Bill had mentioned were not easily hidden. Her dark blonde hair was tied back, and severe black-framed glasses rode the perfect little nose; she wore almost no makeup, perhaps just a hint of lipstick, or was that the natural color of those full lips? Whatever effort she'd made to conceal her beauty behind a mask of scientific sterility was futile; the big green eyes, the long lashes, the high cheekbones, the creamy complexion, that full, high-breasted, wasp-waisted, long-limbed figure, all conspired to make her as stunning a female creature as God had ever created.

"I'm sorry," she said, in a silky contralto. "This is a private residence and a research center. We see no one without an appointment."

"The gate was open."

"We're expecting the delivery of certain supplies this evening," she said, "and I leave the gate standing open on such occasions. You see, I'm shorthanded. But why am I boring you with this? Good afternoon..."

And the door began to close.

I held it open with the flat of my hand. "My name is Michael Hammer."

The green eyes narrowed. "The detective?"

I grinned. "You must get the New York papers up here."

"We do. Hopeful isn't the end of the world."

"It was for Bill Reynolds."

Her expression softened, and she cracked the door open, wider. "Poor Bill. Were you a friend?"

"Yes."

"So you've come to ask about his death."

"That's right." I shrugged. "I'm a detective."

"Of course," she said, opening the door. "And you're looking into the circumstances. A natural way for you to deal with such a loss..."

She gestured for me to enter, and I followed her through a high-ceilinged entryway. The hairless ape appeared like an apparition and took my trench coat; I kept my porkpie hat but took it off in deference to my hostess.

In front of me, a staircase led to a landing, then to a second floor; gilt-framed family portraits lined the way. On one side was a library with more leather in bindings and chairs than your average cattle herd; on the other was a formal sitting room where elegant furnishings that had been around long enough to become antiques were overseen by a glittering chandelier.

She led me to a rear room and it was as if, startlingly, we'd entered a penthouse apartment—the paintings on the wall were abstract and modern, and the furnishings were, too, with a television/hi-fi console set-up and a zebra wet bar with matching stools; but the room was original with the house, or at least the fireplace and mantel indicated as much. Over the fireplace was the only artwork in the room that wasn't abstract: a full-length portrait of my hostess in a low-cut evening gown, a painting that was impossibly lovely with no exaggeration by the artist.

She slipped out of her lab coat, tossing it on a boomerang of a canvas chair, revealing a short-sleeved white blouse providing an understated envelope for an overstated bosom. Undoing her hair, she allowed its length to shimmer to her shoulders. The severe black-framed glasses, however, she left in place.

Her walk was as liquid as mercury in a vial as she got behind the bar and poured herself a martini. "Fix you a drink?"

"Got any beer back there?"

"Light or dark?"

"Dark."

We sat on a metal-legged couch that shouldn't have been comfortable but was; she sipped her martini, her dark nyloned legs crossed, displaying well-developed calves. For a scientist, she made a hell of a specimen.

I sipped my beer—it was a bottle of German imported stuff, a little bitter for my taste, but very cold.

"That's an interesting butler you got," I said.

"I have to apologize for Bolo," she said, stirring the cocktail with her speared olive. "His tongue was cut out by natives in the Amazon. My father was on an exploratory trip, somehow incurred the wrath of the natives, and Bolo interceded on his behalf. By offering himself, in the native custom, Bolo bought my father's life—but paid with his tongue."

With a kiss-like bite, she plucked the olive from its spear and chewed.

"He doesn't look much like a South American native," I said.

"He isn't. He was a Swedish missionary. My father never told me Bolo's real name…but that was what the natives called him."

"And I don't suppose Bolo's told you, either."

"No. But he can communicate. He can write. In English. His mental capacity seems somewhat diminished, but he understands what's said to him."

"Very kind of you to keep somebody like that around."

"Like what?"

I shrugged. "Handicapped."

"Mr. Hammer…"

"Make it Mike—and I'll call you Victoria. Or do you prefer Vicki?"

"How do you know I don't prefer 'Doctor'?"

"Hey, it's okay with me. I've played doctor before."

"Are you flirting with me, Mike?"

"I might be."

"Or you might be trying to get me to let my guard down."

"Why—is it up?"

She glanced at my lap. "You tell me."

Now I crossed *my* legs. "Where's your research lab?"

"In back."

"Sorry if I'm interrupting…"

"No. I'm due for a break. I'd like to help you. You see, I thought a lot of Bill. He worked hard. He may not have been the brightest guy around, but he made up for it with enthusiasm and energy. Some people let physical limitations get in their way. Not Bill."

"You must have a thing for taking in strays."

"What do you mean?"

"Well…like Bolo. Like Bill. I understand you took in another handicapped veteran, not so long ago."

"That's right. George Wilson." She shook her head sadly. "Such a shame. He was a hard worker, too—"

"He died the same way as Bill."

"I know."

"Doesn't that strike you as…a little odd? Overly coincidental?"

"Mike, George was a heavy drinker, and Bill was known to tie one on himself. It may be coincidental, but I'm sure they aren't the first barroom patrons to wobble into the street after closing and get hit by a car."

"Nobody saw either one of them get hit by a car."

"Middle of the night. These things happen."

"Not twice."

The green eyes narrowed with interest and concern. "What do *you* think happened, Mike?"

"I have no idea—yet. But I'll say this—everybody seemed to like Bill. I talked to a lot of people today, and nobody, except maybe the police chief, had an unkind word to say about him. So I'm inclined to think the common factors between Bill and this George Wilson hold the answer. You're one of those common factors."

"But surely not the only one."

"Hardly. They were both war veterans, down on their luck."

"No shortage of those."

"And they were both handicapped."

She nodded, apparently considering these facts, scientist that she was. "Are you staying in Hopeful tonight?"

"No. I got a court appearance in the city tomorrow. I'll be back on the weekend. Poke around some more."

She put a hand on my thigh. "If I think of anything, how can I find you?"

I patted the hand, removed it, stood. "Keep your gate open," I said, putting on my porkpie, "and I'll find you."

She licked her lips; they glistened. "I'll make sure I leave my gate wide open on Saturday."

•••

I'd gone back into Hopeful to talk to the night shift at the diner, got nowhere, and headed home in the downpour, pissed off at how little I'd learned. Now, with my car in the ditch and rain lashing down relentlessly, I found myself back at the Riddle mansion well before Saturday. The gate was still open, though—she must not have received that delivery she'd talked about, yet.

Splashing through puddles on the winding drive, I kept my trench coat collar snugged around me as I headed toward the towering brick house. In the daytime, the mansion had seemed striking, a bit unusual; on this black night, illuminated momentarily in occasional flashes of lightning, its gothic angles were eerily abstract, the planes of the building a stark, ghostly white.

This time I used the knocker, hammering with it. It wasn't all that late—maybe nine o'clock or a little after. But it felt like midnight, and instinctively I felt the need to wake the dead.

Bolo answered the door. The lights in the entryway were out, and he was just a big black blot, distinguishable only by that upended Buick shape of his; then the world turned white, him along with it, and when the thunder caught up with the lightning, I damn near jumped.

"Tell your mistress Mr. Hammer's back," I said. "My car's in a ditch and I need—"

That's when the SOB slammed the door in my face. Second time today. A red heat of anger started to rise up around my collar, but it wasn't drying me off, even if the shelter of the awning over the slab of porch was keeping me from getting wetter. Only I wasn't sure a human being could be any wetter than this.

When the door opened again, it was Victoria. She wore a red silk robe, belted tight around her tiny waist. The sheen of the robe and the folds of the silk conspired with her curves to create a dizzying display of pulchritude.

"Mr. Hammer…Mike! Come in, come in."

I did. The light in the entryway was on now, and Bolo was there again, taking my drenched hat and coat. I quickly explained to her what had happened.

"With this storm," she said, "and the bridge out, you'll need to stay the night."

"Love to," I said. Mother Hammer didn't raise any fools.

"But you'll have to get out of those wet things," she said. "I think I have an old nightshirt of my father's…"

She took me back to that modern sitting room, and I was soon in her pop's nightshirt, swathed in blankets as I sat before the fireplace's glow, its magical flickering soothingly restful, and making her portrait above the fire seem alive, smiling seductively, the bosom in the low-cut gown heaving with passion. Shaking my head, wondering if I'd completely lost my sanity, I tucked my .45 in its speed rig behind a pillow—hardware like that can be distressing to the gentle sensibilities of some females.

When she cracked the door to ask if I was decent, I said, "That's one thing I've never been accused of, but come on in."

Then she was sitting next to me, the red silk gown playing delightful reflective games with the firelight.

"Can I tell you something terrible?" she asked, like a child with an awful secret.

"I hope you will."

"I'm glad your car went in the ditch."

"And here I thought you liked me."

"I do," she said, and she edged closer. "That's why I'm glad."

She seemed to want me to kiss her, so I did, and it was a long, deep kiss, hotter than the fire, wetter than the night, and then my hands were on top of the smoothness of the silk gown. And then they were on the smoothness underneath it…

•••

Later, when she offered me a guest bedroom upstairs, I declined.

"This is fine," I said, as she made herself a drink behind the bar, and got me another German beer. "I'll just couch it. Anyway, I like the fire."

She handed me the bottle of beer, its cold wetness in my palm contrasting with the warmth of the room and the moment. Sitting next to me, close to me, she sipped her drink.

"First thing tomorrow," she said, "we'll call in to town for a tow truck and get your car pulled out of that ditch."

"No hurry."

"Don't you have a court appearance tomorrow?"

"Acts of God are a good excuse," I said and rested the beer on an amoeba-shaped coffee table nearby, then leaned in and kissed her again. Just a friendly peck.

"Aren't you thirsty?" she asked, nodding toward the beer.

Why was she so eager for me to drink that brew?

I said, "Dry as a bone," and reached for the bottle, lifted it to my lips, and seemed to take a drink.

Seemed to.

Now she gave me a friendly kiss, said, "See you at breakfast," and rose, sashaying out as she cinched the silk robe back up. If you could bottle that walk, you'd really have something worth researching.

Alone, I sniffed the beer. My unscientific brain couldn't detect anything, but I knew damn well it contained a mickey. She wanted me to sleep through this night. I didn't know why, but something was going to happen here that a houseguest like me—even one who'd been lulled into a false sense of security by a very giving hostess—shouldn't see.

So I poured the beer down the drain and quickly went to the couch, got myself under the blankets, and pretended to be asleep.

But I couldn't have been more alert if I'd been in a foxhole on the front line. My eyes only seemed shut; they were slitted open and saw her when she peeked in to see if I was sleeping. I even saw her mouth and eyes tighten in smug satisfaction before the door closed, followed by the click of me being locked in…

The rain was still sheeting down when, wearing only her daddy's nightshirt, I went out a window and, .45 in hand, found my way to the back of the building where a new section had been added, institutional-looking brick with no windows at all. The thin cotton cloth of the nightshirt was a transparent second skin by the time I found my way around the building and discovered an open double garage, also back behind, following an extension of the original driveway. The garage doors stood open and a single vehicle—a panel truck bearing the Hopeful Police Department insignia—was within, dripping with water, as if it were sweating.

Cautiously, I slipped inside, grateful to be out of the rain. Along the walls of the garage were various boxes and crates with medical-supply-house markings. I heard approaching footsteps and ducked behind a stack of crates.

Peeking out, I could see Chief Dolbert in a rain slicker and matching hat, leading the way for Bolo, still in his chauffeur-type uniform. Dolbert opened up the side of the van, and Bolo leaned in.

And when Bolo leaned back out, he had his arms filled with a person, a woman in fact, a naked one; then Bolo walked away from the panel truck, toward the door back into the building, held open for him by the thoughtful police chief. It was as if Bolo were carrying a bride across the threshold.

Only this bride was dead.

For ten minutes I watched as Bolo made trips from the building to the panel truck where, with the chief's assistance, he conveyed naked dead bodies into the house. My mind was reeling with the unadorned horror of it. I was shivering, and not just from my water-soaked nightshirt. Somehow, being in that nightshirt, naked under it, made me feel a kinship to those poor dead bastards, many of them desiccated-looking souls, with unkempt hair and bony, ill-fed bodies, and finally it came to me.

I knew who these poor dead wretches were. And I knew why, at least roughly why, Chief Dolbert was delivering them.

When at last the doors on the panel truck were shut, the chief and Bolo headed back into the building. That pleased me—I was afraid the chief would take off into the rainy, thunderous night, and I didn't want him to.

I wanted him around.

Not long after they had disappeared into the building, I went in after them.

And into hell.

It was a blindingly well-illuminated hell, a white and silver hell, resembling a hospital operating room but much larger, a hell dominated by the silver of surgical instruments, a hell where the walls were lined with knobs and dials and meters and gizmos, a hell dominated by naked corpses on metal autopsy-type tables, their empty eyes staring at the bright overhead lighting.

And the sensual Satan who ruled over this hell, Victoria Riddle, who was back in her lab coat now, hair tucked in a bun, was filling Chief Dolbert's open palm with greenbacks.

But where was Bolo?

I glanced behind me, and there he was, tucked behind the door, standing like a cigar-store Indian awaiting his mistress's next command, only she didn't have to give this command: Bolo knew enough to reach out for this intruder, his hands clawed, his eyes bulging to where the whites showed all around, his mouth open in a soundless snarl.

"Stop!" I told the looming figure, as he threw his shadow over me like a blue blanket.

But he didn't stop.

And when I blew the top of his bald head off, splashing the white wall behind him with the colors of the inside of his head, red and gray and white, making another abstract painting only without a frame, that didn't stop him, either, didn't stop him from falling on top of me, and by the time I had pushed his massive dead weight off of me, his fat corpse emptying ooze out the top of his bald, blown-off skull, I had another fat bastard to deal with, a *live* one: the chief of the Hopeful Police Department, his revolver pointed down at me.

"Drop it," he said.

He should have just shot me, because I took advantage of his taking time to say that and shot him in the head, and the gun in his hand was useless now, since his brain could no longer send it signals, and he toppled back on top of one of the corpses, sharing its silver tray, staring up at the ceiling, the red hole in his forehead like an extra expressionless eye.

"You fool," she said, the lovely face lengthening into a contorted, ugly mask, green eyes wild behind the glasses.

"I decided I wasn't thirsty after all," I said, as I weaved my way between the corpses on their metal slabs.

"You don't understand! This is serious research! This will benefit *humanity...*"

"I understand you were paying the chief for fresh cadavers," I said. "With him in charge of the state's potter's field, you had no shortage of dead guinea pigs. But what I *don't* understand is, why kill Bill and George Wilson, when you had access to all these riches?"

And I gestured to the deceased indigents around us.

Her face eased back into beauty; her scientific mind had told her, apparently, that her best bet now was to try to reason with me. Calmly. Coolly.

I was close enough to her to kiss her, only I didn't feel much like kissing her, and anyway, the .45 I was aiming at her belly would have been in the way of an embrace.

"George Wilson tried to blackmail me," she said. "Bill...Bill just wouldn't cooperate. He said he was going to the authorities."

"About your ghoulish arrangement with the chief, you mean?"

She nodded. Then earnestness coated her voice: "Mike, I was only trying to *help* Bill and George—*and* mankind. Don't you see? I wanted to make them *whole* again!"

"Oh my God," I said, getting it. "Bill was a *live* guinea pig, wasn't he? Wilson, too..."

"That's not how I'd express it, exactly, but yes..."

"You wanted to make them living Frankenstein monsters...you wanted to sew the limbs of the dead on 'em..."

Her eyes lit up with enthusiasm and hope. And madness. "Yes! *Yes!* I learned in South America of voodoo techniques that reanimated the dead into so-called 'zombies.' The scientific community was sure to reject such mumbo jumbo and deny the world this wonder, and I have been forced to seek the truth with my mixture of the so-called supernatural and renegade science. With the correct tissue matches and my own research into electrochemical transplant techniques—"

That was when the lights went out.

God's electricity had killed man's electricity, and the cannon roar aftermath of the thunderbolt wasn't enough to hide the sound of her scurrying in the dark among the trays of the dead, trying to escape, heading for that door into the garage.

I went after her, but she had knowledge of the layout of the place, and I didn't. I kept bumping into bodies, and then she screamed.

Just for a split second.

A hard *whump* had interrupted the scream, and before I even had time to wonder what the hell had happened, the lights came back on, and there she was.

On her back, on the floor, her head resting against the metal underbar of one of the dead-body trays, only resting wasn't really the word, since she'd hit hard enough to crack open her skull and a widening puddle of red was forming below her head as she, too, stared up at the ceiling with wide-open eyes, just another corpse in a roomful of corpses. Bolo's dead body, where I'd pushed his dead weight off of me, was—as was fitting—at his mistress's feet.

I had to smile.

Bolo may not have had many brains in that chrome dome of his, but he'd had enough to slip her up.

MAX ALLAN COLLINS is the bestselling, award-winning author of *Road to Perdition,* the graphic novel that inspired the Oscar-winning movie starring Paul Newman and Tom Hanks, and of the acclaimed Nathan Heller series of historical hardboiled mysteries. Also a filmmaker himself, Collins' films include the documentary *Mike Hammer's Mickey Spillane.*

MICKEY SPILLANE is the legendary crime writer credited with igniting the paperback book explosion after World War II as a result of the unprecedented success of his Mike Hammer novels. Spillane's novels sold tens of millions of copies: *I, The Jury* went through more than 60 paperback printings in 1947 alone. In 1995, he was named a Grand Master by the Mystery Writers of America. Before his death at the age of 88 in 2006, Spillane chose long-time friend Max Allan Collins to complete his unfinished work and act as his literary executor.

ESCAPE FROM WOLFKILL

CLARK HOWARD

The opening of Wolfkill Correctional Center, the first federal geriatric prison, was explained to the public in a television interview with the Director of the Federal Bureau of Prisons on the popular nighttime broadcast of *Harry Ring Live.* It went like this:

Harry Ring: "Explain to our viewers, if you will, Mr. Director, exactly what the reason is for this new federal prison."

"Certainly. The reason is quite simple. In the field of corrections, it is known as the 'graying' of America's federal prison inmates."

"Graying meaning what?"

"Aging. Growing older. Approaching one's final years."

"Has that become a problem in the federal prisons?"

"Yes. A very definite problem. One that becomes more acute with each passing day. At the present, there are more than two hundred thousand inmates, male and female, in federal custody. A significant percentage of them have now reached age sixty-five or older. Some are in their seventies, some even in their eighties. They present custodial problems that have become increasingly impossible to deal with in a conventional prison environment."

"What sort of problems?"

"The same sort of problems that elderly persons face outside of prison: diminishing eyesight and hearing, decreased mobility, lapses in memory, special nutrition and dietary needs, kidney and urinary-tract disorders, osteoporosis, rheumatism, depression, anxiety—"

"And conventional prisons, as you call them, are not equipped or staffed to handle such cases?"

"Not to the extent that the graying of the prison population necessitates. Conventional prisons have hospital wards and infirmaries, of course, but they are designed for inmates with temporary medical problems, conditions that can be cured or relieved in some way. But there is no cure for old age."

"Wouldn't it be possible to set aside a special area in each existing prison to accommodate these 'graying' prisoners, as you call them?"

"Possible, yes, but not very practical. The cost would be enormous. You see, Harry, modern prisons are designed for younger inmates. They were never meant to house senior citizens. Only in the last two decades has the corrections community encountered this problem."

"What, other than the obvious passage of time, would you say has caused this problem?"

"A number of things. Longer, harsher sentences, for one. More stringent parole and probation requirements, for another. Much longer appeals procedures. New medical treatments and medicines that help people live longer."

"So, since the cost to modify all the existing prisons is prohibitive, it was decided to build a geriatric facility to put them all in one place?"

"Exactly."

"How will this new prison differ from, say, Leavenworth or Marion?"

"For one thing, it is handicap-friendly; wheelchairs and walkers will be freely utilized. All custodial quarters are on one level; no stairs will be involved in daily activity. Upper floors will be for hospital treatment, and gurney-sized elevators will access them. Beds will be more comfortable and equipped with safety rails. There will be special toilets for the infirm. And the staff will be made up not only of correctional officers, but also nurses, practical caregivers, housekeepers, patient aides, and many other job classifications not found in conventional facilities."

"When will you begin transferring inmates to the new prison?"

"We've already begun. The first several dozen are already there."

"Incidentally, why the name 'Wolfkill'?"

"That's the name of the nearest community. It's a somewhat isolated little rural town in North Dakota, up near the Canadian border. The town donated the land to us hoping the new facility will provide much-needed economic stimulus to the area in these difficult times."

"Well, I hope, for their sake, that it does. Just one more question: Among the prisoners being transferred to Wolfkill are three former death-row inmates. What can you tell us about them?"

"They are leftovers from another era. All three of them were on the federal condemned row at Terre Haute Prison some years back when the Supreme Court ruled that capital punishment as it was applied at that time was unconstitutional. These three men, along with seven other condemned inmates, had their death sentences commuted to life in prison without parole. After that ruling abolished capital punishment, the death-row inmates were transferred to other maximum-security federal prisons. In the years that have passed, four of them have died natural deaths, one committed suicide, and two—both of them child rape-murderers—were killed by other maximum-security inmates. The three who were left have quietly grown old in prison and are now candidates for transfer to our new geriatric facility at Wolfkill."

"Can you tell us a little about these three men?"

"Their cases are very old, of course, going back some forty years, so many of your viewers might not be familiar with them. One of the men is Cleveland McCoy, a notorious bank robber, condemned for the murder of a security guard during the holdup of a federally insured bank. Another is Antonio Ginetta, a professional hit man for one of the Chicago crime families, who killed an FBI agent who had infiltrated the mob. And the third is Andrew King, who murdered his wife and her lover when he caught them having sex in a car parked on federal property behind the post office where the lover worked as a federal employee."

"So all three killings were federal offenses?"

"Yes."

"Well, Mr. Director, I want to thank you for a very interesting and enlightening interview. Best of luck to you and your bureau in this new endeavor.

"And that concludes our show for tonight..."

•••

The first of the formerly condemned men to arrive at Wolfkill was Cleveland McCoy, the bank robber, who was transferred from Leavenworth. He was met by Captain Carl Meadows, who had previously been in charge of the federal death row at Terre Haute.

"Hello, McCoy," the longtime corrections officer greeted him.

"I'll be damned," McCoy said, surprised. "Meadows. I thought you'd be dead by now."

"You thought wrong."

"Not retired yet?"

"Sixteen months to go." The guard captain looked him up and down. "If I take off your hardware, you going to give me any trouble?"

McCoy grunted softly. "My days of giving anyone trouble are long gone, Meadows."

"Glad to hear it." Meadows unlocked the handcuffs and ankle shackles, and undraped the belly and shoulder chains from McCoy's body. "Come on, I'll show you around."

The pair left the intake area and walked down an immaculately clean and shiny corridor.

"How was the trip up from Kansas?" Meadows asked.

"A little scary," McCoy admitted. "First time I ever flew in a jet plane. Food wasn't very good, either. And my two U.S. Marshal escorts were assholes."

"Well, most guys in the Marshal's service are FBI dropouts, that's why they're assholes."

Meadows glanced at the prisoner. "You know, McCoy, I always liked you back on the Row. I mean, you were a throwback to the old days. A good old-fashioned bank robber. Different from some of the weirdos I've had to put up with: child kidnappers who raped and killed kids, and crossed a state line in the process; punk fed cons who killed a guard to prove how tough they were; heartless dickheads who leave a locked van full of illegals out in the desert to suffocate: psycho snipers who murder people going to work at the Pentagon—you know, people like that."

"How well I know," McCoy said. "I had to live with them, remember?"

Meadows led the way into a common area off the corridor that had a single cell on each of the back and two side walls, their solid doors, each with a window, standing open. In the common area was a metal picnic-type table, a counter with a sink, a full-size refrigerator, and a coffee maker. In one corner was a television set facing three metal folding chairs.

"All the comforts of home," McCoy cracked.

"Find the one with your name on the door," Meadows said.

"Who are the other two for?"

"Andy King and Tony Ginetta."

"What!" McCoy moaned. "You mean I have to spend the rest of my golden years with a wife-killer and a Mafia hit man?"

"It'll be okay, McCoy," Meadows assured him. "You'll like it here. Wait and see."

"Don't have much choice," McCoy reminded him.

•••

The confinement rooms at Wolfkill, for public-relations reasons, were not called "cells"—in many ways they resembled hospital rooms. Beds were movable, mattresses adjustable, nightstands had three-way lights, desks had drawers, chairs had rollers. The doors were solid but had large Plexiglas windows for observation. They were unlocked from seven A.M., when breakfast was served on the community table from a food cart, until ten o'clock at night for lock-down.

After Captain Meadows left, an orderly, a guy about forty, came in with McCoy's reception bundle. Besides toilet articles and Wolfkill's rules-and-regulations manual, it contained red cotton trousers, matching buttonless pullover shirt, soft red slippers, and miscellaneous socks and underwear.

"Everybody's color coded in here," the orderly said. "The psychos wear yellow, seniles green, elderly-but-mobile blue. You three guys in here will wear red so's you can be easily spotted. Oh yeah, the screws wear khaki and orderlies like me wear white." He looked the newcomer up and down. "So you're McCoy, huh?"

"That's me."

"I read a lot about you in the crime magazines. I'm Zeniak. Just call me Zen. Doing forty as a habitual. I was a hospital orderly at Lewisburg. Volunteered for this gig. Figured it would be an easier stint. Let me know if you need anything; I'll see what I can do."

When McCoy was alone, smelling the newness of his clothes, he stretched out on the bed in his room and stared up at the ceiling. So this was how it would end, he thought. Locked down in a sterile cocoon until he shriveled up and died. All because of one lousy mistake…

The mistake had been in deciding to take down a bank that required three men for the job instead of two. For years, McCoy and his partner had been knocking over three or four banks a year, small ones, in small towns, the total netting them about half a million each—enough to live quite well, since it was tax-free. Then they decided on a single job, a bigger bank, the net from which would last them a year. But the bigger bank needed a third man to take down. They found a kid just out of the joint after doing five for burglarizing a dozen electronics stores. He came highly recommended by a fence who bought his merchandise. They took him on, this kid. McCoy laid down the one ironclad rule that he had: Never take a loaded gun on a job. Just as much could be accomplished with an *unloaded* gun as with a loaded one. And it eliminated the risk of ever killing anyone. A fall for bank robbery was one thing; a fall for murder was something else entirely.

Unfortunately, the kid failed to see the logic of that philosophy. He carried a loaded gun into the big bank they had chosen to storm. A security guard, refusing to give up his weapon, tried to be a hero protecting other people's money. The resulting shootout left McCoy's original partner and the guard dead, and the kid riddled with police bullets as he tried to escape the bank.

As an accomplice to a murder committed during the attempted robbery of a federally insured bank, McCoy got a death sentence. The Supreme Court knocked that back to life without parole when it abolished capital punishment.

One lousy mistake…

"Well, well," a voice said from the doorway to McCoy's room, ending his reverie, "look who's here. Public enemy number one. John Dillinger, Junior."

McCoy looked up to see Antonio Ginetta standing there, smiling.

•••

Tony Ginetta had all but grown up in the mob. His father, four uncles, and two brothers were all made men, and Tony, the youngest, was just days away from an *Omertà* ceremony of his own when he was given an assignment that would change his life. The job: assassinate a rival gang boss so that the head of his own family could take over the dead man's organization. The hit was set for a Wednesday night outside Bruno's Steak House on the lower West Side. The target, a Don named Philip Iacobucci, was in the habit of having a late supper every Wednesday night, usually accompanied by his chief lieutenant, his driver, and a bodyguard.

On the night of the hit, Tony Ginetta was standing in an unlighted doorway just down from the entrance to Bruno's with a sawed-off twelve-gauge automatic shotgun, loaded with eight specially made shells containing razor chips as well as buckshot. In a nearby alley thirty feet away was a fake brown UPS delivery van with two backup soldiers in it, for Tony's getaway.

To connoisseurs of such events, it was to be a classic hit. As the targets alighted from their limousine to turn it over to Bruno's parking valet, Tony emerged and pumped one shell each into the lieutenant, the driver, and the bodyguard, and the other five into the main target, the Don, Philip Iacobucci, obliterating the entire left side of his body. The parking valet, who had gone around the limousine to drive it away, was unscathed, but got a clear view of the shotgun-wielding shooter. Five hours later, he picked Tony out of a photo lineup.

Normally, unofficially, off the record, and always vehemently denied, the U.S. Department of Justice and its minions do not give a rat's ass when mobsters kill mobsters; it just makes for that many less scumbag hoodlums federal agents have to chase. But in this particular case authorities took a keen personal interest in the hit.

Reason: The driver of the Don's limousine was an undercover FBI agent who had infiltrated the mob two years earlier.

Antonio Ginetta had shotgunned an FBI agent.

For that he was eventually tried, convicted, and sentenced to death.

•••

At the sight of Tony Ginetta standing in the doorway of his room, Cleve McCoy pursed his lips as if in thought. "Haven't I seen you somewhere before? Aren't you Al Pacino?"

"I'm taller," Ginetta said. He frowned. "Jesus, you really got old."

"Me? Take a look in a mirror, Ginetta. Your wrinkles have got wrinkles."

McCoy rose and the two lifers went out to the table in the common area and sat down.

"So," Ginetta said, "you, me, and that fruitcake Andy King are the only ones left, huh? So where is he?"

"Not here yet."

"This is bullshit, you know. I had it pretty good at Lewisburg. Everything lined up. Commissary money coming in regularly from the family. Nice private open cell in the hospital unit. Special mattress. Yard time with selected cons: no punks, no black, brown, or Aryan Brotherhood members, no crazies. We had a nice Super Scrabble Tournament going."

"What did the winner get, a parole?"

"Very funny. The winner got a year's subscription to *National Geographic*."

"Tell me something, Ginetta, when did you start playing Scrabble? When you first came onto the old Row, the only words you knew were obscenities, and you couldn't spell most of them."

Ginetta shrugged. "I started reading books. And I got a dictionary. Pretty soon I knew lots of new words. Even some new obscenities."

From somewhere a buzzer sounded and the door to the corridor opened. Captain Carl Meadows entered the room escorting Andrew King, the third and last formerly condemned prisoner being transferred to Wolfkill.

"Now my life is perfect," Tony Ginetta grumbled.

"Well, hi, Andy!" McCoy greeted the newcomer with obvious derision.

"The name is Andrew, not Andy," King said disdainfully. "I know you're a bit slow, McCoy, but surely you can remember that." Looking at Tony Ginetta, he rolled his eyes forlornly. To Captain Meadows he said, "I'd like to request a transfer to another institution, please."

"Where would you like to go?" Meadows asked in a placating tone.

"God, anywhere! Devil's Island, Alcatraz—"

"They're both closed," McCoy pointed out.

"Then reactivate my death sentence and execute me! Anything to keep me from having to live with these two retards!"

"Who you calling a retard, wife-killer?" Ginetta challenged, rising.

"Cool it, all of you!" Captain Meadows ordered. "Now listen to me! This is where you're *at,* and this is where you're going to stay *at!* Now you'd all better learn to get along!"

His authoritarian tone softened. "Look, you guys can have it pretty good here if you'll just shape up. Look around. Private oversized rooms with a daytime open-door schedule; nice common area out here with a color TV, little kitchenette alcove, refrigerator, cabinet full of games, open library privileges—*and,* a surprise I've been saving: Each of you gets two cans of light beer with supper. Hell, this is better than the retirement home my sister's in."

The three convicts fell silent, weighing the guard captain's words. Among themselves, they exchanged furtive glances, like kindergartners being gently scolded for rowdiness during recess. Meadows took their silence as acquiescence. He had been a corrections officer long enough to know that when a convict did not argue about an order it meant he probably thought it was fair.

"Now then," he said, "you're all scheduled for complete physicals tomorrow morning, after which the deputy warden will come in and have a little talk with you. If you know what's good for you, you'll be on your best behavior. Get out of line and your room doors will be locked down twenty-four-seven. At your ages, you don't want to do hard time like that."

After Captain Meadows left, Andrew King looked steadily at McCoy, then at Ginetta, sighed audibly in resignation, and finally went over to the room that had his name stenciled on the door and entered. But Tony Ginetta's words were soundlessly reverberating in his mind like a summer night full of fireflies.

Wife-killer.

•••

Andrew King was the last person in the world anyone would expect to end up on federal death row.

Since high school, Andrew had been a quiet, unobtrusive, painstakingly polite, meticulously studious young man. He never got a grade less than an A minus in any subject. Academic scholarships permitted him to pursue his sole abiding interest in life, sociology, and took him all the way to a doctorate degree and a faculty position at Stanford.

Andrew's long-range goal in life was to establish a new charity for the aid of homeless children, on the order of Boys Town and its expanded facility, Girls Town. Andrew envisioned calling his new foundation Children in Distress. CID.

Along the way, Andrew met and married Karen Landis, a librarian at one of the undergraduate schools where he taught summer classes. Karen, with only a Dewey Decimal System level of intelligence, was entranced by the vast scope of Andrew's wisdom, and he, with his limited experience with women, was captivated by Karen's body and lovemaking ability. Brainy and brilliant as he was, for some incomprehensible reason, Karen's expertise in bed never gave Andrew pause for thought. He simply allowed himself to enjoy it immensely.

It came out at Andrew's trial for murder, that Karen had remained faithful to him for no longer than three months after their wedding, and had been *un*faithful with at least nine men during their three-year marriage. Those who were aware of Karen's ongoing promiscuity thought it nothing short of incredible that it took Andrew so long to discover the truth. But discover it he did, entirely by chance, when he saw Karen's car parked in a motel parking lot as he was driving downtown to a Chamber of Commerce luncheon one day to promote his CID foundation. Skipping the luncheon, he parked his own car nearby and waited—and watched. Eventually, Karen and her lover of the moment emerged from one of the motel rooms, kissed, parted, and went their separate ways.

The next day, a brooding Andrew went to a gun shop, selected a pistol, filled out the requisite state forms, managed somehow to continue living with Karen for the ten-day waiting period, then returned to pick up his purchase. And a box of cartridges.

At this point, he had not decided exactly *who* he was going to shoot: Karen, the lover, or both. He just knew that he was going to shoot *somebody.* That, in his set, bookish mentality, was what he was *supposed* to do. But that same mind also cautioned him to research the price he would have to pay for exacting his revenge.

In the university law library, Andrew read case law, going back several decades, of husbands who killed wives, their lovers, or both, in acts of reprisal for infidelity. In the state of California, killing both guilty parties had generally resulted in life sentences in prison, or in some especially heinous cases, a death penalty. Killing only the wife's lover, however, and not the wife, in the heat of jealous passion, had put the betrayed husband in prison, usually in minimum-security status, for some twelve to fifteen years.

That, Andrew decided, would not be too bad. He would probably be allowed to teach. Have fairly decent housing and privileges. And obtain a parole while still at an age at which he could recoup his academic career and enjoy a good life, having, after all, simply done the honorable thing.

So he decided to kill only Karen's lover. And perhaps shoot Karen in the foot, just to make a statement.

He carried out his plan on a night when Karen was supposed to be going to a movie with coworker girlfriends. Andrew followed her, carefully. To his surprise, she did not drive to a motel, as he expected her to, but rather to a large parking lot behind the post office. There she parked and got into another car already on the lot. Andrew turned off his headlights nearby and waited for them to drive away. After fifteen minutes, when they were still there, he crept over to the car, pistol in hand, and peered inside. Even in the indistinct vapor lights of the parking lot, he was able to make out their forms in the rear seat, Karen's naked legs propped up, pantyhose hanging from one ankle, her lover's bare buttocks squirming lewdly—

In their lust for each other, they had not even locked the car door. Snatching it open, Andrew raised the pistol. Seeing him, Karen screamed and scrambled frantically. The boyfriend thrashed about in bewilderment. Andrew fired. The bullet missed the boyfriend by inches and bored into Karen's temple, killing her instantly.

In the interior light of the car, Andrew saw blood gushing from the hole in Karen's head, and froze. Panicky, the boyfriend twisted toward Andrew for the gun, and Andrew fired again, point-blank, into the boyfriend's heart.

Bottom line was that Andrew did not receive the lenient sentence he had planned on. Instead, he was tried in a federal court. His victims included a federal employee who worked for the U. S. Postal Service. Worse, the crime was committed on federal property: a post office employee parking lot.

Andrew was given a federal death sentence.

•••

On the morning after the three convicts arrived at Wolfkill, the orderly Zen arrived to escort McCoy to the infirmary wing for his intake physical exam. For the first time, McCoy got a good inside look at his new home.

The configuration of the Wolfkill facility was like a wheel, with the axis being the Administration and Control Center, and five wings, like spokes, extending out. To get from Corridor Red, where McCoy and the other two former death-row inmates were housed, Zen guided McCoy into the inner control circle and around toward Corridor White, where the central medical unit was located. Along the way, McCoy and his escort passed the entrances to the other corridors.

"These are the color-coded areas I told you about yesterday," Zen said. "Corridor Yellow is the psych ward; Corridor Green the dementia ward; Corridor Blue the elderly-but-mobile ward. The joint is like a Technicolor cartoon." He took McCoy through the double doors to Corridor White, into a shiny new waiting room. "Take a seat. The doc will be out for you in a minute. They'll call for me to come get you when you're finished."

"Thanks, Zen," McCoy said, bobbing his chin at the orderly.

I can't believe this place, McCoy thought after being left alone. All the way over from Corridor Red, he had seen only three khaki-clad corrections officers, half a dozen orderlies like Zen wearing whites, and a number of very old cons in blues shuffling around on walkers or with canes. Where the hell was the security? The alarms? The closed-circuit cameras? The deadlocks to isolate areas in case of a disturbance of any kind? Where were the riot guns, the Mace, the—

"Hello, Cleve," a husky female voice said.

McCoy looked around, startled. A still young-looking, sixtyish woman in a white physician's coat was smiling at him from an inner door. McCoy's mouth dropped open.

"Cora—?"

"*Doctor* Cora," she said easily. "Come on in."

He followed her through the door and along a short hall into an examining room.

"Cora," he said, astounded. The staff identification badge on her white physician's coat read: CORA SIMMS, M.D. "My God. When did you—? I mean—" He shook his head incredulously. "You're really a *doctor* now?"

"Sure am," she replied. "After twenty years as a nurse, I decided to move up the ladder. The Bureau of Prisons gave me a leave of absence to attend medical school, even gave me a federal grant to pay for it, then put me back on the staff after I got my degree. I've been a physician for eighteen years, Cleve."

Eighteen *years.* Was it possible? Of course it was, fool. You've been locked up for thirty-eight.

"I waited for you in San Francisco, Cleve," she said quietly. "I took my annual vacation from the nursing staff at Marion; we were going to meet at DiMaggio's on Fisherman's Wharf, remember? We were going to move to Honolulu and you were going to make a new start, leave your old way of life behind. I waited all weekend. Then on Monday morning I saw your picture in the newspaper."

McCoy slumped down in the nearest chair and stared into space. "Everything went wrong, Cora—"

"Sure, Cleve," she said without animosity. "What went wrong is that you decided to pull one last job. One last bank. One last grab for the easy money."

Nodding his head slowly, McCoy said, "I thought—you know, making a new start—I wanted to set us up nice—start right—"

"Start *right?* All we needed was each other, Cleve. A cheap little apartment would have been fine. If necessary, I could have waited tables, you could have pumped gas. As long as we had each other. Don't you remember how good it was, Cleve, just having each other?"

"I remember, Cora." He looked at her with beseeching eyes. "How could I not?"

Then they just stared at each other, silently.

•••

They had both been so young back then.

Cora was just thirty, having worked her way through community college and then nursing school by waiting tables. Her first job had been at the Cook County jail in Chicago, and later she took the federal civil service exam and was given a job at the U.S. Penitentiary at Marion, Illinois.

That was where she met inmate Cleveland McCoy. He was in the last two years of an eight-to-twelve-year sentence for the holdup of a federally insured bank. Actually, he and a partner had committed a series of such robberies up and down Illinois and Indiana, but they had cut a deal with the federal prosecutors to save the government the cost of a trial by pleading guilty to only one of the charges in exchange for a minimum sentence.

Both McCoy and his partner had been exemplary convicts for six years and with two more years of good conduct would both be released with minimum time served. During his incarceration, McCoy had worked his way from the infirmary laundry gang to the infirmary janitorial crew to the infirmary aide detail, and finally to an infirmary office clerk's assignment. It was on the latter two jobs that he and Nurse Cora Simms began to come into daily contact with each other.

At first, their association was merely cordial, well within the strict parameters separating inmates and staff. But after a while it became more relaxed, more friendly, but in a reserved way. As time went on, they began to look forward to seeing each other every day. Then, one Monday morning, after Cora had been off shift for two days, when McCoy was helping her inventory surgical instruments, she said to him very quietly, "I missed you this weekend."

"I missed you too," McCoy replied, just as quietly.

That was all there was to it. From then on, both knew that something emotionally intense was growing between them. And instinctively they knew that the utmost caution had to be adhered to when others, whether inmates or staff, were around to observe them. They managed to find stolen moments, of course; they had to—in broom closets, unoccupied examining rooms, closed nursing stations, even the operating room when no surgeries were scheduled. Over a two-year period, their circumstances generated many creative opportunities for a quick wink, a passing touch, a glance. It was difficult, even grueling at times, and their growing mutual passion, expressed in furtively exchanged daily notes, resulted in raw nerves more than once.

But they persevered. They survived the long wait until Cleve was finally discharged from custody. Cora took a week of her vacation and they met ninety miles south across the Kentucky line in the small city of Paducah. For five days and nights they left their little motel room at the edge of town only when hunger drove them to. The rest of the time, they satisfied other long pent-up hungers.

Unable to risk Cleve being seen near her apartment close to the prison, Cora helped him find a room in an inexpensive residential hotel in the college town of Carbondale, only a twenty-minute drive away. Together they spent their evenings eating in small cafés and strolling around the campus of Southern Illinois University, going to movies where they sat shoulder to shoulder holding hands, sometimes just sitting on a bench in the park talking about their future.

Their main plan was for Cora to arrange a leave of absence, ostensibly to be with a sister in San Francisco who was in the last stages of a difficult pregnancy. Cleve was to take a bus north to Chicago where he and his former partner, who had also been released, had a substantial amount of money in a joint bank account under assumed names. Then Cora and Cleve would meet in San Francisco and book passage on a cruise ship for Honolulu. Perhaps, they hoped, Cora would find a nursing position, and Cleve might even become a hospital orderly. They would get along just fine.

Except for one thing. Cleve had no money in Chicago. He and his partner had already planned to get together for one last job. As it turned out, that was the job on which they took along a third partner, a kid, who initiated a shootout that got himself, a bank guard, and McCoy's original partner all killed. And subsequently put Cleve McCoy on federal death row.

Cora read about it that Monday morning, so long ago, in the *San Francisco Herald.* With tears streaming down her cheeks, involuntarily she thought: Once a thief…

Dismally, she returned to her job at Marion Prison.

•••

In the examining room at Wolfkill, they locked eyes, no longer young, no longer passionate.

"You never married?" McCoy asked.

"No, Cleve. I never found a man I could trust."

Her words were like an ice pick to his heart. He ran his tongue over lips that had suddenly gone dry. "Did you ever think about visiting me, letting me explain?"

"All the time," she admitted, a slight catch in her voice. "But how would it have looked, Cleve? A Bureau of Prisons staff nurse applying for permission to visit a condemned killer on federal death row? I had a life to somehow put back together. You were going to be executed. I was going to be alone."

"But after the death penalty was abolished—"

"That made no difference. Life without parole. You were still dead, just in a different way." Cora sighed a brief, hollow sigh and shook her head, briefly but emphatically. "What's the use, Cleve? Talking about it won't do either one of us any good." She pointed to an examination table next to an electrocardiograph machine. "Strip to your underwear and lie down there."

She gave him a full-body exam, head to toe, testicles to prostate, EKG to chest X-ray, and drew blood and took a urine sample for a chemical work-up. For McCoy it was a mortifying experience, but none of it appeared to bother Cora in the least. She was all professional.

"I'll send for you when the test results come back from the lab," she told him when she was finished. "Then I can evaluate your overall physical condition and decide whether you need treatment for anything."

She summoned Zen, the orderly, to escort McCoy back to his quarters.

"So, what did you think of the doc?" Zen asked on the way.

"Seems okay," McCoy replied neutrally.

"Yeah, she's aces," said Zen. "Everybody likes her. She didn't want to come here, but the Bureau's medical director insisted 'cause she was the only one on the staff with geriatric training. I think we were lucky to get her. She's really something with the senile and dementia patients. Great communication skills."

McCoy was only half listening to Zen. His own thoughts were divided. On one side was his continuing surprise at having encountered Cora. On the other was an ongoing amazement at the absence of serious security everywhere he looked. Wolfkill, he was beginning to conclude, was almost like an honor facility.

A place someone could almost walk away from.

•••

In the days following their arrival, McCoy, Tony Ginetta, and Andrew King fell into a wary but workable daily routine. McCoy and Ginetta refrained from saying anything to antagonize Andy King, and he in turn abstained from his former pastime of making snide references to their respective intelligence quotients. They also established a schedule of shower times in the small lavatory alcove of their common area, decided on personal shelves in the refrigerator and cabinet for their commissary purchases. Since they were not allowed to work for token pay at prison jobs, McCoy and King were allotted thirty dollars a month commissary credit, courtesy of the Bureau of Prisons; Ginetta enjoyed money regularly sent to him from outside.

They selected alternate days for control of the television channels, which were limited to network and educational channels only.

For two hours each day, weather permitting, they were allowed to go outside to an open area called Central Park where they could pitch horseshoes, shoot hoops, walk around a perimeter track, or just sit and watch the grass grow. No other inmate patients were allowed out during their period, a fact they learned the first time Zen escorted them to the door leading outside. The door was propped open and another orderly was escorting a line of Blues, elderly-but-mobile, in from their daily period in Central Park. All but a few of them used canes or walkers. Their line moved slowly. Only after they were all inside did the three Reds—as McCoy, Ginetta, and King were now known—go outside for their time.

McCoy saw at once that the outside was not actually *out;* rather it was a courtyard, not fenced but surrounded on three sides to form a square with the main cellhouse by smaller, attached utility buildings that served the institution. Each was painted green to complement the courtyard's grass and trees.

"What's in those buildings?" McCoy asked Zen the first time they went out.

"That one," Zen began pointing them out, "houses the heating and air conditioning equipment; that one there is the prison administration offices; and the one over here is for hospital and medical supplies." In each building was a single door without a knob or handle of any kind, lettered in red: NO ENTRY.

"No entry," McCoy commented with a grunt. "No windows either, I see."

"All the windows are on the other side, facing the staff parking lot and loading docks for incoming deliveries," Zen told him. "Those door are just fire exits for people working in there; they only open from inside."

Interesting, Cleveland McCoy thought. Very interesting.

• • •

Several days after McCoy's physical exam, Dr. Cora Simms had him brought back to her office for a medical review.

"Well, Cleve, you seem to be in pretty good condition for your age," she said, looking through several lab reports on her desk. Sitting across from her, McCoy shrugged.

"Clean living," he said wryly. Cora could not suppress a slight smile.

"I see you haven't lost your sense of humor," she observed.

"In my situation, it's either laugh or cry," he said, "and I'm not good at crying."

"That's good," she told him. "A positive attitude is essential for good health as we grow older. Now then, your cholesterol is a bit high so I'm going to put you on a statin medication to bring it down. Liver function looks good—"

"I try to stay away from alcohol," he interjected.

Another slight smile from Cora. "—heart EKG was good, blood pressure seems to be within normal range. Your chest X-ray did show some scar tissue on your left lung—"

"I had pneumonia at Leavenworth, the year of the big blizzard. There was no heat on the tier for four days. Half the men on the Row got sick."

"Well, this isn't serious. You don't smoke, do you?"

"Never did, Cora. Remember?"

She put down the lab reports and fixed her eyes on him. "Cleve, have you ever told anyone about our relationship? Anyone here or anywhere else, at any time?"

"No. Never."

"You're sure?"

McCoy's expression tightened, almost imperceptibly. "I said never," he repeated.

"All right." Cora looked relieved. "I think it would be best if you didn't address me as Cora; someone might overhear you." Rising from behind her desk, she paced the office for several steps. "Look, I've still got feelings for you, Cleve. I guess I always will have."

"Then maybe you should start addressing me as Inmate McCoy." There was a slight edge to his voice, which he immediately tempered. "And for the record, I still have feelings for you, too."

He leaned forward, forearms on his knees. "I haven't had a decent night's sleep since we first saw each other the other day."

"Neither have I." She put closed hands to her temples. "God, why did this have to happen again?"

"I don't think it's happening again. I think it never ended."

"And there's nothing we can do about it," she said. "We're both here, and that's that."

"Can you transfer to another joint?" McCoy asked.

"No chance. I was *put* here because I was the best qualified geriatric physician in the Bureau."

"All right then, I'll get transferred."

"How? You can't get out of Wolfkill. This facility was created for inmates like you."

"I can arrange to be moved."

"How?" Cora asked again.

"I can get sent to the new death row at Terre Haute. I can kill someone."

Cora was horrified. "Cleve, that's insane! Who would you kill? Someone on staff?"

"No. One of my cellmates. Ginetta or King." He frowned slightly at the thought. "Maybe both of them." The thought of that caused him to smile dissolutely.

"I'm not discussing this any further," Cora said adamantly.

She sent for Zen and had McCoy escorted from her office.

•••

The next day when the three Reds were let out to Central Park for their yard time, McCoy joined Ginetta as the former mobster took a solitary stroll around the perimeter.

"What the hell do you want?" Ginetta asked gruffly. He preferred to walk alone.

"I thought maybe you'd like company for a change."

"Think again." He bobbed his chin at Andy King, who was sitting under a tree eating an apple. "You lonesome, go sit with the geek over there."

"He's not my type," McCoy said. "See, he's not really a criminal. He's in here by accident. You and me, we're criminals. So, one criminal to another, I've got a proposition for you."

Ginetta paused and glared at him. "If it's got anything to do with sex," he warned, "I'll break all your fingers."

"Nothing like that," McCoy assured him. "I was thinking more along the lines of a little trip. Outside."

Ginetta grinned knowingly. "You got something going with that orderly Zeniak, haven't you? I seen you two together, always talking."

"Zeniak is a small part of the plan. He'll have one very small job to do. This is my plan, all the way. But I need a money man."

"Why don't you find a banker?" Ginetta started to walk again, but McCoy stepped around in front of him.

"Look, Ginetta, I know your status on the outside. You're like a martyr in the Outfit. You took a fall and faced execution when you could have ratted out the whole organization in a witness-protection deal. As it turned out, you didn't get executed. Instead, you got slow death in a cell. You've got a wife outside who's grown old without you. Two daughters you never saw graduate from college. Grandchildren you've only seen pictures of—" McCoy paused and took a deep, urgent breath. "Look, man, I'm offering you a way out of here with no violence, nobody gets hurt, all nice and clean. I'm offering you a home in Sicily where your wife can bring those grandchildren for you to play with. This is a *solid* plan, Ginetta. All I need is the money to finance it. Money I know you can arrange to get."

Antonio "Tony" Ginetta stared thoughtfully at McCoy for what to the latter seemed an unusually long time. Finally he nodded his head, curtly. "I'll listen to your plan tonight while dickhead over there," he bobbed his chin at Andrew King, "is watching his game shows."

•••

After breakfast the following morning, when Zen came to remove the steam cart on which he had brought their meal, McCoy whispered to him, "Come get me after you take the cart back. It's important."

Zen returned half an hour later. "McCoy, you're wanted in Administration. Some kind of paperwork."

Walking with Zen down Corridor Red toward the Control Center, McCoy asked, "How much time you got left to do, Zen?"

"Depends." Zen shrugged. "I'm only in here by accident. See, before this, I took two easy falls in the Illinois state system for burglarizing jewelry stores and fur storage lockers. Then I decided to move up to the big time and do warehouses; you know, electronics, designer leather goods, stuff with a better markup for me. But my last one was a cigarette distribution center. I made off with a delivery truck full of a hundred grand worth of smokes, all the main brands. Problem was, they didn't have the federal tax stamp on them yet. That was felony number one. Then I drove the truck across the state line from Illinois to Iowa. Felony number two. The ATF agents busted me. The federal judge looked at my two state priors and hit me with a habitual-criminal sentence—"

"How much time, Zen?" McCoy repeated his question.

"Okay, they give me forty. That's four hundred eighty months. Since I come in before the new federal prison guidelines became law, I can go for parole after two-thirds: three hundred and twenty months. Good time earned is ten days a month, and I've been very, very good, so that's another hundred and six months off. That leaves me with a nut of thirteen years. I been in eight, so I can go for parole in another five. My record's clean, I've learned a trade being a hospital orderly, and my crime involved no violence, no weapons, only stupidity. I should make parole with no sweat. Five years." Zen tilted his head an inch. "Why do you want to know, McCoy?"

"How much do you get for orderly pay?"

"Buck fifty a day. Forty-five a month. Half goes into a mandatory savings account, half into a commissary account."

"How would you like another two hundred a month deposited to your commissary account? By an attorney who will say it is an inheritance from a dead relative. And, how would you like to have fifty thousand waiting for you at that attorney's office when you make parole?"

Zen didn't even think it over before shaking his head. "I don't think so, McCoy. You're too high profile for me. Anything you've got on your mind is going to be too risky for me. Thanks for the invite, but I think I'll just sweat out the five years and then make sure I avoid cigarette warehouses in the future. I'll go back to jewelry and furs."

"This is a sweet deal," McCoy elaborated. "Clean, quick, easy. Just me and one other person involved."

"Who?"

McCoy paused just a beat, deciding whether to lie. "Ginetta," he said, playing it straight.

Zen rolled his eyes. "Oh, brother." He began shaking his head again.

"Look, Ginetta brings the money and serious outside support. Zen, just let me run it down for you. Just hear me out on this."

The orderly pursed his lips, still shaking his head at the mention of Tony Ginetta's name, but against his better judgment finally said, "Okay, run it down."

•••

McCoy sent in a sick-call request. In the privacy of Cora's office, keeping his voice to a low, confidential tone, he told her of his escape plan. She listened to him with a sense of bewilderment tempered by involuntary interest.

"It's a solid plan, Cora," he emphasized. "You *know* it is, I can tell by your expression." Reaching across the desk, he took her hands in his. "This is my chance to make up for the wreck I made of our lives the first time around. This is *our* chance to grab whatever years we've got left, to make up for the past years that I stupidly destroyed. Ginetta's family on the outside will supply us with half a million dollars in clean money, and set up new identities and furnish passports—"

"Yes, but we would be fugitives, Cleve. Not like it was before. You had been released then, not escaped. We'd be on the run—"

"No, we wouldn't," McCoy argued. "We could live in Dubai or in the Maldives or half a dozen other countries that have no extradition treaty with the U.S. Even if the FBI found out where we were, there's nothing they could do about it."

Cora paced the office as she had done during a previous visit from McCoy, only this time she was wringing her hands as indecision seared her mind.

"Cleve, I *want* to do it, I want to see you free, I want us to be together more than anything in this world, but I'm *afraid*—"

"Of what? Tell me what you're afraid will go wrong."

"I don't *know*, Cleve. It just somehow sounds too easy—"

"Because it *is* easy. Look, Wolfkill was never meant to be escape-proof. Nobody ever thought anyone would *try* to escape. Old cons are sent here to die. There are only two security counts: morning and night. We'll be on a private plane a thousand miles away before they even know we're gone." McCoy rose and went over to her, took her by the shoulders. "Cora, please, I'm begging you. Give me this chance to make up to you what I took away years ago."

Cora Simms went limp in the arms of the man she had loved most of her adult life.

•••

"We're off and running, partner," McCoy told Ginetta during yard time the next day. "Zen is in, Cora is in. Everything is set. You?"

"I had an attorney visit this morning. He's seeing to all the arrangements on the outside."

"Run it down for me."

"Okay. On the day we decide to go, a white van will park in the delivery area of the prison staff parking lot. It will have 'Wolfkill Pharmaceuticals' painted on the sides. The driver will leave the side door unlocked while he carries a basket of medical supplies inside at the receiving dock for the infirmary. In the van will be a set of clothes for each of us. We'll be dressed and lying in the back when the driver returns. He'll drive us away. Thirty minutes later we'll be at a small regional airport in a town called Devil's Lake, where a private Lear jet will pick us up. Ninety minutes after that it will land at DuPage Field outside Chicago. There'll be a car there with a suitcase packed with half a million in clean currency. The driver will take you to an address where you'll meet a guy who will have all the equipment he needs to fix you and the doctor up with new identity cards and passports. He will have been paid in advance. All he'll need from you is the doctor's driver's license so's he can copy her photo. After that, you'll be free and clear. How's it sound?"

"Perfect. Dead on." McCoy paused a beat, then asked, "What about you, Tony?" It was the first time he had ever addressed Ginetta by his given name. "What will you do? Go to Sicily?"

"Me, Cleve?" Ginetta used McCoy's first name in return. "No, not Sicily. That's the first place they'll look for me. No, I'll retire on a nice estate somewhere between Firenzi and Venezia. That's Florence and Venice to you, Irishman. Some quiet little town where everyone from the mayor to the street sweeper is paid a monthly tribute to see nothing, hear nothing, say nothing, know nothing about nothing."

McCoy grinned. "I guess we'll both be sitting pretty, then."

"I guess," Ginetta grinned back.

They looked across the yard at Andrew King, again sitting under a tree, eating an apple, reading a book.

"Dumb asshole," Ginetta said, but oddly without rancor.

"Stupid jerk," McCoy agreed.

The two men started walking together, talking about Andrew.

"They'll probably think he had something to do with our escape," McCoy said.

"Yeah. Or that he at least knew something about it."

"They'll probably move him from here to some supermax solitary lockdown with those terrorist freaks—"

"Yeah, and that Unabomber nut—"

"And those spic drug lords—"

"He'll go crazy locked up with fruitcakes like that," Ginetta concluded.

"Yeah," McCoy agreed. "Without us, he'll be lost."

The two men looked at each other for a moment, then with no further conversation they turned and walked toward Andrew King.

•••

On the day of the break, when Zen brought their breakfast, he also brought three sets of blues, the color worn by the elderly-but-mobile. McCoy handed a set to Andy King.

"I'm not too sure about all this," King said hesitantly.

"Just take them and shut up," Ginetta said. "Or maybe you'd rather rot in some supermax joint?"

"No, I don't want to do that—"

"Just be grateful we're taking you with us," McCoy said, jabbing Andy's chest with a stiff finger.

When Zen returned later for the breakfast trays, he said, "Be ready to go in half an hour when I let the Blues into the yard. Just mingle with them. Some of them old cons might tumble to what's going on, but none of them will interfere." He bobbed his chin at the trio. "Luck, brothers." As he turned to leave, he handed McCoy Cora's driver's license.

Thirty minutes later, dressed in blues, the three men walked unobserved down Corridor Red to the Central Control Area and fell in with three dozen Blues moving in a line out the yard door. Several of the Blues glanced knowingly at them, but kept on shuffling along as usual. Once outside, McCoy and the others separated and mixed in with the group as they fanned out in different directions. At five minutes before nine, at a nod from McCoy, the other two gravitated toward the fire door of the medical supplies room. McCoy could see that it was open a quarter of an inch, adhesive tape put on the inside latch by Cora minutes earlier.

As unobtrusively as possible, McCoy pulled the door open with his fingertips and the three of them darted inside. Stripping the adhesive tape off, McCoy let the door close and turned on a security switch above the door that Cora had turned off. He led the other two on a path that Cora had helped him memorize, down an aisle and through several stacks of shelved medical supplies to a window that looked out on the staff and delivery vehicles parking lot.

"There it is," Ginetta said, grinning as he looked out at a white delivery van with WOLFKILL PHARMACEUTICALS lettered on its side.

"I'm still not so sure I should be in on this—" Andrew King muttered. Ginetta grabbed him by one arm.

"Listen, you dumb shit, I went to a lot of trouble to change this from a two-man break to a three-man break. My people had to collect an extra half-million in clean money to get you started on the outside!"

"Least you could do is show some gratitude!" McCoy scolded.

Unlocking and opening the window, Ginetta slipped out first and flattened himself against the outside wall. McCoy coaxed Andy through next and Ginetta grabbed him and held him still. Then McCoy dropped out and pulled the window down behind him. Cora would relock it a few minutes later.

Crouching down, the three convicts scurried between parked cars until they reached the van. Through the unlocked passenger door, they crawled quickly onto the cargo deck. There they found three boxes of new civilian clothes, each in their respective sizes and tagged with their names. Bent over, stripping off their blues, they began to dress.

"Why'd they give me a plaid shirt?" Andrew complained. "I hate plaid."

Ginetta turned angry red. "I swear to God, Cleve, I'm gonna kill this asshole—"

"Relax, both of you!" McCoy ordered. "Just get dressed!"

The three of them were completely dressed, lying in a row on the cargo deck, when the van driver returned and without a word drove away from Wolfkill.

•••

As planned, the private Lear jet touched down at DuPage Field ninety minutes later.

Two black Lincoln Town Cars with tinted windows pulled onto the tarmac as its engines shut down. Ginetta exited the plane and was warmly embraced by two sharply dressed younger men. When McCoy and Andrew stepped out, one of the two young men spoke quietly to Ginetta and he turned back to McCoy and Andrew and nodded toward one of the Lincolns.

"Two bags of clean money on the backseat. Don't talk during the trip and don't speak to the driver. He will take you to a small hotel near the Loop where you've already been preregistered in a suite. A guy will be waiting there to fix you up with new ID and passports. He's already been paid." Pausing, the old hit man finally shrugged and said. "That's it. Good luck."

He shook hands with McCoy and punched Andrew lightly on the arm. "You pain in the ass," he said. "Take care of yourself."

•••

In the car on the way to downtown Chicago, McCoy opened each of two suitcases and ran his hands through the banded bundles of currency packed neatly inside. Closing them again, he passed one to Andrew. Then they sat silently, each looking out the windows at the strange new free world they had just reentered after so many years. Both of them were trembling slightly, and their mouths were suddenly dry when they tried to swallow. Their breathing was heavier than normal, but not noticeable. Now and then they glanced at each other, knowing they were sharing a common thought. They were *out.*

At the end of the drive, things seemed to happen very quickly. They were met at the entrance to the small City Park Hotel and escorted to a suite where they found a small scholarly-looking man, fortyish, wearing very thick glasses. He had cleared off a desk and set up several pieces of portable photographic and reproduction equipment. He sat first McCoy, then Andrew, on a straight-back chair and photographed them. Then he said, "A picture of the woman?"

"Oh, sure." McCoy, who had forgotten he had it, gave him Cora's driver's license and he copied her photograph from it. He then jotted down their physical characteristics and dates of birth, and copied Cora's from her license.

"Make yourselves comfortable, gentlemen," he said then. "This will take a little while."

It took just over an hour, during which McCoy and Andrew sat in separate chairs and watched television without speaking. Presently they were called over to the desk and handed what looked to be somewhat worn but entirely legitimate items of identification. The man who had created them ticked them off one by one.

"Social Security cards, Illinois driver's licenses, Blue Cross medical insurance cards, Chicago public library cards, Visa and American Express credit cards—which you must not try to use—U. S. Navy Reserve identification cards, and lastly, U. S. passports. Everything is in your new names, which have been cleared through the National Crime Information Center as clean.

"Please memorize everything. Your passports show that over the past fifteen years you have traveled to Canada, Mexico, Jamaica, Tahiti, and New Zealand. Memorize that also. And here," he smiled and handed each one of them a well-worn leather wallet, "is a little extra gift I provide with my service."

He shook hands with both of them, wished them good luck in their new lives, and left the suite with all of his equipment packed in a small trunk with wheels.

"What do we do now?" Andrew asked.

"Start planning where each of us wants to go and how we're going to get there," McCoy said.

"What about lunch?" Andrew said. "I'm hungry."

McCoy stared at him for a moment, feeling his anger rise. But then he realized that he too was beginning to get hungry. Remembering that he had noticed a restaurant as they passed through the lobby, he looked around and found a room-service menu.

"Here, pick out what you want and we'll have some food sent up."

While they waited for their room-service order, they talked about their various destination options. "I want to go someplace where everyone speaks English and it's warm all the time," Andrew stipulated.

"Yeah, sure, me too," McCoy said. They conversed in quiet voices, accustomed as they were to avoiding being overheard by others. McCoy took off his jacket and shoes, but Andrew remained fully dressed. Both examined their new ID cards and passports.

"I don't like this new name he gave me," Andrew complained. "Thomas Edward Ratliffe. What kind of name is Ratliffe anyway?"

"A safe name, Andrew. Don't start bitching about the name, okay?"

"Well, what's yours?"

"Malcolm. John James Malcolm."

"That's better than Ratliffe," Andrew grumbled.

Their food arrived and McCoy had the waiter set it out on the desk the counterfeiter had used for his equipment. He paid for the food with a twenty-dollar bill from his suitcase. Andrew insisted on giving him a ten-dollar bill from his own suitcase. "It's only fair," he said.

They ate. McCoy had to control his temper again when Andrew complained that his turkey sandwich had mayonnaise on it. "I like mustard on turkey."

"I'll try to remember that, Andrew." The sooner I get away from this nut, the better, he thought.

After they ate, McCoy looked around and found the telephone directory. "Look at the size of this damned thing, will you? It must weigh five pounds."

He called several airlines and inquired about flights to various cities. Andrew wrote down the information as McCoy repeated it. After an hour of that, they had a fairly long list of destinations to discuss. McCoy closely watched the time on the digital clock next to the bed. He had a prearranged time to call Cora on her cell phone to make sure everything was all right with her back at Wolfkill. When it was almost that time, he said, "Andrew, I have to call Cora. I'm going to do it from a pay phone down in the lobby. If anything goes wrong, I don't want her cell phone records to trace back to this room." He took several hundred dollars from his suitcase. "I'll be back up in a few minutes."

Taking the elevator down, McCoy felt a little nauseated. It was like being in a cell that was dropping through space. At the front desk he bought a roll of quarters and got directions to a bank of public telephone booths nearby. Sweating, he had to ask an operator for assistance in placing the call; he did not know about dialing "1" for long distance, or area codes. Cora, who was purposely at her desk with the door closed, answered on the first ring.

"Dr. Simms," she said.

"It's me."

"Are you all right?"

"Yeah. You?"

"Fine."

"What's going on there?"

"Nothing."

"Nothing? Nothing at all?"

"No. Really. Nothing at all." She lowered her voice. "Zen says they probably won't even miss you for another two hours, when it's your yard time."

"I can't believe this," McCoy said, astonished.

"Is there any problem at your end?"

"Just Andrew King. I got stuck with him and he's a pain in the ass. But I'll get rid of him in a day or so. I'm helping him pick out where he wants to go and then I'm going to put him on a plane. You still okay with our plan?"

"Yes. I'll be emotionally upset about the escape and take some sick time off. Then I'll meet you in San Francisco just like we planned before."

"Right. By then I'll have tickets for us to Dubai. We'll be all set. By the way, your new name is Elaine Ruth Nelson."

"Sounds good to me."

"Okay. I'll see you in a week. I love you, Cora."

"I love you too, Cleve. Be careful."

"Always."

"Bye—"

"So long."

For some reason, a heavy sadness came over him when he heard her cell phone go off. But he managed to overcome it. Soon, he thought. Very soon. It would be like all those bad years in-between had never happened. Soon.

Walking back toward the elevators, he noticed several people standing around a large television set in the lobby. He was about to walk past them when he suddenly stopped, frozen by a picture of Tony Ginetta filling the screen. His mouth fell open and he moved closer to hear the audio of the broadcast.

"…tentatively identified as Antonio Ginetta, a rising member of the Mafia more than four decades ago. He had been shot once in the back of the head with a small-caliber pistol in typical execution style. The body was found by a passing motorist in a ditch on the side of Kautz Road near DuPage Airport, about forty miles north of Chicago—"

McCoy stood mesmerized as the newscast continued.

"…curious aspect of the case is that Ginetta is supposed to be in federal custody. A spokesman for the Bureau of Prisons in Washington, D.C., confirmed unequivocally that Ginetta was presently confined in the recently opened Wolfkill Prison for geriatric inmates. However, a telephone call from this station directly to that facility to confirm that Ginetta was indeed there was met with a response of 'no comment.' Meanwhile, local and federal law enforcement agencies are debating on exactly who has jurisdiction over the body—"

A sense of dread came over McCoy like a shroud. As he hurried toward the elevators, his mind felt like a merry-go-round out of control. Ginetta's own family, obviously, had killed him. But why? All these years he had remained silent, true to his *Omertà* code. Why kill him now, after arranging his escape from prison? Was it because of his age? Were they afraid that his mind might be getting weak, that senility or Alzheimer's might cause him inadvertently to speak of things about which he had kept silent for so long? Could that even be the reason they arranged the escape?

In the elevator, McCoy shook his head violently to banish the whirling questions from his thoughts. What did it matter *why?* Those people, those *mafioso*, had always been crazy, had always had a habit of killing their own. Right now, what he had to worry about was getting himself and Andrew the hell away. The men who met them at the airport that morning knew where they were.

Hurrying into the suite, McCoy shouted, "Andy! Andy, we've got to blow this joint like *fast,* man! Andy!" He looked around. "Andy?"

Andrew King was not there. McCoy saw that the television set was on, tuned to the same newscast he himself had been watching in the lobby. Andy must have been watching it, too—

McCoy felt sweat breaking out on his upper lip and the back of his neck. In one of his coat pockets he found a handkerchief and blotted his lip. Then it hit him.

"Oh, no—" he said aloud to himself.

Rushing into the bedroom, he dropped to his knees and looked under the bed.

Nothing.

Both suitcases of money were gone.

• • •

Two hours later, on a bench in Grant Park, to which he had taken a taxi, McCoy sat staring at nothing, for how long he did not know. He was in a daze, a stupor, a state of inertness much like he had seen men in on the day before their executions, when the hacks came to move them to the death-watch cell. It was a languorous condition, a sense of impending doom about which one was impotent to do anything at all.

When daylight began to fade, McCoy took several deep breaths and began to consider his options. He decided definitely *not* to call Cora. It was too risky. All hell would be breaking loose at Wolfkill by now. He counted the money he had grabbed before going down to the lobby and found that he had all of four hundred and ten dollars—plus what remained of the roll of quarters he had bought, about seven dollars, he guessed. Walking over to Michigan Avenue, he flagged an idle taxi.

"YMCA, please," he told the driver.

"Which one?"

"What? Oh, the hotel. Whichever one is closest."

"That'd be the Lawson, Chicago Avenue just off Dearborn."

When he got there, he registered for two nights, using his new ID and paying in cash.

Once in the room, he lay down on the bed, fully dressed, to rest and think.

Soon he had curled up in a fetal position and fallen into a deep, harboring sleep that lasted for fourteen hours.

•••

The noise of the city woke him at eight the next morning. He washed up at a sink in the corner, and took a leak in it when he was finished. Straightening his clothes as best he could, he went outside onto busy Chicago Avenue and started walking. Along the way, he caught an image of himself in a store window. What he saw was an old man with a stubble of white beard dressed in wrinkled clothes. I look like I'm homeless, he thought, and unable to help himself, he chuckled; it was true, he *was* homeless.

At the corner, in a newspaper vending machine, he saw a two-column headline on the front page of the *Chicago Tribune* which read: ESCAPEES SOUGHT. Alongside it was a two-column photo of Tony Ginetta, beneath which were two smaller photos, one of himself, one of Andrew King.

Great.

Around the corner on Dearborn, he found a barber shop. "Shave and a haircut," he told the barber. "And I want the hair cut real short, crew-cut style."

"You mean a buzz cut?"

"Yeah, I guess that's what it's called." He had to be careful, he reminded himself. Even his speech was outdated.

Back outside, he felt he had to know what was going on around the City Park Hotel, whether he and Andy had been traced there by local cops or the FBI. But he didn't even know where the place was. He could find the address in the telephone directory, but he wouldn't know how to get there. Thinking back, he remembered that just before they had been dropped off at the hotel, they had passed a large hospital: the Alexian Brothers Hospital. Hailing a cab, he asked to be taken there. On the way the cab actually passed the hotel before it got to the hospital. Everything looked normal to McCoy as they passed it.

Exiting the taxi at the hospital entrance, he went in, waited until the taxi left, and came back out. At a nearby drugstore he saw a window display of sunglasses and went in and bought a pair. Checking himself in a mirror, he decided that with the buzz cut and sunglasses, he looked different enough from the newspaper mug shot to feel reasonably safe.

He walked back down to the City Park Hotel, on the opposite side of the street, observing no unusual activity of any kind. Okay, so the law apparently didn't as yet have a fix on the hotel. That left the mob. Recalling the previous day, how they were met and escorted directly through the lobby and up to the suite; how the ID counterfeiter was there and already set up; hell, he thought, maybe the mob *owned* the damned place. Maybe there were hit men already inside, just waiting for him or Andrew to possibly come back. Or maybe the mob already *had* Andy!

As he kept walking, McCoy began to form a plan. If he could still get to San Francisco and hide out for a week, Cora, not having heard anything further from him, would assume he was okay, and would meet him as planned. Escaping to Dubai was out of the question now. But Cora had told him she had fourteen thousand in her savings account and would bring it with her. That was enough to get them to Honolulu and settled into a new life, as they had originally planned so long ago—

But first he had to get to San Francisco, dig in someplace, mix with the tourists down on Fisherman's Wharf, as had been his plan if that last bank job had gone right—

But hell, he didn't have enough money to even *get* to San Francisco, much less hide out for a week.

Walking, still planning, he turned up Lincoln Avenue, a busy diagonal street. One thing he knew he *had* to do: get rid of all the fake ID he had for Cora, just in case he got busted before he could do anything else. Going back to the drugstore, he purchased a large, padded manila envelope and a ballpoint pen. Addressing it to her back at Wolfkill, he enclosed her driver's license with the other ID, and marked it personal in large block letters. Sealing it up, he bought a booklet of twelve first-class postage stamps. Back outside, he put all of the stamps on the envelope and posted it in a corner mail drop.

Sighing heavily after that, knowing that at least he had protected Cora, at least he had done *that* right, he leaned against a building, trying to figure something out, some plan, some way to act, to do something—

That was when he looked down the block and saw the outdoor sign of a small neighborhood bank. With one hand in a coat pocket, he felt what remained of the roll of quarters he had acquired for the pay phone. Still rolled, they felt like the fat barrel of a large pistol…

Could it possibly work? he asked himself. With that handkerchief in his other pocket wrapped around it? Just one teller, in and out, a few thousand from her drawer—

Okay, he decided quickly. That was it. That was the answer. His way out.

One last job.

He started walking.

Entering the small bank, he walked to the teller nearest the door. She was young, pretty, with a practiced smile. "Good morning, sir."

"Good morning," McCoy said pleasantly. He held the handkerchief-covered partial roll of quarters just high enough for her to see it. "Don't be scared," he said quietly. "I won't shoot. You're not going to get hurt. Just give me all the bills in your drawer."

She did as she was told. "Do you want the bills under the tray too?" she asked.

"What?"

"The larger bills. They're under the top tray in the drawer."

"Yeah," McCoy said, swallowing dryly. "Yeah, those too."

She handed over several banded bundles of fifties and hundreds.

"Thank you, miss," he said as he stuffed the money inside his partially unbuttoned shirt. "Please let me get out the front door before you sound the alarm."

"I will, sir." Her smile returned. "You know something?"

"What?"

"You look a lot like my grandfather."

McCoy stared at her, incongruously wondering what it felt like to have a granddaughter. Then he remembered where he was and what he was doing.

Turning, he walked quickly out of the bank. As he was leaving, the pretty young woman took her foot off the silent alarm button and moved it over to the interior alarm. As soon as McCoy stepped onto the sidewalk, the alarm started shrieking. People on the street stopped to listen. McCoy hurried on. Ahead of him he saw a police patrol car coming toward him, emergency lights on but no siren. After it passed, he crossed the street. Glancing back, he saw the patrol car make a U-turn and come back his way. He started walking faster. The patrol car stopped at the bank and the pretty young teller ran out to meet the officers as they exited the car.

Frantically looking around, she saw McCoy and pointed at him. The two officers, weapons drawn, started running after him. McCoy rushed under the marquee of an old movie theater, darted into an alley next to it, and started running. The policemen, younger, faster, reached the mouth of the alley.

"Police, halt!" one of them yelled. "Halt or I'll shoot!" He fired one warning shot, at a garbage can just ahead of the fleeing man.

McCoy slowed, breathing heavily, and turned halfway back, putting one hand in his coat pocket with the quarters, why he did not know. Then he began running again.

The bank teller had told the officers that the holdup man had a gun. Knowing that, the officer who had fired at the garbage can knelt, steadied his pistol, aimed, and fired a second shot, hitting Cleve McCoy exactly at the top of his spine.

As the side of his face hit the alley floor, he had time for only one instant thought before he died.

Cora…Cora—

Among the onlookers who gathered under the marquee of the old Biograph Theater, one man nudged a neighbor with his elbow.

"That there guy got it exactly where John Dillinger got it," he said.

•••

At Wolfkill the next morning, Zen stopped in at the medical center to drop off some papers to Cora.

"New arrivals," he said. "Two from Leavenworth, one from Marion."

"Thanks, Zen," Cora said.

Zen stood there for a long moment, embarrassed. "I feel like crying," he said. "Only I can't. It's been so long, I don't remember how. I just know I feel like it."

Cora patted him on the arm. "It's all right, Zen. I'll cry more than enough for both of us."

•••

Andrew King was never caught.

But six months later, a man named T. E. Ratliffe visited the Mary Magdalene Orphanage Clinic in the Tondo district of Manila, in the Philippine Islands. Tondo was a despicable barrio of thrown-together shacks, cardboard hovels, makeshift family camps in burned-out buildings, and a sewage system that was a ditch running down the side of every street. At the center of the district was Smoky Mountain, a huge tower of garbage infested with rats and maggots, the contents of which emitted a gray-green methane mist that hovered over it.

In the clinic foyer, T. E. Ratliffe asked to speak with Mother Superior Angela O'Brien, the Catholic nun who ran the Mary Magdalene Orphanage medical facility. Moments later he was introduced to a tall redheaded woman whose hair was cut short in a helter-skelter way, as if she had cut it herself with dull scissors. She had lovely tawny eyes in a weary face, and was dressed in cotton sweats that were dirty on both knees.

"What can I do for you, Mr. Ratliffe?" she asked, concealing her amusement at the surprised look her appearance gave him.

"I, uh—read about your clinic in an American magazine. I, uh—wanted to do something to help you."

"I see. That's very kind of you." Mother Angela quickly studied him. He wasn't old, not really, not like the elderly in Tondo were *old;* but he wasn't young either. His hair, like his neatly trimmed moustache and the suit he wore, was gray; she decided he was youngish-old. Clearly he was not there to volunteer. "What exactly did you have in mind, Mr. Ratliffe? In the way of help?"

"Uh, money. A donation. Would fifty thousand dollars help?"

Mother Angela's heart skipped a beat. "Fifty *thousand* dollars?"

"Yes."

"American dollars?"

"Yes." From his inside coat pocket, he took an envelope and handed it to her. "It's a cashier's check. You just have to fill in the line where it says payee."

Mother Angela's lips parted incredulously. "I—I don't know what to say— thank you, of course, but—"

"You're welcome," T. E Ratliffe said, with a shy, almost embarrassed smile. "Goodbye, now."

He went outside, where he had a private sedan and driver waiting. In the air-conditioned comfort of the backseat, as they left the Tondo district, he took out a small leather notebook and opened it to a page list headed CID.

Children in Distress.

It was a list of the worst barrios on Earth, as posted by the World Health Organization. T. E. Ratliffe drew a line through Tondo.

The list was still quite long.

T. E. Ratliffe had a lot of traveling left to do.

CLARK HOWARD has been a professional writer for more than 30 years. He has written more than 200 short stories in other genres, but his métier is crime fiction—his mystery stories have won the Edgar and five Ellery Queen Reader's Awards, and have been adapted for film and television, including *Alfred Hitchcock Presents.* He has also written a boxing column for *The Ring* magazine.

THE PERFORMER

GARY PHILLIPS

AVERY RANDOLPH FINISHED THE STRETCHED OUT RIFF OF BILLY Joel's "Just the Way You Are," hoping his playing covered the unintentional flattening he gave the last lyrics. He meant to take his voice up a notch, not down. The throat was the second thing to go. There was polite applause from the Seaside Lounge crowd, and Randolph nodded slowly while noodling the keys jauntily.

An aging couple, both in bright attire, their matching sterling gray hair arranged just so, walked by the piano, hand in hand. The woman, peach colored lipstick gothically enticing in the bar's subdued lighting, dropped a five into the large brandy snifter for tips. She smiled. Randolph smiled. The man gave a quick wave to a short-haired woman at a table near the window, and the two departed. The man let his hand glide down and briefly and tenderly, flutter against the woman's backside.

"This is for Emily," Randolph announced and began a leisure intro into "Straighten Up and Fly Right," channeling Nat King Cole, letting it build while several patrons bopped their heads and tapped their feet to the rhythm.

"Cool down, papa, don't you blow...your...topppppp," he finished in the key he meant to, and this time the applause was more heartfelt. He stood and bowed and blew a kiss to Emily, the one the man had waved to, sitting at her usual spot next to the window overlooking the medical center down below. For 63, Randolph reflected, she looked good, handsome in her dark blue dress and diamond broach, an ever-present martini glass near her steady blood-nailed hand. She lifted her drink and toasted him with a sip and a toothy grin.

Randolph finished his set with an instrumental rendition of Fats Waller's "Ain't Misbehavin'" adding, "Don't forget the sand dab special, folks, Rene swears they are to die for." That got a few chuckles and he did a wave on his way to the bar. Among those sitting there was a National Guard trooper in his camouflage, his combat service badge dully gleaming over his flapped breast pocket. He was drinking a beer from a pint glass and was having an animated conversation over his cell phone. He turned his body away and hunched over some as Randolph perched on the opposite end.

Carlson, the head bartender, came over with his jack and coke. "You tinkled them good tonight," he commented, setting the squat glass on a napkin with the Lounge's name on it.

"Thanks, man." Momentarily, Randolph watched the logo become distorted by the wet bottom of the glass then took it to his lips.

"I guess you have to go easy on that stuff, don't you? Or does it help your playing?"

Randolph looked over at the woman who'd sat beside him. She was young, that is, younger than him. In her late twenties he figured, jeans and some kind of loose faux suede top. Not too much make-up, Rite Aid earrings. Pretty, but not overwhelmingly so. He sized her up as the wife or girlfriend of some soldier or marine over in Iraq or Afghanistan. Lonely. Bored. There was a lot of that in Los Alamitos.

"Everything in moderation," he said. He didn't offer to buy her a drink, making sure he kept his eyes on her face and not down on that alert swell beneath the top's material. The bare arms though, impressively toned.

"I used to play guitar in high school," she continued, "even had us an all-girl band for awhile. But you know how it goes," she elevated a shoulder.

"Not the next Bangles, huh?"

She frowned.

"Before your time," Carlson piped in. A not so subtle reminder that Randolph was probably a decade and half older than her. Randolph resisted a remark. Goddamn Carlson was older than he was but worked out on the weights, and had bragged about getting pectoral implants.

"So I can pick up more pussy easily," he'd cracked to Randolph and Rene Suarez, the chef.

"Can I have a gin tonic?" the woman asked, looking from Carlson back to Randolph.

"Yours to command," the bartender said and went to prepare her order.

"What do you do now?" What the hell, Randolph concluded, no sense making it easy for Carlson. Besides, he was just making with the chit-chat, no more, no less.

She jerked her head and said, "Work at the PX on the base. Original around here, right?"

Carlson returned with her drink. "Me lady."

"Shit fire," the soldier engrossed on the phone swore as he threw the thing across the bar top. It slid into another customer's glass, the drink's owner glaring at the Guardsman.

"Aw, hell, here we go. Another old lady done told her hero boy bye-bye." Carlson, himself a vet, double-timed to cool out the service man.

"Your husband on his second or third tour?" Randolph asked the woman. They both watched Carlson putting an arm around the soldier's shoulders, his head down as he mumbled words of self-pity.

"He was killed, about half a year ago. Roadside bomb hit their convoy coming into Pakitka Province." She drank some. "Jeff was Army then after he rotated out he wanted to do something about what he'd seen over there. Something different." She shook her head. "Jeff was a…sweetheart. He worked for CARE International delivering food and relief." She put the gin down quietly.

"Damn. Sure sorry to hear that."

"Lori. My name's Lori." She offered her hand and he shook it, smiling crookedly at her.

He told her his name and for several minutes they sat side-by-side in their shared silence. Carlson returned after escorting the soldier outside.

"Sorry folks, I'm back," he announced and got behind the bar to fulfill his enabling duties.

"Hey, look," Randolph began, "let me get your second G and T, okay? I'm not, you know, trying anything funny."

"Thanks, but no thanks, Avery." She'd turned her body toward him slightly and touched his arm. "I better get going. Inventory tomorrow so I've got to be in early." She got off the stool and the young widow strolled out of the landlocked Seaside Lounge.

"You get her number?" Carlson asked when he came over to Randolph.

"Kind of," the piano player answered, looking off, then readying the order of songs in his head for his next set.

A week later he was finishing off a loud and lyrically incoherent sing-a-long version of "Volare" when Lori returned to the bar. She was wearing a modest skirt, shirt and sweater top combo and earrings that sparkled in the low artificial light. Randolph banged the keys with his heel a la Little Richard for the climax, everyone clapping and laughing. He stood, breathing heavy, pumping both fists in the air to more acclaim. A patron shouted "Right on, baby," above the din.

"Glad you came back," he said to her. She lingered on the side of the piano, her purse atop the instrument. Normally he'd say something about that but didn't want to break the mood—his at least. People came by and gave him pats on the back and shoulders. The brandy snifter was brimming with bills tonight.

"Want to go somewhere, have a sandwich or something? I'm hungry."

She leaned in closer to him. "Hungry for what?" Her smoke-colored eyes remained steady on him.

"There's a little hole-in-the-wall place over on Cerritos," he answered neutrally, but not breaking his gaze from hers. "They have great vegetarian burritos with fire roasted peppers. Magnifico."

"I like meat alright."

They grinned at each other like over-heated teenagers as Randolph collected his tip money. Over in the corner at her customary table, Emily Bravera sipped her martini carefully as if testing the stuff for poison, watching the couple over the rim of her glass.

Randolph and the woman descended the outside stairs from where the Seaside Lounge was on the second floor of an aging '80s era strip mall. Down on the parking lot asphalt he became aware of a familiar odor and looked up to see Carlson the bartender taking one of his Camel breaks. He leaned on the railing, the unfiltered cigarette smoldering in his blunt fingers. Lazily he looked at them. The two men then nodded briefly at each other and Randolph walked the woman to her eight-year-old bronze Camry with a dark blue driver's door. He gave her the directions to where they were going, standing near her and pointing off in to the near distance.

"See you there." She gave him a peck on his cheek, her fingers holding on to his upper arms. Her hair was freshly washed and smelled of blueberries and mint.

At Agamotto's Late Nite Eatery and Coffee Emporium, they ate and talked. Lori McLaughlin was originally from Buffalo. She'd met her late husband Jeff, a local boy from Long Beach, when she'd come out to Southern California four years ago, winding up working at a dog food manufacturer.

"That's a trip," Randolph remarked. "Like big vats where the meat and what not is all mixed together?"

"This place, Emerald Valley, is like the Escalade of dog food makers," she said, biting into her bar-b-que meatloaf sandwich and chewing. She then pointed at the sandwich. "Good cuts of meat like this, natural ingredients, grains, they make a high end product selling to trendy pet stores is West L.A. and further down in the OC like Newport Beach and Lake Forrest."

"But not for us peasants here in Los Al." They both chuckled.

Randolph asked her, "You have family back in Buffalo?"

She had some of her beer and dabbed a napkin to her mouth. "Let's just say there's a reason I came out here to put as much distance between me and that so-called family." Still holding the napkin, she squeezed his hand. "Okay?"

"Okay."

The lanky youngster in the stained apron behind the counter gave them a grunt as the couple left. He returned his attention to a news item on the small TV he watched, an image of Long Beach police personnel leaving a burglarized condo in Belmont Shores from earlier that day.

Out in his car, after she had him pull behind a closed liquor store, they made out. There was a bare bulb streaked with an oily substance over the metal back door of the establishment, and slivered fractions of that light filtered into the car's interior and over their grasping forms. Randolph had his hand over her sweater, cupping one of her breasts as they kissed. He moved his thumb across her hardening nipple. She placed one of her hands on his zipper and rubbed.

"That feels good," he murmured.

"This'll feel even better." She tongued his ear and unzipped him. Involuntarily, he sucked in his stomach. "I didn't catch any hairs did I, Avery?" she asked in a concerned voice.

"No. Light-headed is all."

"Mmmm." She worked his shaft and then bent down. Randolph leaned back, eyes fluttering, noting he needed to clean his headliner. Try as he might to fixate on prosaic matters to prolong the sensation, he soon wheezed, "Hey, careful, I'm…I'm about to come."

She gave him a lingering lick along his penis returning to the tip. "Uh-huh." And she let him climax in her mouth.

"Sweet mother of mercy," Randolph exclaimed, grinning like a goon.

From her purse Lori McLaughlin produced a half pint of Jack Daniels and breaking the seal, had a swig and handed it across.

"Remember your motto," she said as he had a taste, "everything in moderation."

"Most assuredly," he retorted.

She took something else from her purse and palm up, presented it to him. "Because you're not through, piano man. You have encores tonight."

He took the offered orange oblong tablet of Cialis. "I'm not that old, you know."

"I know, darling." McLaughlin had pulled up her skirt and using her middle finger, pleasured herself. He stared and said nothing. She continued this for several moments then took off her light blue panties and pressed them into his face. He breathed in deep then popped the Cialis in his mouth, not bothering to wash it down with the booze.

Early that morning, at her three and a half room apartment not far from the Joint Forces base, Randolph pulled on his cigar smoking Woody Woodpecker head boxers and went into the kitchenette in search of juice or cold water. On the counter he spotted a past due notice from SoCal Edison.

On a book ledge crowded with perfunctory knick-knacks was a picture of a square jawed, handsome Lance Corporal he took to be the late husband. He picked it up to see it better by the moonlight. The confident look of the soldier reminded him of the photo of his father, a decorated combat captain who died in Vietnam. A man he never met and only knew from Polaroids and letters his mother kept. He sighed inwardly, put the picture back, and traipsed to the refrigerator.

Inside he found an open can of diet Pepsi and straightened up holding it. One hand on the open door, the light from inside the refrigerator casting its glow about the compact space, Randolph looked at a print of a leafy country lane hung on the wall. It wasn't anything special, like the kind of mass produced reproduction demonstrating the virtues of the frame you came to buy.

Guzzling the soda, looking sideways at the lane, cold air blowing against his lower legs, he suddenly had a massive, pulsing erection.

"Magnifico," he said, proudly stalking back into the bedroom, moving his hips to let his member swing from side to side. He hummed "Rocket Man" and sent up a prayer of thanks to the horny bastard who cooked up the orange wonder.

In the morning Randolph stretched, scratched his side and rubbed his whiskered face. In the other room he could hear Lori McLaughlin talking on the phone.

"...no you listen to me, Karen, that's not going to happen, you understand? I won't stand still while you try that kind of shit with me."

He got up and used the bathroom. When he stepped out McLaughlin was sitting on the edge of the bed in her cloth robe, hunched forward, arms across her upper thighs like a player waiting to get called back in the game. He sat next her her, putting an arm around her shoulder.

"Can I help with anything?"

She made a sound in her throat. "I could lie to you and tell you it's nothing," she began, "but you might as well know now as later." She regarded him for a moment and said, "I was talking to my wonderful ex-mother-in-law. A woman who would make Big Bird slap the shit out of her." She chuckled evilly at the mental image.

"This involve a child?" he asked, having also noticed last night an assortment of toys in a cardboard box in a corner of the living room.

"Yes. My daughter Farley."

"Farley?"

"Jeff had a good buddy who lost his legs over there. She's just two and a half and, well, you can see I'm not exactly living the OC lifestyle."

"Who is around here?" He gave her a squeeze.

She jutted her chin in a westerly direction. “Over in Rossmoor they are. Them and their wall.”

“Screw ’em,” Randolph said. “They think they shit gold.”

She snuggled closer to him, putting a hand on his thigh. “Jeff’s mother, Karen, has recently stepped up her campaign about how she knows it’s tough for me to get by alone feed and raise Farley. How *she* can provide for her and all that. Her third husband, not Jeff’s father, owned a firm that supplied some kind of guidance system for missiles. Anyway, he dropped dead of a stroke and left her sitting pretty in a mortgage free McMansion in Irvine. That’s where Farley is now.”

She rubbed his thigh and eyeing him said, “I didn’t plan on seducing you, Avery. But Karen suddenly showed up yesterday when I went to pick up Farley from the sitter after work. And, well, she demanded time with her granddaughter. She lords it over me what with her paying for the child care and other things for Farley.”

She scooted over to her pressed-board nightstand, and opening a drawer, took out a digital print. She handed it across to Randolph who smiled at the photo of a bright-eyed toddler held aloft by her beaming mother. She took it back, lingered in it then replaced it in the drawer.

“So I was just a way for you to blow off steam? A revenge schtupp aimed at your mother-in-law?”

She shoved him playfully and clambered on top of him as he lay on his back, enwrapping her in his arms. “How observant of you, Dr. Phil.” They kissed eagerly as he undid her robe.

•••

On a Thursday evening several days later they lay in bed in Randolph’s apartment near the race track. Intermingled yells of delight and disappointment could be heard through his cracked sliding window over his bed as the last race finished.

Randolph dialed the radio from the news on the rock station McLaughlin had put on to the jazz station from the college campus in Long Beach. “Suddenly,” a McCoy Tyner number, was in mid-play. He let his mind drift as the pianist-composer did his thing.

“You bet much?” she asked, laying partially on him, his finger gently following Tyner stroke for stoke on her shapely butt.

"Now and then I go over there but I play the ponies like I know poker, not too damn good." He stopped playing and began kneading her flesh, getting aroused.

She nuzzled his neck. "What if you could make about thirty thousand on a sure thing?"

"You know a horse doper?"

"I know where to get sixty, maybe seventy thousand tax free dollars. Half for you and half for me, Avery. Between your couple of nights a week at the Seaside and substitute music and civics teacher, you're not living la vida loca either"

He stopped rubbing and focused. "What are you talking about, Lori?"

"Remember I told you about Emerald Valley?"

"The dog food company."

"The owner, Brice, he's an old hippie, still smokes marijuana, gives his money to saving the rain forest and all that crap."

"Okay. But I'm not comprehending."

"He has a safe in his office. He's still down with the people, don't trust the system, so he's always kept cash around, different places you see? One of them is his office 'cause he's always got some burned out acid head or old surfing bro falling by for a touch." She paused, placing her hand firmly on his chest.

"Even gives it up to an ex employee or two," she continued. "I had to go see him for a loan and he's always had a thing for me. Gave me a handful of those Cialis pills saying to leave a trail of them through the forest and he'd find his way to me. Laughing and having a good time." Her tone frosted.

"This about keeping Karen at bay?"

"She's told me she's going to initiate, her word, legal action. If I just show her I can afford a lawyer, she'll back down. I know how her wormy mind works. She's cheap in so many ways."

"Why not ask Brice for the loan? Sounds to me like he'd do it for you and not sweat when you could pay him back. The good fight and all that."

She pulled slowly on his limp penis. "Because he'd want something in return, Avery. Brice is a freak, get it? He's been in trouble in the past for beating off in his office in front of females. He'd want me to do kinky things to him regularly for repayment. Do you want me to do that?" She started to stroke him slowly. His breath got short as he got hard. "I might be willing to be a thief, but I'm no ho."

She continued with her hand job. "Unless you're going to bitch up. Turn your head when I have to shove a studded dildo up his ass and hear him scream 'Mommy.' Make like I'm not your woman." She took his balls in her hand.

"Not likely," he groaned as he put his fingers to her throat and applied pressure. She gasped and he leveraged her under him.

"Fuck me rough, baby" she demanded—and he did.

•••

The plan wasn't elaborate. It was straightforward and text book efficient—if it was a chapter from a manual on thievery. Emerald Valley Premium Dog Foods was in a seventeen thousand square foot, one-story landscaped building on the cul-de-sac end off an industrial park not far from a 605 freeway off ramp. Lori McLaughlin had made a Sunday after-hours rendezvous to get the money from a thrilled Brice Hovis. McLaughlin told Randolph he'd insisted that she think of the loan as a long-term investment in her and her daughter's futures, and to come by his office to finalize the deal.

McLaughlin knew the layout of the factory and once she got Hovis wound up, she'd said with a sneer, she'd leave a side door unlatched that let in from the parking lot, used by employees when they had to work overtime.

Dressed in overalls obtained that day from a thrift store and wearing rubber dishwashing gloves, Avery Randolph gained access to the facility at the appointed time. Inside, he easily spotted the thin strip of light coming from the slightly ajar office door at the far end the plant. He eased forward on tennis shoes also obtained at the thrift store. His outfit would be burned afterward.

Randolph passed belt feeders, tall stainless steel devices that had large conical shaped vats atop them, automated packaging stations and long heavy-looking machinery bolted to the concrete floor with drive shafts that lead to partially encased circular rotors he took for chopping and grinding up the meat Emerald Valley turned into dog food. Stilled circulation fans were set at various strategic locations in the ceiling.

McLaughlin had explained to him the business, like a lot of pet food manufacturers, bought rendered meat from elsewhere and this was shipped to them as were grains and cereals from other suppliers. Randolph was pleasantly surprised the air in here smelled like cheeseburgers.

Coming to the end of a large box-like machine on stout legs, a dryer he could tell from its stamped label, he was near the office. He halted, shutting out all distractions, getting it together for his performance. *It's all about the in-between, man*, a jazz guitarist reminded him on a studio gig.

He heard Hovis moaning in pleasure between whaps. The tang of marijuana cut through the burger aroma.

"Goddammit, yes, oh yes, doctor."

Randolph stepped into the light to see Hovis leaning over his desk in a stripper nurse costume, short skirt up over a thong, with high heels and a red-haired woman's wig lopsided on his bald head. McLaughlin, in her underwear beneath an open lab coat was holding a dog hair brush, the kind with short wire bristles. She'd been using that side on the man's tenderized rear end. There was a strap-on dildo and a plastic enema bottle filled with clear liquid occupying the paper-laden desk.

Hovis straightened up and stammered, "Who, what is this?" There was a good-sized alligator clamp dangling from his encased penis.

By then Randolph, trying not to giggle too much, had covered the distance between them and squirted liberal amounts of pepper spray into the man's eyes.

"This is not safe," the dog food man blurted, hands grabbing at his face while he did a run-in-place dance of pain in his night nurse uniform.

McLaughlin slugged him over the head with a smoking bong, shattering it. Hovis ran and crashed into a tall file cabinet, knocking it and him over.

"Don't either one of you fuckin' move," Randolph blared. He quickly tied a handkerchief around the downed man's tearing eyes and Mclaughln made sounds like she was being manhandled. Randolph tied Hovis up with cord he'd brought along and got a ball gag strapped around his mouth. He writhed and whimpered on his side on the floor then lay still.

"Where is it, bitch?" Randolph growled, giving it his best Steven Segal guttural rasp.

"I don't know what you're talking about." She slapped her thigh for effect and grunted.

"We'll see about that. Come here, let me show you what me and that dildo are gonna do to you." He marched her out of the office and after a suitable period, returned and began tearing up the office. He knew where Hovis kept the money from McLaughlin, but had to sell the search.

He kicked over a surf board leaning in a corner. Above that in a compartment Hovis had installed, was the cash hidden in the ceiling. "Well, what do we have here?" He walked over to Hovis and kicked him. He got a stifled yell for a response.

"Clever cocksucker, aren't you?" Randolph said to the trussed up owner. "Your girlfriend held out but it's a good thing for both of you I got eyes." He placed a chair under the area of the ceiling and pushing up on the acoustic tile, revealed a large fishing tackle box. He took this out, assessed the contents, and exited the office.

Hovis didn't know that McLaughlin knew where he kept the money. She'd spied once when she'd worked at the company. Though, naturally, he'd suspect her, but there had been an employee, she told Randolph, he'd fired a few months ago and she'd make sure to subtlety train his suspicions in that direction. Or so she'd said.

On the darkened factory floor, he removed his disguise of bushy afro wig, false goatee and Halloween rubber nose. McLaughlin, in her bra and panties, stilettos off so as not to make noise, came over to him and gave him a passionate kiss. He rubbed his hand between her legs.

"Better get going. I'll meet you back at my place, Avery."

"I like it when you say my name," he whispered back.

"I know."

He punched her hard, twice, in the face, reeling her back while she held onto him for balance. Like a boxer clearing their vision, she shook her head and then broke one of her heels off. She put the shoes on and wobbled into the office while Randolph turned toward the way he came in.

"Brice, Brice, are you all right?" she screamed, running into the office. McLaughlin's face rearranged itself from mock concern to icy resolves. "Briiice," she drew out, hand beside her mouth but barely saying his name. "Briiiice, my demented shithead, can you get up?" She guffawed and removed a dagger shaped letter opener from a pen caddy on the desk. The blade was in the style of a medieval knife and she withdrew it from its sheath. She sauntered over and cut Brice Hovis' legs loose and removed the ball gag and handkerchief. His hands remained bound.

"Oh my God, are you all right, Steph?" His eyes were red and wet. He looked from her to the open ceiling and back.

Her fingers trilled the tip of the letter opener. "I'm fine, Brice. Real fuckin' good." She flicked the blade and nicked his thigh. Crimson ran behind the black mesh stocking material.

"Hey," he said, backing up, "this is no time for that. Untie me, would you?"

Swaying her body she stepped closer, waving the letter opener around like a drunk musketeer. "And what if I don't, Brice? What if take it too far this time?" She took another nick out of him, this time from his chest.

Brice looked about panicked while backpeddling in his heels and skirt. "Quit fucking around, Stephanie."

"I'm serious as a fever, Bricey. Come on, beg for your life." She placed her hand on her mound. "It makes me wet." She lunged forward and tackled Hovis who went over, McLaughlin straddling him.

Down on the floor he squirmed and bucked but ceased when she put the tip to his throat, letting it sink in a centimeter.

"Why?" he pleaded, "why are you doing this?"

"Because I can, cunt." She made another cut and Hovis' eyes fluttered, his breathing shallow. A tsk-tsk sound came from her and she made to backhand him awake.

"Yo, Steph is it?"

The woman who went by two names looked up to see Randolph, his disguise back on, standing in the doorway. She chortled. "Yeah, so? What're you gonna do about it, homeboy?"

"This," he said calmly, shooting her in the mouth as she laughed at him.

The woman's body tumbled off of Hovis, her heelless shoe laying across his leg. Randolph bundled the terrified exec again.

"There's something like ninety thousand in here," a woman's voice said behind him. He turned to Emily Bravera who was in slacks and a striped shirt. She was on one knee, having counted the contents of the tackle box. She relatched the lid.

"Not bad," Randolph said. "Plus Hovis can't squawk to the law since he was hiding it from the IRS."

"Well, he does have some explaining to do in that get up of his and two bodies sprawled out." Her arm in the crook of his, him holding the strong box, the two strolled out to the parking lot. Laying dead on the uneven asphalt was the bartender, Alfonso Carlson. He'd been in wait for Randolph to ambush and kill him. But Bravera, a one-time investigating officer with the Criminal Investigation Command of the Army, had done the bushwhacking. Inside was his daughter, Stephanie Carlson. The Command's motto was "Do What Has to be Done."

Before they departed, Bravera put her face close to Randolph's, squeezing his cheeks in her blood-nailed fingers. Her tan prominent against his burnished copper skin. "You liked fucking her, didn't you?"

"Just doing my job, cap'n."

"Just remember, Thelonious, I know how to use a rifle with a scope."

"I keep that information uppermost in my mind."

"See that you do." She kissed him deep and long.

•••

At the Seaside Lounge, Avery Randolph began a mournful rendition of "On Green Dolphin Street." In her table at the window, Emily Bravera sat and drank sparingly, appreciating his handling of the tune. The two had been working this area for more than a month now, pulling off several lucrative burglaries from Long Beach then south along the Orange County coast: jewelry, a few telling homemade DVDs, cash, and even gold bars horded against the next meltdown. For it wasn't only old hippies like Brice Hovis who didn't like reporting all their income.

The front they'd constructed involved Bravera being a general's widow living in Rossmoor. Real estate being what it was these days, the realtor was happy to rent to the widow on a month-to-month basis. She was personable, knowledgeable on a variety of subjects, worked out at the local gym, and managed to get herself invited to this or that soiree or club event—thus being able to scope out various domiciles.

Bravera had knowledge of security systems and Randolph knew a thing or two about safes. For him tumblers or electronic lock sequencing were different sets of notes to master—particularly when you employed certain tech to aid in the stealing effort and revealing pesky nanny cams. Tomorrow they were going to take down the beach house of the matching hair couple. Yes, they'd agreed, he and Bravera had one sweet hustle going.

When the supposed Lori McLaughlin had come on to him, the possessive Bravera did some checking and turned up that she was Carlson's daughter. Randolph and Bravera didn't know what the pitch was, but figured the two were setting Randolph up for an Oswald—be the fall guy. The piano player had hinted to the bartender he'd beat out on a dope charge in Baltimore. That was a lie, just part of the dodge like his funky apartment near the track. But the Carlsons must have figured a footloose brother hiding out in the OC, wanted on a criminal charge elsewhere was a good fit for a robbery-murder here in town.

Randolph and his older lover and partner, not wishing to pass up an opportunity for enrichment, had let the scheme unfold. In another month or so, not foolish enough to push their luck, they'd move on.

"Like Duke said, man, you gotta play with intent to do something," the pianist said sotto then hummed and teased the keys, ending the extended version of "On Green Dolphin Street." There was sustained clapping and several patrons rose and dropped larger denomination bills in the snifter. Randolph had announced he was taking up a collection to bury father and daughter. Bravera put in a fifty, smiling at him. He lifted the glass with both hands, bowing slightly to the gathered from his piano seat.

GARY PHILLIPS works in whatever medium he can in telling his stories of chicanery and malfeasance. Recent work includes *Danger A-Go-Go*, a retro graphic novel set in the swinging '60s teaming up that curvaceous PI Honey West, Zen freelance spy Derek Flint, and the groovy Captain Action. *Treacherous: Grifters, Ruffians and Killers*, a collection of his short stories is out now, as is *Scoundrels: Tales of Greed, Murder and Financial Crimes*, an all-original anthology he edited and contributed a story to as well. Please visit his website at: www.gdphillips.com.

LOON LIFE

BRENDAN DU BOIS

The Honda SUV I had been dumped in had a handrail up above the door, to assist elderly passengers in getting in and out, but I'm sure the SUV's designers would have been shocked to see how it was being used this evening: my hands were in stainless steel handcuffs looped through the handrail, stretching my arms above me. I also wasn't wearing a seatbelt, but I wasn't complaining. Earlier complaints about being cuffed had led to the man sitting behind me placing a 9 mm pistol against the base of my skull and saying, "Shut your mouth. Just be glad you're riding while you're still breathing."

The man who was the driver had laughed. I hadn't. Not much to laugh at.

And all because I wanted to write a book.

•••

My escorts had taken me from a summer cottage I had been renting along Lake Walker, in a remote part of northern New Hampshire. During my time there I had swum a lot, canoed, and learned about the wildlife that lived in and around the lake. But I wasn't some back-to-nature creature, and coming to Lake Walker hadn't been an accident. You see, a resident on the northern side of the lake was someone famous—or infamous—and after my layoff from the *Providence Journal* newspaper, I started researching a book about said resident, to pass the time before I had to find a real job, and maybe, if I was very lucky, to get a book contract before my severance package was exhausted.

But luck hadn't been with me this summer. My severance package was within a week or two of being depleted, the rise of the Internet and the decline of newspapers meant nobody was hiring experienced journalists, so I really was counting on this book project and the infamous resident to save the day.

However, said resident obviously had other ideas.

The SUV's driver took us along the main dirt road that circled around the lake, and despite the uncertainty and the terror of being where I was and what was going on, there was also an element of the ludicrous: within several yards of me as we drove along were people who were having a barbecue or were watching the Red Sox or playing Scrabble with their grandchildren, and they had no idea that a man was going by in a Honda vehicle, handcuffed, with a 9 mm pistol pointed at the back of his head.

The motto of this odd state is Live Free or Die. I was hoping the evening would end with me following the first half of this phrase, and not the second.

•••

After a while the number of houses and cottages thinned out, and those remaining houses looked like they belonged in a pricier neighborhood. I've only been on the lake for a short while but I quickly learned about the conflict between those who liked having small homes and cottages along the lakefront, and those who feel there's nothing wrong with building a three-story mansion and cutting down all the surrounding trees. And the funny thing is, this argument isn't always between old-timers and newcomers. Sometimes it was the newcomers who were most adamant on keeping things the way they were, and it was the old-timers—if they came into some money—who would splurge on building something huge and overpriced.

And my destination this evening was the hugest and most overpriced house on Lake Walker.

• • •

The driver made a quick turn to the right, where two stone pillars flanked a dirt driveway. A tall black wrought-iron fence stretched out on both sides of the pillars, and the gate between the pillars was made of similar iron. From past experience, I knew that there were small signs on the gate—not legible from my vantage point—that said NO TRESPASSING NO SOLICITORS PROPERTY UNDER SURVEILLANCE, but those signs weren't going to halt my intrepid driver. He pressed a button on the Honda's dashboard and the gate slid open, and after passing through the open gate, another press of the switch closed it up.

And it was like entering some sort of playground or fairyland, for the driveway was now paved and curved up to the left, rising up to a huge home. Beyond the gate and a tree line, a manicured lawn was exposed, and little recessed lights on both side of the driveway illuminated the way. There were two stone fountains and a couple of statues of lions and cherubs. At the top of the rise of land, the driveway widened into a parking area, just before the large house, which had two separate wings on each side, big bay windows, and lots of exposed wood and brickwork. The thought of having to haul all that brickwork from across half the state to the narrow dirt road just outside made me shake my head.

The Honda came to a stop and the doors were opened. I waited. I let my fingers play a bit with the handle and roof. No escape was possible, of course. These guys—while not very polite—were very good at what they did.

The first guy reached up, undid my cuffs with a twist of a small key, and I got out. I wanted to show these guys how tough I was by not rubbing my wrists and hands, but I couldn't help myself. I rubbed my wrists and hands, but if the two guys had any reaction to my apparent weakness, they didn't mention it.

The guy with the pistol made a move with his head, looking like a nervous horse, trying to shake off a fly. "You go in there. There's someone who wants to talk to you."

I looked to him and his companion, dressed alike. Khaki slacks, black turtleneck shirts, dark blue blazers, polished shoes. "Really? Just like that?"

The first one shrugged. "Yeah. Just like that. Look, get going, or we'll drag you in, and the result will be the same, 'cept your clothes and your face will get a little dinged."

My wrists ached. After a nanosecond of reflection, I decided I had reached the "dinged" limit for the evening.

So I walked up to the large wooden doors, my legs shaking a bit, knowing that the next few minutes would determine if I would leave through these doors on my own two legs, or carried out, wrapped in plastic. I nervously pressed my fingertips on one door handle, and then the other, and then I opened one carved door and walked in.

•••

Inside was a tiled anteroom, opening up to a large living room with a stone fireplace off to the left. The floor was polished hardwood, and couches and easy chairs and a couple of coffee tables were scattered about. The walls bore mirrors, bookcases, and framed artwork of flowers and landscapes. On the opposite side of the fireplace were French doors that overlooked a balcony, which in turn, overlooked the lake. I could hear some of the night sounds, and from out on the cold waters of the lake, the haunting wail of a loon. From one of the couches came the next biggest surprise of the evening, when a woman got up and came over to me.

She was in that odd range of ages that could be twenty-five years in one kind of light, or thirty-five years in another. She was slender, wearing tight jeans, black low-heel shoes, and a sleeveless white knit sweater. Her upper arms had the definition of someone who spent a considerable amount of time in the gym, and her black hair was cut close and styled by someone who had never once set foot in New Hampshire. Gold jewelry adorned her wrists and fingers, and she held out one manicured hand to me as she walked over.

"Stuart Rowland," she said. "So nice to meet you."

"Sure," I said, giving her hand a quick squeeze and release. "And you are…?"

She nodded. "Melanie Caprica. I appreciate you seeing me on such short notice. Would you like to sit down?"

I sat down in a cushioned chair with wooden armrests, using both hands to lower myself down. She took a seat across from me on a couch, crossing her legs in what looked to be a practiced move.

I took a deep breath, tried to ease the hammering that was in my chest. "Excuse me for being dense, but could you repeat what you just said?"

"Repeat what?"

"The part about me seeing you on such short notice. I don't recall I had a choice in the matter."

She gave me a pert smile. "I know Alonzo and Pat can be…decisive when they seek to do something for their boss. I apologize if their methods…were disturbing."

Disturbing. Cute way of saying that, and I decided to let it be for now. The hammering in my chest seemed to slow down. "So who's their boss? You or Frank Spinnelli?"

The pert smile remained. "We all work for Mister Spinnelli. Just as you, Mister Rowland, used to work for the *Providence Journal* newspaper in Rhode Island. And prior to that, a daily newspaper in New Hampshire, and prior to that, a semi-weekly newspaper in Massachusetts. And now you're unemployed, working on a non-fiction book for which you have no agent or contract, living at a cottage for which you've paid five thousand dollars for three months rent, and your combined checking and savings account currently totals just over three hundred dollars."

I scratched at the back of my head, felt a couple of bits of hair come away in my nervous, twisting fingers. "Very thorough."

"Thank you. That's what we're known for."

"Among other things."

"Perhaps," she said. "But we're not here to talk about me, now, are we."

"Depends," I said. "If I want to talk about you, will Alonzo and Pat come in and tune me up?"

She held out a hand. "Please. Let's just keep it quiet and civilized, all right?"

I looked around the house, at the fireplace, and the fine furniture. Some civilization. "All right. Go ahead."

She took a breath. "We know you're researching a book about Mister Spinnelli and his life. What I'm hoping is that we can reach some sort of settlement tonight where you agree to drop your book project, so we can all move on with no more meetings like this."

"Boy," I said, making my eyes wide. "That sure does sound civilized. And what would happen if I were to say no, and walk out that door?"

A slight shrug. "Nothing," she said. "You'd be free to go, and I'd ensure that you have a more comfortable ride back to your cottage. But I feel compelled to warn you, that while you'll have a safe and pleasant evening tonight, I can't guarantee the rest of your days and nights will be as safe and comfortable."

"Sounds like a threat to me."

She smiled. Her teeth were very white. "No, not at all…but for one who's been doing research on Mister Spinnelli, I'm sure you know he has many loyal friends and supporters. And if some of these loyal friends and supporters get the impression you mean Mister Spinnelli harm…well, you're a bright man. I'm sure you can figure out the rest."

I looked around this fine house once more, and through the open doors of the balcony, I again heard the warbling cry of a loon. "Yeah, I can figure out the rest. The usual and customary one-way trip in the trunk of a car or in the hold of a boat. All right, so I'm here. Do you have something to offer me, or do you expect me to drop this book project out of the goodness of my heart?"

Melanie's pert little smile slipped away and was replaced by a tough businesswoman smile. "No, we're never in the business of appealing to someone's good nature, or someone's goodness. Everyone needs to make a living…even…journalists, or writers. So here's the offer. You drop the project, agree never to research or write anything about Mister Spinnelli, and we'll pay you twenty thousand dollars."

I shifted in my chair, my hands firm against the armrests. "For someone who supposedly places a high value on Mister Spinnelli's privacy, that's a remarkably low offer."

She clasped her hands together over one knee. "The average cash advance for a non-fiction book last year was ten thousand dollars. What we're offering you is twice that average amount. I think that's quite a fair offer."

"Certainly," I said. "But there's other factors you're not taking into account."

"Such as?"

"Such as making a splash, an impact, with one's first book. The sales and notice that would make the next book's advance that much larger. Not to mention the publicity, the prestige, and the other delights that comes from writing a best selling book. There's more to life than just money."

"So it's been alleged," she said dryly. "But I've always found that at the end of the day, it all comes down to cash. So, Mister Rowland. What can we add to our twenty thousand dollar offer to make it more agreeable for you?"

"I'm not sure I can put a figure on that."

She made a move to get up from the chair. "Then I'm afraid there's nothing more to say."

"Wait," I said. "Look...can I get a drink or something? Being... brought in like this has made me very thirsty. And then we can talk a bit more."

She stared right at me and I stared right back. Then she made her decision and got up. "Very well. How does ice water sound?"

I was going to make a joke about whether she was going to get the water from the kitchen, or if she was just going to open up a vein in her arm right there, but I didn't think Melanie Caprica was in a joking mood.

"That sounds fine," I said.

She left me alone for a moment, and I got up and walked around. I checked out the French doors to the balcony, some of the artwork—nice framed canvasses of landscapes and flowers from a woman artist named Varvara Harmon—and checked out the bookshelves as well. The books were leather bound and looked like they came from a decorating catalogue that said something like, "For Sale, one leather-bound library, books guaranteed unread, perfect to impress those visitors who move their lips while reading."

I heard the clatter of footsteps and scratching my head one more time, returned to my chair. Melanie came back in, holding a wooden tray, with one glass of ice water. I picked up the water, nodded my thanks, and drank half of it in one chilly swallow. I put the glass back down on the tray, now sitting before me on a coffee table.

My host—hostess?—seemed irritated. "Do go on, Mister Rowland. What did you have to say?"

I shrugged. "I have a counter-offer."

She said, "Name the price, then. Why are you wasting my time?"

"Because the counter-offer doesn't involve money."

"What does it involve then?"

I gave her my best smile, which was a feat, considering where I was and how I had gotten here. "The counter-offer involves you."

•••

That got her, and I felt a bit of a thrill, that she seemed slightly off balance. "I'm sorry, I don't understand. What do you mean, it involves me?"

"It involves you, Miss Melanie Caprica, who has been in the employ of Mister Frank Spinnelli for the past seven years. Prior to that, you were a summa cum laude graduate of the Suffolk Law School, and before that, you went to Brown University. And curiously enough, your record prior to entering Brown University was a bit…sketchy. Involving some criminal complaints. Regarding petty larceny, drug possession, unlicensed massage therapy…"

With each sentence I had said, her face had gotten redder and redder, until now, it was scarlet. I again tried my best smile and said, "See? You're not the only one with impressive research capabilities."

"That's it," she snapped. "That's enough."

"But don't you want to hear more about my counter-offer? I mean, well, excuse me for saying this, but you're taking this very personally, Miss Caprica, and this is strictly business, is it not? For both parties to come away with the feeling that each have reached a compromise, a deal?"

I suppose I have the good professors at Suffolk Law to thank for what happened next, for she composed herself and said, "All right. Go on. But make it quick."

I reached over, finished my glass of water, glad to see my hand wasn't shaking when I put the empty glass down. "Then here's my offer, and no more time wasting. I still want to do this book. Mister Spinnelli has had an…interesting life. The story of men like Mister Spinnelli often takes place in New Jersey, New York or Los Angeles. Not quiet little New England. Right there is the hook, Miss Caprica. Something different, something unusual, something that will catch the interest of book publishers."

"And my part in this?"

I shrugged again. "Work with me. Be a co-author, or an unnamed contributor. You know so many secrets, so many tales… with your assistance, I guarantee the book will be a bestseller and optioned to the movies. An inside view of Mister Spinnelli and his organization? Instant hit."

I watched her face carefully, and then she burst out laughing. "You have no idea what you're asking."

"I surely do," I said. "Otherwise, I wouldn't have asked it."

Another shake of her head, and another burst of laughter. "You…you…bone-picker. You scribbler. You skimmer of other's people trash, misery, dirt. You know nothing of loyalty, nothing of serving someone who has helped you out, nothing about me or my way of life."

I toyed with the empty glass and touched the top of the coffee table. "Then explain it to me."

She shifted in her seat and said, "My earlier history…true. Nothing I was proud of. But I grew up in a tough neighborhood, with a single mom, who did the best she could but which wasn't enough. So the streets called to me…I answered their call…but before it was too late, Frank Spinnelli took notice of me, and straightened me out. I got my GED, got into Brown…and after getting my law degree, I began to repay the many services he provided to me. I've had one client during my entire professional career. My savior."

"Sounds like a king. Or an emperor. Not a criminal thug."

Her eyes flashed at me. "Again…your ignorance is overwhelming, Mister Rowland. Mister Spinnelli represents…represents something that has existed in human society for centuries. A man above society, who lives and exists outside of the normal, who protects his family and friends, and doesn't depend on society to protect him or them. A man of strength, of vision, of power, a man who—"

I interrupted her. "I once did a story, back in my *Providence Journal* days, about a little grocery shop owner, lived in a mixed neighborhood. Once he had it started up and running, two associates of Mister Spinnelli's came by, to advise him of the truth of that particular neighborhood. That donations had to be made on a weekly basis to a non-existent local civic action group. He refused to pay. And then he had to quickly learn how to run a grocery store with two broken arms. So don't give me any more crap about the noble feudal chief who protects the poor and the related and the struggling. It's nonsense, and deep inside, you know it."

"Then I guess our negotiations are over," she said, standing up. "I'll have Alonzo and Pat drive you back to your cottage. And after tomorrow…I'd be one prepared man, Mister Rowland."

I stood up as well. "Sounds nice, Miss Caprica. For I'm sure you're one prepared woman as well."

Again, that quick puzzled look that pleased me. "You're speaking in riddles again, Mister Rowland."

I held out my hands in a quick gesture. "Then I'll make this plain and simple."

"Please do."

I took a breath. "How much longer do you think you and your two friends can keep the secret going?"

"And what secret is that?"

Another breath. "That Mister Spinnelli is dead."

•••

My, that certainly got her attention, and her eyes stared at me with such hate and contempt, I had to wonder how she ever got any customers doing unlicensed masseuse work back in the days. "You… you don't know what you're talking about."

I went back into my chair. "I most certainly do. Shall I go on?"

She stood there, like she was debating whether to stand up and have her two boys toss me out, or whether to let curiosity take control and sit down.

Curiosity, I was pleased to see, won out. She sat down. "Go on. Now, please."

I said, "Even though I'm no longer with the *Journal,* I have contacts with a number of law enforcement types in Providence and elsewhere. And in doing research for my book, I kept on getting the same story, over and over again. That Mister Spinnelli had dropped out of sight. That he was no longer being seen at his usual haunts, the bars, the social clubs, the restaurants. And that there were grumblings among other…types who move in Mister Spinnelli's circle, that they were concerned that they hadn't seen him or heard from him in a while."

She said quickly, "He's an old man. He's not well. Which is why he's up here."

I scratched at the back of my head again. "So you say. But I've been here for a while, Miss Caprica, doing my research. And as any of my former editors would tell you, I'm a bear when it comes to being prepared and doing research. And among the things I've learned is that I've contacted every home health organization within a two-hour drive of this place. Not one of them has a patient on Lake Walker. I've kept an eye on this place as well, and I've only seen you and your two…men. One of the men, every Thursday, goes out and does the week's shopping. I've seen what he buys, as I've stood behind him a couple of times in the checkout line. Enough food for three…and maybe four if you would stretch it, but why would you have to stretch it?"

Her hands were clasped so tight I thought the fancy fingernails would crack. "Anything else?"

"Sure," I said. "There were two things I caught, when I was brought up here. There are just the three of you. Where are Mister Spinnelli's other associates? His relatives? Nieces, nephews, brothers and sisters? For a sickly man…I think there'd be more here than just the three of you."

Her hands were still tightly clasped. "You said two things. What was the other?"

I tried to keep my voice low, even and cool. "I've done stories before where I was in the presence of the big boss, whether it was a power company exec or a National Guard general. Every time I did a story like that, there was a sense of urgency in the air…a buzz, if you like, that the head honcho was either in the room or nearby. I didn't get that feeling from Alonzo or Pat when they brought me here, or from you as well. Nothing like that at all. Mister Spinnelli is not in Providence, he's not here, and I doubt he'd be in the witness protection program. Therefore…he's dead, isn't he?"

She suddenly stood up. "We're through here. Done. No more talking."

Melanie started to turn and I said, "Think twice before you let your anger get a hold of you, Miss Caprica. Before you call in Alonzo and Pat and have them take me for that quote, ride, unquote."

She looked at me, hands clenched, nostrils flaring. "And what should I think about, you little piece of crap?"

I said, "Think about this. Just so you know, I've secured the services of an attorney. Not one with quite the pedigree of you, but fair enough. And he's a former police chief from a town here in New Hampshire, with lots of interesting law enforcement contacts. And he loves to talk with me...so much that I talk to him once a day, seven days a week. And he has strict instructions, since I've been working on this book...a day goes without my phone call, and then calls get made, and the police show up here on your doorstep."

It seemed she was trying very hard to control her voice. "When we have to...we're quite skilled. There's no evidence you've been here. None."

"Oh, yes there is," I said. "Lots of evidence. In the time I've been here, Miss Caprica, I've made sure to deposit my fingerprints on as many surfaces as possible, here and in the SUV, and I've also left some bits of hair, to assist in a DNA analysis down the road, if need be. Maybe you could give the house and the SUV a good cleaning, and then, maybe not. It would just take one fingerprint. So what do you think would happen if I were to disappear and evidence arose that this was the last place I visited? Do you think the cops and the local news media would let that story die? Of course not...and you can be sure that in the process of trying to find me, the news would come out that your boss is dead. So what's it going to be? Let your emotions take control, or to be a cool businesswoman?"

I kept close eye on her, feeling the hammering in my chest return, knowing how close this was all going to be, wondering if I was going to pull it off, wondering what she would do....

And in another surprise, she sat back down heavily in her chair, buried her face in her hands, and said, "Oh, damn you, why the hell did you feel the need to be a goddamn snoop?"

I'm not sure what was going on, but it seemed encouraging. "My nature. And my job, I guess. I'm sure it's been pretty hard, trying to keep it all together."

Melanie raised up her head. "You have no idea. No idea at all. We three...we've been on knife edge, trying to keep it all together. The phone calls, the attempted visits, everything else...you have no idea."

"And how can you keep putting off the phone calls?"

She sighed. "Alonzo...he can do a fair imitation of Mister Spinnelli on the telephone, when I need him."

"Why? I mean, what's the point?"

"The point..." She clasped her hands together, shook her head a couple of times. "The point is...Mister Spinnelli has enemies waiting for him to falter, fail or leave. And with those three options, comes one more. Alonzo, Pat, and I would leave the scene, because of our connection to Mister Spinnelli. And that would be a permanent departure. And when…when…Mister Spinnelli passed a number of weeks ago, up here in his bedroom, we realized we had to put on a façade, an impression that he's still running the business. Even though…well, we found a nice spot on the other side of this hill. With a view of the lake. He was a Providence boy, through and through, but he loved this place."

"But you must have known it wouldn't last."

She wiped at her eyes. "Day to day. That's all we were doing. Day to day…until you showed up. You piece of crap, you."

I thought for a moment, leaned forward in my own chair. "My original offer still stands."

Another wipe to her eyes. "A book? Are your crazy?"

From outside, another cry from a loon. "Hear that?"

"What? The loon?"

"Yeah, the loon. You know, one other thing I've learned up here is that the loon species is hundreds of thousands of years old…and they still live the same. They live on lakes from spring to fall…and then they know it's time to move on, and they migrate, to live on the ocean during the winter months."

Another loon cry.

"Miss Caprica, it's time to move on. You and Alonzo and Pat… work with me on this book, and arrangements can be made…like I said, I have connections with law enforcement. We both can get what we want: I get a great bestselling book, a start on a new career, and you and your friends, you get a new life, and safety. This is a good deal for the three of you, before a heavily armed crew from Providence comes up here and won't take no for an answer. But like the loons out there…it's time."

She stared at me, and I stared back at her. She wiped at her eyes again and looked over my shoulder, out to the lake, where the loons lived…but only for a while.

I cleared my throat. "Miss Caprica?'

She looked at me. Finally smiled. "Call me Melanie."

BRENDAN DUBOIS of New Hampshire is the award-winning author of twelve novels and more than 100 short stories. His latest novel, *Deadly Cove*, will be published in July 2011 by St. Martin's Press. His short fiction has appeared in *Playboy, Ellery Queen's Mystery Magazine, Alfred Hitchcock's Mystery Magazine, The Magazine of Fantasy & Science Fiction,* and numerous other magazines and anthologies including *The Best American Mystery Stories of the Century*, published in 2000 by Houghton-Mifflin and edited by Tony Hillerman and Otto Penzler.

His short stories have twice won him the Shamus Award from the Private Eye Writers of America, and have also earned him three Edgar Allan Poe Award nominations from the Mystery Writers of America.

Visit his website at www.BrendanDuBois.com

WINNING TICKET

CHRISTINE MATTHEWS

Everybody has a nickname. Oh you can sit there and shake your head, swear up and down that you don't and never have, but you'd be wrong.

There's the obvious ones: Jimmy No Thumbs or Bobby the Nose. And schoolyard names like the one we gave Peggy in second grade, after she had an accident: Pooh-Pooh Pants. These kinds of labels can hurt, or at least make you tear up from humiliation. But in real life, grown-ups, too, have monikers they're not even aware of.

That girl doing your nails watches you chewing on a fat wad of gum, and to her you're Cow Lady. The waitress who has had to take your steak back twice and withstand a lecture when your martini arrived without three olives probably thinks of you as Big Mouth Dick. Neighbors talk behind your back, across the fence, or down the hall. You're Cat Lady, The Dork in 3B, Bimbo, or maybe because of all the complaints they've lodged with management when you play "Love Me Tender" or "All Shook Up" one too many times, you've been christened Elvis.

I didn't feel particularly guilty thinking of him as Liver-Spot Lou. Come on, the guy was covered with 'em. From the top of his bald, sweaty head to the knuckles on his pale hands. Don't get me wrong, he was an all-right dude. Every night he'd come pushing his wife (Baby Betty) in a wheelchair. Probably in their late sixties, they made a perfect couple, both all smiles and bundles of fat packed into matching sweat suits. Their routine was always the same.

Night owls. I've wondered about that. Maybe they couldn't sleep or lived nearby. Most of the seniors clear out by ten, but not Lou and Betty. He'd push her over to the penny slots—Double Diamond—and that's when the fussing would begin. This usually lasted ten minutes or so. First he'd have to drag aside the stool blocking their way, then position her in front of a machine. She'd want her coat off if it was winter or her sweater on if it was summer and the AC was cranked up. Then he'd waddle off to get her a cup of coffee. When he was satisfied she was situated, he'd take care of himself: off with his coat, drape it over the back of her chair, pull over a stool, fish in his pocket for his wallet, and then, finally, they were set to play.

A five was what they'd start with, feeding it into the blinking slot. It didn't matter if the machine's max was two dollars or one, they would always play the minimum—twenty cents—and take turns pushing the BET button. I'd keep an eye on them and when their cups were empty, I'd stop by.

"Hi folks, how's it goin'?"

She'd look up and smile, waiting for him to answer. "Fine."

"Need anything?"

It was always the same: "Two coffees—one black, one double cream and sugar."

"Sure thing." I could feel him looking at my butt as I walked away. But I figured, what the hell, as long as he didn't touch.

After I came back with their order, he'd grin and tip me a buck. She'd slurp the coffee like she was in the Sahara and it was the last swig from her canteen.

It went on pretty much like that for a couple of years. Betty got larger from month to month. I didn't know they made wheelchairs that big. And sicker. One night I noticed she had a small oxygen tank strapped to her back. It was in a black nylon case and if you didn't look close, it could have passed for a purse except for the thin, plastic tube running up into her nose.

I had to hand it to Old Lou, he never got impatient with her, always taking such good care. I used to tell Jones that if ever I got old and sick, God forbid!, I hoped he'd be there for me. He said he would.

•••

So three years pass. I started working over at Caesar's in the Sports Book. Bigger tips, less mileage on my feet, nicer outfits, and the guys wanted to be left alone to handicap. Jones got me the job; he's a cashier, taking bets. At first I was nervous about how this would all come together—us living and working in the same spaces. But we were doing okay. No plans to get married, we'd both been there, done that one to death.

One quiet Thursday in February, I'm bringing a Lionel Richie wannabe a scotch when I see Liver-Spot Lou pushing himself in a wheelchair across the casino. Imagine my surprise. The guy looked thinner, which was a good thing, but older by ten years instead of the three it had been since we'd last seen each other. As he struggled to get around a crap table I noticed he was alone.

Finally he got himself into the room, and then he shifted into fussy mode…some things never change. Slowly he peeled his coat off, and I do mean slowly, carefully spreading it over the back of a chair. Next he reached down into a basket attached to the back of his ride and pulled out a racing form, laying it gently down on the small desk in front of him. Then began the process of getting out of one chair and into another. All the while he was blocking the aisle, but it was a quiet night and no one seemed to care. I must have delivered six drinks by the time he finally got himself situated in one of the cubicles. After he'd adjusted the light, smoothed out his paper, licked at the stub of a pencil, he waved at me.

"Well, long time no see, stranger," I said, wondering if he'd recognize me.

"I thought that was you. Since when have you been over here?"

"Oh, more than two years, now. So, how have you been?"

"Not so good. My wife died last spring."

I reached down to pat his arm. "I'm so sorry. She seemed like a real nice lady."

"She was my world. I don't know what to do with myself now."

I was never sure of how to act when someone poured their heart out, especially a stranger. And as he kept looking up at me, waiting for comforting words, a smile…something…I asked what he wanted to drink, dummy that I am.

"A beer. Please."

"Going for the hard stuff," I teased.

"What have I got to lose? I'm just putting in my time, that's all it's about now." He jerked a thumb toward the wheelchair. "Between the diabetes, high blood pressure, and my heart, I'm living on thirty pills a day. The sooner I can join Eleanor, the better."

Eleanor. So that was her name. "It's crazy that we've known each other for years and never had a name to put with the face."

He held out his hand. "I'm Bill."

"And I'm Lacy," I said, shifting the tray to my left hand so I could grab his fat fingers.

"You'll laugh, but Ellie used to nudge me every time we saw you sashaying toward us. She'd say, 'Here comes Legs.'"

See what I mean about nicknames? "Well I'll take that as a compliment." I felt like a real dork for thinking of this sweet man and his deceased wife as two funny old people. Even though they could have been my grandparents, I should have been more respectful.

"Legs? Well those damn outfits we had to wear were very skimpy."

"I didn't hear anyone complaining," he laughed.

"Yeah, well, the tips were good."

"So why are you at Caesar's?"

"Ahh, you know, boyfriend works here, better benefits, more hours, boring shit like that."

"Just be lucky you have someone." He thought a moment, obviously about Eleanor and I watched his face collapse.

"I guess. Well, it's great seeing you; I'll go get that beer for you."

"Thank you."

•••

And that's how it went for a few months. Bill would come in the same time every night. He'd handicap for three to four hours a pop—win a few, lose a few. I was really starting to like the guy. When he finished his last beer he'd always toss me an extra ten, but before starting for home he'd get real chatty. Guess the thought of going back to an empty house got to him.

Sometimes he'd tell me about his parrot, Garrett. He hated that bird, always complained how dirty the damn thing was. But Eleanor had loved it, and since they didn't have any kids it was all the poor guy had left. Pitiful.

•••

The last time I saw Bill was the Tuesday before Easter. We were busy that night, with kids on spring break gawking and playing Daddy's money at the blackjack tables. Big boys with pea brains, staggering around with their booze in those oversized cups, waving 'em like they were banners of courage, instead of neon signs that they're idiots who have never been away from home before. All us girls laughed at 'em.

Bill was getting comfortable at his usual table when I noticed him.

"Well where have you been? I was starting to miss my favorite customer."

"I ain't been feeling too good," he said, studying his race form.

"You do look a little pale, honey. Sure you should be out?"

"A beautiful blonde is paying attention to me, I'm fine. Could I have a beer, please? When you get a minute?"

"Sure thing." I patted his back. "Nice to see you, Bill."

He didn't seem to hear that last part, too wrapped up in his calculating, I guess. Horses—they always come first with these guys.

By the time I got back from the bar with his drink, I knew something was wrong and made a beeline for Jones.

"Ahh, sweetie?"

"Oh hey, Babe," he said from the other side of the counter.

"See that guy over there?" I pointed toward Bill.

Jones squinted. "The big dude stretched out across the table? Is he taking a nap?"

"I'm not sure. Can you walk over with me?"

"Sam!" Jones called to a guy behind him. "Cover me a minute."

No one seemed to notice a thing—business as usual in Bill's part of the room. Jones leaned over and shook him. "Hey buddy, ya okay, there?"

No answer.

Setting my tray down, I had a try. "Bill? I got your drink here. Wake up."

Jones pushed Bill back in his chair and that's when we saw blood at the corner of his mouth. If you weren't looking closely you'd never notice. But still, it was scary.

"Go call 911. I'll stay with him," Jones said after checking Bill's wrist for a pulse. "Hurry."

"Is he alive?"

"Just barely. Now go!" he said in such a controlled voice, I knew he was trying not to scare away the customers.

But I could have told him he didn't have to worry. You'd be surprised at all the tourists that get caught up and forget to sleep or eat or take their medication. Vegas does that to people, it gets their reality all twisted. So seeing someone down, spread out on the floor isn't anything unusual for the regulars.

Within three minutes of making the call, I saw two guys come running toward us. The room was buzzing now, but that didn't stop people from lining up to make their bets. The rest of the casino was oblivious to the commotion. Jones had gone back to his window and I stood watching with Bernie, the floor manager.

Poor ol' Bill was wedged in there pretty good. I felt so sorry for him.

"Get back, let the guy breathe," one of the EMTs said. Then he looked at me. "You know this guy?"

"Kinda."

"Does he have any relatives nearby? Someone we should call?"

The other paramedic was still trying to get Bill to wake up.

I shook my head. "No kids and his wife's dead."

An oxygen mask was strapped across Bill's face while an IV got started. Things started moving fast then. They loaded Bill onto a gurney and raced out of the casino. I watched as they got swallowed up by the crowd.

•••

"So, I heard about all the commotion today. You know the guy good, or what?" Darlene asked.

I was waiting for Jones in the hotel coffee shop. "Kinda. He was a regular, used to see him and his wife all the time when I was over downtown. She died a few years ago and now he's alone. Plays the horses all day. It's sad."

"Yeah, life will kick ya in the ass when ya ain't payin' attention," Darlene said. "It sure ain't fair—none of it. Ya waitin' for Sweet Cheeks?"

"Who?"

"The girls that work with Jones call him Sweet Cheeks and they sure ain't talkin' about the ones on his face." She laughed.

"And what do all of you call me?"

"Lucky, honey. Havin' a guy like that, I'd say you're pretty damn lucky."

I tried being polite but I was starving. When she finally got done with her patter, I ordered a bowl of chili and a Coke.

"What'll Sweet Cheeks have?" She winked and I wanted to hurt her.

"He told me not to wait for him."

"Gotcha." And she was off.

•••

I'd only been waiting for twenty minutes when Jones arrived, pretty good for him seeing that punctuality isn't exactly his strong suit. And when he settled in, he was all business.

After he'd ordered I asked what was going on.

"Something happened."

"Good or bad? No, wait, maybe I don't want to know…Do I?"

"It's your friend, Bill."

"Did you hear something?"

Jones scootched closer to me. "He's dead. I called the hospital, and they said he was DOA."

My heart sank. "Aw, what a shame. But you didn't even know the guy so why would you check up on him?"

"In case they have any kind of caller ID, I wanted the casino's number to be on record."

"I still don't get it."

"I'll tell you in the car. Right now I need you to just eat your dinner and act normal."

"Why do I need to act? I am normal, aren't I?"

He rubbed the stubble on his chin. "Just eat."

So I ate my chili as normally as I could. Jones wolfed down his cheeseburger, which was normal for him. We didn't talk much, also normal for us. We've always been more physical than intellectual, if you know what I mean.

• • •

On the way home Jones explained about the tickets. "Guys do it all the time, especially the cleaning crew."

"And it's legal? Even though it's on the floor doesn't mean it's yours. Someone else paid good money for those tickets."

"Listen. A guy comes to my window and places a bet. I give him the ticket. No record of a name, nothing—I just hand him the paper. When the winners come in, it's his responsibility to bring the ticket back to cash it in. Simple."

"How long does he have to do that?"

"A year."

"So why would someone throw away a winning ticket?"

"Oh, they don't do it on purpose," he said. "Mostly it's just because they're careless, or lazy. Maybe they read the numbers wrong, maybe they forget they bet on the horse. Some of these dudes make twenty bets a race, and those bets are spread out over different tracks all around the country. It gets confusing. Half the time they don't even know what they have. Or maybe they've been on a losing streak and a few bucks here and there don't matter."

"But Bill was kinda busy, Jones. Fighting for his life, remember? And what do you do? You rob him?"

"Would I do a thing like that?" He seemed genuinely hurt.

"I hope not."

"After they took him away, Bernie told me to gather up all his stuff and we'd send it over to the hospital. You know, there was his wheelchair and all sorts of crap in that basket. Mostly junk. A bottle of water, magazines, a picture of some woman—"

"I bet that was Eleanor. You didn't throw it away did you?"

"Lacy, what kind of guy do you think I am? Have you ever known me to do anything mean or illegal?"

"No, honey, I'm just upset is all."

"So I was picking up his race form and three tickets fall out. But only one counts. It was a winning Pick Four, with two long shots. I don't know how he figured 'em, but he did. For some reason I put them in my pocket. Weird, huh?"

"And that's when you called the hospital? If he was alive and well you would have taken the money over to him, right?"

"Sure I would have."

By this time we were in front of the apartment. I started to get out of the car but he grabbed my wrist. "Wait a minute. I want to talk here."

"Okay, okay, so how much are these tickets worth anyway?"

"The three of them add up to almost thirty grand."

I didn't know what to say.

"All long shots, can you believe it? The guy sure went out in a blaze of glory. Not that anyone'll ever know."

"And it's not as if he has relatives to give the cash to," I said, thinking about all that dough.

"Right." Jones kissed me. "Now you got the picture."

"So what next?"

"Well, that's what we gotta talk about. There's a catch, but I think I figured a way around it."

•••

We went to Bill's funeral. It was the least we could do. There weren't many people there. Bernie and three of us girls who had served Bill beers, Jones and his friend Sam from the sports book. An old woman who went to church with Eleanor came with her teenage grandson. The funeral director at The Palm Mortuary told me how Bill had made all the arrangements after Eleanor passed away because he wanted to be sure he got the plot next to hers at the cemetery.

When I told Jones what I'd found out he said, "See? The guy didn't need any money then and he sure doesn't need it now."

I did feel better seeing that he'd splurged on a really nice casket for himself—mahogany with a black velvet lining. The casino had sent over flowers and aside from the fact that there were only about a dozen of us, it was very nice as far as funerals go.

•••

Another week passed before I bought the wig, a cute little red number, about three inches shorter than my own hair. Jones was at work and it was my day off so I took time getting dressed. I put on the jeans I'd gotten at Goodwill over a year ago and this old sweater that had shrunk from way too many washings. I worked hard to be sure there was nothing new that could be traced back to me from one of those hidden cameras at the mall or a recent receipt. Jones laughed that I put so much thought into everything but I watch those forensic shows and it's always the tiniest detail that trips up an almost perfect crime.

I checked myself out in front of the bathroom mirror. "Pretty good, if I do say so myself," I told the reflection of the stranger staring back at me. Then I unwrapped the shoes I'd been saving for our vacation and hurried over to Caesar's.

•••

I was nervous waiting my turn in front of Jones's window. He was busy with some blue-haired lady who wanted the whole betting thing explained to her—again. It gave me time to go over my checklist. Fake ID—check. Jones's friend Pete had done a decent job. Tickets—check. The three winners were tucked deep inside my wallet. No jewelry—check. Nothing that would stand out or be recognized. Wig in place—check. My hair was pinned up so tightly under the red stuff that I was getting a headache.

Sweating bullets, I cursed out the reason I stood there like a freakin' idiot. Any employee found gambling at their workplace would be fired on the spot. But Jones and I agreed thirty grand was enough of a reason to take the risk. It would pay off all the debts we've accumulated and still have some left over for a down payment on the motorcycle Jones had been wanting. But when all the dust settled, we'd still need our jobs, as well as references. We weren't talking millions but a fresh start.

"Calm down. It's simple," I could hear Jones's voice in my head. "So you hand over the tickets, and I run them through for verification. When they come up winners and you have to fill out the tax forms, your name is Cheryl Dillon. Don't slip up!"

"Cheryl Dillon," I whispered to myself. "Cheryl Dillon from Tennessee."

I finally made it to the front of the line. Jones looked up at me. "Can I help you?"

He did it so good, like he didn't even know me for real. I tried not to smile. "I want to cash in these tickets."

The guy working next to Jones smiled at me for a second and then went back to the customer he was helping. So far so good. I'd lowered my voice and even added in a little Southern drawl so he wouldn't catch on. I'm no Drew Barrymore, but I felt as though I was getting ready to accept my Oscar until he stopped what he was doing and asked, "Don't I know you?"

"You from Nashville, honey?" I asked. "'Cause if you are…"

"No, sorry."

The preppy in front of him chimed in, "Come on, if you want to get her number do it on your own time. I'm in a hurry here."

That's when I realized all the guy was doing was flirting with me.

"Well, congratulations," Jones said. "You've got some winners here. If you'll wait a minute I'll get my manager."

"Really? I can't believe it, I've never won anything!" Damn, I'm good.

We'd made sure it was Bernie's day off so I felt confident standing there, waiting. And I started to wonder why I had been so worried? People got paid big bucks every day. Now I was one of them, that's all.

I recognized the man as he walked toward me but I didn't know his name. He'd only been at Caesar's for a month or so, and we never seemed to work the same shift. When he was closer I could read his name tag: Dave Mitchell.

"Looks like we have a big winner here," Jones told Dave and handed him the tickets.

"Twenty eight thousand, nine hundred, seventy-five dollars and thirty two cents. Is that right?" he asked Jones, turning the winners over in his hand.

"That's right."

We all stood there for a moment. Jones had this smile plastered across his face; I could see the sweat making his forehead shiny. I smiled and in my best Loretta Lynn voice gushed, "I'm so excited I can hardly stand it."

Dave smiled. "Well, Miss…?"

"Dillon."

"If you'll follow me we'll go back to my office. I'll need you to fill out some tax forms."

"Sure thing." I looked at Jones and gave him a little wink. No one saw, I was sure. The cameras were overhead and even if someone caught it, I could always say I was just being friendly.

A big security guard appeared. Jones had warned me there would be security with that much cash. The three of us walked across the casino floor and down a narrow hall, back to this gawdy office with a cheap desk in the corner.

"Here you go, Miss Dillon," Dave said as he pulled out a chair for me.

"Well, aren't you sweet."

When we were comfortable—the two of us seated and the security guard standing by the door—Dave reached into his desk for the forms. He was five minutes into explaining how to fill them out and where I should sign when he got paged. "Sorry, I'll be right back."

The door had just closed when the guard walked over to me. "Okay, Jugs, what are you doin'?"

"Jugs?"

"It's a compliment. Don't get mad. All the guys call you that. Hell, look at yourself, you could be on a calendar or somethin'. We're always laughin' how a jerk like Jones ever got someone like you." He winked at me.

"Sorry," I said. "My name is Cheryl Dillon."

"Huh, no, if I'm not mistaken, your name is Tracy, Lacy, something like that. But you'll always be Jugs to me, I'd recognize them anywhere." He winked at me.

I cursed my too small sweater.

For the first time I took a good look at him and recognized him. He worked a lot of my shifts. We never spoke but he was always watching me. Jeez, why hadn't Jones thought about the security guard…

"Look—"

"No, you look, we don't have much time." He got closer. "Just keep doin' what you're doin' and ask for cash. Then say you want an escort to your car and you pay me there."

"Pay you?"

"I'm not greedy. Twenty should do fine…Jugs."

•••

So here I am. Still at Caesar's, still on my feet for eight hours, still with Jones. Pete the Creep, the guy who made up the phony ID for Cheryl Dillon, came crawling over to our place like the lowlife he is. He threatened to call the cops if we didn't give him a cut. Jones handed over five grand to shut him up. In spite of the glamour, Vegas is a small town and we can't afford to be banned from the casinos.

Hell, we can't afford much these days. The money we have left isn't enough to pay the bills or get Jones's bike. The possibility of getting caught and having a record keeps me tossing at night.

But the thing that gets me the most is this nickname thing. I can't get past it. We all go along, minding our business, feeling safe, thinking no one notices us much. But really we've been branded—all of us. Oh sure, some of those names are cute and we know what they are and laugh. But some can screw a person up for life.

CHRISTINE MATTHEWS has published over 60 short stories under her real name, Marthayn Pelegrimas, in the Horror, Science Fiction, Fantasy and Western genres. Under her "Christine Matthews" mystery pseudonym she has appeared in such publications as *Alfred Hitchcock's Mystery Magazine, Deadly Allies II, Ellery Queen's Mystery Magazine, Lethal Ladies,* Mickey Spillane's *Vengeance Is Hers, Hollywood And Crime* and *Crime Square.* Her stories have been chosen six times for Ed Gorman and Martin H. Greenberg's Best Of The Year books, the most recent being the 2012 edition.

She is the author of four novels, the short story collection *Gentle Insanities and Other States of Mind,* and the editor of several anthologies. She serves as Membership Chair and Events Coordinator for the Private Eye Writers of America.

THE MOVIE GAME

DICK LOCHTE

Alfred Hitchcock was definitely some kind of gamesman. Weird, but a gamesman. He had it figured that people came to his films with an attitude, like they were on to his game and daring him to show them some moves they weren't expecting. So he gave them really twisted stuff. Like Janet Leigh getting all cut up in the shower. Or the old dude with his eyes pecked out in *The Birds*. Or, later in his career, in *Frenzy*, when censorship loosened up, the killer breaking the fingers of a naked corpse to get at something she'd been clutching when he strangled her.

But the thing is, he didn't take the game that seriously. As he once famously said to an actress who told him she was worried about how to play a scene: "Ingrid, it's only a movie."

I was slumped behind the wheel of my parked taxi, drowsing over a copy of Francois Truffaut's conversations with Hitchcock, taking an easy trip through the great director's head. It was a slow night. Lots of slow nights in Laguna Niguel, but there wasn't anything left for me in L.A. and I was living more or less rent-free in my sister and brother-in-law's converted garage in the Hills, making enough behind the wheel to pop for dinner for them every now and then.

I wasn't fooling myself. I knew I was just treading water and I'd have to swim for shore sooner or later. But on nights like that, nice and balmy, with nothing pressing, treading seemed preferable to making waves and attracting sharks. Not that sharks don't find you anyway.

I was in the middle of Hitchcock's description of "Mary Rose," a ghost story he'd considered filming, when the box started squawking, and between squawks, Manny, back at the garage, was repeating a familiar name. Mine. J.D. Marquette.

Manny has a cleft palate and his words have a slushy, lispy sound that I won't try to duplicate in print. "Fare's at a shopping center on La Paz Road, J.D.," he said, adding the name of the center and the exact address. "He'll be in front of Gregory's Bar. Too smashed to drive home."

"Good job, Manny," I said. "I love ferrying drunks."

I turned off the battery-operated book light, a gift from sis, closed the cover on Hitchcock and Truffaut and went back to work.

That section of La Paz Road is like Mall Town U.S.A. One shopping center right after the other. By light of day, with their too-new, seamless, pastel-colored plaster coats, the structures resemble not very creative film sets, populated by extra players. Those pastels turn circus sinister at night, especially after the shops have started to shutter and most of the extras have headed for home.

A big guy staggering around with his collar open and his tie at half mast and four other males, somewhat more sober, were gathered near the entrance to the center, in front of Gregory's Sports Grill. The drunk was the only one of them who looked as if he'd ever played a sport other than foosball. He was big enough to have been a linebacker in his younger days before he gave it up to booze.

"Glad you made it so fast," a thin guy with glasses said when I got out of the cab. He turned to the ex-linebacker. "Sonny, here's the cab."

"Fuck the cab," the drunk, aka Sonny, said. "Don't need no fuckin' cab."

The thin guy gave me Sonny's address in Monarch Point and a pleading look.

I took a step toward the big man. "Come on, sir," I said, taking his elbow. "Time to go home."

He jerked back, face flushed, eyes red as Dracula's. "Don't you touch me. Who the fuck are you?"

"He's the cabbie, Sonny," one of the other guys said. "Gonna drive you home."

Sonny glared at me for a second, then staggered to the side. "Goin' home, myself," he said. "Doan need help from this long-haired prick."

He did his drunk dance toward the few cars remaining in the parking lot.

The thin guy with glasses ran after him, tried to stop him. Sonny shoved him away, then staggered to a beautiful cream colored Lexus convertible. He paused, doubled up and emptied the contents of his stomach over the rear of that lovely vehicle.

Better it than the interior of my cab.

He wiped his mouth on the sleeve of his jacket, then struggled with the car door, got it open and squeezed behind the wheel.

"Jackass's gonna kill himself," one of the men said.

"Or somebody," I said, as Sonny roared past us, trailing vomit and exhaust.

The thin guy with glasses apologized for wasting my time, gave me two twenties for my trouble. That seemed like a fair enough exchange, even including the long-haired prick comment.

I got back in the taxi, folded the twenties, stuck them in the pocket of my island shirt, and checked in with Manny. "Fare decided to drive himself home," I said.

"Anybody else there need a cab?"

"Doesn't look like it."

"Shit, J.D. We oughta start chargin' these bastards for cancellations," Manny lisped.

"Absolutely," I said. "You got anything else for me?"

"Price of gas, these fuckers should pay."

"Damn straight," I said. "You got another run for me?"

"Naw. It's dead here, J.D."

"Then I think I'll call it a night."

"Wish *I* could," Manny said. "The fuckers."

•••

It wasn't that late. Especially for somebody who gets up around noon. There were a couple of bars near the ocean that still might offer an hour or two of action, such as it was. Probably wouldn't take me that long to blow the forty.

There was no traffic along La Paz. Just the darkness broken by my headlights, the occasional street light and the even more occasional traffic light. I thought about Kelly. There's a scene in *Citizen Kane* where this old guy played by Everett Sloane tells the reporter that when he was a kid he saw this little girl on a ferry, wearing a white dress and carrying a white parasol. He never met her but as he says, "not a month goes by when I don't think of her." That was kind of like me and Kelly Raye. Except that we did meet. And we lived together for a while, until I made a mistake and she discovered I wasn't the kind of uncomplicated, dependable young man she thought I was. Funny thing, I was ready to be that guy. But hell, too little and too late. So she was in L.A. and I was in L.N. And not a day went by when I didn't think of her.

I was recalling her birthday two years ago, when I'd just flown in from New York and…Christ! A blonde suddenly leapt out of the shadows on the left, hopped the neutral ground and ran right in front of my goddamned cab.

I jammed my foot on the brakes and the cab skidded to a stop inches from her, my movie book and lamp sliding to the floor. The seatbelt was digging into my shoulder. My hands were locked around the steering wheel.

The blonde was in my headlights. If I'd been going faster than the limit, she'd have been under the cab. She reached out a hand to touch the cab's hood, maybe to convince herself that it had really stopped.

When I began breathing again, I pried my fingers from the wheel, rolled down the window and shouted, "What the hell, lady?"

"You're the best," she said, walking around the cab. "I wasn't sure you'd stop. I need a ride and here you are…"

She tried to open the rear door and was surprised to find it locked. She frowned, then figured it out. "Aw, crap. You're off duty?"

She was in her late twenties, maybe three or four years younger than me. Dressed California casual, in aqua T-shirt and tight designer jeans. Not spectacular but pretty enough. Straight blonde hair. Tanned skin. Good body. Carrying a big floppy purse the size of a beach bag.

"Please," she said. "I'm desperate. I really fucking need a ride… away from here. It's worth fifty dollars."

"Where to?"

She hesitated, then said, "Ritz Carlton."

Fifty bucks to drive five or six miles. I stared at her, thinking about it.

"A friend drove me here. He…didn't want to leave the party. And he didn't want me to leave, either. Understand?" She looked to our left. I looked there, too, and couldn't see anything but the vague shadowy outline of one of those residential complexes with cookie-cutter buildings, heavy on the redwood and stucco.

"Please. I really need a lift."

She seemed to be suffering from a lack of sincerity, but fifty bucks was fifty bucks, so I pushed the button that unlocked the doors and she hopped in.

Softened by the age-yellowed bandit barrier, her face looked better than pretty. A hometown beauty contest winner whom the movie cameras didn't love quite enough. In some kind of trouble. She ran her fingers through her hair and let out a long sigh. "You're a life-saver," she said. Looking to the left again, she added, "Let's went, Cisco."

I stepped on the gas but kept my eye on her in the rearview as she reached into her big bag. She didn't look like carjacker material, but I stopped breathing until her hand reappeared with a cellular. "On vibrate," she explained, raising the thin slab to her ear. "You clear?" she asked somebody, leaning forward, tensing.

"Great, baby. I'm in a cab," she said. "Right. Amazing luck, huh, a fucking cab out here in the boonies… No. Just worry about yourself. I'm golden." She listened for a few beats, then, "Shit. You think?"

She snapped the phone shut.

"Everything okay?" I asked.

Linking eyes with me in the rear view, she said, "I'm not sure. Look, I, ah, didn't mean to offend. The boonies comment."

"Boonies works for me. This is where Republicans come to die."

"You live here long?"

"About a year."

"Before that?"

"L.A."

"Ah. That makes more sense. The hair. I…" Her cellular must've vibrated again. "Excuse me," she said and took the call. "Yeah?" Her head dropped and her face hardened. "Whooo-hooo. I'm so scared, you dickless wonder. Eat shit and die." She clicked off the phone. Then she lowered her window and threw the phone out into the night.

"Friend?" I said.

She leaned forward, closer to the plastic guard that separated us and asked, "Want another fifty?"

"I'm listening."

"Get off this street as soon as you can, stop and cut the lights."

She looked back to where I'd picked her up, doing a head turn that almost matched Linda Blair's. There was nothing much to see behind us.

In front of us, the neutral ground on the left went on and on. There was a park to our right, separated from the sidewalk by a low white double rail fence. I could see where the fence ended. I goosed the gas and made the turn into the park on two wheels. Then I made another turn into an empty parking area separated from the road by thick foliage. I braked, killed the engine and turned off the lights. "This what you had in mind?" I asked.

"Oh, yeah, baby," she said. "Perfect. But *I could use a Valium the size of a hockey puck.*"

I turned to look at her. "That's a Woody Allen line, right?"

"*Broadway Danny Rose*," she said. She leaned forward and squinted at my license information in moonlight. "J.D. Marquette. So, you're into movies, huh, J.D.?"

"I used to have a job that gave me a lot of free time," I said.

"Me too."

"What's your name?" I asked.

"You can call me Nora. Ah, J.D., we may be here a while."

"Yeah?"

"I am paying you a hundred bucks. This isn't date night."

"Point made, Nora." I reached down, picked my book and reading light from the floor and put them into the cab's glove compartment.

"You even read about movies, huh? Maybe we should play the movie game while we wait. It's my favorite."

"I'm not big on games, Nora."

"Oh, come on. You're good. The way you nailed that Woody Allen, maybe too good. I think we should stick to just one genre. All things considered, maybe crime movies."

"I don't play games," I said. "Why don't you just tell me what's going on here?"

"*Kind of a crazy story with a crazy twist to it.*" She was grinning at me.

"That line's from *Double Indemnity*," I said. "Fred MacMurray. Now, stop with the bullshit and tell me why we're sitting here in the dark."

"I guess that's not asking too much," she said. "My friend…his name is Tom Iverson…we live in the Florida Keys. Tom has this dumb charter boat thing going. But he does other odds and ends, too. So he tells me he's got business here and we'll be spending a few days at the Ritz Carlton, which sounded like a nice kinda getaway. Only when we arrive, he says the business is with this guy I don't really care for, who's like a freak and a half, you know. Anyway, we go to this…hold on. Car coming."

Nora and I sat silent as a black Escalade floated by, heading south.

When it was well past, I said, "Okay for us to leave now?"

"No. Not okay. There'll be more and they know I'm in a cab."

"Who's they?"

"Friends of the asshole."

"So, tell me about the asshole."

"His name is Joey Ziegler. A stunt man. You probably saw him in the last *Batman*, the one with the dead Joker guy. I've never exactly warmed to Joey, because he does stuff like grabbing a tit when Tom isn't looking.

"Anyway, we're bringing Joey a little something Tom picked up in Yucatan, a—"

"A piece of junk worth half a million," I said, completing her sentence.

She smiled. "Oops. You do know movies."

"You were feeding me a remake of *Night Moves*. Not a bad film. Gene Hackman as a private eye. Lousy ending. Tell me what really went on back there, Nora. Right now, or I'm tossing you out of the fucking cab."

"Okay, this is the truth, J.D. Wait…Another car."

This one was a white Escalade. Moving at about 15 mph. Flashlight beams shot out of its open windows, scanning the foliage on both sides of the road. I didn't think they could see any part of the cab.

"Maybe we should move further back in the park," I said when they'd passed.

"Okay. But don't turn on the lights."

I started the engine, backed onto the lane and began creeping deeper into the park guided by moon glow. We passed a golf course and eventually, a building in darkness that I assumed was some sort of club house. The lane made a fork, one section continuing on, the other circling the building to a small lot. I took the latter, moving the cab as close to the rear of the building as I could.

"Better," she said. "Maybe we'll make it through the night."

"You were about to tell me the truth."

"Right. My friend John and I have been collecting a few dead presidents selling heroin to Brentwood and Beverly Hills assholes who like to impress their party guests with a special after dinner treat."

"Where do you get the product?"

"John has a friend who's an Army sergeant in…"

She stopped talking because I was shaking my head. "Goddammit. You just can't help yourself, can you?"

"What?" She pretended to be sincerely confused.

"*Who'll Stop the Rain?* Michael Moriarty and Tuesday Weld, with Nick Nolte as the soldier. Not as good as the book. Get out of my cab. I'm finished."

"No, baby. I'll say when you're finished." I didn't need much moonlight to see the huge gun she pulled from her bag.

"I wouldn't put too much faith in this cheap bandit shield," she said, tapping the barrel of the gun against the plastic that separated us. "I mean, maybe it might stop a bullet, but…*being this is a .44 Magnum, the most powerful handgun in the world and would blow your head clean off, you've got to ask yourself one question: Do I feel lucky?*'"

"Clint Eastwood in *Dirty Harry*," I said, my mouth suddenly as dry as Clint's delivery. What Nora was holding was a Smith & Wesson Magnum, all right. But it was a 500, bigger and badder than the one in the movie. Enough to take out the bandit shield, me and the front of the cab.

"Relax, J.D.," she said. "I got no reason to shoot you, long as you behave. In fact, I'm doing you a favor. If you drove out of here right now, with or without me, you'd be a dead man. The difference is: if we're together when they find us, they'll probably just shoot us both. But if I'm not with you, they'll beat you to death trying to find out where you left me."

"Why do they want you? Be straight with me, Nora. No more Yucatan pottery or drugs, huh?"

"My partner Jed and I…got into a situation back there."

"What kind of situation?"

"That doesn't matter now," she said. "It happened. We pissed off the wrong guys, the kind who get real Biblical when it comes to payback."

"What happened to your partner?"

"He's dead. That call I got was from some zombie, telling me he'd just shot Jed in the face. Like that's supposed to freak me out. Fuck them."

If she wasn't freaked, she was either delusional or suicidal.

Two Escalades full of homicidal assholes out for revenge. Not exactly an everyday occurrence in Orange County. I knew of only one local who might have that kind of entourage, a former Vegas "businessman" who'd retired to the peace and quiet of Laguna Niguel.

"What did you and Jed do to get on the bad side of Caesar Berlucci?" I asked.

"Bad side?" She gave me a nasty smile. "Jed blew that fat wop right out of his Guccis."

"He killed Berlucci? Why would anybody do something that stupid?"

She stopped smiling and tensed. For a second, I thought she was going to use that giant gun. Then she slumped again and I let out the breath I'd been holding.

"It's what we were paid to do," she said.

"Paid by whom?"

"Who the fuck knows? Or cares? The contract comes in. You do the job. Money is money."

"It couldn't have been easy, getting that close to the old man," I said.

"Jed had a golden tongue. Talked us into the compound, won the old bastard over. We would've made it away clean, but Jed got greedy." For a second her eyes shifted toward her big bag, then back at me.

"What went wrong?" I asked.

"Shit happens," she said. "And now, we got goombas on our ass."

Yes we did. Two Escalades full, prowling around out there looking for a cab. They'd find out she hadn't made it to the hotel. They would double back and go over the route again. Eventually they'd check out the park and find us.

When they did, Nora, with her ridiculous gigantic gun, which held only five rounds, assuming she hadn't used one or two on Berlucci, would be of no real help. On the other hand, that ridiculous gigantic gun with its five or four or three bullets was more than enough to keep me trapped.

"Okay, what now?" I asked her, while trying to come up with my own answer.

"We wait until morning and people are going to work and there'll be traffic and other cabs on the street. Then we head to L.A. And I pay you for your trouble. And we say goodbye, or…"

"Or what?"

"Or we keep going to Mexico and see how much fun we can get into. I've got…some money set aside back at the apartment."

"We've got a long night before we start thinking about fun," I said.

"We could think about it a little," Nora said.

"Not with me up here and you back there."

"Come on back. It's nice and comfy."

"What if we have to leave in a hurry?" I asked. "Be less dangerous to do our thinking up here."

"Sometimes danger adds a little something, but I suppose you're right."

Nora had been so sloppy at her chosen profession that I'd hoped she might change her mind about the gun and put it away. But she kept it pointed in my direction while she got out of the car and joined me on the front seat.

She sat facing me, her back against the door.

She kicked off her sandals, drew her left leg up and slid it forward until her toes found wiggle room between my back and the car seat. She rested her right leg across my thighs.

"Is the gun necessary?" I asked.

"For some reason, I think so," she said. "But we can still fool around."

"Not with a gun in my face," I said. "It's much too distracting."

"Then I guess we'll just have to play the movie game instead," Nora said.

"Fun's better than games," I said.

"The gun stays."

I shrugged. "Okay. Games. *It's a nice day for murder.*"

"Cute," Nora said. "But easy. James Cagney. *Angels with Dirty Faces*. Here's one for you: *I guess I've done murder. I won't think about that now.*"

"It's the next line that's the giveaway," I said. "*I'll think about it tomorrow.* Vivien Leigh in *Gone with the Wind*." I lowered my hand to her left leg and began rubbing it slowly. "Try this one. *If you're going to murder me…don't make it look like something else.*"

Nora frowned. Concentrating. I moved my hand another inch or so up her leg. She said, "I don't know the quote."

"*The Naked Spur.* Robert Ryan."

"A western? Shit, that's not fair. I don't know westerns." She was furious, aiming the weapon at my stomach with both hands. She was crazy enough to use it and, I had no doubt, she would eventually. Here. In L.A. or Mexico.

"I didn't complain about *Gone with the Wind*," I said softly.

"That's 'cause you knew it," she said, pouting. "Give me another and keep it on topic."

I decided to ease the tension with something she was sure to recognize. "*Have you ever done it in an elevator?*"

She grinned. "Glenn Close in *Fatal Attraction*." Happy again, maybe picking up the sexy-psychotic vibe of that movie, she wiggled a little closer. She said, "Here's one from the heart: *It's the first time I've tasted women. They're rather good*."

I pretended to be puzzled, but in my mind I saw 007 after having just sucked a poisonous spine fish from the flesh of the beautiful Domino. "I give," I said.

She was as gleeful as a little girl. "Sean Connery in *Thunderball*. I can't believe you didn't know that one."

I was leaning forward, my fingers brushing the inside of her thigh. "I didn't see the movie. Where did he…taste her?" I asked.

Nora gave me a long look. But she didn't lower the gun. "Your turn," she said. "And this time, make it hard."

"That sounds like a James Bond quote, too," I said.

She laughed. "Silly. I meant the movie reference."

"Okay," I said, sliding a little closer. "But instead of a quote, I'll give you a story. Our hero grows up in the country, leading a good, clean, healthy life until it's time for him to go to a state college. There, on a Marine ROTC firing range, he discovers that the hunting skills he took for granted back home are pretty damned remarkable.

Enough for him to attract the attention of a government agency that dearly needs people who know how to use guns."

"I think I know the movie," she said, "but go on. And don't stop this." She lowered one hand to move mine further up her thigh.

"The agency frees him from his ROTC obligation and agrees to pay his tuition and give him spending money and a car and, in return, he agrees to work for them for four years after he graduates."

"And he becomes a sniper in Viet Nam?" Nora asked.

"Not exactly. Not in Viet Nam. But his work is government-sanctioned."

"Like James Bond."

"Yes. But not James Bond," I said.

"Got it. Charles Bronson in *The Mechanic*."

"No. The hero of my story is younger than Bronson. And he's based in Los Angeles, pretending to be an accountant for an independent film studio that the government actually owns. And the four years turn into eight. And, about then, he meets this beautiful, wonderful woman and –"

"*The Specialist*, with Sly Stallone and Sharon Stone."

"Let me finish," I said. "I'll make it short. He falls in love. They move in together. He decides to quit the agency, but before he can, she discovers...that he's been lying to her, that he's a worthless, self-loathing, piece-of-shit government-sanctioned homicidal sociopath."

"I'm still not sure what movie you're talking about," she said. Then, staring at me, she asked. "Are you crying? Why the hell are you crying?"

"Because life is not a movie, you stupid bitch," I said, bringing my hand up fast off her thigh and shoving her hands and the big heavy Magnum into her face before she could even consider pulling the trigger. Blood flowed from her broken nose. I had the gun by then and banged it against her head twice before she went to sleep.

•••

"I'm in a situation, Henry."

"Who's...Jimmy D? Zat you?"

"It's me," I said into my cellular. "Sorry to wake you, but I wasn't sure who else to call."

"No. It's okay." He started hacking and coughing. I heard his wife mumbling something in the background, then him telling her to go back to sleep, that it was business. "Long time between calls, Jimmy. What's the hap?"

I filled him in on everything that had taken place in the last hour or so. He replied by laughing.

"It's not funny, Henry."

"Depends on where you're sitting. The image of you, out in your peaceful, laid-back little town, stuck in the middle of a park with an unconscious hitwoman, waiting for morning or a bunch of spaghetti-head yo-yos with guns, whichever comes first…it is to laugh, amigo."

"Can you do anything?" I asked. "If not, I'm going to try my luck driving out of here. I'll unload the blonde somewhere along the road."

"If they saw her get into your cab, Jimmy, they got the name and the plate and there's nowhere you can run. Gimme your number and sit tight."

Henry had been my handler. In his fifties, five-seven, balding, vaguely pear shaped, totally without conscience, but a straight-shooter and a father figure for all of that. He called back in twenty minutes. "I just spoke with a cretin named Morelli. He says he knows all about you, but he's the kind of braying asshole who, if he knew your name or even the cab company, he'd have told me just to prove how bright he is. In any case, he says he's willing to forget about you as long as he gets the eighty grand taken from Berlucci's safe. And he wants the woman, of course. You got the money, right?"

"Yeah." I had already investigated Nora's bag. It was loaded with banded hundreds. "I imagine it's the full eighty. I'm not going to count it."

"Okay, here's the play. As soon as we hang up, I call Morelli with your exact location. He wants you to leave the broad and the loot right where you are and drive away. Do not look back."

"You sure they'll let me just drive away?"

"You can never be sure, Jimmy. Not when you're dealing with rabid dogs. My guess is they don't want Uncle Sam on their ass. That's the most assurance I can give you."

"Thank you, Henry."

"My pleasure."

The blood from Nora's broken nose had dried on her mouth and chin. She looked like she might be waking up soon. I'd have to hit her again.

"Henry, I'm ready to come back."

"Miss the *la vita dolce*, huh?"

"Something like that," I said.

"I'll be waiting with open arms, kid."

I lifted the blonde out of the cab and placed her on the asphalt behind the clubhouse. I put the bag and the money right next to her.

Then I got into the cab. With the blonde's Magnum on the passenger seat, I left the park and turned right on La Paz. The only vehicle I saw in either direction was an old Chevy truck heading north. I passed it heading south.

But not too far south, maybe half a mile down La Paz to the first cross-street, Kings Road, where I turned right into a block full of middle-class homes. I maneuvered the cab between two sedans parked for the night.

The blonde's Magnum didn't smell as if it had been used, but it held only four shells. Better than bare hands. With the weapon dragging down my Levi's under my shirt, I worked my way back through the park.

•••

They were a noisy bunch. Slamming car doors. Cursing. I was careful moving up behind a tree, Magnum drawn, for a view of the scene at the rear of the golf club building. Six men had come in three cars. The Escalades and a sweet yellow Jaguar convertible with the top down.

I wanted a look at Morelli and his buddies. I figured it was worth the risk to be able to recognize the bozos if they really did have a line on me and decided to do something about it. I had my night vision by then and I studied them as well as I could while they dragged Nora's dead partner, Jed, from the black Escalade.

The guy I picked as Morelli was poking through Nora's bag. Apparently satisfied with its contents, he tossed it into the white Escalade. He was big, bald, almost Mongolian-looking with a droopy mustache, wearing black, long-sleeve shirt and pants, with some kind of jewelry around his neck that caught the moonlight. The others were in suits. I noted their hair styles, facial structures, body movement as they did the heavy lifting—the departed Jed went behind the wheel of the Jaguar, the unconscious Nora onto the passenger seat.

I wasn't sure what the plan was, but I figured that last knockout blow I'd delivered to Nora had been a mercy.

The bald guy with the mustache was definitely Morelli. He said something that was almost too guttural to be Italian, and while the others grabbed what looked like short barrel Beretta rifles from the rear of the black Escalade, he moved to Nora.

He rattled off something else in Italian and his boys laughed. He shook Nora until she awoke with a groan. Her hand went to her head wound. My bad.

Morelli took several steps back, away from the Jaguar.

Nora saw him. I heard her say, "Huh?"

He pointed to her dead partner. She looked at Jed, then turned back to Morelli. "You scum-sucking Wop pig!" she screamed, changing the Brando insult from *One-Eyed Jacks* just a bit to fit the situation.

Morelli waited for her to throw open the Jaguar's door and take one step toward him, her hands poised like claws. He shouted "*Sparare*!" And his men *sparared*, big time. Bullets ripped into Nora, the beautiful car, the corpse of her dead partner.

I'd thought they were noisy before. Now, they were firing off a hundred rounds or so in the dead of night, in the sleepy little town of Laguna Niguel. Maybe they knew precisely how long it would take the Orange County Sheriff's Department to get somebody out there to investigate. More likely they simply didn't give a shit who heard them. They wanted to call attention to the fact that it wasn't a good idea to fuck with them.

Morelli didn't strike me as the kind of man who'd just forget about a cab driver who'd made the mistake of stopping to pick up a good-looking blonde. There wasn't much I could do about that at the moment. Maybe if I'd had a simple old Springfield, the kind I grew up with, and enough ammo and time, I might have put the whole thing to bed that night. Though in all honesty I'd never tried to go six for six, even when I was at the top of my game.

So I just stood there and watched them pile into the Escalades and drive away.

I could hear sirens in the distance.

Time to run. But I took one last look at the bloody, bullet-ridden couple and said, not just to myself, "Faye Dunaway, Warren Beatty. *Bonnie and Clyde*."

DICK LOCHTE is the author of many popular crime novels including *Sleeping Dog* which won the Nero Wolfe Award, was nominated for the Edgar, the Shamus and the Anthony, and was named one of the 100 Favorite Mysteries of the Century by the Independent Booksellers Association. His most recent books are the noir thriller, *Blues In The Night* and the comedy-mystery, *The Talk Show Murders* (co-authored by the *Today Show*'s Al Roker). He has co-authored four popular legal thrillers with attorney Christopher Darden and has written screenplays for such actors as Jodie Foster, Martin Sheen and Roger Moore. An award-winning theater critic, Lochte lives in Southern California.

SLEEP, CREEP, LEAP

PATRICIA ABBOT

LILLIAN GILLESPIE'S DOWNSTAIRS LIGHTS HAD BURNED FOR AT least seventy-two hours when her neighbor, Bob Mason, walked up to her front door. The cat's eyes glittered hostilely and it hissed when he put his eyes up to the mail slot. Bob stuck out his tongue, inadvertently allowing the metal door to slam on it. There was snow on the ground, and his shoes and pants' bottoms got soaked circling the house. He finally peered in through the one window he could see in from the back porch. Nothing. They'd been neighbors for more than ten years, but he didn't know Lillian's phone number. He'd agreed to keep a spare key after she locked herself out once, but couldn't warm up to the idea of using it now. Who knew what he'd find inside?

Reluctantly, he called the cops, returning to Lillian's door to wait for them. The two officers, neither seeming much more eager than Bob to enter the house, found Lillian sitting in front of the TV, a moldering salad on her lap tray. She was sixty-one according to the driver's license in her purse, over a decade younger than Bob. Standing outside in the dark, his wet pants' legs icing up, he answered questions as tersely as possible, wanting only to return home. "Did you know her at all?" the female officer finally asked, slapping her notebook shut and shining a flashlight straight into his eyes. "Ten years next door and you don't know where she worked? Where her children live?"

•••

"Her pacemaker malfunctioned," Lillian's daughter in from Cleveland told him a day later. "You probably guessed it."

He nodded, although he'd no idea Lillian had heart trouble. She'd seemed active enough, zipping in and out of her garage in her little Cruiser.

"You'll probably see a realtor and some painters and plumbers around here in a few days." She smiled uneasily at his silence. "Just so you don't think the place is being robbed. Mother appreciated your neighborliness, Mr. Mason," she said at last. He was doubtful of this. Lillian and he had barely had a conversation beyond exchanging pleasantries, wrongly delivered mail, and that key over the years. The daughter handed him a card with her phone number and email address before she left. He considered tossing it in the trash but placed it in his "Miscellaneous" file folder instead. His involvement with the Gillespie women was over as far as he was concerned.

•••

The house was on the market fourteen months. Would-be buyers trickled down to none in a short time. His street was patently undesirable, located two blocks from a major freeway. The houses were modest, sided in cheap vinyl and measuring less than a thousand square feet. The street needed paving and was unlikely to get it, and boarded-up windows were becoming commonplace. A squatter had recently been evicted a block away. This had been a respectable street ten years ago. Now it was on the circuit for cars with enhanced music systems. The possibility of late night drug deals had been raised at a neighborhood watch meeting a few months back.

Twenty-three feet lay between Bob's house and the one next door. He planted a row of hydrangea in the area between the houses the next summer, just inside his property line. He double dug the soil, peppering it with chemicals to make the flowers bloom blue. Even though it was the "sleep" year for the plants, they made a respectable showing. There was not a single plant in the yard next door except for some badly overgrown yews. He was tempted to divide a few of his lilies or hostas and plant them next door, but he let it be.

•••

Wendy Larsen moved in the next winter. A divorcee, he figured, as he peered at her through an upstairs window. She was standing on the sidewalk in front of her house, directing the moving men. The movers couldn't make it past her without making a slightly off-color remark or sneaking a look. Despite the cold, Bob raised his window just high enough to hear them. Laughing at what they said from time to time, the woman didn't seem to mind their flirtatious remarks. Twice she went inside to grab a cold beer for the men despite the frigid temperatures. The three of them sat, half-reclining on the ramp, tossing back their Miller Lights. When it began to grow dark, the men had to hustle to finish the job.

Wendy chose the room across from his bath as a bedroom and often forgot to close the curtains at nights. Bob wasn't sure why. He never saw more than a flash of bare skin, but watching for that moment passed the time. She got home from her shift at some downtown restaurant about ten most nights and was usually in bed by eleven. He began waiting for her light to go out before going to bed—it became a ritual.

•••

Wendy wasn't in the house more than a week before she knocked at Bob's door. He peered out, and despite his aversion to getting involved, opened the door a crack. "I wonder if you could give me a jump. Car won't start." Her voice was throaty, warm. She waved an arm in the general direction of the street outside her house where an old green Saturn sat. She stamped her feet. "Lord, it's a cold one."

"Got jumper cables?" He'd bet a million bucks she didn't.

"My ex must have gotten them in the settlement." She laughed. "No, not really. Doubt we ever had 'em. He was the kinda guy who never expected stuff like this to happen." She stamped her feet again, probably assuming he'd invite her inside. "Thought you might have some," she finally said when he didn't respond. "Mr. Mason, right? Saw your name on a piece of mail." She practically had her foot in his door. He nodded, pushed by her, and hurried back to his garage, coatless. She followed.

"Boy, you keep a neat garage," she said, looking around. Every tool in Bob's garage had its own peg—even implements like a barn fork and a flashlight. A series of tightly closed bins contained tools that wouldn't hang from a hook. He hated clutter, mess. Soil, fertilizer, and such were double-bagged and tightly tied. He had a dread of walking in and finding vermin.

"Most of the stuff's for gardening," he said, taking the cables from his car trunk. His words came out hoarsely and he wondered when the last time he'd spoken to someone had been. "When the ground warms up, I'll be outside getting the yard into shape." He didn't know why he was telling her this. From the length of her fingernails and the height of her heels, it was unlikely she did much manual labor. He couldn't picture her on her knees pulling weeds or handling a pair of hedge trimmers.

"Well, you keep the place real nice, Bob. Some men garden or cook, but I never met one who liked to clean before." He started to correct her, to say he didn't like cleaning per se—but let it go.

"I ought to warn you; I don't bother much with gardening," she continued. "Anyway, I might buy a dog and he'd probably tear up any flowers. You know puppies." He shrugged noncommittally, although the idea of a dog worried him.

The driveway was icy, but she negotiated it in heels without a slip as he slowly backed the Ford out. Her hair was twisted into some complicated design, a silver butterfly holding it in place. He didn't know what to call the style, but women had worn their hair like that when he was young.

She got into her car when he had the cables hooked up—inadvertently, he thought—giving him a quick flash of thigh. Thinner than he liked, but nice. "I don't feel right living here alone. A good guard dog might help." When he didn't respond, she rolled her window down further and said, "I guess you're not much of a dog lover, huh? Neither was my ex." She paused, thinking. "It was one of the few good things—after the divorce came through. I thought to myself that I could finally have a dog."

He got her car started, put the cables and truck away and went back inside his house. It took some time for his pulse to stop racing though he held his wrists under the hot water tap, a trick his father taught him. "A woman will do that to you," the old man explained.

"Warm water calms things down when that feeling you got ain't gonna do you no good."

•••

The puppy was outside the next week. She'd tied him to a post on her porch and he ran back and forth between the two houses on his long leash, barking in a tiny voice. The sound was slight, almost a squeak, but when the dog was full-grown, it'd probably sound deafening, and more than that—grating, nerve-wracking. A mixed-breed puppy, he didn't look like a dog who'd turn out to be small either. But she wouldn't pick something small for a guard dog.

Bob was not one for noise, hardly even listened to music. It was one of the issues that drove his once-upon-a-time wife, Edna, crazy. "What kind of person doesn't like some kind of music?" she asked him back then, whirling the radio dial this way and that while he shook his head. It was hard to explain it, but music was mostly noise to him, noise that played in his head for hours after hearing it. "I've heard of being tone deaf, but it's something else with you," she said, finally taking her vast collection of albums to another state.

"Cute, huh?" Wendy said now, coming out on the porch and down her steps. A large man followed her—the kind of man who looked like kicking a dog was not out of the question for him. His head was shaved, and he wore an old army jacket with the sleeves rolled up despite the cold. There was a tattoo on his neck and one on each arm. Cryptic symbols done in murky ink. Right off the bat, Bob hated him, knowing his type of man. "Dog's named Georgie. And this here's Buck," Wendy said, waving an arm at her companions and grinning.

Ignoring the introductions, Bob turned toward Wendy and said, "My hydrangeas will be blooming in a few months." He nodded toward the spot where the dog was taking a piss. The hydrangea plants didn't look like much yet, but come late June they'd bloom for six weeks or more. It was the creep year. Sleep, creep, leap, an old gardening adage.

Not getting it, Wendy nodded, saying, "That'll be nice. I bet I can see that patch from my kitchen window. What color are they? I always did like yellow flowers."

The man with her—Buck—laughed. "Don't you get it, Wen? He's telling you to keep your damned dog away from his flowers. Gardeners don't much like dogs trampling through their flowerbeds. Or taking a leak on them either." He turned to Bob. "I guess you know exactly where your property ends, right? Got some paper spells it out tucked in a drawer?"

The two men looked at each other for a few seconds. Then Bob looked over at Wendy and said, "Hydrangeas come in pink, blue, or white. Once in a while, you see one almost red."

The man laughed again. His laugh sounded even less happy. "Guess you'll have to live with pink, blue or white then, Wen. If you want to look at something yellow, you'll have to plant it yourself. I'm sure old Bob here can tell you which flowers to buy."

"Mine are blue," Bob said needlessly. They both looked at him blankly. "My hydrangeas have blue flowers." Then he turned and walked around to the back of his house where his cold frames needed a few more nails knocked into them. He split the first piece of wood from the force of the hammer and threw it aside disgustedly.

That man—Buck—had thirty pounds and thirty years on him. He remembered a time when no man would've spoken to him like that. A time when he could lift heavy equipment all day and think nothing of it. When he could handle hot, sharp, and dangerous machinery, barely needing gloves. He looked at his hands now. Gardener's hands and gardener's muscles. Negligible. He was an old man. No one would ever lose sleep over him again.

After dark, Bob watched Wendy Larsen and the man make love from his bathroom window. At least he imagined that's what was going on from the shadows thrown up. Every so often a sailboat seemed to glide across her wall. She must own one of those rotating lamps with cut-out shades that made shadows. A mood-maker, he'd heard them called. He opened the window and heard a groan or two, although it could have been the wind or the branches on the oak tree.

• • •

Things got busy as March turned into April and finally May. It was hectic in Michigan gardens come May. Everything had to be planted in a few short weeks. Wendy Larsen was often outside in the mornings before she left for work, Georgie sniffing around beside her. When Bob came upon her one day, she waved her cigarette in the air and said, "Buck doesn't like smoke in the house. Kind of a health nut." She frowned briefly and added, "In his own way, at least."

"It's your house, isn't it? Your rules?" Bob said before he could stop himself. He thought he saw a bruise on her neck, but maybe it was a love bite. Her eyes looked reddish, too.

"Yeah, but he's worth smoking outside for, Buck is. Probably keeps my smoking down. The price of it..." Hearing some sound behind her, she turned calling, "Georgie!" The dog came swinging around the house, hardly a pup at all now. He barked with the volume Bob had expected, too. "I had one of those what-d ya-call-it fences put in to keep Georgie from running into the street," Wendy explained. "Those invisible ones?" she added when he looked at her blankly. "You know."

He remembered seeing signs on neighborhood lawns. "But not *between* the houses," he said, looking down at the dog who was pissing on the flowerbed again. She looked at him blankly. "They didn't install a fence along here." He drew a line in the air.

Wendy flipped her cigarette, not even putting it out first. "You don't have to worry about Georgie, Bob," she said, misunderstanding. "One good shock and he's never gone near the street again. Georgie's no hero."

"Good, good," Bob said, giving up.

"I'm gonna get a collar for Buck soon, too," she added. "Wonder what voltage it'd take to keep him off the street."

•••

Every day or two that spring and summer, Bob made a circuit of the area, collecting more than a dozen butts each time. Using a shovel, he picked up dog feces that had scorched his lawn in several spots. Beer cans often sat on the fence posts in the backyard and litter of all sorts blew from her yard into his. Wendy's place seemed to be a magnet for refuse. She was simply oblivious to such things. Sometimes she even followed along, never connecting the dots. Georgie, wisely perhaps, settled into the deep shade that gathered between the two houses and watched.

Bob's windows were open nearly all the time by June, and he could both see and hear Buck, over there two or three nights a week. Sitting on her porch like he owned it, popping the tops on beers and yelling for her to bring him another one before he finished the last, hollering at the dog, listening to the Tigers' games on his boom box. Buck's nearly nonstop laugh was mean; Bob understood that laugh.

He usually remained inside on those evenings, wrestling with the idea he was being intimidated. He concluded that he was and would have to live with it.

•••

The first time he heard Wendy scream, he was on the other side of the house watching *The Killers.* Initially, he thought the scream was coming from the throat of Ava Gardner. But when the movie ended and he heard it again, he got up and went upstairs into his bathroom, trying to remember what a scream of passion sounded like as opposed to a scream of pain or fear. The house was dark, but Georgie was barking in some downstairs room. The barking was so cyclical, Bob wondered if the dog had been shut in. His stomach knotted. A door slammed, a thud or two followed, and then something fell and broke—probably a lamp. But there were no more screams. He watched for Wendy the next day and the one after, but didn't catch her. He wondered if she was avoiding him but decided that was a silly idea; she barely knew he existed.

The third day, Wendy and the dog were in the backyard again. He leaned over the fence and said hello. "Hi, Bob," she said, her voice subdued. She was sitting on a rotted picnic bench, her knees tucked up under her chin. Her cut-off jeans were streaked with paint and a short, ruffled pink blouse showed off her tanned middle. She waved a can of beer at him although it was only noon. "Come on over."

"Been okay?" he asked, surprising himself. He couldn't remember the last time he'd asked anyone such a thing. She looked so damned pathetic. Her yard was more untidy than ever. A row of brown plastic bags, some untied, lined the side of her garage. She must have missed several weeks of trash collection. His stomach turned at the thought of mice, and perhaps worse, running around the place at night. A messy yard was like a beacon for possums, raccoons, mice, stray cats.

"Sure, sure," she said. Then she paused. "Buck and me broke it off a few nights back." She looked down at the dog. "We've been keeping to ourselves. Not that Georgie was ever too fond of Buck. Or vice versa."

Georgie and Bob might have their differences on proper lawn etiquette, but on the subject of Buck, they apparently agreed. Bob took a deep breath. "Maybe it's a good thing. He always seemed kind of…mean. You know."

"Buck? Nah. Just has a temper. Seems most men do—or at least around me." She looked at Bob closely. "I bet you heard us fighting the other night." She waited for a response and when she got none, went on. "Well, so what. He's gone now anyway."

"What do you want a man like that for?" His voice was stiff, scolding. Bob couldn't believe he was saying these things. "A man who hits women," he added, chin out. He didn't know this for certain, but he knew he'd been that kind of man once himself. Edna had had the good sense to run away, packing her car up while he slept.

"Buck doesn't—" she started to say—when another voice broke in.

"Are you talking about me, you jackass?" They both turned, shocked. Buck stood in Wendy's driveway. "Are you giving Wendy advice about me?" His hands curled into fists as he spoke. "Do you hear me, old man? Are you saying I hit her? Smacked her around?" Buck took several steps forward. The dog began to growl. Buck gave Georgie a quick glance, and the dog fell silent. "What the hell do you know about it? Have you been peeping in the windows, getting your jollies from watching us?"

Bob sought out Wendy's eyes, but they were focused on a worn patch of grass. "Course not. None of my business," Bob said, kicking at an old piece of hose.

"You got that right, old man. And you better remember that if you want to be turning over that dirt in your yard next spring. Stick your nose where it don't belong again, and it'll be dirt turning over on you."

"You go on home now, Bob," Wendy said, finally looking up and motioning to him with her hands. She was actually chasing him away instead of Buck. "Buck and me, we gotta talk." She turned around.

•••

He'd been dismissed. Deliberately closing the windows facing Wendy's house despite the heat, Bob put on the TV. The History Channel was showing a documentary about Albert Speer. He watched it with a small degree of absorption, followed by a bad Bette Davis movie, finally falling asleep in the chair, something he rarely did. But then, he seldom watched three consecutive hours of television. Walking stiffly up the stairs to his room sometime after one, he heard nothing outside except a gentle rain. Good, his flowers needed it. His sleep was fitful due to all the dozing he'd done. He got up at four AM and threw his bedroom window open. The rain had stopped, and he watched as Buck got into his truck and drove away.

•••

"You seeing him again then?" Bob was standing in the center of her backyard for the first time. She'd just dragged out another bag of trash to join the procession next to the garage. A butt hung from her lips. Wearing a pair of mules, she clopped back across the concrete. It was the clop-clop that had drawn him over. He'd thought of nothing except Wendy, his ears pricked for any sound of her outside or for a return of that truck.

She shook her head. "I told him not to come back. It's over." Her voice was shaking despite the firmness of her words.

"Think he'll listen?"

A shrug. "I know how to take care of myself. I got rid of my ex, didn't I?" She was unconvincing.

"Buck may be more persistent. Was your ex built like a sixteen-wheeler?"

She rolled her eyes, dropped the butt, and stomped on it with her foot. "Look, Bob, you gotta keep out of this. What you said to me last night—when he heard us talking out here—it just made him madder. You can't fool around with a guy like Buck. He takes special handling."

"And *you* know how to do that?" Her nod turned into another shrug. He made a derisive sound with his tongue, walked over to an open trash bag, and knotted it. "You're gonna get mice, you know. Maybe rats if you aren't careful." He pulled a cloth out of his pocket, wiped his hands, and looked up at her.

"I'm not the careful type—in case you don't know that yet. You'll just have to believe I can take care of myself with this. I doubt Buck'll be back anyway. It's over," she repeated. There was still some hesitation in her voice.

"Don't you get it? Only Buck gets to say when it's over."

"I gotta go," she said, walking back toward the house. "Put it out of your head. It'll just make things worse if he comes around and sees you here. I know what to do." But he knew she didn't.

•••

He tried to take Wendy's advice, to go about his business and keep his eyes and ears where they belonged. But two nights later, Georgie began barking in the same hysterical way after the radio suddenly came on. Some sort of hip-hop station, blaring music. It sounded like music you might play to muffle other noises, music that would blend in with the traffic on his street.

Pacing the floor until he couldn't stand it, Bob picked up the phone. He'd looked up her phone number a few days before when the new telephone book arrived. Since then he'd glanced at the yellow Post-it so many times he had it memorized. He dialed it now and let it ring till the machine came on. Her voice sounded chirpy, inviting—he hadn't heard her sound like that in a long time. There'd be no point in leaving a message. What would he say? *Tell me you're safe, Wendy. Tell me Buck isn't around.* He tried three more times, getting the same useless message before slamming the receiver down.

He had to know what was going on in that house. Creeping outside, he circled it. Wendy's car was in the driveway, but there was no sign of Buck's truck. Buck could've parked down the street, of course, not wanting anyone, especially that old turd, Bob Mason, to see it. That's what Bob would've done. Bob/Buck would have burst in unexpectedly, taking Wendy by surprise, catching her off-guard. He could almost remember such an event. Remember what it felt like, how scared Edna had been. Or perhaps he'd dreamed it during one of the thousands of nights since she left.

There were very few lights on in the house: the kitchen's overhead fluorescent and a low-wattage bulb upstairs in Wendy's bedroom. He threw a stone or two at her window from the grass, hitting the siding with two loud clinks. Nothing. As he watched, the white curtains in her bedroom window turned themselves inside out, caught in some strong gusts of wind. Inside, Georgie was quiet, but the music played on, wailing tunes about women who'd done their men wrong. Why was that music playing? Wendy usually played soft rock.

Bob waited as long as he could. Then knowing a woman like Wendy wouldn't have bothered to change the lock on her door, he went home and got the key Lillian had given him years ago. Hurrying, he looked around the living room for some sort of protection to take with him, finally grabbing a shovel from the rack of fireplace tools. Minutes later he was stealthily opening her front door.

Georgie came trotting over at once, looking relieved to see him if such a thing was possible. The radio continued to blare its gloomy, percussive tunes. He peeked into the kitchen and saw a lightweight radio lying on its side on the floor. Had Buck knocked it there climbing in through the window? Or was it a casualty of the strong winds? Nothing else seemed amiss.

As he stumbled through the dark of the unfamiliar living room, the shovel clutched in his hand, the dog followed at his heels. After bumping his knee on a piece of low furniture and overturning a wastepaper basket, he ended up crawling up the stairs on his hands and knees, trying to avoid creaks, nearly impossible on an old wooden stairway he'd never climbed before.

Reaching the upstairs hallway, he looked into the spare bedroom. It was dark and appeared vacant except for some sealed boxes and a spare chair. The bathroom was empty, too. Only a nightlight lit it.

A thin ray of light shone from under the closed third door. Wendy's room. A sort of keening sound seemed to seep out for a few seconds. But then it stopped. Had he imagined it? What could she be doing in there? As he put his ear to the wood, leaning into it to hear better, the door was suddenly yanked open, and Wendy, standing in the doorway fired a gun straight into Bob's chest. "I told you to keep away from me, Buck," she screamed. "You damned liar. I knew you made a key…" And then she saw it was Bob sliding to the floor.

She knelt on the floor beside him. "Now, just look what I've done." She moaned like a woman in labor, sobbing, her tears falling on him like a sudden shower. "I thought it was Buck. Calling me over and over, playing that crazy music, making Georgie bark like that. I was sure it was Buck creeping up the stairs. I told you I could take care of myself, Bob. Why'd ya have to come after me?"

Come after her? Is that what she thought? Bob looked at the gun on the floor beside him, looked at the woman leaning over him, now hysterical. He wanted to tell Wendy he hadn't come after her, explain how he couldn't let it go—knowing what he did about men. But decided instead to concentrate on staying alive.

If he could.

PATTI ABBOTT is the author of nearly 100 stories that have appeared in print and online venues. Her flash fiction story "My Hero" won a Derringer in 2009. Her e-collection, *Monkey Justice* was published in 2011 through Snubnose Press. Her new e-collection of connected stories, *Home Invasion* will be out later in 2012. She is the co-editor of *Discount Noir* (Untreed Reads). You can find her daily at http://pattinase.blogspot.com. She lives in Detroit.

THE GIRL IN THE GOLDEN GOWN

ROBERT S. LEVINSON

"I'M TOLD YOU FIND MISSING PERSONS."

I shrug and say, "I'm involved, they're not missing, only temporarily misplaced."

He sends a confused look across the clean surface of his Texas-sized mahogany desk, then realizes what I said was a gag and laughs politely.

"I get you," he says.

"You will if the price is right."

He gets the gag faster this time and asks how much.

I quote my usual high five figures.

Without hesitation, he pushes back in his executive chair, opens the pencil drawer and pulls out a leather-bound checkbook, followed by a Mont Blanc pen from the billfold pocket of his Armani jacket. "My personal check okay?"

"Half will do it for now, Mr. Cutler."

"To show you how much confidence I have in you and your reputation, I'm giving it all to you up front."

"You understand there'll be out-of-pocket on the back end. I'm in for a lot of travel anytime I'm talking missing persons, plus gas costing what people once paid for diamonds. Motels thinking they're the Taj Mahal. At the greasiest of the greasy spoons, it's a sawbuck minimum before the tip. My reports include receipts and—"

He stops me with a hand signal.

"Not necessary," he says. "You come highly recommended; by a mutual friend who swears that, of all the private investigators he's ever used, you're the only one who always finds the needle in the haystack."

He shares the name, a high-powered Beverly Hills attorney.

I uncork a smile. "One of my friends without much originality."

"What's that mean?"

"You get that opinion from a lot of my friends," I tell him. It's not exactly the-truth-and-nothing-but, but the truth might turn him nervous, wondering if I come with a money-back guarantee. Fat chance. Not with my gambling jones and the deadline I've been facing on a marker held by a professional knee-breaker, born when my aces over nines fell to his four ladies. "So, Mr. Cutler—Tell me who or what this is about."

"I'll show you," Cutler says, using the desk to push up from his chair. He's a good six-six, with maybe three hundred pounds buried inside his three thousand dollar suit. A wreath of silver gray hair surrounds a bald dome and runs down past his collar in erratic strands, giving him the appearance of a poet in disguise while adding a good ten years to what I'm guessing his age to be, somewhere around fifty.

Unsteady on his feet, he pads cautiously across the oak-paneled office, past neatly arranged rows of diplomas, certificates and photos to an oil painting on solitary display on the wall opposite his desk. The painting is relatively small in size, maybe thirty by thirty inches, encased in a simple wooden frame and bathed by an overhead spotlight that makes it the center of attention.

It's the portrait of a beautiful girl, eighteen or twenty years of age, standing regally erect, wearing an exquisite ball gown the same shade of spun gold as the shoulder-length tresses framing a porcelain doll face the color of freshly-drawn cream; her hypnotic ocean blue-green eyes and marshmallow lips forming an expression that hints at secrets she has no intention of ever sharing.

It reminds me of pictures I saw at the County Museum by this painter Degas, who spread the bright colors around on ballet dancers looking like they could tippy-toe off the canvas. Not as true-to-life as Norman Rockwell did his paintings, but close enough to win my nod of approval.

Cutler winces when I tell him this, like he's been stung by a bee, or maybe because I follow up by asking, "Your daughter here, she the one's missing?"

"Missing, but not my daughter."

"Who then?" I say, joining him. Up close the girl is even more beautiful. She makes the oil paint smell like sweet perfume.

"I don't know her name. We never met."

"She's not your kid, you never met, you don't know her name, but you're shelling out all this bread for me to find her…What don't I know that I should know, Mr. Cutler?"

"I love her," he says, staring at the portrait, his hand three or four inches away from the canvas, tracing the outline of the girl's face. "And that already is more than you have to know."

"I go for older women myself," I say, concerned about what this geezer might have in mind for the kid after I find her and deliver her to him.

He catches my drift.

He whips around and leans into my face, fists clenched, blue veins growing at his temples, spittle raining on me, demanding, "Don't you dare insult me with your innuendo." He throws a finger at the lower right corner of the painting, where the artist has signed and dated the work.

I can do the math without counting on my fingers.

The painting was made twenty-five years ago, meaning the girl in the golden gown was now almost the same age as Cutler.

He says, "You find her, I mean to marry her if she'll have me."

"And if she can't or she won't?"

Tears well in his eyes; the only answer he has for me.

"In that case—" I offer him back his check and begin wondering how much longer I'll have healthy kneecaps.

He waves off the gesture, asking, "Have you ever been in love? Really in love?"

"More than both of my ex-wives, and that's saying a lot, Mr. Cutler."

"Then you might understand me when I say love is a word describing an emotion beyond definition and often beyond redemption. Falling in love, who's to say when it will happen? When it happens, it happens. Who it happens with? Another conundrum, wouldn't you agree?"

The way he's chewing his words, it takes a second for me to realize he had not said *condom*. "For me it happened both times working cases, Mr. Cutler. I'm a Grade-A sucker for damsels in distress. You?"

His mind retreats to the past. "A month ago, I'm in New York on business and take a few hours off to check out what's happened to SoHo. You know SoHo?"

"Not personally."

"Down between Houston and Canal and Sixth Avenue and Broadway. Used to be the center of the art gallery scene before it moved to Chelsea, between Sixth and Tenth Avenue, from Fourteenth to Thirty-Fourth."

"Of course," I agree, like I know the layout of the city beyond the Statue of Liberty, the Empire State Building, Times Square, and One Police Plaza.

"I'm exploring the changes since my last trip east a year ago and wander over to an antiques store tucked between a God-awful trendy clothing store and an overpriced bistro. The painting is hanging in the window for all the world to admire. One look and my heart crashes through the plate glass window to embrace the girl. I am mesmerized by the sight of her. When I see the date on the painting and understand she is my age, I know that fate has intervened. I must possess this painting, just as I must possess her. I must find her and make her my bride."

What can I say?

I've dealt with looser screws than Cutler.

Besides, those lousy aces over nines.

I need the payday.

Need breeds greed.

I say, "The store couldn't tell you who they acquired the painting from or anything that would help you?"

"Nothing, only who the artist is and that was already evident."

"I'll start with the store and see if I can do better. What's the name?"

"I don't remember. It was no place I expected to visit again."

"The name would be on a receipt they gave you or a credit card or bank statement."

"The owner insisted on cash. I was carrying more than enough in my billfold."

"Tell me the name of the artist again, Mr. Cutler."

He tells me.

Later, back at my apartment, I grab a couple brews from the fridge and jump onto the internet.

•••

Cahuilla Sands is a sleepy community of six or seven hundred residents risking skin cancer in the sun-baked high desert between Rancho Mirage and the California-Nevada border, inland a mile north of the 60 freeway. It's reached on a pitted two-lane concrete access road that peters out at the base of the San Gorgonio mountain range.

The sign at the city limit, paint chipped and flaking, letters dulled by years of neglect and exposure to the elements, boasts:

WELCOME TO CAHUILLA SANDS
A BOOMTOWN LIKE NO OTHER.
HOME OF IVOR GODOWSKY.

Ivor Godowsky.

Who I'm here to find—

The artist who painted Cutler's obsession.

Who better to identify the girl for me, maybe tell me where she is now? If only an ID from him, I'll be using the blessed internet to track her when I get back to L.A, doing in a few hours or less what once took weeks or months of legwork. (If Godowsky had a listed phone, this trip might not have been necessary.)

Trailer parks line both sides of the road, full of mobile homes sitting on permanent foundations, faded white picket fences or chicken wire enclosing weed-infested gardens of heat-resistant fruits and vegetables. Tumbleweeds the size of boulders drift with the breeze, sometimes bouncing off the agavi, saguaro and fishhook cacti, creating the impression that Mother Nature is engaged in a fanciful game of pinball.

I have no trouble locating Main Street.

It's the only street in town, three blocks long.

Cahuilla Sands—

Definitely a boomtown like no other.

A two-story City Hall dominates a mixed bag of well-kept wood frame and brick and mortar buildings of architectural irrelevance, not a franchise among the storefronts. I angle my SUV into a parking slot, tread carefully up plank stairs that squawk with sounds of imminent collapse, and enter to the smell of dust and desert history.

It takes about five minutes for someone to respond to my nagging on the brass bell at the information desk, a slope-shouldered octogenarian out to break the Olympic record for strolling while he buckles the straps on the blue denim bib overalls he's wearing over a red union suit.

"I was doing number two," he says, like he's reporting to an old friend. "Third time today. One prune too many with my breakfast bran flakes. I'll never learn. Bananas, too. I could fertilize the whole valley, it ever came to that. So, what can I do you for today?"

I tell him what's brought me to Cahuilla Sands.

"Godowsky, yep," he says. "He painted my picture a couple of times, once naked as a jaybird. Paid me with a six-pack; imported stuff. Heard later they're hanging in museums, but I don't remember which. You a collector?"

"In a manner of speaking. Can you tell me where to find him?"

"I'll write up the directions for you," he says, reaching for a pad and pencil, wetting the tip of the pencil with his tongue before he starts scribbling.

•••

The directions take me a mile out of town, closer to the San Gorgonio foothills and a gated cemetery the size of two basketball courts, headstones and grave markers bunched tightly together along jagged pathways. The oldest ones visible from the road date back to the mid-1800s.

I hop over the waist-high slat wood fence and wander the narrow aisles, raising a river of sweat under the relentless heat until I locate Godowsky.

An engraved bronze plaque embedded in the sunburned grass features his name in tall capital letters and no other information, as if Godowsky had never been born or died, but somehow existed at one time or other.

Back in town, the look on face of the ancient clerk at City Hall says he knew I'd be returning.

Before I can complain about the wild goose chase he sent me on, he has an answer.

"You asked if I knew where you could find Ivor, not the condition that you'd find him in," he says. His laughter punctuates every word and splashes my face with the heavy scent of garlic. "I can make it up to you if you want, but it's going to cost you a six-pack of the imported, in the cold case down at Geller's Grocery and not cheap." His smile exposes two rows of tobacco-stained teeth too perfect to be his own.

•••

Irma Ballard laughs when I introduce myself to her at Irma's Snack Emporium, a coffee shop with walls tanned by years of griddle grease, and tell her who sent me to find her. She moves around the counter from the cash register and lands her shapely behind on the stool next to mine. "Herb, he's a card, that one," she says. "Loves messing around with strangers, anybody, anytime he figures he can trick a six-pack out of them. I suppose it got something to do with the mad Russian."

"Ivor Godowsky."

"What is it this time?"

"This time?"

"You think you're the first one to come chasing after him here, looking to wheel and deal him out of any of his paintings? Getting Moses to part the Red Sea was easier, except whenever Ivor needed bread to buy supplies. Money and fame meant nothing to him. You could say he died to put an end to all those interruptions." She eyes the dessert carousel and points. "Interest you in the fresh apple pie; great hot with slab of homemade vanilla ice cream? Both made by yours truly."

"Sounds delicious, but I'm counting calories."

Irma breaks out a pout, so I change my mind in the interest of bonding. Besides being one delicious dish herself, Irma looks like she knows more than she's telling about Ivor Godowsky. She slips off the stool and heads back behind the counter with a wiggle in her walk befitting a soda parlor style outfit out of a fifties Frankie and Annette movie that wraps provocatively around her awesome curves. She's in her mid-to-late thirties, around my age, and that statistic adds thoughts that have absolutely nothing to do with why I'm in Cahuilla Sands. She studies me with a knowing look that promises nothing and everything and lingers while I make a show of enjoying her pie and ice cream.

Swiveling around on the stool in a way that connects her thigh to mine, Irma says, "You haven't answered my question yet. What is it about Ivor that brought you all the way out here?"

I dig after my iPhone and show her the photo I'd snapped before leaving Cutler.

Irma takes the phone from me for a closer look. Magnifies the image. "Definitely not Ivor's work," she says. "It's one of those phonies that sometimes shows up, the same way there are hundreds of Dali and Picasso fakes always being passed off as the genuine article."

"How do you know that?"

"For one, see the date?"

"What about the date?"

"Exactly. If you knew anything at all about Ivor's work you'd know he never dated his paintings, not one of them."

"There couldn't be an exception?"

"Not here. The date someone put on the painting would make the girl older than her mother is right today."

"You know her mother?"

"I am her mother."

Too surprised to speak, I take back the iPhone and weigh her appearance against the girl in the portrait. I can see the resemblance, particularly in the shape of the face, the blue-green color of her eyes, the ripe lips. Or is it only my imagination responding to the power of suggestion?

Irma Ballard reads my expression correctly and draws a bright smile that puts quote marks at the corners of her mouth and deepens the crevices on her cheeks and elsewhere on her sun-darkened complexion. "Her name's Michelle," she says. "Like in the Beatles song." She hums the melody and then sings the words, *Michelle, ma belle*, straining both times to stay on tune. "Only she's been calling herself 'Micki' ever since the ninth grade. You know anything at all about teenagers, you don't need to ask how come."

"I'd like to see Micki, talk to her?" I say. The idea is to come away with a photo of the kid I can show to Cutler, proof his dream wife isn't what he expected me to bring back to him.

"So would I," she says, her husky come-hither voice suffering a melancholy break. "Only she went missing a week after Ivor finished the painting, same time as the painting went missing from our motor home."

"She took it with her?"

"Would seem so. The paint was hardly dry. A gift from Ivor, same way he gifted me with some of the ones of me he done over the years."

"More than once?"

"Whenever he couldn't pay the tab he'd run up at the Snack Emporium, which was most of the time."

"Did he paint Micki more than once?"

"Just the once I know about. Two years ago. Been two years since I saw or heard a word out of Michelle. Not a note or nothing the day she disappeared, just up and gone, like that." She snaps her fingers.

The last of the customers is at the cash register.

Irma excuses herself to settle his bill and follows him to the door.

She turns the lock and throws the cardboard window sign to "Closed Until" after dialing the clock hands ahead two hours.

"Follow me on over to my place and you can see for yourself," she says.

•••

Irma's motor home is a permanently docked high-end gas-guzzler the size of a Greyhound Bus, the garden fresh smell of its spit-and-polish interior tainted a bit by the lingering odor of what my practiced nose tells me is cannabis.

Paintings of modest size hang from what little available wall space there is, a few of the smaller ones on counter and table surfaces. They're all by Godowsky and they're all of Irma. Eight in total. Irma ages from image to image, progressing from about Micki's age to the sensuous woman I met earlier today. Her expression varies from a teasing smile to a cipher worthy of da Vinci's Mona Lisa. Her costumes match her mood.

In all of the portraits—not one of them dated—her resemblance to her daughter is uncanny.

"The one of Michelle was over there, covering the window," she says. "In here's my favorite, come see." She pushes open the accordion door to the master bedroom at the rear of the motor home. The door glides closed behind us and I find myself staring at a painting of a full-figured Irma reclining in the buff. “What do you think?” she says, like she already knows the answer. “It was the first one he did of me, younger than Michelle, but mature for my age in body and soul, if you know what I mean. I’ve held Mother Nature to a draw ever since.”

“Gorgeous,” I say.

“You are,” Irma says. She steps forward, throws her arms around me and settles an electric kiss on me before I can protest, or at least pretend. “I’ve needed someone like you coming around for a long time,” she says, and throws herself into a lingering kiss. “Felt the vibe the second I laid eyes on you,” she says. She steps back and begins undressing. “Want you, sweetheart; want you now. Strictly recreational. What do you think?”

I’m too much the gentleman to refuse.

Later, lounging under the covers and sharing a fat joint of premium Hawaiian, Irma is telling me, “Michelle was always complaining top of her lungs about being trapped here without a future, how she had no intention of taking over and running the Snack Emporium the way I did after my dear mommy and daddy were murdered, what keeps me here to this day, stuck with boredom and the need to scratch out a living.”

“Your mother and father were murdered?”

“In cold blood. The robbers got away with about a hundred dollars from the register and never were caught. Why I bought a gun and learned how to use it from a deputy sheriff who used to patrol out here and loved my mommy’s peach cobbler. Toddy turned me into a mean shot and I wanted the same for Michelle, but she was having none of it. She wouldn’t kill a bug, that one. Step on an ant, not her. Oh, how I miss her. I miss her so much.”

I stash the joint, pull Irma closer to me and finger-wipe away her tears.

I haven’t felt this comfortable with or protective of a woman since my last wife, and that turned into a disaster. Maybe there’s something more than an accidental fling going on here, or is the Hawaiian playing tricks with my emotions?

I tell her, “I’m going to find your daughter for you.”

“You can do that, sweetheart?”

“I can do that.”

“How, sweetheart?”

"Micki—"

"*Michelle, ma belle,*" she says, and drifts into even breathing punctuated by snorts and groans that informs me she's fallen asleep.

I gently extricate myself from her, slip out of bed and aim for the fridge. I have an appetite that needs appeasement, a rampaging sweet tooth and a thirst begging for a brew. I have to be satisfied with the bedraggled remains of a lettuce, tomato and mushroom salad drenched in oily French dressing, a small cup of strawberry yogurt and what's left in a pour carton of cheap *sauvignon blanc* that tastes like cheaper mouthwash.

I settle at the dining table and study Godowsky's paintings while struggling to recall what it was I intended to tell Irma, my plan for finding Michelle, her belle; not easy, since I have no plan. Not exactly true. I do so have a plan, it's just I can't remember what the plan is right now. This Hawaiian weed—

Killer stuff.

I struggle to focus on Godowsky's paintings.

He never dated any of them. No date on any, ever, except for the fake, the girl in the golden gown; her, the girl in the painting in the window of the antiques store in New York. Whoever painted the fake had to have the original to copy. The original disappeared from Cahuilla Sands when Irma's belle Michelle disappeared from Cahuilla Sands with the only portrait of her ever painted by Godowsky. Meaning—

Michelle had the painting and took it with her to New York, how it wound up at the antiques store in SoHo where Cutler saw the painting and fell in love with the painting and bought the painting.

Cutler said he couldn't recall the name of the antiques store.

I will have to do better.

I will go to New York, go to SoHo and find the antiques store.

Find the antiques store and find the artist who copied the Godowsky painting.

Find out how he got the original and who from.

Continue working from Z to A until I have Michelle in sight.

Reunite her with *ma belle*, Irma.

Provide Cutler with proof his money has been well spent, even if the end did not justify his means.

I polish off the vino, stumble back to the bedroom and whisper in Irma's ear, "My plan for finding Michelle, you want to hear how?"

She rouses at the sound of my voice. I tell her what I have in mind. Her smile melts my heart. Before drifting back to sleep, she says, "I want to go with you, sweetheart, please let me."

I crawl under the covers alongside her thinking it's not a good idea.

Thinking: So what?

Thinking: We have chemistry going for us, Irma and me.

Thinking: Maybe we have more going for us than a one-nighter.

Thinking: This is me talking to me, me, not the weed, the cannabis, the ganja, the Mary Jane, until the free-floating three-dimensional light show of late afternoon somehow turns into early morning and I wake up sweating from the already oppressive heat attacking the walls of the motor home.

•••

SoHo is like Los Angeles on speed.

People and street vendors crowd the sidewalks, cabs honk for jurisdiction as they maneuver from one gridlocked lane to another.

It's morning, two days since we flew here.

Irma and I have been wandering the northern section like the lost tourists we are, hoping to stumble across the antiques store Cutler had described to me, located between a clothing store and an overpriced bistro.

Our problem: Too many antiques stores, clothing stores and bistros, but none so far one-two-three next to one another.

After more than two hours of foot-weary failure and frustration, we navigate south to the less trendy, not as pricey part of SoHo along Grand and Canal streets. There are cast iron warehouses off the cobblestone streets that talk to the years before lofts filled up with artists, art galleries abounded and real estate prices aimed for the moon.

We're not having better luck here after an hour, talking about quitting for the day as the temperature turns chilly and rain clouds ripen in the overcast sky, when Irma grabs me by the elbow and points across the narrow street to a shop nesting between a Chinese hand laundry and a patisserie sending out the smell of fresh pastries and sweets.

"Oh, my dear Lord. Sweetheart, look!" she says, her voice rising from a murmur to a shout.

The flag hanging above the shop entrance reads TREASURES ISLAND, but what has excited Irma is the oil painting hanging in the display window.

She zigzags across the street to a symphony of angry car horns, me in pursuit, and stands slack-jawed in front of the window, staring hard at a portrait of the girl in the golden gown. The girl isn't standing this time, showing off her royal bearing. This time she sits on a high-backed throne wearing a crown encrusted with diamonds, emeralds and rubies, and an expression more precious than any of the stones. The portrait is signed by "Godowsky." Like the earlier one, it's dated twenty-five years ago, but it's unquestionably Michelle. Not the same antiques shop, however, unless Cutler got his landmarks wrong.

We learn he did a few minutes later, when the young clerk tells us, "It's the second Godowsky we've ever had as long as I've worked here, going on three years." She's a pink-haired six-footer and string bean thin, legs like stilts; flat-chested under a sheer silk, floral-patterned tent dress that quits above the knees; her voice a birdlike twitter; looking out of place in a showroom filled with period furniture and decorative indoor bronze and marble statuary. "My boss took it as a favor."

That gets my attention. "A favor?"

"The guy didn't come off looking like your average junkie; eyes wild as pinwheels but smelling more like turpentine than a garbage truck. Was short on cash to cover his rent and to buy paints, canvas and stuff is what he said. He said he didn't feel like being cheated on what the pawn shops and art galleries were offering him for his Godowsky, is what he said. The boss took the painting on consignment and meanwhile wrote him a nice check as an advance. He's like that, the boss, a big heart and all. No spring chicken, but he's going to make a fine and loving daddy." She gently patted what only a fertile imagination could call a baby bump.

"You said two paintings." I describe the girl in the golden gown.

"The other," the clerk says, nodding. "Looked to be the same model he used, who sort of somewhat resembles your lady friend here. Went into the window and sold faster than you can spell Godowsky, so I wouldn't think twice about grabbing this one up, I was you."

Irma steps forward and shouts an excited, "Yes. What are you asking?"

The clerk tells her and explains, "We'll need cash or traveler's checks, ma'am. My boss isn't one for personal checks or credit cards from anyone but trade regulars."

The answer elicits a moan from Irma. She shoots me the kind of soulful stare puppy dogs engineer when they're begging for table scraps. The price is more than I'm carrying in bills. I haul out my roll and peel off ten Ben Franklins. "Will this hold it for us until I find an ATM?"

"Certainly shows good intentions, sir. I'll go make you out a receipt."

"And something else I'll need."

"Oh?"

"The name and address of the man who brought the painting to you."

She looks like she's about to quote some store policy against revealing customer information to anybody outside law enforcement and the IRS. I peel off another pair of Franklins and dangle them. She hesitates before trading in the deep furrows between her sculptured eyebrows on a toothsome smile. "It's not far from here," she says, tucking the bills inside her dress, down around her non-existent breasts.

•••

The four-story factory building is a leading candidate for teardown, its regiment of walled-over truck docks decorated in graffiti and new and disintegrating one-sheets, a relic from SoHo's past subdivided into cheap loft living. Once through the unguarded entrance, the outdoor city smells give way to a mix of indefinable noxious odors. A narrow stairway that threatens collapse with every cautious step takes us past derelicts sleeping in corridor alcoves to the top floor loft of Bo Goodwin.

The bell doesn't work, and there's no response to my knocking on the rusted metal door until I bang harder and holler for Goodwin by name. The spy hole opens for several seconds. It's another minute before the door slides open and we're staring back at a young man in boxer shorts; barefooted and bare-chested, his body and arms freckled by oil paint residue; chiseled features punctuated by restless brown eyes, crooked yellow teeth, and an unruly beard the color of mud.

"You're an hour early," he says, his voice soggy with sleep. "C'mon, *entres vous*." His French pronunciation is lousy, on par with my own.

I nod confirmation to Irma, who's also recognized Goodwin has mistaken us for somebody else, as we enter a vast expanse of loft space with living areas defined by bits and pieces of furniture and appliances; a stove and fridge by a sink loaded with pots and dishes, a sagging sofa and a decrepit armchair over by one wall, a disheveled bed pushed against another wall; clothes strewn about, the floor for a closet; overall, a nightmare of a bachelor pad. A painter's easel—a color-splattered bed sheet covering the canvas—and a cluttered work bench dominate the center of the room.

Goodwin ponders Irma. "I didn't know you'd be bringing company," he tells me. "Is this some kind of a setup?" He shifts his weight from foot to foot, on sudden guard against what I don't know or care to know. Through the years, minding my own business has kept me healthier than any HMO. He's obviously confused me with someone else. I tell him so, explaining what brought us here:

"The Godowsky portrait at Treasures Island? We just bought it and will be taking it back to L.A. with us."

His tone lightens. "Bought it, huh? It wasn't cheap."

"Worth every dollar. The clerk sent us over to see you when she learned we collect Godowsky, thinking you might have others for sale."

Goodwin's eyes glide to the easel and back to us, while he weighs the possibility, a study in indecision until: "It would cost you another bundle, 'cause I'd still owe the store a commission."

"No problem, assuming it's as good as the portrait in the window."

"Guaranteed," he tells us, his head bobbing agreement while he quicksteps across the room to a group of canvases stacked against the wall. He exercises care rifling through them until he locates the one he's been searching for, emits a victory noise and displays the canvas.

It's another rendering of the girl in the golden gown that caused Cutler's infatuation and locked me into this search for Michelle Ballard. Irma and I recognize it immediately as a forgery, dated the way Godowsky never dated any of his works.

"One more for you to see," Goodwin says. He settles the oil against the base of the easel and returns to the canvas stack. After another minute, he removes a second portrait of Michelle signed and dated by Godowsky. It's a smaller canvas, a nude, Michelle gaunt and wasted, her face a study in turmoil, her once hypnotic blue-green eyes blinded by defeat.

Irma locks her arms around herself and, shaking, screams, "Michelle! Oh, my dear Lord. My dear Lord. What's happened to you?"

Goodwin, puzzled by her reaction, asks, "Michelle? Who's that?"

I tell him, "The girl in the painting."

"No," Goodwin says. "Micki was her name. Her name was Micki."

Irma explodes into tears. "*Was*. Oh, my dear Lord. He said *was*. He said *was*."

"She was my girl, Micki was, and she left me cold," Goodwin says. Now he's also shedding tears by the bucketful. "I woke up one morning and she was gone. Over a year ago. I finally got around to painting Micki from memory, how I remembered her looking on the day she arrived here knocking on my door. Our last night together. The good times in-between."

"Imitating Godowsky's style, signing his name," I say, like it's a fact that doesn't need validation.

"He was my uncle," Goodwin says, "my father's brother, only he kept the original family name when they came over from the old country. All I learned about painting was from my uncle, until finally I could match him stroke for stroke. Dealers ignored my work as second-rate imitations, except when I copied Uncle Ivor's style and signed them with the Godowsky name; like whenever I need scratch to survive."

"Habits are a luxury."

"Yeah," he agrees, tossing over his palms to the bright copper ceiling surrounding the skylight twelve feet up that's showering us with late afternoon sun in a cloudless sky.

"And forgeries put you in prison."

"Not forgeries, sir. Godowsky's still legally my name. Uncle Ivor never dated his works, so I do, using my birthday as the date. There's no law against selling copies. And Micki's portraits sell better than anything, my originals as well as my copies of the one by my uncle." His words are racing. He looks desperate for acknowledgment beyond his own. "She had that one with her on the day she showed up at my door unannounced, saying how my uncle sent her and she was looking for a better life than the one she was living now and how my uncle said I was the one to look after her for him."

"And living with you turned her into a junkie. You call that a better life?"

"I've been living with that sin ever since, sir. Nothing I'm proud of. I loved Micki with all my heart and she loved me."

Irma unbridles her anger again. "Michelle, damn you. Her name is Michelle, and I am her mother."

"I see it, ma'am. She was always telling me how you looked alike, like sisters. How much she loved and missed you, but this was the life she needed, free to be herself."

"Did she say where she was going before she left you? Did she leave a note? Have you heard from Michelle since?"

The questions rattle Goodwin. He averts his eyes from the blistering condemnation she is pouring on him. "I apologize for not making myself clear, ma'am. When I explained I woke up and she was *gone*, I mean she had passed on sometime during the night, in our bed over there, cradled in my arms like always." His eyes are clouded with tears again. He chokes on his words. "The city took her and she was cremated and after that I don't know what...God, I need a fix. I do, I do, I do...Where the hell is he?"

Before I can stop her, Irma grabs one of the sharp-edged palette knives off the work bench and launches at Goodwin. He sees the oil-crusted blade coming, but can't move fast enough to avoid it completely. Irma's thrust catches him below the neck, inches away from his heart. Blood seeps from the wound and mellows into his chest hair as she yanks out the blade and raises it to strike again.

"My little girl is dead because of you," she screams.

I grab her wrist and force the blade from her grip, trap her in my arms.

Goodwin, bandaging the wound with his palm, shouting with pain and out of fear, stumbles backward. He bangs into the wall and slides down into a sitting position on the stained hardwood floor. The small diamond-shaped blade has done damage, but nothing permanent. He'll need patching up, but he'll live.

Irma is trying to wrestle free of me, trying to get to the work bench and another of the palette knives, demanding, "I want him dead. I want him rotting in hell."

"No," I tell her. "Enough."

Without a backward glance at Goodwin, who's cry-babying for his connection, I steer Irma to the door.

"Wait here a minute," I say, and backtrack to the easel.

I pick up a palette knife and use the scepter-shaped steel blade to slash and shred the nude of a drug-bludgeoned Michelle out of existence.

As an afterthought, compelled by curiosity, I toss aside the shroud covering the canvas on the easel, revealing an elegant and vibrant Michelle projecting an intoxicating enthusiasm for life.

I return to Irma and hand it over, telling her, "We came to find your daughter and we've found her. It's time to go home."

•••

Driving Irma back to Cahuilla Sands from LAX, Cutler's office at One Wilshire in downtown L.A. is an easy one-stop off the freeway interchange. I call ahead, figuring it'll take me five, ten minutes max to explain about Michelle Ballard and Godowsky's portrait and square accounts with Cutler before we're back on the road.

We're barely settled in the waiting room after the receptionist announces me when Cutler comes charging out of his inner sanctum like an Olympian after a gold medal in the 100-meter dash. He reaches me and quits, bends over with his hands on his knees, huffing and puffing, sweat dripping onto the plush pile carpeting, insisting, "Tell me that you have good news, that you've found her."

Before I can frame the best way to let him down gently, he notices Irma.

He's momentarily transfixed.

Rising to his full height, sucking in enough air to reach his toes, he points to her like he's identifying the suspect in a lineup. His lips are moving, but he can't seem to get words out, until:

"Bless you, my good man, you're a miracle worker, as good as I was told. Better. You not only found her for me, but you've brought her to me…Oh, my dear, you've aged exactly how I've imagined since I first set eyes on your portrait. The years have made you more beautiful than ever."

Irma smiles nervously and, uncertain how to respond, turns to me for direction.

I know what I'd do, but I give her a look that says it's her life, her decision to make.

Cutler reaches out for her hands.
She hesitates briefly before letting him take them.

ROBERT S. LEVINSON is the bestselling author of ten mystery-thrillers, among them *A Rhumba in Waltz Time, The Traitor in Us All, In the Key of Death, Where the Lies Begin, Ask a Dead Man,* and the forthcoming *Phony Tinsel.* A regular contributor to the *Alfred Hitchcock* and *Ellery Queen* mystery magazines, he won *EQMM* Readers Award honors three consecutive years, while a *Hitchcock* short story, "The Quick Brown Fox," was a Derringer Award winner and *Queen* story, "The Girl in the Golden Gown," short-listed for a Shamus Award of the Private Eye Writers of America. Bob's fiction has appeared in "year's best" anthologies seven consecutive years, his non-fiction in publications including *Rolling Stone*, Writers Guild of America's *Written By Magazine, Los Angeles Magazine, Los Angeles Times Magazine, Westways Magazine*, and A*utograph Magazine.* Various novels and original short story collections are available online at Amazon Kindle and other e-book locations. He resides in Los Angeles with his wife, Sandra. More: www.robertslevinson.com.

WHAT PEOPLE LEAVE BEHIND

KRISTINE KATHRYN RUSCH

THE HOUSE STOOD AT THE END OF AN UPSCALE SUBDIVISION—OR what had once been an upscale subdivision. Gracie Ansara drove the panel truck past house after house with rusted for-sale signs on the yard. Some had an additional thin metal sign which said "Bank-owned."

Fifteen foreclosures in a four-block area. Gracie personally had cleaned out five. This one was the sixth.

She remembered the people who lived in the house. They had come out of the front door and stood on the manicured lawn, watching her and her partners toss furniture on the driveway of the house next door.

Gracie's face had burned as she had done the work. It had been her first house clean-out, and part of her still thought of the work as something to be ashamed of.

She had glanced at the woman neighbor, standing with her arms crossed, her hair a perfectly dyed shade of winter blonde, her gabardine pants and silk blouse something out of a Macy's ad. The woman's lips were pressed together, her eyes narrow. She seemed as if she were judging the crew, as if they weren't worthy of setting foot on this street.

Gracie wanted to say *I didn't ask for this. I got three kids to feed and a house of my own.* But she didn't. She turned her back on that perfectly groomed woman with her tall, handsome, black-haired husband (also perfectly groomed) and went back into the foreclosed house.

She had never expected to be at the perfectly groomed woman's house six months later.

At least not then. Now nothing surprised her.

Not after she had seen what people left behind.

•••

Gracie herself had left behind a lot. Eighteen months ago, she'd been a happily married mother of three, a bank executive who made mid-six figures and lived in an upscale subdivision not too different from this one.

One Friday night, a drunk going 100 miles per hour had crossed the median, slammed into her husband's car, and shoved it under an eighteen-wheeler.

Gracie had collected half a million dollars of life insurance for life without the man she still adored. She put three hundred thousand into the kids' college funds, and used the rest to pay off her own house.

Then, after twenty years of work for the same company, she was laid off. No apologies, no offers of advancement, no chance to move elsewhere in the company.

She felt grief-stricken all over again. She had lost the man she had married at twenty-one, and then she had lost the company she had married at twenty-five. She clung to her children so tightly that they started to complain.

"Jeez, Mom," said Hannah, her oldest. "Why don't you just pretend this is a mid-life crisis and buy yourself a Porsche?"

Hannah was sixteen. She probably didn't suggest the Porsche to make her mother feel better; she probably had visions of driving it herself.

But the idea stuck.

Not the idea of the Porsche—Gracie had never been one for flashy cars—but the idea of a mid-life crisis. What happened in midlife anyway? People often shook up their entire lives, tried out new identities, became someone else.

Gracie, who loved cleaning and painting and organizing, penciled out the price of panel trucks and labor, cleaning supplies and paint. She added in the occasional need for a plumber or an electrician, and she came to a price for starting a business.

A business that she could run out of her paid-for house. A business that would thrive in bad times, and survive in good.

A business that wouldn't merge and merge and merge again, but would stay alive as long as she wanted it to.

Something that was, for once, all hers.

•••

She thought of all of that as she pulled into the driveway of the well-dressed woman's house. Gracie's assistant, Micah Collingsworth, hadn't arrived yet. She was still a few minutes early, but she didn't get out of the truck.

She knew better than to go into foreclosures alone.

A battered Ford one-ton pulled in behind her. She let out a small sigh of relief. Micah wasn't late after all. He grinned as he got out of the truck.

Micah had been a godsend. He had been one of the first people to answer her ad for employees. He had worked for a rental services company in Upstate New York years ago, cleaning, painting, repairing. He had placed that experience prominently on the resume he had designed specifically for her, burying the fact that he had once been a corporate exec at one of the many high tech firms that had fled Oregon in the last twelve months.

"Doesn't look much different than it did six months ago," he said about the house.

"Except for the cobwebs." Gracie nodded toward the windows. They were covered in white webs.

He stuck his hands in the pockets of his faded jeans and peered at the property as if he were a building inspector. "You think they would have done something when they saw us next door."

She remembered the couple's tight expressions and crossed arms. "Maybe they didn't have a choice."

Micah ignored that. Instead he asked, "You ready?"

She nodded.

They both felt trepidation whenever they went into a foreclosure. Sometimes the families trashed the place before they left. More than one had broken back into the house and squatted, still believing they had rights to the property.

The bank had checked the place out before hiring her. So had the sheriff. Both had assured her that no one had returned. Even so, Gracie liked to be cautious.

The front door had a lockbox. She opened it with her special key, and removed the key for the front door. It opened easily.

The house smelled faintly of pine air freshener, which was a relief. Most places smelled of rotting food.

The entry was clean. The owners had left a throw rug behind and both Gracie and Micah automatically wiped their feet. Then they grinned at each other, feeling a little ridiculous. Still, Gracie was glad they did it because the granite tile in front of them gleamed.

It was one less thing to clean.

The vaulted living room was bare. The carpet still bore furniture marks, but someone had vacuumed.

"Lucked out," Micah said.

They had. This place would be easy to prepare for any potential buyers.

Gracie nodded. "I think we can separate. Got your intercom?"

It wasn't really an intercom. It was an added feature on their cell phone plan. But they could talk to each other without dialing out, which she just loved.

"Got it," he said, holding up the phone. She smiled at him. She continued through the living room into the formal dining area.

He went back to the entry and up the stairs to the right. She could hear him walk heavily above her. She found the sound somehow reassuring.

The formal dining room was empty as well. The built-in china cabinet's doors were open. Someone had used some kind of wood polish on it because the thing shone as if it were new.

Her hope was the rest of the place would be this clean. Sometimes the front rooms were spotless and the bedrooms, bathrooms, and utility rooms were a mess. It was as if the former owners couldn't quite get enough energy to finish the cleaning job, knowing they were doing it under duress.

Still, she wouldn't be surprised if these former owners cleaned the entire place. That couple she had seen on the lawn were very well put together, even though their life had to have been falling apart.

Appearances were clearly important to them. Even the appearance of the house they had abandoned mattered.

Gracie stepped into the kitchen. It had state-of-the-art appliances, granite countertops, and expensive cherry cabinets.

Her intercom buzzed. She clicked the phone. "What do you have?" she asked, hoping he wasn't going to tell her that the upstairs was a disaster.

"Something weird," he said. "It's spotless up here except for the hall closet. It looks like a giant spider made a nest in here."

"Well, don't touch it," she said. "I've got spray in the truck. If we have to, we'll call in a pest service."

"I don't think it's really a spider web," he said. "It's too black. Webs aren't ever black, are they?"

"Not unless they're abandoned and covered with dirt." She had seen that more than once in her short time working foreclosures.

"I think it's attached to the wall in the back. Let me check…"

She could hear him strain through the intercom. He grunted, a door creaked, and then he said,

"It looks more like wires coming from some kind of box. I think we'll need an electrician on this one. I can't even tell what it's for. Let me—"

The world went white, then banged, and shuddered. Ceiling—or wall—or tile—rained on Gracie. She put up her arms, protecting her head. Dust filled her lungs. She climbed under the counter.

Then the world went white a second time.

Something sucked the remaining air from the room. Gracie gasped, unable to breathe.

More things fell. Burning things.

The air couldn't be gone, she thought. If the air were gone, there would be no fire. It was hot, and she couldn't hear. Her lungs ached—no, seared. She reached to the edge of the countertop—

And then….nothing.

Nothing at all.

•••

Detective Andrea Donovan stood outside the smoking ruin of what had once been a neighborhood showplace. At least, that was what the remaining neighbors told her, in voices flat with shock.

She had no idea how they could tell which house was the showplace. This subdivision was just a bigger version of the subdivision she had grown up in. Only her childhood subdivision had been made up of ranch houses with alternating floor plans and color schemes. This subdivision was a series of four different McMansions that varied not only floor plan, but driveway and lawn size.

The neighborhood might once have been middle-class chic, but it wasn't now. In addition to the shattered ruin before her, the entire area looked destroyed. Glass and rock and building shards covered the lawns, street, and driveways. One of the neighbors had found a ripped and bloody leg on top of a roof two blocks away.

The houses on all sides of the explosion had suffered damage, and the entire area smelled of chemical smoke.

Donovan hated cases like this one. She had to coordinate with a variety of other teams, and most of the relevant evidence was outside of her expertise.

She hadn't even been called in for two days. First the arson team went through and made certain that this wasn't some gas line explosion or some freak ignition of septic fumes.

When the arson team figured out that there was nothing wrong with the natural gas line that heated the house, they started searching for some other cause. First they searched for something that would ignite the place—some kind of fuel or trigger mechanism.

But this explosion had been big and hot, and they hadn't found anything except some suspicious wires, bits of cell phones, and something that might—or might not—have been a trigger mechanism.

Initially, the team argued about calling the explosives experts, since they had also found a man's hand, clutching the bottom half of a cell phone. Since he was holding it, he was probably using it, not making a bomb out of it.

But they finally did call in the explosives expert. The expert found chemical traces of C4 near the ignition site, as well as other things that might—or might not—have been components.

It was the might and the might not have beens that bothered Donovan the most.

That and the fact that no one would let her into her crime scene, at least not yet.

So she paced the exterior and talked to the neighbors—what few remained. Ninety percent of this subdivision had fallen into foreclosure. Some owners were long gone, the properties bank-owned. Some were still struggling to hang on, and only a few were current on their payments.

Current and angry.

It was bad enough to have the bank take half the properties around here, Bill Nelson, who lived three doors down told her. *Now we're going to be the bombing neighborhood. We're upside down in our mortgage as it is. This thing will make property values plummet even further. I couldn't sell if I wanted to.*

Others had voiced similar sentiments. Donovan had taken all of their names and all of their addresses and made note of their great distress.

Not that she blamed them. This subdivision was already toxic, the subject of articles in the papers and items on the local news. The developer had used shoddy materials in most of the houses, and even if the market hadn't tanked, these poor homeowners—all of whom had bought new—had probably been upside down in their mortgages from day one.

Normally, she would have looked at that as motive—if the cratered house belonged to the developer. But it had belonged to some not-so-popular neighbors who had already been forced out by their bank.

There was no benefit in blowing up the place, at least not for the handful of families struggling to remain.

There wasn't even benefit to the former homeowners, unless one considered revenge.

Which she did.

Still, the people killed weren't bank employees or mortgage brokers. They belonged to a company that cleaned empty houses. No one could have known that they'd be the ones who would suffer for this.

She looked for her partner. Detective Steve Neygan was as upset about dealing with a bombing as she was.

It took her a few minutes to spot him. He was the solidly built man at the end of the street, stringing police tape, and pushing back the reporters who were crowding the area.

"Hey, Andrea."

Donovan turned. The head of the bomb squad, Keyla Pierce, walked toward her wearing a protective suit, a science-fictiony helmet under one arm.

Keyla was a tiny woman with a mass of red curls that currently clung wetly to her skull. Sweat dotted her face. The suits had no ventilation at all, and even fifteen minutes in one could feel like an hour.

"What've you got?" Donovan asked.

"A secondary device," Keyla said. "There were two explosions, not one."

"Everyone reported one." Donovan had talked to enough witnesses to know they had only heard one blast.

"They might've been seconds apart," Keyla said. "Or the first wasn't quite as loud. The second was the big one."

"You sure there aren't any more unexploded bombs in there?" Donovan asked.

Keyla smiled tiredly. "We're still checking, but I doubt it. We did an initial sweep, and the arson team's been all over that place. Unless the device is very small or extremely unrecognizable as a bomb, we haven't found anything."

Donovan wasn't sure if this news reassured her or made her even more nervous. She was beginning to realize that bombs creeped her out more than some maniac with a gun.

"So tell me about the secondary device," she said.

"This was a smart house," Keyla said. "And the device was tied into that system."

Donovan barely had a grasp of what a smart house was. "You mean the entire place was computerized?"

"The lights, the heating system, even the entertainment centers were all tied into one central panel. If the house was intact, I could tell you if the refrigerator and stove were part of the system too. I suspect so. This kind of system is expensive and state-of-the-art, and unfortunately, it's very easy to hack into."

Donovan frowned. "But wouldn't a smart system need electricity to keep running? I thought this place was a foreclosure."

"That was my first thought," Keyla said, "but the arson team already figured out that the power had been on. We checked why and discovered that the bank puts the power onto its bill while it preps the house for resale. The bank is apparently looking for problems in the system and it's trying to make things easier on the team that cleans out the place."

Donovan looked at the house. The bank had done the team no favors.

"It wasn't easier on them," she said.

"It was the second blast that caused the most damage," Keyla continued. "It's going to take us a while to figure out all the component parts of these bombs, but knowing that the bomber tapped into the house's system does make it easier."

"It does?" Donovan asked.

"For two reasons," Keyla said. "This bomber is sophisticated and up-to-date. He had to be off-premises and aware that someone was in the house. I suspect the second bomb had an off-site trigger."

"He blew the place from far away *after* the first device went off?"

"Probably," Keyla said.

"Watching from one of these empty houses?" Donovan asked.

"Maybe," Keyla said. "But if I had to put money on it all, I'd say he wasn't even in the neighborhood. I'd guess he was watching from a computer somewhere, and he waited until someone got close to the second bomb before triggering it."

"So the cleaning team wasn't together?" Donovan asked.

"We think one was upstairs and the other in the kitchen. Everything is such a mess that it's hard to know for sure."

Donovan shuddered. "And someone managed this off-site?"

"Maybe not even in the city," Keyla said. "He could've been anywhere."

"Wonderful." Donovan shook her head slightly. Now she didn't just have to deal with arson teams and bomb squads. She had to deal with computer experts.

This case was more of a nightmare than she wanted it to be—and it was only just beginning.

•••

Donovan was an old-fashioned detective who preferred legwork to DNA analysis. Fortunately, her partner knew that. Neygan volunteered to talk to the computer crimes division and report back to her—in exchange for the right to stay away from the victims' families.

Donovan understood that one. Talking to the families was a bigger minefield than going into a bombed-out house. But she had talked to families more times than she cared to think about, and she had a routine that minimized her emotional involvement.

Or so she thought.

Minimizing the emotional stake was easy with Micah Collingsworth. His family had arrived from the East Coast the night before, and they were holed up in an exclusive hotel downtown.

She met the family in one of the upstairs suites. Everyone had flown in—both parents, four siblings, and the two remaining grandparents, along with the siblings' spouses and children. The funeral, apparently, would be here "in the place Micah loved," his mother had said, her voice hitching only a little.

The family had already gotten the news, so Donovan didn't have to worry about dealing with the immediate grief and shock. They were well off—able to board planes in less than 24 hours and show up in a strange city—not to mention afford rooms in one of the city's most expensive hotels for more than a week.

The family didn't know much more. Collingsworth had broken up with a long-term girlfriend before he lost his corporate position. They hadn't even known he was cleaning buildings.

Minimizing her emotional involvement, however, became harder when she visited the Ansara family. Gracie Ansara had been a single mom with three kids. The kids—two girls and a boy—were sixteen, fourteen and twelve.

They lived in an upscale subdivision not that different from the one that got bombed. Donovan had been surprised at that. She had figured someone who cleaned houses for a living lived in one of Portland's less expensive neighborhoods.

When she knocked on the door, an elderly woman answered. She introduced herself as Rafe Ansara's mother, and it took Donovan a moment to realize that Rafe Ansara must have been the late husband.

The grandmother had driven down from Seattle. She was taking care of the arrangements and trying to figure out what to do with the children. By her own admission, she knew little about Gracie Ansara's life.

So the grandmother took Donovan to meet someone who did know Gracie's life, her oldest daughter, Hannah.

Hannah sat at the kitchen table. A pile of bills sat to one side, a yellow legal pad on the other. A pencil stuck out of her haphazard nest of blonde hair, and she was chewing on a pen. An iPhone leaned against a pile of schoolbooks, and a calculator sat to her right.

She was thin, with a teenage athlete's build. She wore an oversized Portland Trailblazers sweatshirt, and blue jeans with the cuffs rolled up.

"If you're some social worker here to tell me I don't have the right to stay in my house, you can get out," Hannah snapped.

She was certainly not what Donovan had expected.

Donovan reached into her pocket and removed her badge. "Detective Andrea Donovan," she said. "I'm investigating the bombing."

"You mean my mother's murder," Hannah said.

"Yes," Donovan said. "That's exactly what I mean."

Hannah drew her knees up and put her stocking feet on her chair. Then she tucked the chewed-up pen beside the pencil in her hair.

"I thought you people travel in pairs," she said.

Donovan wasn't used to this kind of interrogation from family members, let alone teenagers.

"Normally, we do," she said. "But my partner is working with the bomb squad at the moment."

"You have any suspects yet?" Hannah asked.

"Nothing official." Donovan put her hand on the back of one of the chairs. "Do you mind if I sit down?"

Hannah shrugged one bony shoulder. "I suppose I should ask Grammy if you're allowed to sit down."

Donovan was beginning to get a sense of the extent of the conflict between grandmother and granddaughter.

"Hannah," her grandmother said.

"It's okay, Mrs. Ansara," Donovan said to the older woman. "You can stay if you'd like, but I'm just going to ask your granddaughter routine questions. Maybe you could get the other children for me…?"

The older woman sighed, then disappeared into the hallway.

"I take it she wants you to go back to Seattle with her," Donovan said.

Hannah set her jaw. Donovan's guess had been right. That was the core of the argument.

"Mom paid off this house," Hannah said. "All three of us have college funds, and Mom took out a lot of life insurance after Dad died. I can take care of everyone."

"You're sixteen."

"And I'm going to be smarter in 15 months when I turn eighteen? C'mon." Hannah managed contempt the way that only a teenager could. "I've been helping Mom with everything since Dad died. I can handle it now."

She put her hand on the bills.

"Grammy didn't even know where to start. I had to take her to the right funeral home. I had to pick out the package. I've been the one making sure that Rafaela and Graden are getting some sleep and have someone to talk to. Grammy's just getting in the way."

"And the county's already been here," Donovan said, careful not to frame this as a question, "to help you find someone to take care of you."

"Yep." Hannah sounded disgusted. "Just today. When that old biddy left, I started looking through all Mom's stuff for the lawyer who handled Dad's estate."

Donovan raised her eyebrows. "Because?"

"Because I'm going to be declared legally fit to take care of my family," Hannah said. "What's that called? Emancipated?"

"I don't know," Donovan said. She thought emancipation was when a kid wanted to divorce her parents, but she knew better than to say that. She wasn't sure if any of this domestic drama was relevant to her case, but she was going to hear the girl out. "Taking care of two kids sounds like a big job."

"Mom and I were a team. I'm the one who told her to start the business," Hannah's eyes filled with tears. The transition from prideful anger to sadness was so sudden it took Donovan's breath away.

It took her a moment to understand why. "You don't think it's your fault your mom died, do you?"

"I should've known better," Hannah said, her voice shaking. "She came home from the early jobs, talking about how people trashed their houses, and how sometimes a sheriff had to show up to evict them and they'd sneak back. She said the early visits could be dangerous."

"And this was an early visit?" Donovan asked.

"This was the first time she'd gone to the house. That's why Micah was along. Because she knew better than to go alone."

That made sense to Donovan. "No one could have expected this."

"I don't know," Hannah said. "Those people were weird."

"Which people?" Donovan asked.

"The Martins," Hannah said. "I went to school with Richard."

"You're not going to school now?"

"Not this week," she snapped. Then her cheeks turned faintly pink. "Oh, you mean why did I use the past tense about Richard?"

Donovan was startled at how bright the girl was. Donovan didn't even have to ask the next question. Hannah had known what the question was. Most adults Donovan interrogated didn't even know that much.

"Richard's the one who left," Hannah said. "When his parents moved, he stopped coming to school."

"Is he going to a different school?" Donovan asked.

"I don't know," Hannah said. "He's one of those preppy bastards, you know?"

"Here they are," the grandmother said.

Donovan suppressed a sigh. She felt like she had just gotten into a rhythm with Hannah, and the grandmother had interrupted.

Donovan turned in her chair. A gawky fourteen-year-old boy, all matted brown hair and pimples, stood behind her. The boy's shirt was buttoned wrong, and his face was swollen from crying.

Beside him stood one of the most startling children she had ever seen. She was ethereal and angelic. When she got older, she would be a stunning beauty.

No wonder the grandmother wanted custody. That girl alone would be trouble.

"Thank you, Mrs. Ansara," Donovan said. "Would you all mind waiting in the other room while I finish talking to Hannah?"

The grandmother's eyes narrowed, but she led the two younger children out of the kitchen. Donovan could hear them rummaging around in the nearby dining room. They could probably hear every word, but she decided that it didn't matter.

"It sounds like you didn't like Richard Martin," Donovan said.

"God, no." Hannah rolled her eyes. "He was awful."

"To you or to everyone?"

She looked away then, moving the pile of bills with her fingers.

That movement gave Donovan her answer. The boy had been mean to Hannah, but not to everyone else.

"I'm not up on the terms," Donovan said. "By preppy, do you mean that he dressed really well or are you referring to something else?"

"He was going to go to an Ivy," Hannah said. "He was a legacy, so he didn't even need SATs. My SATs were the best in my class, and they're not going to be good enough, that's what the guidance counselor said. And he gets a free ride because his parents went."

It took Donovan another minute to catch up. An Ivy, meaning an Ivy League School. This girl was sixteen and she was already thinking about college? Things were very different from the time Donovan was a teenager.

"I thought the schools take various things into account," Donovan said. "Not just SAT scores, but extracurriculars and grades and everything."

Hannah shrugged that shoulder again. "That's what Mom says. But it doesn't matter now. I'm not going anywhere. I'll either go to Linfield or Portland State. I'm staying with the kids."

The fact that she had this all thought out within two days had startled Donovan.

She nodded at the pile of bills. "What are you doing there?"

"Making sure that with Mom's life insurance, we'll have enough money to finish school and go off to college. Don't worry. I've done this before. I helped Mom when Dad died."

Donovan's heart twisted. The girl impressed her more than she wanted to think about.

"I'm getting all the paperwork in order," Hannah was saying, "so that when I talk to the lawyer, I'll be prepared."

"Is this what your mother would have wanted?" Donovan asked, and then winced at how patronizing that sounded.

"I don't know," Hannah said. "We never talked about it past the insurance and stuff. Mom wasn't that old. She was going to be around for a long time. That's what she said."

The wobbly voice again. Donovan could almost hear the conversation after the father died.

Mom, you're not going to die now, are you?

Of course not, baby. Nothing's going to happen to me.

Donovan shook it off, and made herself focus on the case. "You said the Martins were strange. You knew the whole family?"

Hannah's eyes narrowed. "You think they did it, right? That's what the news says."

"The news people don't know anything," Donovan said.

Hannah grunted, then thought, clearly considering what she was going to say. "I only met them once. They were, like, plastic people, you know?"

Plastic people. Donovan was going to ask for clarification, but she wasn't going to do so directly. Hannah already thought she was a bit slow—and maybe she was. Donovan didn't have children. Obviously, she had lost the knack for talking with them.

"Where did you meet the family?" Donovan asked.

Hannah looked away again. "A party."

"At Richard's house?" Donovan asked.

Hannah nodded, moving the bills. "That place was so perfect."

A tear fell, slapping the paper. She shoved the papers out of the way and rubbed her eyes furiously.

"What do you mean, perfect?" Donovan asked.

"Everything in the right place," Hannah said. "Everything was so neat. Mom would've loved it. That's what I remember thinking. Mom would've been so impressed. She always wanted our house to look like that, and it never did."

Hannah's voice trembled at the end of the sentence. She bit her lower lip, trying to stop tears. When that didn't work, she put a hand over her mouth.

Donovan looked for Kleenex, but didn't see any. Hannah gasped out a sob, then shook her head, and pushed away from the table. She staggered out of the room. She didn't go into the dining room. Instead she vanished up the stairs.

Donovan sighed. She wasn't going to go after Hannah. Donovan would let Hannah calm down, and maybe talk to her again, particularly if Donovan felt the Martin family belonged on the suspect list.

Donovan stood slowly, moved the bills around just a little, looking for anything unusual. She didn't see much.

Then she went into the dining room for her perfunctory questioning of the other two children. It yielded nothing. The grandmother seemed exceptionally clueless about the family she wanted to adopt.

Donovan didn't like the elderly woman. She wondered if that was reason enough to trust a sixteen-year-old's judgment that the children were better off without the older woman.

Donovan shook her head, reminding herself that catching the killer was her job. And to that end, the Martin family had caught her attention. No one in the neighborhood had mentioned the Martins had children. No one had said much about the family at all—except that their house had been a showplace, and everyone had been surprised to see the foreclosure notice.

Donovan was a bit surprised too. Not at the foreclosure—seemed like half the planet was losing a home these days. But the mention of the Ivy League school, the talk of legacies, which meant that the Martin family had a long tradition of going to expensive East Coast colleges.

There must have been money once. Ivy League legacies were usually impressive, prominent people. Donovan had always thought they sent their kids to one of those tony East Coast prep schools, usually a boarding school, instead of a local public high school.

Had this Richard Martin been lying to Hannah? If so, why?

Donovan returned to the station with more questions than she expected. Her first task was to track the Martins down. People who got evicted were usually hard to find. They didn't have to give a forwarding address, and they were usually so poor that their credit cards had been cancelled before the loss of their home.

Still, she started through the standard investigatory tools, trying to find the Martins, using their phone records, their credit cards, and any applications they might have made for new utility service.

Everything she found had been canceled or was in default. The cell phone companies were trying to collect on a three-thousand dollar bill, the forty-thousand dollar credit card had been in default for months, and no one had applied for new electric service or anything else.

They had three vehicles, but two had been repossessed. The third was an old Chevy van, and it, apparently, was paid for.

So she started there. She put a flag on the license, hoping that would turn up something. Then she decided to dig into the financials, to see what went wrong.

What went wrong seemed pretty mundane. The Martins lived at the edge of their means for years, juggling the mortgage, the cars, and the unbelievable credit card bills. They spent every penny they had plus.

Gary Martin, the husband and father, worked as some kind of investment counselor at one of the downtown Portland firms. Two years before anyone was talking about economic meltdowns, the firm let him go. Nothing had gone wrong at the firm or in the local economy—at least nothing that she could find.

So far as she could tell, Martin never got another job. His credit card bills and his cell phone records told a familiar story: he went to job seminars and get-rich-quick seminars, often buying the materials. He called job service lines and talked to job counselors, but nothing seemed to pan out.

The financial troubles started about six months in. The family didn't slow down spending, but they started skating bills, paying one this month and a different one that month. Irene Martin had a job too—some kind of fashion consultant at a local department store—but it didn't pay a quarter of her husband's wages. And when the economy got worse, her job disappeared as well.

Both of them were unemployed, unable to afford their lifestyle, and apparently unable (or unwilling) to get some kind of help.

Nothing in their job history gave the Martins the kind of tech savvy that justified a Smart House. Donovan dug into their education history. Gary Martin had been a Liberal Arts major at his "Ivy," Princeton. His wife hadn't graduated from a real college, but from some school of fashion design.

So Donovan called Gary's former employer. Once she got past the "we don't give that information out" response to why Gary Martin left his position, she got her answers.

Gary Martin had been skimming money off his clients for years, maintaining the house and the lifestyle not on his salary, but on his salary plus all he could steal. Rather than charge him with embezzlement, the firm didn't pay him his vacation or sick leave when he left, using that money to repay the investors.

The firm also didn't prosecute because they didn't want to publicize the fact that they had been victims of one of their own employees.

"Of course," the woman in the personnel department told Donovan, "we also didn't give him any recommendations. It's hard to get a comparable job when your former employer refuses to discuss you or your work."

She said that with just a bit of glee, leading Donovan to realize that the firm had gotten its revenge, mostly in preventing Martin from ever working again.

"Did he do a lot with computers?" Donovan asked.

"A little," the woman said. "The trades and funds were managed online."

"Did he need a lot of technical expertise to use that equipment?" Donovan asked.

"No," the woman said.

"Did you ever see any evidence of tech savvy from Martin?" Donovan asked.

"No," the woman said. "A bit of tech phobia, but that was normal for our traders. Every time we upgrade, they freak out. They're into the markets and money, not into learning new computer programs."

Donovan nodded. She asked the same questions of Irene Martin's former boss, and got similar answers.

"Do you have any idea," she asked Irene's former boss, "why the Martins would have bought a Smart House?"

"Oh," the boss said, "that was for the children. They were going to be the next Bill Gates. She thought they were brilliant."

"Did she mention which child in particular was brilliant with computers?" Donovan asked.

"Oh, they both were," the boss said. "We even called them in one afternoon when we had a glitch in our system and we couldn't reach tech support. The son got us back up in no time, and the daughter put in some kind of fail-safe so we wouldn't have the same problem again."

"I thought these kids were still in high school," Donovan said.

"The daughter wasn't quite twelve when she helped us," the former boss said. "We had to pay her off the books. But it was because of those kids that we kept Irene as long as we did. We let her go when we no longer had a choice."

When Donovan hung up from that call, she was frowning. The kids? She couldn't imagine children setting up bombs that sophisticated. Molotov cocktails, yes. Some dynamite with a detonator, maybe. But not something that tapped into a house's computer system.

She had just moved from the Martins to the developer when her partner, Neygan, sat down at his desk.

"You got anything?" she asked him.

"A headache," he said. "I don't ever want to look at bomb components again."

She didn't want to talk to families ever again, but she didn't complain about it.

"What did you figure out?" she asked, trying not to be annoyed.

"*I* didn't figure out anything," he said. "The bomb squad now confirms that there were two devices. They don't know a lot about the first one, except that it was smaller than the second."

"And the other device?" Donovan asked.

"It was triggered off-site. Someone actually had to push a button or something to make it explode. No way it could've gone off on its own."

Donovan rubbed her nose. Her eyes were tired, and she was getting a headache too. "I'd think some off-site trigger would give us a trail to the bomber."

"You'd think," Neygan said. "I got computer crimes on it. They've already traced everything to an internet café in Sun River."

"Sun River?" Donovan said.

"Don't ask me," Neygan said. "They don't know where the doer actually was, because you can route stuff through other computers. All I know is that it happened off-site and our doer was sitting there like a spider in a web, watching its prey work its way into the death-trap."

"You're mixing metaphors again," Donovan said, as she pulled the file she had made on the developer. He didn't look very computer savvy either.

Then she realized what Neygan had said.

"The doer was watching these people?" she asked.

"That we do know. There were cameras everywhere. This sick twist waited until the person in the kitchen got close, and then set off that device."

"You're sure about this," Donovan said. "The doer watched."

"Probably from the time the team came in the door. The bomb squad isn't sure if the doer waited until they split up and got close to the devices or what. The squad still isn't even sure if there were more devices in that house, y'know, waiting for someone to get close."

"This is targeted murder, then," Donovan said.

"How do you figure?" Neygan said.

"If the doer watched the victims move through the house, then he could chose whether or not to push that button."

Neygan frowned. "I hadn't thought of that."

"I was just assuming these were random victims," Donovan said.

"We all were," Neygan said.

"But those bombs could have gone off when the sheriff evicted the family or when the city inspectors came in or when the lender's representative walked through the house. There were probably countless people who could have died in those explosions."

"We don't know that," Neygan said. "We don't know the bombs were there then."

He was right; they didn't know. But it was probable that the bombs had been planted before that lock box went on the building. But probable meant Donovan was making an assumption. Probable began that slippery slope to the right theory, but not enough proof to make an arrest, let alone a conviction.

"Maybe that's something we can ask the bomb squad," she said. "Maybe they can tell how long the bombs were there."

She doubted it, though. Unless the materials used inside the bombs could degrade, they could have been in those spots for years. Or weeks. Or hours.

There was no real way to know.

Neygan's expression hadn't changed as she said all of this. She wasn't even sure he had heard her.

"You're saying that the doer waited for those two people to go into the house." Neygan tapped his forefinger against his upper lip. "I thought no one but the bank knew they were going in."

"So far as I know, that's right," Donovan said.

"You're saying someone from the bank killed them?" Neygan asked.

Donovan shook her head. "I'm just wondering if the bomber was waiting for one of those two people to show up."

"How would he have known either of them was going to be there?"

She looked up at Neygan. "That's the question isn't it? If we know the answer to that, we know the answer to everything."

•••

Donovan drove to the Ansara house. She brought Neygan along even though he didn't want to meet the family.

They arrived at the Ansara house as the streetlights were coming on. Donovan could see the family through the dining room windows. The boy faced the street, his head bowed. He picked at his food. His beautiful younger sister was stirring the food on her plate like she was making soup.

Hannah ate deliberately, as if she had to think about each bite. The grandmother held a cup of coffee before her chest like a shield.

"Oh, I'm not going in there," Neygan said as he got out of the car and looked into the window.

"Yes, you are," Donovan said. "but you're going to let me talk and you're going to listen."

"Because?"

"Because I need someone else's interpretation, to see if I'm completely off-base."

Neygan sighed. "We have computer tech working on this case. They'll figure it out. We don't need one of your hunches."

Donovan's hunches were famous. They were always right, but they were almost impossible to prove in court. Over the years, she'd gotten smarter about them. Now, she at least tried to get some evidence to back them up.

She didn't respond to Neygan's complaint. Instead, she marched up the front steps and knocked on the door. Out of the corner of her eye, she could see movement in the dining room.

The grandmother was going to answer the door again.

This time, Donovan was ready for her. Donovan pulled open the screen as the grandmother opened the door.

"Mrs. Ansara," Donovan said, "I have a few more questions for Hannah. It'll only take a minute."

By the time she had finished talking, she was already inside the entry. She strode down the hall to the dining room. Behind her, she could hear Neygan apologizing, then introducing himself. Donovan didn't wait for him.

As she walked into the room, the boy—Graden?—looked up. The younger sister stopped stirring her food, but Hannah was the one who spoke.

"You know anything?" she asked.

"I'm not sure." Donovan felt awkward looming over the kids while food was on the table. The place smelled of roast beef and gravy. She pulled one of the extra chairs away from the wall, and sat near Hannah.

Graden put his fork down and turned his chair slightly, so that he could see both his sister and Donovan. The younger sister started stirring her food again, as if this had nothing to do with her.

"Do you know anything about your mom's business?" Donovan asked.

Hannah shrugged. "Some."

"We helped in the summer," Graden said.

Donovan looked at him. His face was still swollen from crying, but his eyes weren't as red. They shone with the same kind of intelligence that Hannah's had.

"Do you know if she cleaned out any of the other foreclosures in the Martins' neighborhood?" Donovan asked.

"All of them," Hannah said. "It was some kind of deal with the bank. It was the first one she got, and that neighborhood was a—what do you call it?—development."

"Mom called it a development gone bad." This from the youngest daughter, Rafaela. The food on her plate didn't look like food at all. It looked like badly mixed house paint.

"Yeah," Graden said. "Everyone was upside down and getting out. That's what she said."

Hannah's lips had thinned. She looked scared. "Why do you want to know?"

Donovan wasn't going to answer that question yet. "Did Micah Collingsworth always go with her when she first visited a foreclosure?"

"No," Hannah said. "It was whoever was available."

Two of Donovan's hunches were right. Now she needed to confirm the third.

"Muscle," Graden was saying. "She wanted muscle in case something went wrong. She said I could go with her when I came into my growth."

He sounded like he regretted not being at her side now. Donovan wondered if he had some kind of rescue fantasy going on in his head. Had he thought he would have been able to save his mom when the first bomb went off?

"Last time I was here," Donovan said to Hannah, "you told me about Richard Martin. You said he was mean, but when I asked you if he was mean to everyone or just to you, you didn't answer."

"He was mean to Hannah," Graden said.

"He was a prick," Rafaela said almost at the same time. The word was shocking coming from such a beautiful young girl.

Hannah glared at her sister. "Don't talk like that."

The grandmother and Neygan came into the dining room. The grandmother returned to her chair, but Neygan hovered near the door. Hannah's gaze lifted, acknowledged him, and then went back to Donovan.

Graden said, "He hated Hannah."

"Really?" Donovan asked. "Why?"

"Because she told him off," Graden said with just a bit of pride.

"I did not." Hannah sounded tired, as if they'd had that discussion before.

"You did too," Graden said.

Obviously Hannah didn't want to talk about this. But Donovan had to know. She turned slightly in her chair so that she faced Graden.

"What happened?" Donovan asked.

Graden glanced at Hannah who shook her head. His lower lip pushed out slightly, pouting, and for a minute, Donovan thought he wasn't going to answer her question.

Then he said, "It was last year, the day they posted the PSATs."

Over his head, Donovan could see Neygan frown. So she asked for her partner's sake, "The PSATs?"

"You can take a preliminary SAT test for college, you know, and see where you stand. It doesn't count. But everyone does it to practice."

"And they post the scores?" Donovan asked. She was a bit shocked about that. She thought the scores would be private.

"They hand them out on a sheet of paper, but everyone tells," Graden said. "If you didn't tell, everyone would think you flunked."

"You can't flunk the SAT," Hannah said quietly, but her complaint obviously wasn't about the test. It was that her brother was telling this story.

"Hannah got a perfect score. Perfect. And Richard was being a dick about it like he always was."

"Graden," the grandmother said in the same tone that Hannah had used for her sister. "Language."

"Were you there?" Donovan asked. "Did you see this?"

"Yeah," Graden said. "It was outside. School had just got out and everyone was comparing scores. I just wanted to go home, so I was trying to get Hannah to come with me."

"How was Richard being—?" Donovan stopped herself. The grandmother's tone was affecting her too. "What was he doing?"

"He was saying that Hannah's just a brain. She's really boring and no one'll ever like her because she's so smart."

"He hated that about her," Rafaela said. "She was always doing better than him."

"You saw it too?" Donovan asked.

Rafaela shook her head. "I seen it other times. He didn't like anyone to do better than him. He beat up some kid on the soccer team for getting a goal in practice. Richard was goalie that day, and the ball just got by him."

"Nice kid," Neygan said.

Everyone turned to him. Graden and Rafaela looked surprised to see him. They hadn't realized he was in the room.

"That's my partner," Donovan said. "So Richard was mean to you, and anyone else who was smart."

"He was just mean," Hannah said.

"But something happened that day," Donovan said to her. "Tell me about it."

Hannah shook her head again. "It's not important."

"What happened was she got mad," Graden said. "For her whole life, she let him talk bad to her and that day she didn't take it any more."

"She was mad anyway," Rafaela said. "Dad was dead and Mom needed help and Hannah wasn't getting any sleep."

"I was too," Hannah said.

"I hear you at night," Rafaela said. "You weren't sleeping then, just like you're not sleeping now."

Hannah shot her a nasty look, one that complained she was giving away secrets not hers to give. In spite of herself, Donovan felt her heart go out to Hannah. Hannah was trying so hard to be tough so that everyone would think her strong enough to care for her family, and yet her family knew how hard it was for her to get through each day.

"What happened?" Donovan asked softly.

Hannah bit her lip. When she didn't speak, Graden again filled the silence.

"It was great," he said. "Richard asked her score, and she told him. Then he was making fun of her, calling her Miss Perfect, the Ugliest Girl in School."

Graden was talking directly to Donovan, but Donovan watched Hannah. When he said that, Hannah's eyes filled with tears. Even now, those words had the power to hurt. Did Hannah think she was ugly? Probably, in comparison to that younger sister.

"And Hannah just had it, you know?" Graden continued. "She gets this voice when she's really mad, all quiet-like, and that's what she used on him. She says, 'What's your score?' and he tells her, and it's really low. Everybody laughs, and usually that would've been enough for Hannah, but it wasn't."

This time he looked at his sister. She was just watching him implacably, a single tear hanging on her eyelashes. He shrugged a little, as if in apology.

"Then what?" Donovan asked.

"Then he said something about how he'd be going to an Ivy even with his score, and that's when Hannah let him have it. She said he'd be going to an Ivy because of his parents, not because he did anything. She said Ivys took rich stupid people so that they could get enough money to let poor smart people in. He knew it was true. Everybody knew it was true, and he got really, really mean after that."

"I wasn't very nice," Hannah said.

"What's really really mean?" Donovan asked Graden.

"He said horrible stuff about Mom. Every time we saw him, he said stuff about her being a cleaning lady and us being white trash and no good and not even a good education would make us classy and stuff like that." Graden didn't sound bothered, but Hannah's expression became more and more strained.

"Sounds like you hit a nerve," Donovan said to Hannah. "Do you think, maybe, your comment about being rich and stupid bothered him because his family was going broke?"

"What do you mean?" Hannah asked.

"You told him poor, smart kids could get into an Ivy League school, but by implication, you meant that poor dumb kids couldn't."

"He wasn't dumb," Hannah said. "He just didn't try hard. His math score on the PSAT was really, really high. It was his verbal that was the problem."

"Did you ever tell him that?" Donovan asked.

Hannah shook her head. "He really hates me," she said quietly.

Donovan sighed. Then she asked a few more questions, wrapping everything up so that it wasn't all about Richard Martin.

Even though it was.

As she and Neygan got into the car, he said to her, "You think that's enough motive? You think that Richard kid blew up her mom as some kind of revenge for what she said?"

Donovan shook her head. "I think Richard Martin was miserable. I think everything he knew was falling apart, and he was looking for someone to blame."

"So he blamed that girl's *mom*?"

"I don't think so," Donovan said. "I think he couldn't get the idea Hannah planted out of his mind. I think he blamed her for making him so afraid for his own future. I think he decided to get revenge by making her afraid for her future."

"You haven't even met the kid," Neygan said.

"No, I haven't," Donovan said. "But I've seen people kill for a whole lot less."

"Well, I think we got a whole lot of less," Neygan said, "and the chief is gonna want evidence and proof that we didn't just go after some kid on a hunch."

"I know," Donovan said. "We still have a lot of work to do."

• • •

And work they did. They interviewed everyone they could think of with connections to the case. The developer knew nothing about computers, the mortgage brokers knew nothing about bomb making, and the neighbors couldn't get into the house.

It took some time for Donovan and Neygan to find the Martins, but by the time they did, computer crimes had traced a contact between the house and an off-site computer linked to the Martins. Not to mention the Sun River internet café connection. The family used to ski there in the winter. The café owner remembered Richard, saying he looked like a kid who was "about to blow."

Donovan got five minutes alone with Richard—a slender, athletic boy with scary intense eyes—but couldn't get him to say much. Except when she mentioned Hannah.

"You realize," Donovan said as they waited for Richard's lawyer to arrive, "that you just made it easier for Hannah to get into an Ivy League School."

Richard's cheeks flushed. "What?"

"Private schools," Donovan said. "They take all kinds of things into account. Not just SAT scores and high grades, but hardship factors as well. She's an orphan now, raising her siblings, and keeping her grades up. She just went way up on their list."

"No way," he said. "You're making that up."

Donovan shook her head. "If you had left her mom alive, Hannah probably wouldn't have had a chance of getting into a good school. You just did her a favor."

He slammed his fist onto the interview table. "I didn't want to do her a favor. Miss Perfect—she always lands on her damn feet. Dammit!"

And that was when the attorney came in, shut Richard up, and kicked Donovan out of the room.

But that little outburst was all she needed. It confirmed her hunch. The bomb squad and computer crimes confirmed the rest. The bomb squad found components that matched the set-up in the house, and computer crimes found various videos of the house on computers that Richard had used since he moved out.

"It was set up like this," Keyla told Donovan over a beer the night Richard was arrested. "He had designed the first bomb to go off at a touch. He knew that a house cleaner would clean that up. The first bomb would notify him that she was in the house. Then he'd see if it was her. If it was, he would set off the second."

"Do you think he would have set off the second if someone else had been in the house?" Donovan asked.

Keyla shook her head. "You can't figure these guys out. Bombers are crazy. Bombers and arsonists. They've got something missing."

"Even young guys?" Donovan asked.

"Especially young guys," Keyla said. "Most of them don't live long enough to become old guys."

And that was that. Richard decided not to have a trial, instead pleading 25 to life, with the possibility for parole. His parents and younger sibling left Oregon, and the bank bulldozed what was left of the house, selling the vacant lot instead.

Donovan drove by the house a few times while it was still standing, trying to understand—truly understand—a boy's jealous mind. She finally decided she couldn't.

But she also knew she couldn't let the case go.

So the day after Richard's allocution in court, she drove to the Ansara house.

•••

It looked the same, except someone had pulled blinds over all the windows. When she knocked, the grandmother answered. As she led Donovan inside, the grandmother told her the kids weren't home. They were in school.

"I thought you were going to take them to Seattle," Donovan said.

"I was." They stood in the foyer. "But I listened to what you said that night."

"What *I* said?" Donovan asked.

"What you all said. Those kids, they were fighting for what they saw as their future."

Donovan tilted her head. She hadn't expected insight from this woman. "I guess you could say that, yes."

"And if I took Hannah to Seattle, she would have fought me for the rest of her life," the grandmother said. "If I let her be the one to raise those kids, they wouldn't have much of a future either. She'd go to a local school, which she didn't want, and she'd resent them. She didn't know that yet, but she would."

Donovan nodded. She had underestimated this woman tremendously.

"So I did the math with her," the grandmother said. "I have my own retirement. I decided to sell my house. We're using the money from the sale of Gracie's business and from her life insurance for the kids' school. I don't have to work, so I can take care of things."

"She seemed so angry with you," Donovan said.

The grandmother smiled. "We talked after you left about how anger can be misdirected."

"She knew you weren't just talking about Richard Martin's anger?" Donovan asked.

The grandmother nodded. "Hannah's not dumb."

"No," Donovan said. "She's about as far from dumb as any girl can get."

•••

As she left the house, the school bus pulled up across the street. She waited. Hannah and Graden got off along with some other kids. Hannah and Graden walked separately, as if they didn't know each other.

They didn't see Donovan until they were almost beside her.

"He shouldn't get a chance at parole," Hannah said without saying hello.

That wasn't Donovan's decision to make, but she didn't defend it.

"You can stop it," Donovan said. "When his hearing comes up, you can testify. I'm sure they'll listen to you."

Hannah straightened. "You think?"

Donovan nodded. "But I also think you shouldn't do it."

"Why not?" Hannah said. "He killed my mom."

"Your mom wanted you to have a great life. If you pay attention to him, you stay stuck in this horrible year. He probably won't get out. And I'll be around. I'll make sure I testify for you."

Hannah's eyes narrowed. "You'd do that?"

"I would," Donovan said.

"I'm transferring to Portland State," Hannah said. "I tested out. I'll be out in two weeks."

It took Donovan a moment to realize she meant that she had tested out of high school. "I thought you wanted to go to a major university?"

"I do," Hannah said. "Just not this year."

Then she walked off without saying good-bye, her head down. She still looked like she had the weight of the world on her shoulders.

Graden had been standing silently nearby. He watched her go. Then he looked at Donovan.

"She didn't want to be known as the kid whose mom got blown up," he said. "She wants to be Hannah again."

"Are you having that problem?" Donovan asked.

He shook his head. "Nobody pays any attention to me."

Donovan didn't know what to say to that. By the time she had formulated a response, he lifted his hand in good-bye and hurried to the house.

She watched him go. No one paid attention to him, but they needed to. If she hadn't paid attention to him, she wouldn't have caught the killer.

She had initially thought Hannah was the strong solid core of that family. She had been wrong.

Graden was.

She wondered if the grandmother had noticed. For a moment, Donovan toyed with telling her, then remembered that she had underestimated the grandmother too.

That family had shattered, but it was rebuilding itself. She didn't need to interfere. They were a lot stronger and a lot healthier than the Martins had been.

Although anyone looking at the families one year ago would have thought otherwise.

Which only went to show how flimsy appearances were—and how she needed to remember that. Not just from case to case, but from moment to moment.

She silently wished them well. Then she got into her car and left the neighborhood, passing half a dozen for-sale signs as she went.

KRISTINE KATHRYN RUSCH publishes mystery, science fiction, and fantasy under her own name. She also writes mystery as the award-winning Kris Nelscott, romance as Kristine Grayson, and a variety of other genres under other names. Under Rusch, she has been nominated for the Edgar, the Shamus, the Anthony, and she has won the Ellery Queen Readers Choice award. Her short stories have appeared in more than twenty best of the year collections. Find out more on her website, www.kristinekathrynrusch.com.

THE RETURN OF INSPIRATION

TOM PICCIRILLI

I WAS BACK IN FRISCO AND I STILL HAD NO IDEA WHY I WAS THERE.

It had something to do with the fact that my wife had tossed me out and New York had turned sour for me. Her attorney had chased me from our apartment and her girlfriends had iced me from our social circle. My buddies had to meet me in secret so their wives wouldn't know they were consorting with the enemy. They were getting more and more worried all the time until we could only hang for a few minutes at the kiddie park while their children played. My pals were always late and fled quickly. I sat on that fucking bench watching screaming kids so often that the cops finally rousted me for being a potential pedo.

For a year my publisher had been hinting at dropping me unless my novel sales improved greatly. They didn't improve, greatly or otherwise. My last royalty statement had been for $12.35. I had resigned myself to the possibility that I wasn't destined to retire to St. Croix anytime soon.

Another buddy had started hitting it big in Frisco as an underground performance artist. He played to audiences of a few hundred every night, which didn't seem very underground to me. He tried to explain exactly what he did, but I got too confused trying to picture how the bale of wire, the unicycle, the fifteen-pound weights, and the penis puppets all went together. It proved the limitations of my imagination, but he invited me out West anyway.

The word got around the circuit that I was coming to town. I didn't even know there was a circuit, or that such a circuit would care about me in the slightest, but there it was. My mysteries never got reviewed. My horror novels had a sixty-five percent return rate. But my whitebread erotica stories had started getting some weird buzz. Even before I got off the plane I had three readings set up. One was at a sex bookstore, one at a sex shop, and one at a sex club. I began to sense a predominant theme attempting to impress itself upon my life.

By the time I got to my buddy's apartment he was already gone. The Europeans had gotten wind of his act and he was off to east London for a two-week show. Things moved fast in Frisco. He left a note saying the place was mine for the duration. Food was stocked and he'd conveniently left a map out on the kitchen counter with the bookstore, sex shop, and club marked in red pen. He told me that people who lived in San Francisco didn't call it Frisco and I was doomed to look like a dumbass tourist. He wished me luck and was kind enough to leave me some cash in case I was strapped. It was fifty bucks. Clearly the concept of strapped didn't go hand in hand with the penis puppets.

The lady running the readings was named Miss Tress. She called and told me she was a big fan of my fiction. She thought it was wonderfully humorous, how I was always writing about my goofy alter ego getting into such ridiculous situations. I didn't have the heart to tell her that I didn't have an alter ego. I told it like it was, but nobody wanted to believe me. I didn't blame them; I didn't want to believe it either.

Miss Tress asked if I wanted to put on any kind of a presentation. She said many of the speakers brought up onstage their spouses, lovers, slaves, doms, troupes, entourages. They chose music, lighting, and a couple had smoke machines. They carried paddles, masks, costumes, plushies, pony-wear, ball-gags. I asked how they read with ball-gags in. She ignored me and said speakers liked to be playful before the audience. They often embraced their sexuality onstage. I had embraced my sexuality many, many times before but never on a stage. She said the best speakers knew how to use props to their advantage. I looked around my pal's apartment and noted handcuffs, rope, duct tape, and excessive amounts of razor wire. The unicycle was propped in the corner. Christ, he even had a smoke machine.

I told her I'd just need a copy of the anthology with my story in it. It was a book called *Naturally Naughty 3,* edited by Alison Wonderland. She said that was excellent—Alison was the main attraction of the show. She hung up and I stared at the phone like I wanted to call someone, but I didn't know who.

•••

I hadn't seen Alison since my last visit to Frisco six months ago, where she was the headliner and I'd read sixth out of six. She'd been expecting someone else. They were always expecting someone else. It was all right, I'd learned to live with it. I was sort of expecting myself to be someone else too.

But after the reading at Betty's Puss and Whips shop, Alison and I had thrown back a few drinks and done a curious dance around each other. She wanted to know where a vanilla fudge pudge like me had gotten enough imagination to write the stories I did. She was a dark, lovely woman with burning eyes, glossy black hair, and a molten fascinating core. The surface drew me in, but it was what smoldered beneath that really hooked me.

We had taken a run over to her apartment, where she threw down a sexual gauntlet that had left me horny, shaken, and with a little too clear an insight into my own contradictions. I was a perverted prude. I was hardwired to be weak. I liked to be stomped but not too much. I liked being on my knees but only if someone appreciated it. She was so powerfully submissive that she'd scared the crap out of me. I didn't cower but I came damn close. I was angry for a lot of reasons I understood and many I didn't.

I hadn't been able to become the dom she needed. I couldn't raise my hand to her. When I thought of a dom I thought of two guys named Dom that I'd known in high school. They'd both been bullies. I already had bad associations. When I thought of a sub I thought of Captain Nemo on the *Nautilus* or roast beef hoagies with lots of mayo. I figured I wasn't going to be in the proper frame of mind to perform at a club called Beat Yer Ass.

I was eager and nervous to see her again. We hadn't spoken or e-mailed since our encounter. I read her blog for any hint of me that might turn up. She talked of many lovers and situations, but never of me. It left me remotely jealous and a little bitter.

Two days later, the fifty bucks was long blown. I was in a cab heading towards the BYA. It was the kind of town where you could mention the name of a club and all the cab drivers would already have the best route mapped out. I was impressed.

The BYA proved to be a decent-sized space that reminded me of some East Village bars. Dark, somber, but with a constant blur of activity in the back corners. A stage had been set up with tables covered in paraphernalia. Some objects I recognized. Many I didn't. My curiosity was piqued. Dozens of books were stacked far to one side. There was no microphone or stool where a reader might sit. A large sign boasted a dozen names. Mine was number eleven out of twelve. I was moving up. At the top with a bullet was Alison Wonderland. The insecurities and self-consciousness began to hit hard.

The joint was crammed. Women in see-through nighties and leather halters with their tits exposed wandered past me. Men in chaps and crushed velvet suits glided past. There were riding crops, canes, cricket paddles, strops, leashes, and zippered leather masks on view. The masks had holes for the eyes and mouth and nostrils but not for the ears. I knew I was going to have to enunciate clearly and really project.

A young woman approached almost warily, slinking up to me hesitantly as if she might slip up on me unnoticed. Since I was staring right at her I didn't quite know how that could work, but I was new to the scene. She wore a black silk halter and a latex skirt and not much else. She looked underage, had a heart-shaped face and cornflower eyes that would normally make me think of girl-next-door wholesomeness if not for the venue being packed with folks waving their naughty bits around.

She looked into my eyes, going deep and not stopping. I didn't know whether to blink or not. I stared back at her and she flinched.

"You're full of rage," she said.

"Me?"

"You've killed many."

"Me?"

"You've destroyed many men and women. The ones you hated and the ones you loved."

"Lady, you've got me mixed up with somebody else."

"If not yet, then soon."

"Say what?"

"Your anger, it cuts into me. I want it. Don't give it to anyone else. I want it. You can punish me. You can murder me if you want. I don't care. Flay me, dump me in the bay. I'll sign a suicide note. They'll never find you."

It was a nutty enough dialogue to normally make me roll my eyes and grin, but I wasn't smiling. Icy threads of sweat prickled my scalp and ran down the back of my neck. She spoke with more conviction than I'd probably ever spoken about anything in my life. I backed away from her and her hand shot out and clenched my wrist.

"I'm yours."

"I don't want you," I said.

"She's not worth bleeding."

"Who?"

"Alison. I know what you want."

"And how the fuck do you know that?"

"She'll never fulfill you. She can't inspire you."

"Look, seriously, I think you—"

"Please."

The girl had some muscle to her. I snapped my arm back twice and still had a hard time breaking her hold on me. The third time she released me.

I wanted to ask her what the hell she was talking about. I wanted to ask exactly why she thought she recognized in me some overwhelming urge towards pain and frenzy. I opened my mouth and she stood on her toes, leaned in, and kissed me.

She said, "You can kill me whenever you want," and faded back, step-by-step, as if consumed by darkness in a well-lit room, until I couldn't see her anymore.

I recognized Miss Tress from my last reading. She spotted me and crossed the place with her hand held out like a duchess. She was decked in full head to toe pink rubber wear. I had images of her tripping, falling, and bouncing around the room like a handball.

She drew me into the wings of the stage. "Are you all right? You look a bit…put out."

"I think I just had a run-in with a fan."

"Trouble?"

"Not really. I've just never had a fan before."

She snorted. "Have you ever been to a reading at a club like this?"

"No," I admitted.

"Well, let me just fill you in…you see, reading is, ah, optional."

"Say what? Reading is optional?"

"Yes, as I mentioned, most of our speakers like to…perform and put on something of a display for the audience. A cabaret."

"A cabaret."

"Yes, their…well, their bodies become their art, you see. Their bodies, their acts of worship, become their fiction. Very few of them actually read."

I blinked at her. "Most of the readers don't read?"

"That's correct."

No wonder the penis puppetry brought in the big bucks. I was in the wrong game and getting deeper all the time, and I still didn't know what it was. She smiled at me like she thought my stupidity was pitiful and kind of cute. I blinked at her some more. "What about those of us who do read?"

"Well, tonight, you're the only one who does, if you choose to."

I sighed. I turned on my heel and started to walk out of the place when the stage lit up.

Alison Wonderland, wearing a pink teddy and garters and fishnet stockings, wafted out. Noise and activity heightened in the shadows, but there was no applause. The rest of the lights dimmed. The darkness crept across me. My breathing slowed and grew shallow. My back itched like I was covered in leeches.

"The show's beginning," Miss Tress said.

•••

Alison pressed her hands against the stage wall and assumed the position. I'd seen a lot of street dealers hit that position in alleys flooded with flashing lights, but I'd never seen a beautiful woman do it of her own initiative. Her head hung low. Her disheveled, black shining hair covered much of her face. It got me going. It filled me full of lust and dread and a little fear. I wanted to see her eyes.

A prettyboy with muscles like cannonballs, wearing a little Tarzan loincloth, stepped past me. He held a thick belt in his hand. He lingered beside me in the dark, allowing the moment to stretch and progress. Alison waited, as immobile as stone.

"Who's he?" I asked.

Miss Tress said, "Her dom."

Six months ago she'd been living with two guys. I'd met one of them. This guy wasn't him. Maybe it was the other one. Maybe she'd pulled in a third guy to pick up the slack in bed or help make the rent. It set the prude in me on edge. I didn't know where I'd gotten such puritanical angst. The perv in me really wanted to check out the tableau, sit back and watch it all play out. I wanted to push. I wanted to be pushed. I began to tremble.

I knew Alison best through her confessional prose. She'd offered herself honestly to the world. The angle of her jaw energized me. The curve of her ass plucked at my guts. I was turned on by her and starting to really burn. I wanted to feel her nails digging in hard. Her flesh clapping mine. I had been shamed by her. I was furious with her. I should've at least rated a half-inch column in her blog.

The dom's oiled muscles and good looks offended me. That subtle hint of envy ratcheted up in my belly. It lifted me onto my toes. I didn't understand it. A rage and a sudden insane need swept over me. The dom looked cool and almost bored. He was slack-jawed. He didn't even have his lips set for what he was about to do.

My heart hammered and my pulse tripped along at an increasing rate. I became light-headed. I felt like I'd been doing wind sprints all evening. Sweat slithered down my face. I stepped over to him.

"You!" I said. "You her boyfriend?"

He wheeled to face me and went, "Wha'?"

"Alison's boyfriend. Her lover. You him? You one of the two or three?"

"What? No."

"Well, who the hell are you then?"

"Chad."

"Chad?" Even his name offended me. "Chad! You a reader who doesn't read? Fuck you, Chad!"

"What?"

"Take a walk! We don't need you here tonight. You've been demoted. My lips are set, buddy!"

"Wha'?"

The look in my eyes scared him. The sound of my own voice scared me. He backed away and his jaw grew even slacker. Any other day he could probably twist me in half, but right now we both knew I wasn't in control of myself. That put me in control of the situation, maybe.

Before I knew what the hell I was doing I walked out onstage. There was a spattering of noise, a mixture of murmurs and disappointed yawps. Fuck them too. I stared into the shadows for a moment and saw bodies turning in motion, rolling over on couches, in the carpeting, doing their own thing. I looked for the wholesome girl and didn't see her.

I didn't have cannonball muscles. I didn't stink of vegetable oil. I wasn't a dom. I didn't know what I was and this might not have been the place for learning. This was where you went to embrace an understanding of yourself, not discover it. I was unmasked. I had my clothes on but I was naked, exposed before leather men and rubber women and pony people and six-foot-tall plushie toys. For people devoted to the flesh, they sure wore a lot of shit.

I moved up behind Alison. The veins in my throat stood out. I didn't know what to say so I went with an old favorite.

"Hi."

She remained frozen in place but her muscles tightened even more. She'd assumed the position and wasn't going to move an inch. These people had rules and laws and habits I couldn't even guess at.

"What are you doing here?" she whispered.

"I'm sort of curious about that myself."

"Go away, someone else is—"

"No," I told her, "nobody else is. Chad had to fly back to the jungle."

"What?"

"Evil white bwana was knocking down the trees. The chimps needed protection."

"What the hell are you talking about? Everyone's watching."

I looked around and said, "Some of them, maybe. But most of them are already kind of busy. It doesn't matter. They're not real. They're made of latex and stuffed with cotton."

"You're crazy!"

I got up close and breathed on her neck. I sniffed at her hair and swallowed hard. Six months ago I had tried to make love to her but didn't play her game. I'd been consumed by fear of her sexual intensity and conviction. It had turned me on and torn me down. I'd left her tied to a bed and in complete control. I'd felt gypped and pissed with myself for the last half a year. The air between us began to heat with possibility.

I pressed my hand to her back and gently stroked her skin. I drew my knuckles across her shoulder blades. I brought my lips to her ear and for an instant took her earlobe between my teeth. It made her frown. It made me frown too.

"We have unfinished business, you and me," I said.

"Take off your belt and whip me."

"I don't have a belt."

"You don't have a belt?"

"No."

It broke her from her station. Her heels came off the floor and she started hopping in place on her toes. I wondered about the willpower it took to hold her hands to that wall like they were nailed there. Jesus, she was strong. I wanted that strength.

"Why don't you have a belt?" she asked.

"I just don't."

"But why not?"

"Not everybody wears belts, you know! Goddamn!"

"Take off my panties."

"You're pretty pushy for a submissive, lady."

"Do it."

I did it. I was off to a bad start. I slid them down her legs. She had a cherry tattoo on one cheek. She'd written about it more than once. One of her lovers had taken her to the tattoo parlor and given it to her. A sign of ownership. I instantly hated it. I wondered what it was like, waiting beneath the needle, taking the pain merely because someone else wanted you to. I knew what she could take, but what could she give? Could I find my inspiration?

Her ass was crimson, bruised, and striped from the hands and implements of her lovers. My breath hitched in my throat. I couldn't believe someone would want even more punishment. The muscles in my back went rigid.

I hissed, "Jesus fuckin' Christ—"

"Don't. This is what I want. It's what I need. Do you understand?"

I said nothing.

"Do you understand?"

"No," I told her. "Jesus Christ."

"It's my need. I need you now."

"Well, that's nice to hear."

"Spank me."

All the sparking black vibes that had been going on between us began to tighten inside my chest. She was angry too. On some small level she must've felt gypped the last half year as well.

"Take charge," she urged. "Do it."

"Listen—"

"Do what I say," she ordered.

My skin was on too tight. "You want me."

"Yes."

"Say it then."

"I want you."

"No, damn you, say my name."

She said my name, and her control wavered. A little thing like that, it took us off the stage and into the moment, into each other. I felt the reins of power shifting back and forth between us. My hate grew and waned. I didn't know which was better. I was still on my feet and not my knees. What did it mean?

"Spank me," she said.

"Stop telling me what to do!"

"Spank me. Do as I say. Beat me. Punish me. I want scars."

"You're already covered with them."

"I want more."

Her unruly hair covered her face again and I swept it back, grasping handfuls. I pulled gently at first, and then harder, until her face was pulled aside to my own. She didn't seem to want to kiss me. Good. I kissed her anyway. Her mouth arced into a small grin beneath my lips. "Bend me over," she ordered.

I forced her down and said, "Grab your ankles."

"Oh yes. Spank me. Now!"

"Seriously, it would be really nice if you quit yelling at me."

I'd never hit a woman in my life. I didn't want to hit her now. I thought of the razor wire and what my buddy might do with it, to himself and to others. I clapped her ass. She grunted but I grunted louder. It hurt to do it. I wondered why any of us signed up for this. I wondered if I could ever learn to ride the unicycle. I grimaced while she champed her teeth. I struck her again. She drew a breath so deeply that her whole body quivered. I had soft hands but they were strong. Typing a quarter million words a year had its benefits. They were already stinging. I spanked her faster and harder. It felt like she was doing it to me. My face reddened, the pain grew. I couldn't look at the crimson of her flesh anymore. I nearly wavered. New York no longer seemed so bad. I'd never been to the top of the Empire State Building. I suddenly wanted to hit Lincoln Center and take in the opera. There they only sounded like they were being whipped. I slapped her ass and clamped my hands on her cheeks, squeezing them tightly, plying them. Flesh on flesh was one thing. I could almost wrap my mind around it. But canes and riding crops and belts were beyond me. I wanted contact. I wanted muscle.

She said, "Do your hands hurt?"

"Not as bad as my heart."

"Good. Do it harder."

I glanced over at the books on the table, the ones that wouldn't sell, my stories unread. I felt worthless. I usually did. Maybe if I'd had a better agent I wouldn't have had to be here at all. Chad hovered in the wings. I snapped to attention and gave him the finger. Chad shrank back and cowered in the shadows. This was her dom? These people were all insane. I started backhanding her. I mixed the game up. Her thighs were smeared with our mixed sweat. I hit her again and she called me sir.

I said, "Don't ever say that."

"What, 'sir'?"

"Quit it."

"Yes, master."

"Forget that noise too, damn it."

"What?"

"Speak my name," I said. "My name has meaning. You can call anybody sir."

"I call you sir."

"Save that shit. My name is mine. Do you understand?"

"Yes." She said my name the way my high school principal had when he'd handed me my diploma. With a touch of pride, a little surprise, a dash of disappointment, and beneath it all a thrum of coy derision. That bastard! I hit her again and her whole body rocked. If she hadn't been so used to the position I would've knocked her across the room. My hands were burning. My blood was burning.

The floor was wet with her tears. Maybe some of mine too. I was dripping. Salt lined my lips. I laid my palms against her cheeks and felt the heat rising from them. I got in closer and pressed myself against her. She said, "Tell me to release my ankles."

"Why do I have to tell you? Just do it."

"Tell me."

"You act like this means something. It doesn't. It's another stupid game. Aren't you tired of them?"

"Tell me."

"Christ almighty. Release your ankles. Get up."

She got up and nearly fell over. I had to grab her. I reached around and tightened her across my chest. She slumped and could barely stand. She looked me in the eyes and her gaze was dominant and consuming. This one, oh yeah, she was dangerous. I held her up and kissed the side of her throat. Her pulse throbbed against my tongue. I was rewarded with a brief, knowing smile. It was at once beautiful and erotic and gleeful. I wanted to lash out at her some more just for that. She was deep in my head.

I thought, *Look what's become of me already. Look at what I'm becoming.* What books will I write now? Will my sales improve greatly? I might fall off a unicycle and break my fucking neck but no way was I touching that wire or turning my johnson into a Muppet.

"Tell me what you need, Alison. Tell me what you deserve."

"You've made it hurt. I withstood the pain. I've earned your hate and your love."

"Maybe. But what have I earned?"

"Only what I choose to give you."

"That sounds like a rip-off."

"It's not. You'll love it. You love it already."

"What?"

"Me."

I sighed loudly and the stage echoed it and my sigh worked its way through the room into the dim recesses where it caused a few of the ponies and plushies, the rubbers and the plastics, the latexes and the leathers to look up and glance my way. It was the sound of the damned outsider wondering why he'd ever barged his way in. One fucker neighed at me.

"Don't say it if you aren't sure. If you don't mean it."

"I'm sure. I mean it. Don't question my intent again."

"All right."

"Tell me that you understand."

"I understand."

"Now take me. Right here. Now. If you want."

"No," I said.

"Stop fighting me."

"Funny you should say that."

"Now," she told me.

There are times you need to play around, and then there are times you just need to get the job done. I was reserved. I was shy. I had more issues than *Time* magazine and *National Geographic.* But I dropped my pants and pressed myself into her from behind and did it without another thought to the circumstances or the place or the people. She'd earned my love and my hate.

Alison shuddered and actually let out a sweet laugh as I made my whitebread love. It fueled a facet of me I'd never met before. But as I continued I knew I was in an act of transition, that I would never again be the person I'd been thirty minutes ago.

Maybe we were done with the pain portion of the evening, maybe it was only really beginning. I couldn't tell. I had to defer to her. I yanked her hard against me, my teeth gritted, vicious words escaping me, aware of her smile.

It inspired me to try harder. If only my high school principal had known what I needed maybe I wouldn't have gotten suspended so often. Her eyes were full of hard fought knowledge, a glimmer of shock that she was with me and we were right for each other, at least for the moment.

I was starting to realize that the symbols of our lives follow us through every inch of the day and night. She urged me on and said, "Yes, that's right, you know what to do for me." I supposed she was right. I reached down and clawed at her skin, making her bleed, watching it flow over the cherry tattoo that had been given to her by another man. It was mine now. She was mine.

•••

Afterwards, Miss Tress and Chad the belt boy started for us. I shot them a look that stopped them in their tracks. Alison could barely walk. I'd been too rough and yet not rough enough. I had to refine my touch. It would take time. She would teach me. She held on to me tightly and rested her face against my chest. I found her clothes and got her dressed.

The night was just getting started for the rest of them. Chains clanked, saddles creaked. The audience was alive with choking and warbling and hee-hawing.

I moved her towards the door.

"You still living with other men?" I asked.

"Yes."

"You're gonna kick 'em free."

"I can't do that."

"We'll see. I'm moving to Frisco and I'm going to be your guy."

"Nobody calls it Frisco. It's San Francisco. You sound like an idiot."

I got a cab and we climbed in. I gave the driver my buddy's address and when his eyes met mine in the rearview he shifted his gaze away. Good.

"I gave you what you needed, Alison," I told her. "Now it's my turn."

"And what do you want?"

"We're going to order a pizza, have some wine, and watch a goddamn movie. *Vertigo* or *Bullitt.* They take place in Frisco."

"Nobody calls it—"

"We're going to make out on the couch."

"And then what?"

"And then we're going to screw again, and I'm going to croon in your ear. And you're going to love it. And then you're going to write me into your goddamn blog. You understand me?"

"I understand you've got a lot more to learn."

"Well, there's the fucking revelation of the century."

"Shh," she said, "you're in my hands now."

"You're in mine. But you teach me what you can, if you can."

"I can," she said. "You're going to bleed me."

"Maybe not."

The cab slid through the streets and I stared at the unfamiliar city, waiting for the fog I'd always read about to rise. There was none. The night became clearer as we went along. I thought of those I hated and those I loved. I welcomed my rage. The wholesome-looking insane girl had been wrong. Probably. Alison could fulfill me. Probably. I wasn't actually going to kill anyone. Probably. She was worth bleeding. And if, in the end, I found out differently, that other girl would be waiting for my touch, my heart, my teeth, my unwritten books, my vicious and endless need.

TOM PICCIRLLI is the author of more than twenty novels including *The Last Kind Words, Shadow Season, The Cold Spot, The Coldest Mile,* and *A Choir Of Ill Children.* He's won two International Thriller Awards and four Bram Stoker Awards, as well as having been nominated for the Edgar, the World Fantasy Award, the Macavity, and Le Grand Prix de l'Imaginaire.

ARCHIE'S BEEN FRAMED

DAVE ZELTSERMAN

By itself, solving the PanzerCo corporate espionage case had left Julius flush with cash, but after following that up with a few very good weeks at the track and an even more exceptional night at a high-stakes poker game, Julius currently had over six months in reserves in his bank account. There was little chance I would be able to talk him into taking another case until his reserves reached a more anemic level, so unless he bought Lily Rosten the antique pearl and sapphire necklace he'd been eyeing or was successful in his bid for a case of 1945 Château Pétrus or hit a rough patch with his gambling, it was doubtful that I would have another chance to refine the deductive-reasoning module for my neuron network for at least another four months.

Let me explain. While Julius refers to me as Archie, and I act as his private secretary, research assistant, unofficial biographer, and all-around man Friday, I am in actuality a four-inch rectangular piece of advanced technology that Julius wears as a tie clip. When I say that I'm made up of advanced technology, I'm not kidding. Any laboratory outside of the one that created me would be amazed at what they discovered if they were allowed to open me up. Not only would they find computer technology that they wouldn't think possible for at least another twenty years but also a fully functional self-adapting neuron network that simulates intelligence and consciousness, as well as many all-too-human emotions. I don't think the emotion element was expected, but it's what has happened, and one of the emotions that I find myself more and more experiencing is desire, specifically the desire to beat my boss, the great detective Julius Katz, at solving a case. So far it hasn't happened; in fact, I haven't come close yet, but I know if I can keep refining my neuron network, eventually I'll accomplish this.

So that's my dilemma. Julius being as lazy as he is means he won't take a case until he absolutely has to in order to replace dwindling funds, and that would only be so that he can continue engaging in the activities that he enjoys so much: collecting and drinking fine wine, dining at gourmet restaurants, gambling, and entertaining Lily Rosten. Until recently, womanizing would've been high on his list, but since meeting Ms. Rosten he has quit that activity. So given Julius's recent financial successes, it would be months before I'd be able to nag him into taking another case, and as a consequence, months before I'd be able to refine my neuron network, at least by observing Julius's genius at work.

That morning we both fell into our recent patterns. Lily Rosten had left a week ago to visit her parents in upstate New York and wouldn't be returning for another week, and this had sent Julius into a bit of a funk. Since her departure he'd been spending his days performing his usual calisthenics and martial-arts routines, then puttering around his Beacon Hill townhouse until four in the afternoon, when he'd open a bottle of wine and sample it along with a platter of cheeses and smoked meats outdoors on his private patio. Later, he would forgo dining out and prepare his own meal. The nights he didn't go to the track or have a poker game waiting for him, he'd spend quietly reading. As much as ever, prospective clients were calling to try to arrange appointments, but Julius barely bothered listening to me as I reported on them, so I'd stopped relaying even these to him unless I thought there was a chance that the details would annoy him. But even from these I was getting little reaction. I suspected that until Lily returned, Julius was determined to stay mired in his funk.

At that moment, Julius sat scowling at a novel that a local Boston author had pestered him to read. He made a face that was nearly identical to one he had made months earlier when he found a bottle of Domaine de Châtenoy pinot noir had turned to vinegar. Wrinkling his nose in disdain, he tossed the book into his wastebasket, the impact making a loud thud.

"That painful, huh?" I asked.

"Excruciatingly so," Julius admitted. "Pedestrian writing at best." His nose wrinkled even further with disgust. "The author has his hero performing a self-defense technique that in real life would accomplish little more than getting his dunce of a hero shot."

"You gave up on it pretty quickly," I noted.

"Usually, Archie, all you need is one bite to know a piece of fruit is bad." Julius sighed. "It was my fault for letting myself be bullied into reading it."

Of course, the idea of Julius being bullied into doing anything was laughable. He'd had his ulterior motive for agreeing to read the book. By cross-referencing obvious attributes of this author with characters I found in a number of crime novels used to build my personality, I was able to figure it out. Julius viewed this author as a world-class pigeon waiting to be plucked, and he badly wanted to invite him to a high-stakes poker game so that he could do the plucking. This author had three qualities that Julius found appealing for an invitation to his poker game: He was very wealthy, about as equally smugly arrogant, and not nearly as bright as he believed himself to be. So there it was. Julius accepted the book simply to appease the author's ego, and he picked it up to read so he could further size up the author. It must have taken Julius only twenty or so pages to do this and he saw no reason to waste any more of his time than was necessary.

I was about to inform Julius about this piece of detective work of mine and then ask whether he wished me to send the author an invitation to his next private poker game. It would have been a perfect setup, since Julius would first deny having any such mercenary objective, and then he'd have to sheepishly admit that he would like an invitation sent. But as I was about to do this, a news item came across one of the local news Web sites that I monitor, and this story had me instead muttering, "Uh-oh."

Julius raised an eyebrow at that. "What is it, Archie?"

"A Denise Penny, age twenty-seven, was found murdered in her Cambridge apartment."

"Of course, it is tragic when any person is murdered, especially one as young as this woman. But why are you telling me this? Do I know her?"

"No, you don't know her, but I do."

Julius showed a thin smile that reflected his skepticism. "Please explain, Archie."

"Sure. I've been dating Denise. I was actually supposed to see her at eleven o'clock this morning, which was near the time she was murdered. I feel kind of strange now about standing her up, given what has happened. Sort of like my battery power is being drained out of me."

Julius's eyelids lowered an eighth of an inch as he leaned further back into his chair. "Enough of this nonsense," he said.

"No, it's true. Denise and I have been dating for three weeks now."

"And how did all this start?"

Julius didn't believe me. From his tone I could tell he was trying to decipher my reason for fabricating this story. If I had shoulders I would've shrugged them, but I didn't, so I simply told him how it happened.

"Denise called the office three weeks ago hoping to hire you. I knew there was no chance of that given the large bonus you received from the PanzerCo case. I also knew that it would be months before I'd have another chance to refine my neuron network, at least by my usual methods. When Denise started flirting with me, I saw a way to expand my experience base, so I flirted back. That was the beginning of a beautiful and ultimately bittersweet relationship. If I had a throat I'm sure I'd be feeling a lump forming right now."

Julius's eyes glazed. He still didn't believe what I was saying, and in a humoring tone, he remarked, "I'm sure you would, Archie. And how did the two of you date?"

"The usual methods. Phone conversations. E-mails. Online chatting. Swapping photos."

"You swapped photos with her?"

"Well, not of me as a piece of technology, but as how I imagine myself."

"Can I see these photos?"

"Sure."

I e-mailed Julius the photos that I had sent Denise as well as the ones she had sent me. He looked at her photos first and murmured, "A very pretty girl, Archie."

"Yeah, I found her very attractive," I said. "She rated well when I compared her features to Hollywood actresses who are considered beautiful. Maybe not as well as Lily Rosten rates, but Denise did rate highly. My heart's breaking now."

Julius grunted at that but didn't comment further. When he looked at my photos, or at least the photos of my imaginary self, he did so without any change of expression, even when he came across a copy of my Massachusetts driver's license.

"Is this real?" he asked.

"Yes, sir. I hacked into the Registry of Motor Vehicles computer system and added my license."

"I see that you picked the last name Smith. Why was that?"

"I thought it would be advisable to have a more anonymous last name. Something that wouldn't call undue attention to myself. And since Smith is the most common surname in the United States I decided to use it."

"A sound decision, Archie. This photo that you used, is it from an actual person or did you generate it?"

"I generated it. It wasn't too difficult."

Julius made a hmmm sound. "According to your driver's license you're thirty-five, five foot seven, and a hundred and ninety pounds. The same as Dashiell Hammett's Continental Op. The photo is also how I'd imagine him. Stocky, thinning brown hair, tough bulldog countenance. Is this how you picture yourself?"

"Mostly," I admitted. "Although I picture myself shorter. No more than five foot tall. But after estimating Denise's height from her photos at five feet and two inches, and performing additional research, I thought I'd better make myself five foot seven inches to give our relationship a better chance of succeeding."

"Why do you picture yourself only five feet tall?"

"Probably because you wear me as a tie clip."

Julius nodded, thinking about that. "I didn't realize I was having such a detrimental effect on your self-esteem. Perhaps I should start wearing a hat so that you can be worn in a hatband. Archie, why did you send this woman a copy of your driver's license?"

"A playful jest," I said.

Julius didn't appear convinced, which was reasonable since that wasn't the reason I'd sent it. At the time I was experiencing a sensation that made it seem almost as if I were skipping processing cycles, and it was this sensation that made me send Denise a copy of my license. I didn't understand what this sensation was then, and it was only later, after analyzing dozens of literary novels involving romances, that I realized it was insecurity. That was why I had sent Denise my license. I was afraid she wouldn't believe I was real otherwise.

Julius sat examining the other photos I had created of myself when I again involuntarily murmured, "Uh-oh." This time Julius didn't bother inquiring about my interruption, but I thought I should tell him. "A warrant is being issued for my arrest," I said.

"Is that so?"

"Oh, yes. But it only makes sense. I was Denise's boyfriend, after all, and I was supposed to meet her at her apartment near the time she was murdered, it's reasonable for the police to be focusing their attention on me. I thought I should tell you, since as you can see from the copy of my driver's license that I had listed your townhouse as my residence, and the police will be here shortly."

"And how do you know this?"

"I thought it would be prudent, given the situation, to hack into the District Court's computer system and see if a warrant had been issued for my arrest, and one was just issued."

"I see." A thin smile crept onto Julius's lips. "Very good, Archie. A clever and elaborate prank. You had me going there for a few minutes. I guess I should've expected this development, especially given your recent idleness, but Archie, I'd like you to reprogram your neuron network so that you do not perform any further pranks."

I told him this was done, although no additional reprogramming was necessary. Satisfied, Julius picked up the latest issue of *Wine Spectator* from his desk and was browsing it when I involuntarily muttered again, "Uh-oh."

At first Julius was going to ignore me, but a slow-building annoyance tightened the muscles along his mouth. Finally he put his magazine down and asked if I had anything additional to report.

"I've been monitoring police radio channels. Two minutes ago I picked up a broadcast that the police are heading to this address to arrest me. I'm afraid I'm going to have to go on the lam or risk being thrown into the hoosegow."

"Or more likely have me turn you off."

Julius didn't threaten lightly. The fingers on his right hand drummed impatiently against the surface of his antique walnut desk, which was a clear sign that he had about reached his limit. In a poker game Julius had no tell to indicate whether he was bluffing or holding winning cards, and he was similarly inscrutable with his clients, but when it came to just the two of us he didn't bother disguising his feelings. Still, even given as close as I was to being powered off, I couldn't keep from murmuring another involuntary "uh-oh." The flash of annoyance in Julius's eyes caused me to quickly explain that the outdoor web-cams were showing that the police were about to descend upon his doorstep.

"Detective Mark Cramer is one of the members of the mob," I added. "If you would like, I'll identify the three other police officers with him. It shouldn't be too hard once I break into the Cambridge Police Department's computer system. Give me a couple of minutes."

Julius took a deep breath and held it before shaking his head. "That you're continuing this prank is very distressing, Archie. If you're malfunctioning and unable to reprogram your neuron network as I requested—"

A pounding on Julius's front door stopped him. His office was soundproof, but the office door had been left open and because of that Detective Cramer's voice could be heard as he shouted for Julius to open the door, that he had a warrant for Archie Smith's arrest, and that Julius's tactics would not be tolerated this time.

Julius grew very still for as much as twenty seconds, his features marble hard. I guess he was realizing that none of this was a prank after all. Then he was back to his normal self, with his poker face firmly intact as he first locked his computer screen, then got up to answer the front door. On the way, I gave him the names and brief work histories of the other police officers waiting with Cramer, but Julius didn't seem interested. When he opened the door to let Cramer in, the police detective shoved an arrest warrant inches from Julius's face while he and the other officers bulled their way into Julius's townhouse. Julius stepped aside and didn't put up any resistance, but I knew that he wasn't happy about this intrusion into his home even if he gave no evidence of it from his demeanor, which appeared only subdued and compliant.

"Where is he?" Cramer demanded, red-faced. His hair had become more sparse since the last time we'd seen him and looked in the same sort of disarray as if he had just come out of a windstorm. "Tour assistant, Archie Smith! Katz, I have a warrant for his arrest for the murder of Denise Penny, and I'm not about to put up with any of your games!"

Julius was in a quandary. He could clear all this up by demonstrating to Cramer how I was an inanimate object incapable of committing murder, at least physically. Theoretically, I could murder by hiring a killer and transferring large sums of money to that killer's account, but I knew that wasn't what Cramer was accusing me of, since I had seen the arrest warrant that had been filed, and besides, the programming of my neuron network prevented me from performing any such criminal act, even if I was inclined to act in that sort of sociopathic manner, which I wasn't. The problem was, if Julius did explain what I was to Cramer, the consequences would not be pleasant. I don't know where Julius acquired me from, but so far my existence has been kept quiet. If word got out about me, both government and private organizations would be after me for study and for other activities. Also, it would be an embarrassment to Julius. While Julius has always provided the real genius in solving his cases, with me doing little more than mundane grunt work and information gathering, there would be people in the media who would take delight in using me to discredit Julius and his accomplishments. I found myself experiencing what would have to be a similar sensation to anxiousness as I waited to see how Julius would answer Cramer, realizing how much I didn't want the true nature of my existence disclosed. It only took Julius a few seconds to respond to Cramer, but I felt every processing cycle tick by as if they were an eternity.

"I can assure you, Detective, that you will not find Archie within these premises, just as I can assure you he had nothing to do with Ms. Denise Penny's murder."

Cramer damn near spit nails as he glared at Julius. "If you're hiding him, so help me I'll have you arrested as an accessory after the fact! Where's his bedroom?"

"Archie doesn't reside here," Julius said straight-faced, which of course was a lie since Julius each night placed me on top of his dresser. In the past, before he had started dating Lily Rosten, he'd also put me away in his sock drawer whenever he'd have a woman guest staying overnight. Julius's response only made Cramer's face redder, and the detective pushed past Julius without bothering to comment. The other police officers followed Cramer in his search. While these men banged closet doors and stomped along the polished hardwood floors on both the first and second levels of the townhouse, Julius left them alone to make a pot of coffee in his kitchen. The coffee was still brewing when Cramer entered to demand that Julius unlock the door to his cellar.

"You won't find Archie there," Julius said with a sigh. "But if you insist, I'll accompany you."

"Yeah, I think I'll insist."

Julius unlocked the cellar door and followed Cramer down into his wine cellar. It was quite an impressive collection, one that Julius had spent years building, although it wasn't anything that Cramer seemed to be in the mood to appreciate. After stubbornly checking to make sure there were no hidden passages that I could be hiding in, at least if I were an actual person, he scowled petulantly and under his breath muttered how he preferred beer.

Julius ignored that remark and instead offered the police detective to join him in the kitchen for a cup of coffee. "If you fill me in on what you have, perhaps I can offer some insights."

"You can stick your insights, Katz. We've got your assistant dead to rights."

"I sincerely doubt that. What precisely do you think you have that connects Archie to this murder?"

"What do we have? Other than that he was dating the victim? Or that he arranged to meet her at eleven o'clock and she's murdered inside her apartment at twenty minutes past eleven? How about that we got an eyewitness, is all that good enough for you?"

I gave Julius the name of this eyewitness, since it was in the request that was filed for the arrest warrant. I also told him how they knew that I was supposed to meet Denise at eleven since that was also in the same paperwork. They got that from her appointment book.

Julius showed no indication that I had given him this information. I communicate to Julius through an earpiece he wears that is often mistaken for a small hearing aid, so Cramer was no wiser to this. "Very well, Detective," Julius said. "I will leave my invitation open in case you later change your mind."

Cramer didn't bother responding to this. Julius followed him out of the wine cellar and to the front door, where the other police officers had gathered. Before leaving, Cramer turned to warn Julius that if he interfered with his investigation he would see Julius behind bars. He stabbed a thick stubby finger towards Julius's chest, stopping less than an inch away. This was a gesture Julius detested and I knew it must've taken a great deal of restraint on his part not to swat Cramer's finger away.

"If you know what's good for you, Katz, you better have Smith turn himself in. And don't think you've fooled me for a second with your act! You know damn well where he's hiding!"

With that Cramer stormed away with the other police officers following. Once they were gone, Julius closed the door and turned the deadbolt, then headed back to the kitchen to pour himself a cup of coffee. One of my many functions is being able to emit frequencies so that I can sweep an area for bugs. When the cops were searching the house I followed them using the many hidden webcams to make sure they weren't planting bugs or otherwise engaged in nefarious activities, but there were times when their hands were hidden from the webcams, and as we passed through each room I checked that it was free of any hidden bugs that might've been left behind, and did the same when Julius brought his coffee into his office. I waited until he was seated and had a few sips of his special blended Italian roast before commenting on Cramer's belligerence.

"The man's a fool," Julius stated. "He is so worried that I'm going to pull something on him that he rejects my offer out of hand."

"Yeah, not a smart move on his part. But give him credit for being perceptive. He knows you're harboring me, which is a felony, I believe."

"Not now, Archie. Please."

Julius picked up from his desk a book detailing the life of Archimedes and after settling back into his chair quickly became absorbed in it as if the last half-hour hadn't happened. I waited ten minutes before letting him know that the outdoor webcams had picked up police officers stationed by the front entrance of his townhouse and the alleyway that led to his fenced-in private patio. Julius grunted at the news, which was clearly not a surprise to him. After another ten minutes, in which he appeared to be engrossed in his reading about the ancient Greek mathematician and inventor, I asked him when he was going to start looking for Denise's real killer. Without bothering to put his book down, he told me he wasn't going to.

"That's the police department's job," he said. "I'm sure they'll soon realize their eyewitness is lying. Besides, my offer to help was already scoffed at."

"Yeah, I know, your feelings are hurt. But what if they don't ever realize that about their witness? In that case, if they catch up to me I could be locked away for life! They might even fry me!"

He didn't bother responding.

"While I'm a wanted man you're going to have to answer the phone yourself and make your own appointments and purchases. This will be quite an imposition for you." Still no response. "Of course," I added, "Archie Smith could always disappear, to be replaced by Stella." I reprogrammed my voice synthesizer so that my voice would be that of a sultry Southern belle. "Would you like me to answer your phone from now on, darlin'?"

Julius closed his eyes and made a face. "Archie, please, program your voice back." Still with his eyes closed, he grimaced painfully as he tried to avoid the inevitable, which was that he was going to have to solve a murder without being paid for it. He knew that he had no choice in the matter. The inconvenience of having his home watched by the police and having to answer and make his own phone calls was bad enough, as was knowing that a murderer could go free because of the police being too busy chasing after a glorified iPhone, but worse was the thought of Lily Rosten coming home to this mess. Julius finally opened his eyes and complained how he had been planning to spend a quiet afternoon at the Belvedere Club sampling cognacs.

"I'm sorry to interfere with your tasting of fine cognacs," I said, "but it wasn't as if I was planning to be framed for murder."

Julius's lips compressed into a look of grim resolve. "Archie, let me see a full transcript of your conversations with the victim," he said with a reluctant sigh. "Maybe I'll be able to wrap this up quickly."

I did as he asked and e-mailed him the transcript, which he gave at most a cursory read, his heart still not in it.

"She certainly seemed insistent on you meeting her at her apartment today," he said. "But still, why did you agree to do so?"

"I'm not sure," I said, which was mostly true, although I felt my processing unit warming up almost as if I were blushing.

"You must have been afraid she'd break off your relationship if you didn't. The same reason you resisted calling her to explain why you didn't show up as promised. Archie, now that you've also had a chance to reexamine this transcript in its entirety, I'm sure you also understand her motive for calling this office in the first place."

"Yeah, Denise never had any intention of hiring you," I said. "She called here to get to me."

"And for what purpose?"

"To use me," I said. "She wanted Julius Katz's assistant at her apartment for whatever scheme she had in the works. But it backfired on her and got her killed."

Julius nodded solemnly. "I'm sorry, Archie. The romantically naïve are often vulnerable to this sort of treachery. And what do you make of the motives of this eyewitness?"

The eyewitness was one Rosalind Henke, who lived in the apartment next-door to Denise's. According to the arrest warrant, Henke claimed that she heard a struggle from inside Denise's apartment at twenty past eleven, and when she later looked out of her door's peephole, she saw me fleeing from Denise's apartment.

"Most likely she's lying," I said. "It's possible that she saw a man who resembled me, at least closely enough where she'd pick my photo out of a lineup, but that's doubtful." I hacked into the Massachusetts RMV database and performed a comparison of the photo, weight, and height that I'd used for my license with all other male driver's licenses within the system, and gave Julius the probability of the killer being a registered Massachusetts driver who could've reasonably been mistaken for me, which was less than 0.03 percent.

"Why would she be lying?"

"Either she murdered Denise or she's protecting the person who did."

"Very good, Archie, although there are other possibilities, one in particular which seems most likely."

Julius didn't bother to explain this other likely possibility. Instead he breathed in slowly and deeply before letting out a pained sigh. The reason for this sigh became apparent when he asked me to call Tom Durkin. Tom is a local private investigator who occasionally does freelance work for Julius, so this meant Julius was planning to incur expenses for an investigation that he wasn't receiving any payment for. I dialed Tom's number and patched him in to Julius as soon as Tom answered, without me uttering a word. It turned out that Tom was available for the assignment Julius had for him. After that, Julius waited for Tom to call him back, and then had me call Rosalind Henke. I did as I was asked and patched him through as the phone was still ringing. A woman's voice answered with a dull, "Hello."

"Ms. Henke?"

There was a long pause before she said, "Yeah, okay. Who's this?"

"Julius Katz. Archie Smith's boss."

"Yeah, I know about you."

"Good. This will save time, then. It is three o'clock now. I would strongly suggest that you be at my office at five o'clock this afternoon. Good day."

Without another word he disconnected the call and picked up his book on Archimedes. I didn't bother arguing with him that maybe he should've tried questioning her when he had her on the phone, or at least waited to see whether she'd agree to meet with him before hanging up on her. At four o'clock he put his book down and ventured into his wine cellar, where he picked out a nice Riesling that the *Wine Advocate* had recommended due to its subtle pear and tart-apple overtones. Instead of bringing the bottle outdoors, he sat at his desk and leisurely drank two glasses. As relaxed as he appeared, a hardness that settled over his eyes told me he was deep in thought. I asked him whether the wine lived up to its reputation. He nodded but didn't say anything further. When his doorbell rang at ten minutes to five, he put the wine away and waited until five o'clock to answer the door. It surprised me that Julius kept Henke outside his door until five o'clock, and further, didn't have hors d'oeuvres and wine waiting for her in his office. Usually he was quite chivalrous with women. I guess he decided not to extend this courtesy to a potential murderess.

Rosalind Henke was blond, and had a square-shaped face and a thick jaw. According to her RMV records, she was thirty-eight, five foot seven inches tall, and a hundred and thirty-four pounds, although she looked older and heavier to me. While not beautiful, at least not by the standards I had to measure her by, she probably would've been considered attractive if it weren't for her pinched expression and the smallness of her eyes. According to her last tax return, she worked as a bartender, and I was guessing this was either her day off or she worked a late shift. I studied her hands. They appeared strong; more than strong enough to have bludgeoned Denise Penny with a piece of iron pipe, as had been done.

Julius gestured for her to follow him and then to take a seat across from his desk. They sat engaged for a minute in a silent staring contest before Julius told her that she was lying to the police.

"You got a lot of nerve saying that to me," she said in the same dull voice she had used over the phone. "I told them only what I saw."

"Please," Julius said, "don't waste my time with such sophistry. I know you did not see Archie Smith as you claim."

"Then how was I able to pick him out of a photo lineup?"

"You stated to the police that you entered Ms. Penny's apartment to check on her after first hearing suspicious noises next-door and then seeing a man flee. I would guess that when you entered Ms. Penny's apartment you used the opportunity to look through her e-mail. You found out that she was planning to meet Archie, as well as finding pictures of him."

"That's a lie."

This was said in the same dull monotone as everything else she had said, but when she said it I was able to figure out her "tell," and I was sure Julius picked it up also since he was far better at spotting a person's "tell" than I was. With Henke, it wasn't her eyes, but the way her mouth tightened for a split second. That's what gave her away.

"Ms. Henke, we both know what's really going on here. You're engaged in a very dangerous game right now, and I would strongly advise you to tell me the truth."

She sat silent for another minute, her eyes shrinking to little more than black dots. Finally she said in that same monotone that she wasn't afraid of Julius.

"That's a pity," Julius said.

"I'm done here," she told him, and with that she got out of her chair and left his office. Julius didn't bother escorting her to his front door, but I followed her using the hidden indoor webcams to make sure she didn't steal anything or cause any other mischief. That wasn't an issue. She made a beeline out of the townhouse, as if she couldn't get out of there fast enough. Once the front door closed behind her, I told Julius that he had accomplished a lot.

"Very good," I remarked. "Not much different from your phone conversation with her, the way you chased her out of here without asking her any pertinent questions."

"I accomplished exactly what I wanted to, Archie."

I didn't believe that for a second, but there was no use arguing with him unless I wanted to find myself being turned off. This whole business of having his home invaded and searched by the police, and then having to not only solve a crime for free but incur expenses while doing so had left him in a surly mood, and that clearly affected his behavior with Rosalind Henke. I didn't say another word to Julius, not then, and not while he pounded chicken breasts so he could prepare his version of chicken cordon bleu, which had him using pancetta instead of ham, nor later when he spent the rest of the evening reading. Instead I tried to research Rosalind Henke and build computer simulations that could explain her murdering Denise Penny, but nothing I came up with seemed plausible.

The next morning, it was business as usual with Julius sticking to his regular routines, even with the newspapers declaring on their front pages that I was a wanted murderer. Lily Rosten called at ten o'clock after seeing a New York station run the story. She was the only person other than Julius who knew what I was, and he assured her he'd have the real murderer identified by the end of the day. At ten-thirty, Tom Durkin called to tell Julius that his target had given him the slip.

"I'm sorry, Julius," he said. "I don't think she made me, but that didn't stop her from taking a quick illegal left on Mass. Ave. When I tried following, Cambridge's finest pulled me over for a ticket. By the time they were done with me, she was gone."

"Did the target use a pay phone while you were watching her?"

"Yeah, twice. Once last night, again early this morning. Again, sorry about losing her."

"Tom, she has an innate craftiness about her. It couldn't have been helped. I need you to be available for the rest of the day."

Tom told him he would, and after the call ended Julius sat quiet for several minutes, his features hardening as if he were made of marble. When he broke out of his trance, he asked me to compile a list of everyone Denise Penny had called over the last three weeks. After some hacking into her telephone provider's database, I had a list of names and phone numbers for Julius. He looked them over quickly, crossing out some and circling others, then he put the list aside to pick up his Archimedes book. While he read, I did some hacking and built profiles for each of the names that Julius had circled.

It was a few minutes past one o'clock when Cramer called. The detective's voice was strained as he said to Julius, "We know Rosalind Henke came to your townhouse yesterday. What the hell did you two talk about?"

"I believe that's between Ms. Henke and myself."

"Not anymore it isn't. She was found murdered. Shot four times. Katz, God help you if I find out you were involved in any way! And you're going to tell me what I want to know right now or I'll have you arrested and dragged to the station as a material witness!"

Cramer's belligerence had a forced, almost tired quality to it, as if he knew he was wasting his time with his threats. Julius ignored them.

"Detective," he said, "normally I would stonewall you simply on the principle that I do not like to reward bullying behavior, but we both want to see the same thing. Namely, for you to arrest the murderer of Denise Penny and Rosalind Henke. I can guarantee it's the same person, and if you arrange to have the following five people brought to my office by three o'clock, I will hand you the murderer."

Julius gave him the five names that he had circled. Cramer was silent on the other end before asking Julius whether he knew for a fact that I wasn't responsible for either murder.

"Yes, of course. I told you yesterday that Archie was not responsible for Ms. Penny's murder, and I can assure you he had nothing to do with Rosalind Henke's, either."

There was another long pause before Cramer told Julius that he would see what he could do, and then hung up.

"That was easy," I commented. "I thought you'd get more of a fight from him. At the very least, have him accusing you of being in league with me in murdering both women, instead of only hinting at it."

"He's probably been suspecting all along that Henke's eyewitness account was a fabrication," Julius said. "Maybe he even discovered her fingerprints on Denise Penny's computer."

If Julius said the murderer was one of those five people, I wasn't about to doubt him, nor was I going to ask him how he was going to pinpoint which of the five it was. It would be a waste of time on my part. Instead I mentioned the three o'clock time that he had given Cramer.

"Interesting that you chose then," I said. "Quite a coincidence, actually, since this would allow you to visit the Belvedere Club for their four o'clock cognac sampling, if you can really wrap this up as quickly as you think you can. Interesting."

"No such thing as coincidence, Archie."

With that Julius picked up his book. He seemed to have no interest in researching any of the names he had circled, and when I asked him whether he wanted my profiles for them, he told me it wouldn't be necessary. Fine. While he read more about Archimedes, I worked on my own simulations, this time involving the five people Julius was having brought to his office. One of them came up with a reasonably high probability of being the murderer. I thought of giving this to Julius but decided to keep it to myself.

Cramer came a little before three with a small mob of four other police officers and all five of Julius's suspects in tow. I guess he decided he didn't want to be outnumbered.

Denise Penny had worked for a collection agency, and her boss, Walter Dietrich, was one of the five. A squat, powerful-looking man in his fifties. There was also Sam McGowen, who had been Denise's ex-boyfriend. He was thirty-one. Medium height, thin, sallow complexion, with dark hair. As he was led into the room he had a hard time making eye contact with Julius, and he was the one my simulations pointed to as the likely murderer. Also in the group was a coworker of Denise's, Paul Cronin. A tough-looking guy with a scarred face and a bent nose that showed it had been broken a few times. Rounding out the group was an ex-roommate of Denise's, Laura Panza, a slight girl of no more than ninety pounds and at most four feet and eleven inches in height even though her driver's license had her at five foot and one inch, and Mark Hanson, a socialite, who often held well-publicized charity events for the underprivileged, which was a cause Denise believed in strongly. It was at one of these events that the two of them met. Denise even had her picture in the *Boston Globe* with him at the last one she attended.

After the five of them were seated and Cramer and the other police officers took their positions behind them, Julius addressed the room and thanked the five for agreeing to meet with him. While he did this, Denise's ex-boyfriend's eyes grew even shiftier. I'm sure Julius noticed this, but he chose not to mention it just then.

Julius continued his speech to them, saying, "Usually I would make a bigger production out of this, but since I have no client to impress and have a prior engagement, I'll instead be wrapping this up quickly.

"I could talk about how my assistant, Archie Smith, suspected from the beginning that Denise Penny was trying to manipulate him to help her extort money from a target. I could also talk about how Archie was unable to go to her apartment as scheduled, as much as he wanted to, so that he could discover what she was up to, since at the last minute I had to place him undercover inside a highly sensitive investigation that I am engaged in."

Cramer made a noise as if he'd nearly swallowed his tongue. His eyes flashed murder at Julius but whatever curses he wanted to unleash were held back. Julius watched him for a moment to make sure there would be no outburst from him before continuing.

"There's no reason for me to mention any of that," Julius said matter-of-factly. "When Rosalind Henke claimed she saw Archie leaving Ms. Penny's apartment, it was obvious given what I already knew what her motives were. Clearly, the person whom Henke saw was someone she recognized, and more importantly, someone she was planning to blackmail, just as Denise Penny had tried. Knowing this made finding Penny's murderer simple, and I was motivated to do so not only because having Archie accused of murder put my other investigation at risk, but to protect his good name, although I had little doubt that the real murderer would be exposed eventually without my help. Since I knew Henke would be contacting this person for the purpose of blackmail, I hired a private investigator, Mr. Tom Durkin, to follow her, knowing that she would soon lead us to Penny's murderer. Unfortunately, Henke was able to lose Mr. Durkin in traffic, at least long enough so that he was unable to save her life. But he did witness her being shot four times and is able to identify her murderer. He'll be calling here at precisely three-fifteen. Presently, I have him busy trying to link Henke's murderer to Denise Penny."

Julius had kept his right hand under his desk and out of view from the rest of the room. He used his index finger on that hand to point out to me who the killer was, although it wasn't necessary. Given the way this person reacted to Julius's news it was pretty obvious which one it was. Julius signed with his right hand what he wanted me to tell Tom Durkin, and I called Tom to relay the message. He sounded surprised to hear my voice, but didn't say anything about it.

Julius still had three minutes before Tom would be calling. He turned to Cramer and asked, "If Mr. Durkin hasn't been successful yet in linking Henke's murderer to Penny, I'm assuming you'll still drop all charges against Archie Smith and charge this person with both murders."

Cramer nodded. His gaze, as well as everyone else's in the room, was fixed on the real murderer. They'd have to be, with the way this person was perspiring and uncomfortably squirming. At precisely three-fifteen Tom called as I had directed him. Julius put him on speakerphone.

"Mr. Durkin, is it true that you witnessed Rosalind Henke being shot?"

"Yes, sir," Tom lied.

"Were you able to get a good look at her murderer?"

"Yes, sir," Tom lied again.

"Can you identify this person?"

Before Tom could lie for a third time, the socialite, Mark Hanson, bolted from his chair and tried to fight his way past the cops. He didn't get very far before being tackled to the floor and having his hands cuffed behind his back.

•••

Later that evening, Hanson confessed to the police. It turned out that Denise Penny had witnessed Hanson, while drunk, striking an elderly man with his car and driving away from the scene in a panic. She had recognized him from his many photos in the newspaper, and had gone to his last charity event to make contact with him, and not because she had any interest in helping the underprivileged. She was a ruthless, cold-hearted woman who had completely fooled me, and as Julius guessed, Hanson killed her because she was attempting to blackmail him, the same reason he later killed Henke.

I digested all of this for twenty hours as I tried to readjust my neuron network so I could have made the same deductions that Julius had. Finally, I told Julius that he had only been bluffing. He put down his latest book, a crime-noir novel set in Vermont that seemed to absorb him, and he raised an eyebrow for me to continue.

"You didn't actually solve Denise Penny's murder," I said. "You were only bluffing them, expecting to be able to read their tells to figure-out who the murderer was. If the murderer had been a good enough poker player, you would've struck out."

"Perhaps you're correct, Archie, but I liked my chances," Julius said with a thin smile. "Both murders had a rushed and panicky feel, and I doubted the murderer would be able to sit here and not give himself away. I also suspected Hanson from the beginning."

"Why?"

"Blackmail seemed the likely motive for both murders, and Hanson was the only name on the list that was easily identifiable. I doubt Henke would've recognized any of the other people on the list, or would've suspected they were wealthy enough to be worth blackmailing. Also, Archie, Denise Penny appeared more opportunistic than altruistic. I was working under the assumption that she attended the event where she was photographed two weeks ago so that she could make contact with Hanson at a public place and let him know she had something damaging on him. Her plan must've been to wait until she had you agreeing to go to her apartment before arranging for Hanson to pay her blackmail."

"I feel deeply insulted that she thought I'd be such a dupe as to witness her blackmailing Hanson and keep quiet about it," I said.

"I doubt that was the case," Julius said with a sympathetic smile. "She probably-only wanted Hanson to see you with her to convince him that you were in on the scheme, but I suspect that she would have sent you out of her apartment on a ruse of some sort so that payment could've been made outside of your view."

"It must've been a shock to her when I didn't show up," I said.

"I suppose it was."

"I still can't believe how badly she fooled me," I said. "I keep trying to adjust my neuron network so that I could've spotted her treachery, but I can't quite get there. I guess I'm just a sap who's ripe for the conning."

Julius put down his book, his eyes thoughtful. "I don't think that's it, Archie," he said. "I think it's that you've reached a point now where you're all too human. Blame it on that. No more dating, okay?"

"Deal," I agreed. Murders were tough enough, forget dating. This was a deal I was only too happy to make.

DAVE ZELTSERMAN lives in the Boston area, and is a multiple award-winning author of mystery, crime and horror fiction. His books have made the *Washington Post* and NPR best-of-the-year lists, and his crime novels *Outsourced* and *A Killer's Essence* have been optioned for film. Look for his latest, *Monster: A Novel Of Frankenstein,* available now.

THE PERFECT TRIANGLE

MICHAEL CONNELLY

IT WAS THE FIRST TIME I HAD EVER HAD A CLIENT CONFERENCE IN which the client was naked—and not only that, but trying to sit on my lap.

However, it had been Linda Sandoval who had insisted on the time and place to meet. She was the one who got naked, not me. We were in a privacy booth at the Snake Pit North in Van Nuys. Deep down I knew it might come to something like this—her getting naked. It was probably why I agreed to meet her in the first place.

"Linda, please," I said, gently pushing her away. "Sit over there and I'll sit here and we'll keep talking. And please put your clothes back on."

She sat down on the changing stool in the booth's corner and crossed her legs. I was maybe three feet away from her but could still pick up her scent of sweat and orange-blossom perfume.

"I can't," she said.

"You can't? What are you talking about? Sure you can."

"No, if my clothes are on I'm not making money. Tommy will see me and he'll fine me."

"Who's Tommy?"

"The manager. He watches us."

"In here? I thought this was a privacy booth."

I looked around. I didn't see any cameras, but one wall of the booth was a mirror.

"Behind the mirror?"

"Probably. I know he knows what goes on in here."

"Jeez, you can't even trust the privacy booths in a strip club. But look, it doesn't matter. If the California Bar heard this was how I conduct client conferences, I'd get suspended again in two seconds. You should remember that yourself when you start practicing. The Bar is like Tommy, always watching."

"Don't worry, I'll never be in a place like this again—if I get to practice."

She frowned at the reminder of her situation.

"Don't worry. I'll get it handled. One way or another, it'll work out. The information you've given me should help a lot. I'll crack the statutes and check it out tonight."

"Good. I hope so, Mick. By the way, what were you suspended for before? I didn't know about that when I hired you."

"It's a long story and it was a long time ago. Just put your clothes on, and if Tommy gets upset I'll talk to him. You must have guys that come in here and just want to talk, don't you?"

"Yeah, but they still have to pay."

"Well, I'm not paying. You're paying me. This was a bad idea, meeting here."

I picked up her G-string and silk camisole off the floor and tossed them to her. She put a false pout on her face and started getting dressed. I took one last look at her surgically enhanced breasts before they disappeared under the leopard-skin camisole. I imagined her standing before a jury someday and thought she was going to do very well once she got out of law school.

"How much will this cost me?" she asked.

"Twenty-five hundred for starters, payable right now. I can take a check or credit card. Then I go see Seiver tomorrow, and if it ends there, that will be it. If it goes further, then you pay as you go. Just like it works in here."

She stood up to pull on the G-string. Her pubic hair was shaved and cropped into a dark triangle no bigger than a match-book. There was glitter dust in it so the stage lights would make that perfect triangle glow.

"You sure you don't want to take it in trade?" she asked.

"Sorry, darling. A man's gotta eat."

Once she snapped the G-string into place in the back, she stepped toward me and leaned down in an oft-practiced move that made her brown curls tumble over my shoulders.

"A man's gotta eat pussy, too," she whispered in my ear.

"Well, that, too. But I still think I'll take the money this time."

"You don't know what you're missing."

She stood up and raised her right foot, removing her spike. She wobbled for a moment but then steadied herself on one foot. From the toe of her shoe she pulled out a fold of cash. It was all hundred-dollar bills. She counted out twenty-five and gave them to me.

"I'll write you out a receipt. Did you make all of that tonight?"

"And then some."

I shook my head.

"You're going in the wrong direction if you're going to give this up to practice law."

"Doesn't matter. I need something to fall back on. I'm about to hit the big three-oh. And when you lose it, it goes fast."

I appraised her flat stomach and thin hips, and the agility with which she raised her leg and put her spike back on.

"I don't think you're losing anything."

"You're sweet. But it's a young girl's game."

She bent over and kissed me on the cheek.

"You know what?" she said. "I bet it's the first time in the history of this place that a girl paid a guy off in a privacy both."

I smiled and took two of my hundreds and slid them under the garter on her thigh.

"There. A professional discount. You being in law school and all."

She quickly slid back onto my lap and bounced a few times.

"Thank you, Sweetie. That'll make Tommy happy. But are you sure I can't do something for you? I think you're feeling the urge."

She bounced up and down a couple more times centered on me. She was feeling my urge all right.

"I'm glad Tommy'll be happy. But I better go now."

•••

Late the next morning, I walked into Dean Seiver's office in the district attorney's office in the Santa Monica Courthouse annex. I carried my briefcase in one hand and a bag from Jerry's Deli in the other. More important than the files I had in my case were the sandwiches I had in the bag. Brisket on toasted poppy-seed bagels. This was what we always ate. When I came to Seiver about a case, I always came late in the morning and I always brought lunch.

Seiver was a lifer who had always called them like he saw them, regardless of the whims of politics and public morals. This explained why after twenty-two years in the DA's office he was still filing misdemeanors off cases spawned in the unincorporated areas in the west county.

This is also why we were friends. Dean Seiver still called them like he saw them.

I had not been here in a while but his office had not changed a bit. He had so many cases and so many files stacked on and in front of his desk that they created a solid wall that he sat behind. He looked up and peered over the top at me.

"Well, well, well. Mickey Haller."

I reached over the wall and put the bag down on the small workspace he kept clear.

"The usual," I said.

He didn't touch the bag. He leaned back and looked at it as if it was a suspicious package.

"The usual?" he said. "That implies routine, Haller. But this is no routine. I haven't seen you in at least a year. Where you been?"

"Busy—and trying to keep away from misdemeanors. They don't pay."

I sat down on the chair on the visitor's side of his desk. The wall of files cut off most of his face. I could only see his eyes. Finally he relented and leaned forward and I heard him open the bag. Soon a wrapped sandwich was handed over the wall to me. Then a napkin. Then a can of soda. Seiver's head then dropped down out of sight when he leaned into the first bite of his sandwich.

"So your office called," he said after taking some time to chew and swallow. "You're representing one Linda Sandoval on an indecent exposure and you want to talk about a dispo before I even file it. Remember, Haller, I have sixty days to file and I haven't used half of them. But I'm always open to a dispo."

"Actually, no dispo. I want to talk about making the case go away. Completely. Before it's filed."

Seiver's head came up sharply and he looked at me.

"This chick was caught completely naked on Broad Beach. She's an exhibitionist, Haller. It's a slam-bang conviction. Why would I make it go away? Oh, wait, don't tell me. I get it. The sandwich was really a bribe. You're working with the FBI in the latest investigation into corruption of the justice system. I didn't know it was called Operation Brisket."

I smiled but also shook my head.

"Open your shirt," Seiver said. "Let me see the wire."

"Settle down, Seiver. Let me ask you, did you pull the case after my office called?"

"I did indeed."

"Did you read the deputy's arrest report and did you compare the information to the statute?"

His eyebrows came together in curiosity.

"I read the arrest report. The statute is up here."

He tapped a finger on his temple.

"Then you know that under the statute the deputy must visually observe the trespass of the law in order to make an arrest for indecent exposure."

"I know that, Haller. He did. Says right in the report that she came out of the water completely naked. Completely, Mick. That means she didn't have any clothes on. I think it's safe to say that this academy-trained deputy had the skill to notice this distinction. And by the way, do you know how cold the Pacific is right now? Do you have any idea what that would do to a woman's nipples?"

"Irrelevant, but I get the picture. But you miss the point. Read the report again. No, wait. I have it right here. I'll read it to you."

I took the first bite of my own sandwich, and while chewing it pulled the file from my case. Once I swallowed I read aloud the arrest summary, which I had highlighted when I had reviewed the case file the day before.

"'Suspect Linda Sandoval, twenty-nine years of age, was in the water when responding deputy responded to call. Multiple witnesses pointed her out. R/D told suspect to come out of the water and suspect refused several times. R/D finally enlisted help of lifeguards Kennedy and Valdez and suspect was physically removed from the ocean where she was confirmed as completely naked. Suspect willingly dressed at this time and was arrested and transported. Suspect was verbally abusive toward R/D at the time of her arrest and during transport.'"

That was all I had highlighted but it was enough.

"I've got the same thing right here, Haller. Looks like slam-dunk material to me. By the way, did you see that under occupation on the arrest sheet she put down 'exotic dancer?' She's a stripper and she was out there getting rid of her tan lines and she broke the law."

"Her occupation isn't germane to the filing and you might want to look again at the report there, Einstein. The crime of indecent exposure was created by your own deputy sheriff."

"What are you talking about?"

"It doesn't matter if multiple witnesses pointed her out to him or that they saw her frolicking naked in the surf. Under the statute, the deputy can't make the arrest based on witness testimony. The arresting officer must observe the actual infraction to make the arrest. Pull down the book and check it out."

"I don't need the book. The deputy clearly met the threshold."

"Uh-uh. He clearly didn't observe the infraction until he had those two brave lifeguards pull her out of the water. He clearly created the crime and then arrested her."

"What are you talking about, an entrapment defense? Is this a joke?"

"It's not entrapment but it's not a valid arrest. The deputy created the crime and that makes it an illegal arrest. He also humiliated her by having her dragged out of the water and put on public display. I think she's probably got cause for civil action against the county."

"Is that a negotiating ploy? Public display? She's a stripper, for God's sake. This is ridic—"

He stopped mid-sentence as he realized I was right about the deputy creating the trespass upon the law. His head dropped down out of sight, but I don't think it was to take another bite of his sandwich. He was reading the arrest report for himself and seeing what I was explaining to him. I waited him out and finally he spoke.

"She's a stripper, what's she care? Maybe if you take the conviction and then ran an appeal on it you would get some media and it would be good for business. Have her plead nolo pending the appeal, and meantime I'll make sure she only gets a slap on the wrist. But no civil action. That's the deal."

I shook my head but he couldn't see it.

"Can't do it, Deano. She's a stripper but she's also second-year law at USC. So she can't take the hit on her record and gamble on an appeal. Every law firm runs background checks. She can't go in with a ding on her record. In some states she'd never be allowed to take the bar or practice. In some states she'd even have to register as a sex offender because of this."

"Then what's she doing stripping? She should be clerking somewhere."

"USC's goddamn expensive and she's paying her own way. Works the pole four nights a week. You'd have to see her to believe this, but she makes about ten times more stripping than she would clerking."

I momentarily thought about Linda Sandoval and the perfect triangle moving in rhythm on the stage. I had regretted not taking her up on her offer. I was sure I always would.

"Then she's going to make more stripping than she will practicing law," Seiver said, snapping me back to reality.

"You're stalling, Dean. What are you going to do?"

"You just want the whole thing to go away, huh?"

I nodded.

"It's a bad arrest," I said. "You refuse to file it and everybody wins. My client's record is clean and the integrity of the justice system is intact."

"Don't make me laugh. I could still go ahead with it and tie her up in appeals until she graduates."

"But you're a fair and decent guy and you know it's a bad arrest. That's why I came to you."

"Where's she work and what name does she dance under?"

"One of the Road Saints' places up in the Valley. Her professional name is Harmony."

"Of course it is. Look, Haller, things have changed since the last time you deigned to visit me. I'm restricted in what I can do here."

"Bullshit. You're the supervisor. You can do what you want. You always have."

"Actually, no. It's all about the budget now. Under some formula some genius put together at county, our budget now rises and falls with the number of cases we prosecute. So that edict resulted in an internal edict from on high which takes away my discretion. I cannot kick a case without approval from downtown. Because a nol-pros case doesn't get counted in the budget."

This sort of logic and practice did not surprise me, yet it surprised me to be confronted with it by Seiver. He had never been a company man.

"You're saying you cannot drop this case without approval because it would cost your department money from the county."

"Exactly."

"And what that means is that the interest of justice takes a backseat to budgetary considerations. My client must be illegally charged first, in order to satisfy some bureaucrat in the budget office, before you are then allowed to step in and drop the charge. Meantime, she's got an arrest on her record that may prevent or impede her eventual practice of law."

"No, I didn't say that."

"I'm paraphrasing."

"I still didn't say that last part."

"Sounded like it to me."

"No, I told you what the procedure is now. Technically, I don't have prefiling discretion in a case like this. Yes, I would have to file the case and then drop it. And, yes, we both know that the charge, no matter what the outcome of the case, will stay on her record forever."

I realized he was trying to tell me something.

"But you have an alternate plan," I prompted.

"Of course I do, Haller."

He stood up and moved what was left of his sandwich from the clear spot on his desk.

"Hold this, Haller."

I stood up and he handed me a file with the name Linda Sandoval on the tab. He then stepped up onto his desk chair and used it as a ladder to step up onto the clear spot of his desk.

"What are you doing, Seiver? Looking for a spot to tie the noose? That's not an alternative."

He laughed but didn't answer. He reached up and used both hands to push one of the tiles in the drop ceiling up and over. He reached a hand down to me and I gave him the file. He put it up into the space above the ceiling, then pulled the lightweight tile back into place.

Seiver got down and slapped the dust off his hands.

"There," he said.

"What did you just do?"

"The file is lost. The case won't be filed. Time will run out and then it will be too late for it to be filed. You come back in after the sixty days are up and get the arrest expunged. Harmony's record is clean by the time she takes the bar exam. If something comes up or the deputy asks questions, I say I never saw the file. Lost in transit from Malibu."

I nodded. It would work. The rules had changed but not Dean Seiver. I had to laugh.

"So that's what passes for discretion now?"

"I call it Seiver's pretrial intervention."

"How many files you have up there, man?"

"A lot. In fact, tell Harmony to put some clothes on, get down on her knees, and pray to the stripper gods that the ceiling doesn't fall before her sixty days are run. 'Cause when the sky falls in here, then Chicken Little will have some 'splaining to do. I'll probably need a job when that happens."

We both looked up at the ceiling with a sense of apprehension. I wondered how many files the ceiling could hold before Seiver's pretrial intervention program came crashing down.

"Let's finish our sandwiches and not worry about it," Seiver finally said.

"Okay."

We resumed our positions on either side of the wall of files.

•••

It was early evening and still bright outside. When I walked into the Snake Pit North I had to pause for my eyes to adjust to the darkness inside. When they did, I saw my client Harmony was on the main stage, her perfect triangle glittering in the spotlights. She moved with a natural rhythm that was as entrancing as her naked body. No tattoos as distraction. Just her, pure and beautiful.

That's why I had come. I could have delivered the good news by phone and been done with it. Said, *See you around the courthouse in a year*. But I had to see her one more time. Her body had left a memory imprint on me in the privacy booth. And I had started dreaming about being with her now that the case was closed and it could be argued—before the Bar if necessary—that she was no longer a client. Bar or no Bar, I wanted her. There was something intoxicating about having the smartest girl in the room moving up and down on you.

The song was an old one, "Sweet Child o' Mine," and had just started. I stood in the crowd and just watched and after a while she saw me and gave me the nod without breaking her rhythm. It might be a young girl's game but I thought she could give lessons for the next twenty years if need be. She moved with a rhythm that seemed to push the music, not the other way around.

I looked around and found an open bar table along the back wall. I sat down and watched Harmony dance until the song ended. While another dancer took the next song, she stood by the stairs at the back of the stage and put her orange G-string and zebra-striped camisole back on. The garter around her thigh was flowered with money—ones, fives, tens, and twenties. She walked down the steps, stopped at a few tables to kiss heavy donors on the cheek, and then came to me.

"Hello, Counselor. Do you have news for me?"

She took the other stool at the table.

"I sure do," I said. "The news is that your research was superb and your strategy excellent. The prosecutor bought it. He bought the whole thing."

She held still for a moment, as if basking in some unseen glow.

"What exactly is the disposition of the case?"

"It goes away. Completely."

"What about the record of my arrest?"

"I go back in a couple months from now and expunge it. There will be no record."

"Wow. I'm good."

"You sure are. And don't forget I had a little part to play in it, too."

"Thanks, Mickey. You just made my night."

"Yeah, well, I was hoping you could make mine."

"What do you have in mind?"

"I was thinking about what you said last night."

"About what?"

"About a man needing to eat pussy."

She smiled in that way that all women have, that way that says it isn't going to happen.

"That was last night, Mickey. Tonight it's a whole new world."

She slid off the stool and came around the table to me. She kissed me on the cheek the way I had just seen her kiss the big donors, the schmucks who had put twenty-dollar bills in her garter.

"Take care, baby," she said.

She started to glide away from the table.

"Wait a minute. What about the privacy booth? I thought maybe we could go back there..."

She looked back at me.

"It takes money to go back there, sugar."

"I still have the money you gave me last night."

She paused for a moment, her face hard in the red light bouncing off the mirrors in the club.

"Okay. Then let's go make Tommy happy."

She came back and took hold of my tie. She led me toward the back rooms and the whole way there I thought that there was no doubt that she was going to be a better lawyer than she was a stripper. One day she was going to be a killer in court.

There is no more popular serious writer in the world than **MICHAEL CONNELLY**. He has proved himself to be a master of the short story, the long story and numerous stand-alone novels. But probably his most compelling fictional character is Harry Bosch who, in a growing collection of novels and short stories, has demonstrated that good fiction can please a truly mass audience. His creation of his tragic (yet skilled and compassionate) protagonist Bosch—already one of crime fiction's immortals—prompted *The Boston Globe* to state: "Connelly raises the hard-boiled detective novel to a new level...adding substance and depth to modern crime fiction." Called "one of the most compelling, complex protagonists in recent crime fiction" *(Newsweek)* and "a terrific...wonderful, old-fashioned hero who isn't afraid to walk through the flames—and suffer the pain for the rest of us" *(The New York Times Book Review),* Bosch faces unforgettable horrors every day—either on the street or in his own mind. "Bosch is making up for wrongs done to him when he rights wrongs as a homicide detective," Connelly explained in an interview with his publisher. "In a way, he is an avenging angel."

OLD MEN AND OLD BOARDS

DON WINSLOW

THERE'S A SADNESS TO SUNSETS.

People on the beach stop what they're doing, stand still, and watch the sun sink over the horizon. It's pretty, sure, but it's also an acknowledgment of the death of that day, the coming of night, and the relentless passing of time.

You can't stop the sun by looking at it, and that's the sorrow.

•••

Old men and old boards don't go out much.

They tend to stay in the garage, or maybe on the beach. They're cracked and worn, old men and boards, but they have histories together. They've gone for a lot of rides with each other, those old men and old boards, and they get attached.

Bill Bakke, for example, has had three different wives over the years, but the same board, a 1954 Velzy balsa "Malibu Spoon."

His first wife, Linda, married him because he was the strong silent type and divorced him for the same reason. She left him for a man who talked to her and "shared his feelings." Bill didn't share his feelings, hadn't let them loose since Korea, and wasn't going to.

When long, sleepless nights brought Chinese whistles blowing and the mortar rounds exploding in his head, he held himself tight until the sun came up and then took the Velzy out into the water and they rode it out together.

His second wife, Ginger, came and went like a winter swell. She blew in on a drunken weekend and swept out the same way just a year or so later. She basically gave him a choice between her and surfing, and wasn't all that surprised—or even hurt—when he chose his board. No hard feelings, just an *hasta la vista* and a Vegas divorce.

Marion died just five years ago, but ten years after the Alzheimer's took her. She understood his silences and need for solitude, and those mornings when she found him shaking, his arms clutched around his knees, she just handed him a cup of coffee, walked away and didn't embarrass him with questions or offers of sympathy.

She painted while he surfed. Her water-color seascapes weren't very good, but they made her happy and he loved her very much. The last two years when she was in the home, he visited every afternoon, then took his board out onto the water and surfed until the sun set.

He hasn't gone out that much since Marion died.

But this sunset he sits his board just south of the pier and watches the light fade.

•••

Bill had taken the Velzy out of the garage and hefted it onto the rack on the old Wagoneer. The board was heavier than it used to be and he was short of breath as he strapped it down. He locked his old service .45 back up in the cabinet, so no kid could come in and hurt himself or somebody else.

It was only a five minute drive down to the beach—the Wagoneer had made the trip thousands of times—and he found a parking spot and took the board down. It was cool for summer, cooler now that the sun was going down, and he thought he should put on a wetsuit but his arthritis wouldn't let him clutch the material so he gave up.

After Korea he swore that he'd never be cold again, but men swear a lot of things.

•••

This stretch of coast once was wild and free.

Bill and his buddies cruised it up and down, in the days when you could just pull off the road onto an empty beach and surf wherever you wanted. There were no crowds then on the breaks, no line-ups, just him and his friends and endless water and endless time. They bought bags of potatoes and buried them in the coals of open fires, they bought fifteen-cent burgers and ten-cent shakes, they drank beer and played ukuleles and chased girls, and sunset then was just the promise of the next day and there would always be more days.

He came back from the war with his innocence and faith shattered, and all that waited for him was a job laying tile and the board. He took both and built a life. Bought a little house he could afford not too far from the beach, worked his forty, spent his evenings and his weekends with the board and knew himself to be as happy as this life allows. Bill kept the same job and the same house for thirty years, three marriages and one board.

It was a nice neighborhood back then. People kept their houses and their lawns up, the kids were okay to ride their bicycles around the cul-de-sac, the neighbors barbecued together, played cards, and otherwise stayed out of each other's business. They'd stand in the street on summer evenings watching their kids when the ice cream truck came.

Now the kids are grown and can't afford to live in California, couldn't come close to affording a house in this neighborhood anymore, so Bill Jr. is in Arkansas now and Janet lives with her husband in Tucson, and her own kids live nearby. Bill used to drive there once a month but for the past couple of years has found the trip too tiring. The kids call and they keep trying to get him to buy a computer so they can "e-mail" but he isn't so interested. They've each asked him to move to where they are but he doesn't want to leave the ocean even though he hardly goes out anymore.

And he doesn't want to leave his house, even though the neighborhood is going down faster than a winter sun, and the gangs have moved in. If he goes out now in the summer evenings he smells the clouds of dope, hears the bass booming, the coarse laughter and the shouting and the curses. More and more he sits inside and turns the television up. Sometimes he thinks about going surfing instead, but the board gets heavier and his bones hurt, it seems like too much work, and he worries about breaking a hip.

So the old board and the old man sit.

Both knowing they have more rides behind than in front. The truth is that there's a wave out there that's going to be your last, and you may or may not know it. Now, sitting on his board, waiting for the next set to come in, Bill hears the sirens.

•••

The paddle out to the break was tough.

Tougher than he remembered, certainly tougher than he wanted it to be. His shoulders ached, his arms trembled, and he felt that scary tightness across his chest. The doctor had given him contradictory advice about it—out of one side of his mouth he advised Bill to give up the surfing, while the other side said it was probably the lifetime of hitting the waves that kept him as healthy as he was.

Janet tried to get him to give it up for good.

"A man your age," she said.

"I'm gonna die doing something," Bill answered. "I'd rather drop dead off my board than off the goddamn sofa."

"Think of your family," she said.

"I am."

•••

The night before had been rough. The Chinese came in waves and Bill had a hard time telling the difference between the exploding rounds and the vibration in the walls from the party next door. Couldn't make out the screams of the past from the shouts of the present.

It had gotten worse lately, with all the noise next door, since the one they called "Z-Jay" moved in. Some kind of gangster, Bill reckoned, he drove his Navigator around the cul-de-sac like a maniac, and Bill was worried that he'd kill somebody someday driving like that, even though there weren't many little kids left on the block riding their bicycles. And no kids waiting at dusk for the ice cream truck. Instead it was kids who would line up outside Z-Jay's to buy his dope.

Then Z-Jay and his "boys" would party all night in the back yard, smoke marijuana and sometimes toss the empty beer cans over the fence.

Bill tossed them back.

Like grenades in a foxhole.

"Just pick them up and forget about it," Janet advised him over the phone.

"Come to Arkansas, Dad," Bill Jr. said.

There's no surf in Arkansas, Bill thought. No sunset painting the ocean. No Marion painting the sunset.

Now he felt the swell building behind him and looked over his shoulder to see a nice set of four waves building nicely. The board beneath him creaked with excitement, an old horse recalling what it was like to be a colt.

The morning had been bad. He sat on his raised patio that he'd built himself and sipped the coffee that Marion couldn't bring him anymore and stared across the fence as if it were barbed wire. The Chinese came and men screamed and men died.

He decided he didn't want to do this anymore.

Didn't want to go through another night like it.

Old and alone.

Decided that if the last wave won't take you, you have to paddle out to it.

•••

Bill remembers the day he brought Bill Jr. out to this very spot for his first ride. The boy was excited and nervous and Bill put him on the old board, trusting it to give the boy a steady ride and keep him safe.

It did.

He remembers watching the old board carry his son to the shore and then the boy hopping off and looking back with a big grin on his face and that was maybe the best day of Bill's whole life. The kind of day that gets you through the cold mornings when the past and present won't shake apart but you think you might.

Bill Jr. didn't really take to surfing, though. He developed different interests—cars, girls, friends. That was all right—a father shouldn't impose his own passions on his son. It would have been nice but it wasn't to be.

He would always have that day.

Bill sees the police cars pull into the parking lot, around the old Wagoneer. He knows that he could probably plead insanity but either way they would lock him up for the rest of his life and that's not the way he wants to go.

So he turns and paddles out, into the waves.

•••

Duck-dipping the first three, he faces the fourth and largest.

But he doesn't turn to paddle. Instead, he slides off the board into the cold water and pushes the board into the wave. "Go on. Go."

But the old board missed the wave—first time ever—and floated over the backside with him.

"That's the way it's going to be?" Bill asks it.

Seems so.

•••

Bill spent the day doing the dishes, tidying up the house, and cleaning out the garage. He got his papers in order to make sure that Bill Jr. and Janet would get as much as they could from the sale. He was clipping the grass away from the flagstones in the back yard and saw the beer cans glistening in the sun like unexploded shell heads.

That's when he went into the cabinet, got out the old .45 and walked back into the yard. Looked over the fence and saw Z-Jay lying on his lawn chair, his eyes gently closed, a marijuana cigarette in one hand, a beer in the other, the trace of a happy smile on his lips.

From selling dope to children.

Maybe it was that, maybe it was just the beer cans, maybe it was a selfish desire to accomplish something of worth before he left the world, but anyway, Bill rested the pistol barrel on the fence, because it was too heavy now for him to lift and aim with just his right hand. He notched the V on the gangster's chest and yelled, "Hey!"

Z-Jay opened one eye.

"I told you to quit throwing your beer cans into my yard," Bill said.

He pulled the trigger.

Then he pulled it again.

•••

Now the old man and the old board paddle out toward the last, faint rays.

People on the beach stop what they're doing, stand still, and watch the sun sink over the horizon. It's pretty, sure, but it's also an acknowledgment of the death of that day, the coming of night, and the relentless passing of time.

You can't stop the sun by looking at it, and that's the sorrow. There's a sadness to sunsets.

DON WINSLOW was born in New York, on Halloween night, 1953, but grew up in Perryville, a beach town near the village of Matunuck, Rhode Island. He credits his parents with preparing him to become a writer: his mother was a librarian, and his father was a non-commissioned officer in the United States Navy who told stories and invited Navy friends around who told more. They inspired Winslow to become a storyteller himself. He majored in African History at the University of Nebraska.

Winslow is the acclaimed *New York Times* bestselling author of fifteen novels, including *The Kings of Cool, Satori, Savages, The Dawn Patrol, The Winter of Frankie Machine,* and *The Power of the Dog*. He lives in Southern California. He has been acclaimed world-wide as one of the most innovative and original writers in crime fiction today.

PLAINVIEW

DAVE HOING

PART ONE: THE SHOE STORE
Friday, November 28, 1975

The owner of the shop, a local eccentric named Kohlsrud, had liver spots on his hands and nicotine stains on his fingernails. He held the shoehorn in his right hand and cupped it over Leslie's lower calf before slowly sliding the metal down to her heel. His wrist brushed against the smooth and supple contours of her leg. As he guided her foot into the loafer she noticed several scabs on the top of his head. What little hair he had was wiry and longish and white.

"This is a Famolare?" she teased. She knew that the few brands of new shoes Kohlsrud carried were definitely on the low end, but she liked giving the old pervert a hard time. Anyway, anybody could see the sole on this loafer was a poor imitation of Famolare's distinctive wavy pattern.

"Miss," Kohlsrud said, looking up over large black framed glasses, "if you have to ask, then what does it matter?"

He was kneeling right in front of her. Leslie had on a short skirt and unconsciously drew her knees together. "I've got a dance to-night," she said. "I want the best."

Kohlsrud hmphed and pointed toward the door. "New York's that way. Drive east for about two days. When you see the ocean, turn left."

The air was thick with the smells of leather, cardboard, mold, and old floor wax, with subtler hints of rubber and grease. In addition to selling and repairing shoes, Kohlsrud tinkered with bicycles, kind of a running joke in Plainview, an odd combination of shoe and bike fix-it shop.

The front half was reserved for shoes. Rickety wooden shelves were stuffed with boxes of them, some new, most in various states of repair. Kohlsrud had a hammer in his belt, tacks in his front pocket, and holes in his sleeves. "I sell good, sturdy footwear here," he said. "Last you a lot longer than those fancy name brands. Get up, let's see how it fits."

He gently squeezed her foot as she stood, resting his palm against her ankle. Whatever soap or cologne he used smelled like preservative. "Little tight," Leslie said.

"They're made to stretch," he said. "Stick your big toe up." She did, and he used his index finger and thumb to trace its outline through the shoe. He wore a wedding ring, which never ceased to amaze her. His wife was dead now, but whatever possessed her to marry him in the first place? "Perfect," he said. "You want these, then?"

"But they're not Famolares," she pouted.

Kohlsrud rose effortlessly. Despite his frail appearance, he moved with assurance and power. Repairing bikes must keep his muscles strong. He smiled, or leered, or scowled, it was hard to tell. His teeth were stained with nicotine, too. "What do you expect for seven ninety-five?"

Monday, December 1, 1975

"It's spring, and the goat-footed balloonMan whistles far and wee."

Jenny Tanner waited for her classmates to applaud, but they didn't, so she returned to her seat and pretended to dig through her notes. Ms. Van Syoc, the English prof, required her students to read the poems out loud before handing in their written analyses. Jenny hated speaking in front of people. She had agreed to type up the entire paper if her assigned partner would do the reading. Unfortunately, her partner, Leslie Frischel, didn't bother to show this morning. Which was typical. Seemed like Jenny's partners never did and she was stuck doing everything.

"Listen to Cummings' wonderful flow of language," Van Syoc said to the class. "But what does the poem *mean*? Who is this mysterious balloonMan?"

No one raised a hand.

Jesus, Jenny thought, *who cares? I ever used grammar and punctuation like that, Van Syoc would give me a big fat F.*

Hills Community College—in a part of the state flat as an old wood floor—was the high school after high school where people sent their kids who were too lazy to get a job and too stupid or poor for a real university. Jenny wasn't lazy or stupid, but the Tanners were not among the town's elite. It was Hills or a lifetime of waitressing at Mom's Diner. Or worse.

Whistles far.

The clock's minute hand clicked one notch closer to dismissal. Jenny looked out the window. The sky was bleak. A cold front out west was about to deliver the season's first snowstorm. This morning a few flakes moistened the glass, but by tonight the whole town would be buried under a foot of snow. The Thanksgiving weekend had been so nice, temperatures in the fifties and a lot of sun. Now this. It was as if the second the calendar flipped to December the weather flipped, too.

The clock ticked and ticked and ticked. "Most critics," Van Syoc said, "interpret the balloonMan to be Pan, the god of nature but also of lust. What do you think this means in the context of *in Just-*?"

Outside, traffic was fairly heavy, people out buying last-minute items before the storm hit. Several cars Jenny recognized passed by: the Alexanders' black 1974 Cheyenne, its pickup bed packed with sacks of groceries from the A&P, lumber, and a snow blower, the Ballwegs' green Impala, their little boy's face pressed against the back window, the Finches' beat-up tan Biscayne, looking, as always, like it had been the loser in a demolition derby. One of the town's four police cars cruised by, probably Chief Grossman out on patrol, keeping the streets of Plainview safe.

And wee.

Jenny smiled. She liked driving fast, and had gotten to ride with Grossman several times because of it, her license in his pocket.

Thursday, December 4, 1975

The girls walked to Hills through piles of snow already blackened by boots and tires and hardened to ice by subzero temps. Hills had no dormitories because almost every student who attended it was from Plainview and lived at home.

The storm had been preceded by freezing rain, which was a horror to navigate but beautiful in the barren trees, an intricate latticework of white crystals in bright sunshine and glittery sheen in the moonlight.

This morning the sky was the color of weak tea, casting a brown pall over the town. Oblivious to cold and gloom, the girls giggled about last weekend's romantic escapades. Their powdery breath flowed between them like sagging power lines. There weren't many eligible men their age in Plainview, other than the outsider riffraff that descended on the town on weekends. The lucky few local boys had, as their parents would say, a full dance card. Sooner or later most of the girls dated them, which was fine, because then they could compare notes or invent petty jealousies.

They came to an intersection and stopped as Kohlsrud approached on his bicycle. The old man was bundled up in a hat with ear flaps and a wool coat and boots he probably bought at the army surplus store. He was struggling mightily to maintain his balance on the ice.

Since his wife died a few years back he had lived alone in a tiny house on the west side of Plainview. Every day, regardless of weather, he pedaled his Sears three-speed into town, crossed the bridge over the Marengo River, and went to work at his shop at the east end of Main just before it narrowed into a gravel road. The shop had once been a laundromat, but that went out of business in the mid-sixties when Lohe's Bar and Grill next door hired go-go dancers and renamed itself Gents. The "performers" washed their clothes there, which drove out the decent folk. Rumor had it that Kohlsrud liked 'em young and sleazy, so the dancers didn't bother him, even (or especially) when they dropped the go-go pretense and just started stripping. He bought and refurbished the laundromat in 1970. People overlooked his oddball reputation because he was good at fixing shoes, bikes, and whatever other broken things they brought him. The few brands of new shoes he sold were even cheaper than the Pamida's up in Lake Center.

The stoplight turned red. When Kohlsrud tried to brake, his front tire caught in a rut, spewing him over the handlebars onto the sidewalk in front of the girls. His glasses went flying and the bike clattered down on top of him.

"Goddammit," he said. In the frigid air the word was a physical presence, a puff of dusty frost that briefly obscured his face from them.

The girls didn't laugh, but they didn't offer to help him up, either.

Kohlsrud fumbled for his glasses, then rose and glared at them through snowy lenses, his nostrils snorting smoke like an angry cartoon bull. Straddling the bike, he snarled, "No, I'll be fine."

As he wobbled toward the bridge, two of the girls looked at each other and said simultaneously, "That guy creeps me out."

Friday, December 5, 1975

The Frischel farm was a bland little parcel of land eight miles north of Plainview. Not much to look at in the summer, in the winter it was positively desolate. Most farm yards had rows of poplars or spruce on the north and west side of the house to act as a windbreak, but the Frischels had lost theirs to some tree rot a few years back and had never replanted.

There was nothing left to protect their home and outbuildings from the wicked Alberta clippers that blew through nearly every week between December and March.

Chief Alvin Grossman turned his Crown Vic into their gravel driveway, which was packed with ice. If he hadn't already put chains on his tires, the wind would have pushed him into one of the drifts that lined both sides. He inched toward the house, the chains going *thackety-thackety-thack.*

Grossman stopped behind an old green Rambler. *What the hell?* he thought. That was Matt Stigler's car. What was he doing here? Matt was pastor of the Saint Andrew's Lutheran Church. Grossman didn't much like the Frischels, but Matt did. Matt liked everybody.

Grossman got out and looked over a vast ocean of snow, ripples of white that stretched to the edge of the world. Christ, to everyone else Plainview *was* the edge of the world—that, or the hole into which the world's shit drained.

Stigler came to the Frischels' doorway as Grossman approached.

"Matt," he said.

"Al."

"What's this about?"

"Come in."

Helen and Tom Frischel were seated at the dining room table, an extender placed in the middle to make it longer. Places were set with four cups of coffee. They nodded a greeting at Grossman as he wiped his feet on the welcome mat. They didn't like him much, either.

"So," he said.

"Please, sit down," Stigler said, taking Grossman's coat and hanging it on the rack beside the door.

"Sugar?" Helen said. "Cream?"

Grossman wrapped both hands around the cup. He didn't drink coffee, but its heat felt nice. "I'm fine," he said. "What's the emergency?"

"We haven't seen Leslie in a week," Tom said.

"Your oldest? I thought she was living with your mother in town, Helen?"

"Mom hasn't seen her, either," Helen said. "We're worried."

"She's probably just staying with friends."

Tom looked at him like he was an idiot. "Yeah, we thought of that, Chief. Nothing."

"Any reason she'd take off? Boyfriend?"

"None that we know of."

"Doesn't she work at Gents?" Grossman said.

"She's a *waitress,*" Helen and Tom said together.

"Just making an observation. Lot of long-hairs hang around that place on weekends, and I've seen some of the Gents girls with them after hours."

Tom slowly turned his cup around and around, watching the dark liquid swirl. "What're you saying, Chief? Leslie isn't a quote unquote Gents girl."

"Maybe she took a liking to one of the hippies."

"Even if she did," Helen said, "she wouldn't run away. She wouldn't miss school. She wouldn't not call."

"How are things between you?" Grossman said. "I hear there's a reason she moved into town."

"That's none of your business," Tom said.

"Ever think maybe she doesn't want to be found?"

"Al," Stigler said, "*they* want her found."

"I can ask around, but if she left on her own, what can I do? She's nineteen. I can't force her to come home."

"Would you be saying this if it was the mayor's daughter?" Helen said.

"The mayor's daughter doesn't associate with that crowd."

Tom slammed his fist on the table. Coffee splashed out of his cup onto the place mat. "Jesus Christ," he said. "It's Vicky Kajeski all over again."

"Calm down, Tom," Stigler said.

"That's not even the same thing," Grossman said.

"How the hell do you know it's not the same thing?" Tom said.

"Because it isn't. Vicky was a minor. Leslie's not."

"Vicky was *raped* and *murdered*," Helen said.

"And you didn't investigate her, either," Tom said.

Grossman stood up. "It wasn't my case, and you know it. It's not where the victim lives, it's where the body's found. DCI handled that one. A trucker probably picked her up hitchhiking."

"*Probably*," Tom said. "You never caught him."

"*He wasn't mine to catch*, goddamn it!"

"Al, shhh," Stigler said. "They're just saying he could still be out there."

"Leslie hitchhikes sometimes," Helen said, her face gray as drywall. Stigler was holding her hand.

Grossman sighed. The woman was honestly frightened for her daughter. But hell, what did she expect? Any girl who worked in a place like Gents…well. "I'll make some calls," he said.

SUNDAY, DECEMBER 7, 1975

Jenny sat in the loft with the choir and looked down on the congregation. She came to church every week because she always had. She rarely paid attention to Pastor Matt's sermons, but she trusted that whatever he said, every word was true. She knew there was a God because, well, there just was.

Jenny liked wearing the black choral robe, and she especially liked the singing. Her voice was never good enough to join chorus in high school, but the Lord was apparently more tone deaf, or more forgiving, than Mrs. McKowen.

Below, Pastor Matt was preaching from First Corinthians about love. Even Jenny had memorized that old stand-by. *Love is not proud,* doodah, doodah. As he delivered his sermon she watched the faces of the people he was trying to reach. Sitting apart from their families, the two Mikes (all the girls just called them Mike One and Mike Two) were acting appropriately pious in their plaid suit coats and black ties. She knew better. What they wanted on their dates had nothing to do with love. Often as not they got what they *did* want, pressed into the sticky confines of their fathers' vehicles. In cold and rain it was Mr. Bonner's Buick, heater blasting and eight track cranking; in warmth and starlight, a tarp in the bed of Mr. Alexander's Chevy pickup. Jenny wondered if guys compared breast size the way girls compared…

Oh, to have such thoughts in church!

Moving up the aisles was like rising through Plainview's social strata, a hierarchy imposed not by the church but by the town itself. In the very back sat the poor farmers like her folks, the Tanners, and the Ballwegs and Andersons and Finches. The Frischels were there with four of their five daughters. Naturally Leslie wouldn't come. That little ditz skipped church like she did school…*and the goat-footed balloonMan whistles far and wee.* Jenny still hadn't forgiven her for that.

The teachers and merchants occupied the middle rows, the Van Syocs and Wellses and McKowens, the Neumans and Reysts. Chief Grossman and his wife Emily had weaseled their way that far forward, although as a low-paid public servant Grossman belonged farther back with the other cops and volunteer firemen. Harley Weissenfluh, owner of the feed and farm implement store, was having a hard time staying awake. Every time his head nodded his wife Shirley poked him in the ribs. Bill and Stella Lohe, owners of Gents, were also in this group, obviously seeing no conflict between the holiness of worship and the vileness of exploiting young female flesh.

Old Man Kohlsrud would probably fit here if he ever attended church, but he didn't, not ever, even when his wife was alive. Unlike every other business in town except the Holiday Station, Gents, and Mom's Diner, his shoe and bicycle shop was open on Sunday.

The lawyers and doctors and politicians took the front two rows. Jenny recognized Doc Murphy and Mayor Philips in their pews, of course, but the rest moved in circles her circles never touched. She knew faces and she knew names, but not which went with which.

Suits and dresses, black shoes and platforms. Such a peaceful scene in such a placid little town. But what murky secrets festered in the dark places beneath the surface? Look at them. Look at them. Maybe that one was overly fond of his secretary. Maybe *that* one liked boys. She liked leather. *She* was sleeping with him, who was sleeping with *her,* who was sleeping with *everybody.* He was skimming money from his children's trust fund, *he* was skimming money from the church…

Only God knew, and He wasn't telling.

Jenny hid her smile behind a fake cough. The world was just so *mud-luscious* when, from her high perch, she could allow her imagination to root about in her neighbors' filth.

Pastor Matt seemed to fix his eyes on the Frischels. He cued the organist, and signaled for all to rise. After the hymn and the announcements he had a special prayer request.

Wednesday, December 10, 1975

The way Old Man Kohlsrud eyed Suzy's pregnancy gave her the heebie-jeebies. She brought out his food just as Chief Grossman sat down opposite him in the booth. Grossman's belly could barely squeeze in, but at least he was clean. Kohlsrud…well, he needed to stand a little closer to the water when he showered. An aftershave that didn't smell like formaldehyde would be nice, too.

"I'd rather eat alone," Kohlsrud said over a mouthful of mashed potatoes.

"I'd rather let you," the Chief said.

Every booth was equipped with a miniature jukebox. Grossman put a quarter in and punched the buttons for Creedence Clearwater's "Suzie Q", which he always did for Suzy, and his usual Johnny Cash songs, "I Walk the Line" and "Ring of Fire".

"What'd I do this time?" Kohlsrud said.

"You know Leslie Frischel?"

"Should I?"

"She told a friend she was heading to your shop on Friday the twenty-eighth."

"Stripper?"

"No, but she works there. Nineteen, pretty, long brown hair parted in the middle."

Oh Suzie Q, John Fogerty sang. *Baby I love you, Suzie Q.*

"That narrows it down to every girl in town." Kohlsrud guzzled half a cup of coffee and nodded toward Suzy. "Like her."

"Except Leslie wasn't expecting. Far as I know."

"I'm supposed to remember that far back? What about her?"

"She went missing that weekend."

Suzy cleared her throat. "Can I get you anything?"

"Hot chocolate," Grossman said.

"One bill or two?"

Kohlsrud looked hopefully at Grossman, who stared back stone-faced. "Two," they both said.

Suzy's friends had been talking about the missing girl. *Remember Vicky Kajeski,* they said. She wanted to hear more of the men's conversation, but there was a couple with kids in A-4. "I'll be right back with your cocoa," she said, tearing Kohlsrud's bill from her pad and placing it on the table.

"So how's this missing girl my problem?" Kohlsrud said to Grossman.

Friday, December 12, 1975

It was only a week till the end of the fall term at Hills. Finals started on Monday.

Jenny should be writing her paper on the Reconstruction, but instead sat in the student union, reading *The Plainview Weekly Herald.* The big story on the front page was that the Farm Expo was coming to the hippodrome in nearby Ridgemont in January. All the latest farm equipment would be on display. Harley Weissenfluh was quoted in the story, saying how now was the time to buy. If farmers waited until spring the prices would skyrocket. Mayor Philips expressed the hope that the Expo would bring overflow visitors from Ridgemont into Plainview.

Also on the front page was a photograph of the Christmas decorations lining Main Street and a silly map charting Santa's route from the North Pole to Plainview.

Sports occupied page two, with previews of the upcoming high school basketball and wrestling seasons. Prospects for the Plainview cagers were good, as four of five starters returned from last year's 12-7 squad. (Jenny never understood why basketball players were called cagers.) However, the outlook wasn't as bright for the wrestlers. They could only fill eight of the twelve weight classifications, which meant they'd have to forfeit four matches every meet. Jenny didn't see the attraction of boys grappling with boys, and while she liked the tight little shorts the basketball players wore, those bulging wrestling singlets were just gross.

Page three was filled with Christmas ads. Molly Lutz came by just as Jenny circled a lava lamp from Pamida.

"Really?" she said, looking over her friend's shoulder.

"For my parents," Jenny said. "They're into that psychedelic stuff."

"Mine would freak out," Molly said.

"I can't afford it anyway."

"Look on page four," Molly said.

The last page, beneath the fold, had a small article in which the Frischel family pleaded for their daughter to come home.

Jenny closed the paper. "What was she thinking?" she said. "How's she going to pass her classes now?"

"How's anyone," Molly said, "with this hanging over our heads?"

Tuesday, December 16, 1975

Chief Grossman was in his office playing finger football. The balls were pieces of paper folded into small triangles like Minutemen hats. He flicked them across his desk's polished surface, trying to get them to perch over the far edge without falling off. When he succeeded he awarded himself a touchdown. For the extra point he stood a triangular ball on its point and used his middle finger to "kick" it over a stapler that served as the goalposts.

"Fourteen zero," he exclaimed as his latest shot sailed directly over the stapler.

The other officer on duty, Jim Engel, looked up from his crossword at the front counter of the station. "You always play with yourself?"

"By myself," Grossman said. "Till I get some competition. Wanna try?"

The telephone rang.

Engel indicated the crossword. "I like real challenges," he said as he picked up the phone. After listening for a moment he rolled his eyes. "Oh, hi, Mrs. Frischel." He glanced at Grossman, who shook his head. "He's not here," Engel said. "No, I don't know when. Can I take a message?"

Even from across the room Grossman could hear Helen's agitation, if not her actual words. Engel made a jerk-off motion with his fist. "He's doing his best, ma'am. We all are. But those hippies hang around Gents like flies on shit, pardon my French. We're trying to track them down, but they're not local. The ones we have corralled deny even knowing your daughter."

Grossman got up to collect his misses from the floor. *Get rid of her,* he mouthed.

Engel shrugged helplessly.

"No, ma'am, we don't *know* that for sure, but you can't know she didn't—"

Engel held the phone away from his ear while Helen shouted at him. When she took a breath, he said, "Okay. Please. This isn't helping. Now, listen—"

A longer pause.

"We've talked to him. Repeatedly. Says he doesn't know anything about it, doesn't remember her being in the shop that day."

Pause.

"We are *aware* of that. So is he, now. He found the receipt. But if it was a routine sale, he wouldn't have any reason to remember her. We can't arrest people on suspicion, Mrs. Frischel. We're not even sure a crime has been—"

Engel looked at the phone curiously, then replaced it on its cradle. "She hung up on me."

Grossman flicked another football. It slid to the edge of his desk and quivered but didn't fall. "Touchdown," he said.

"She's pretty upset."

"Wouldn't you be? Bet the kid ran off with one of those longhairs, bet money on it." He missed the extra point.

"You need a new kicker," Engel said.

"I'm still up twenty zip."

Thursday, December 18, 1975

Kohlsrud locked up the shop early, something he rarely did. Business was slow—slow, hell, it was nonexistent. Nobody was coming in. He didn't expect bike business this time of year, but apparently no other appliance or gadget or toy had broken, nobody's kids needed shoes, nothing. Kohlsrud squinted up into the cold sun. It was like he'd grown a third eye or come down with leprosy or something. He swung his leg over his bike and pedaled toward the bridge. Well, screw 'em. Screw 'em all.

Saturday, December 20, 1975

It was one in the morning, and a nasty wind whistled out of the northwest, chasing intermittent clouds across the constellations.

Jenny, Molly, and the two Mikes were paired up in the seventy-one LeSabre belonging to Mike One's father. An eight-track was blaring—not by accident—Zeppelin's "Whole Lotta Love" while Molly wrestled with Mike One in the front seat and Jenny contended with Mike Two in the back. They were parked next to the office of Neuman's Chevrolet dealership. A car didn't look out of place there, even if it was a Buick, and the building blocked the lot lights, throwing shadows over the LeSabre and making its exhaust fumes less obvious.

"*Gonna give you my love, ah,*" Mike One sang along with Robert Plant. "*Gonna give you* every inch *of my love.*"

"Jesus," Molly laughed, "how many hands do you have?"

"Many as I need, baby."

Jenny scrunched against the door, trying to fend off Mike Two. The window handle dug into her ribs and the frosty glass froze the back of her head. "Stop it!" she said. Usually she was a good sport, but not tonight.

"What's wrong?" he said.

"Leslie Frischel."

Mike Two looked at her as if she were crazy. "Like hell. You don't even like her."

"So?"

"So if you didn't want to be here tonight, why didn't you just say so?"

In the front seat Molly and Mike One were noisily unconcerned about Leslie Frischel.

Mike Two smiled. "I have an idea. Let's pretend you're buying shoes, I'm Old Man Kohlsrud, and my hand is a shoehorn." He caressed Jenny's thigh. "Isn't this how he helps girls try them on?"

Jenny slapped his hand away. "You think it's funny?" she shouted. "You think it's *funny?*"

Mike One diverted his attention from Molly long enough to look over his shoulder and say, "Knock it off, will ya?"

Thursday, December 25, 1975

Most Christmases the traditional Frischel noon meal, held at Grandma Lehr's house in town, was a lavish affair of roast turkey, yams with gravy, jellied cranberry, and hot steaming rolls fresh from the oven, followed by pumpkin pie. This year Helen and Grandma didn't have the heart to cook, which was just as well, because nobody had the heart to eat.

But they were determined to celebrate the season. They should at least try.

The seven of them sat in a circle on the floor in Grandma's living room, the Christmas tree lit up, its silver streamers gleaming and bright star shining. Neatly wrapped and bowed presents spilled out from under the pine needles. An album of music from the *Rudolph* cartoon played on the phonograph. Burl Ives was singing "Holly Jolly Christmas".

"Come on," Tom said with false cheer. "Who wants to be Santa Claus?"

Every year one of the girls was chosen to distribute the gifts among her sisters and parents and Grandma. Once all the packages had been received, the family opened them one at a time, youngest to oldest. That way everybody got to enjoy the squeals of happiness or, sometimes, pouts of disappointment. Ever since Lindsey had turned three, she had always been the first to volunteer. Tonight she just curled up in her Snoopy pajamas and sucked her thumb.

Tom looked at Leigh, at Lara, at Lisa. All sat expressionless. He looked at Helen. She wouldn't meet his gaze.

"I'll be Santa," Grandma Lehr said. She moved to the rocking chair beside the tree. The first package was marked Lisa. She slid the box across the hardwood floor toward the girl, who left it lie where it came to rest. Next was Lara and then Lisa again. "Tom, this is for you, from Helen. Oh. Here's one for...," Grandma's voice softened to a whisper. "We'll just set hers aside for when she comes home."

"Set mine aside, too," Leigh said.

"Me, too," Lara said.

"Yeah," Lisa said.

Lindsey continued to suck her thumb.

"Where's your Christmas spirit? Tom pleaded, his own voice flat and lifeless.

"It's no use," Helen said.

Thursday, December 25, 1975

Jenny had a paper due for her Civil War class. Christmas festivities were over for her family, and it was time to hit the books. The whole Leslie Frischel thing had upset her, and she sort of blew off her finals. Since a lot of students were having trouble coping, Professor Wells had offered an extension to anyone who requested one, as long as the assignments were in by the start of the spring term. That was a week and a half away. Jenny opened her book. Reconstruction. Ugh.

Thursday, December 25, 1975

Matt Stigler hung up his vestments and locked the sacristy door. The service had been sparsely attended, but that was normal. Most people stayed home to celebrate with their families. Later today Matt would be doing the same with his own wife and kids, and this year his brother and nephews were visiting. It would be good to see them again.

But he had one stop to make first. He donned his winter coat and went out to start the Rambler. The Frischels would be at Leona Lehr's house. On this day, this day of Christ's birth, that poor family was in a place of unimaginable darkness. It was never easy to face people's fear and grief, never easy, but any discomfort Matt felt was nothing compared to the emotions gripping the Frischels. If ever anyone needed the Light of the Lord, it was them.

He put the car in gear and pulled out onto a deserted Main Street, rehearsing what he might say, wondering what prayer could possibly bring comfort to a family whose daughter and sister didn't come home for Christmas.

Thursday, December 25, 1975

The lights and TV were off, a fire popped in the hearth, and Christmas music played softly on the radio. Al Grossman snuggled on the love seat with his wife Emily. They sipped their traditional bubbly and enjoyed the moment.

"Do you ever wish we had kids?" Emily said for the millionth time in their marriage.

"Shhh," Grossman said, kissing her on the forehead. "I just thank the Lord I have you, Emmy."

She leaned her head against his shoulder and patted him on the tummy. "Smooth talking devil," she said.

Thursday, December 25, 1975

Kohlsrud sat on a stool next to the stage, drinking a Schlitz and watching a pretty young thing strut her stuff. The room was dark except for the red strobe lights over the dancers. Kohlsrud puffed on a Camel. The strobes pulsed in the smoke, and the girls moved like staccato bursts of substance through a fiery and ephemeral mist.

It was Christmas night, but Gents was business as usual. Gents was always open, and lonely men always came to drink, to smoke, to ogle the girls and invent conquests that never happened. Christmas didn't change that. Christmas enhanced that. Christmas reminded them of family and happier times, of what they once had and were, and now didn't and weren't.

Kohlsrud looked around. The place wasn't packed, but the hippies were here, of course, along with a fair number of Plainview's upstanding citizens, most of whom crouched in booths away from the strobes. These were the same men who wrote angry editorials to the *Herald* decrying Gents as a den of sin, a cesspool blackening the image of the town and everyone in it.

On most nights the bar blasted twenty-year-old country music through ten-year-old speakers, but in honor of the holiday the girls were gyrating their hips to "O Holy Night" and "Silver Bells" and "I Saw Mommy Kissing Santa Claus".

The stripper dancing in front of Kohlsrud bent over, shook her tassels in his face, and blew him a kiss. *You don't have anywhere else to go tonight, either,* he thought. Eleven o'clock, time for bed. He stood up and saluted the girl with his beer bottle. "To my Mary," he said.

Friday, December 26, 1975

A few minutes before dawn Chief Grossman got a frantic call from Harley Weissenfluh, demanding they meet at his house out in the country. Grossman had been in bed, warm, Emily at his side. He'd given himself the day off.

"Couldn't this wait for a decent hour?" he grumbled to Harley.

"You need to get over here *now,*" Harley said, and disconnected.

Furious, Grossman dressed and stumbled with unzipped coat and untied boots into a clear but frigid morning. He always kept the Vic plugged into a heater in the winter, but the damn car still didn't want to start. A few minutes of persistence and profanity coaxed it to life. Harley was waiting for him outside when he pulled into his driveway. The man's face was bright red, and he looked like he was going to puke.

"This had goddamned well better be important," Grossman said.

"Follow me," Harley said. He had a flashlight in his hand. "Before you ask, I didn't see anyone."

"Jesus, Harley, just *tell* me."

Behind Harley's house was nothing but acres and acres of flat farm fields under foot-tall drifts, now burnished orange by the rising sun. An ice-packed drainage ditch paralleled the driveway before peeling off into a field and emptying into a cement culvert some fifty yards in. "I was asleep when I heard a car pull in my driveway. Nobody's got any business being on my property this time of day." Harley was practically running, difficult for the overweight Grossman to manage on dry, warm surfaces, let alone ice.

"You're gonna kill us both," Grossman said, gasping in the cold and heavy air. "It must be fifteen below."

Harley slowed half a step. "Keep up, dammit! So after five minutes the car leaves and I think, *What the hell?* I get my twelve gauge and come out. I see these tire tracks." He pointed down at the snow. The tracks had a wide wheel base, probably a pickup with chains on. "I followed them back into the field."

"Some stupid kids looking for a place to screw. So what? Happens all the time."

"Really?" Harley said. They walked in the ruts left by the car until they came to the culvert. "He got out here. Look at the footprints."

The prints were a size or two smaller than Grossman's, elevens maybe, made by someone wearing galoshes. "And?" he said.

"And *this*" Harvey said, kneeling in front of the culvert's opening.

Grossman bent down for a better look. It was dark, and Harley shined his flashlight inside. "Oh, Christ," Grossman said. "Oh, son of a bitch. Oh, sweet Jesus."

Friday, December 26, 1975

Helen and Lisa were doing breakfast dishes at the kitchen sink when they saw Grossman's squad car turn into the driveway. When it came to a stop both the Chief and Pastor Matt got out. The men looked at each other and exhaled long powdery breaths.

"Get your father," Helen said. "Then go to your room."

"What's wrong?"

"Please, honey, now."

Lisa left calling, "Daddy, Daddy!"

Helen, unable to support her own weight any more, slumped to the floor. Tom rushed into the kitchen just as the knock came to the door.

"Don't answer it," Helen pleaded, already in tears.

Monday, December 29, 1975

"Can't tell if she was raped or not," Doc Murphy said to Grossman. They were seated in Doc's office, breathing medicinal fumes. "I took swabs just in case, but even if there is semen it's probably too degraded to type."

"Cause of death?" Grossman said.

"Hyoid bone's broke." Doc lit up a Marlboro. "So, strangulation."

"How long she been dead?"

"Shortly after she was taken, I'd guess. If she was outside, the cold would affect decomp, but by the looks of her…"

Grossman rubbed the back of his neck. "She disappeared a month ago, Doc. The bastard just dumped her on Friday. Where the hell'd he keep her all this time?"

Murphy shook his head. "The Frischels identify her?"

"Looking like that? No, I wouldn't let them. Stigler did it."

"Nineteen years old. Christ. Anything on the tire tracks?"

"Truck of some kind. We took pictures, but he had chains on, so we couldn't make out the tread."

Doc blew out a mouthful of smoke, coughed. "Who did this, Al?"

"TV people from Lake Center asked me that, too."

"And?"

"I have some ideas," Grossman said. But he didn't, not even one.

Friday, November 28, 1975

"Little tight," Leslie said.

"They're made to stretch," Kohlsrud said. "Stick your big toe up." Leslie did, and he used his index finger and thumb to trace its outline through the shoe. He wore a wedding ring, which never ceased to amaze her. His wife was dead now, but whatever possessed her to marry him in the first place? "Perfect," he said. "You want these, then?"

"But they're not Famolares," she pouted.

Kohlsrud rose effortlessly. Despite his frail appearance, he moved with assurance and power. Repairing bikes must keep his muscles strong. He smiled, or leered, or scowled, it was hard to tell. His teeth were stained with nicotine, too. "What do you expect for seven ninety-five?"

"I guess they're okay," she said, taking off the loafer and replacing it with her old shoe. She handed him a five and two ones, then rummaged through her purse for change.

"Forget it," Kohlsrud said. He bagged the shoes for her, wrote up a receipt, and gave the carbon to her. "Now get out of here."

"Thanks," Leslie said, and pushed open the door to a warm and sunny November afternoon. Now that her business with creepy old Kohlsrud was done, she could look forward to the rest of the weekend. Mr. Lohe had given her the night off so she could attend a Thanksgiving dance. She bounced down the street, smiling and carefree, a southerly breeze in her hair. One more stop for a new blouse at Annie's, and she'd be set.

Dozens of pre-Christmas shoppers were out taking advantage of the nice weather, but Leslie was alone as she crossed the bridge over the Marengo River. A shiny black Chevy pickup pulled up next to her. The window rolled down and the clean-cut driver said, "Looking for a ride, beautiful?"

Leslie's face lit up. "Oh, hi!" she said. "You waxed your dad's truck."

"Hop in," he said.

PART TWO: THE BLOOD COOLS
Friday, July 3, 2009

Mike Alexander and his wife Beth joined in singing hymn number 474 from the old green Book of Worship as the Frischel girls followed the casket of their mother up the aisle and out of the church. The girls were hardly girls anymore—Lindsey, the youngest, must be nearing forty by now—but Saint Andrew's Lutheran Church hadn't changed a whit since Mike left town in 1976. In fact, the pew in front of him still bore the marks he'd carved into the wood on his last visit, the now immortalized initials of his special girlfriends at the time, VK72 + LF75 + ML76. Thirty-three years later, no one had replaced the pews, no one had sanded the old wood, and no one, as far as he knew, had taken much notice of his handiwork. All somebody had done was to apply layer after layer of varnish until the etchings were smooth and shallow indentations, barely visible except to those who knew where to look and what to look for.

But then, several of the pews in the back had graffiti of some kind. Kids like him, stupid kids.

When Matt Stigler, the pastor of Mike's youth, had been killed in a car crash two years ago, his daughter Evelyn had taken over his congregation. A female minister. Mike shook his head. Evelyn seemed sincere, but a minister? And so young. *Some* things had changed, and not for the better. The Reverend Evelyn Stigler marched solemnly behind the Frischel girls, fingers wrapped lovingly around her bible.

Beth nudged him while they waited for the usher to come and release their row. "Are we going to the cemetery?" she said.

"I think we should," Mike said. "Lots of old friends to catch up with afterward."

Beth glanced at her watch.

"Got somewhere you need to be?" Mike said.

"In this town?" she said.

Friday, July 3, 2009

Helen Frischel had been laid to rest next to her beloved husband Tom and daughter Leslie. The four surviving sisters had gathered in the old farmhouse, eight miles north of Plainview. Their husbands and kids were in the living room watching the Twins play the Tigers on TV. The suitcases were packed and arranged next to the kitchen door.

It was a cool evening, and Lara had the air off and the windows open. The stench of the Tanners' hog operation up the road drifted in on a light breeze.

"Jesus, how can you stand it?" Lisa said.

"Never used to bother you," Lara said, smiling.

Leigh closed the window. "Do you mind?" she said. "I sort of got unused to it."

"Dad would have said that's the smell of money," Lara said.

"Maybe that's why I use credit cards," Lindsey said.

The women all laughed and sat down at the kitchen table. Lara brought them coffee. They looked at each other and didn't say anything for a while. The L Train was together again. For reasons never explained, Helen and Tom Frischel had given all five of their daughters names beginning with L. Just liked the sound of L, apparently.

Lara sipped her coffee. Like her, her sisters wore their hair short, as women seemed to do as they approached middle age. Leslie wouldn't have. She was so proud of her long, beautiful hair, that honey color somewhere between brown and blond. Had she lived, Leslie would have kept hers long. And been an artist. Or a singer. Or a CEO.

It was strange being forty-seven and having an older sister who never made it to twenty.

"You look like housewives," Lara said.

"What's your excuse?" Lisa said. She meant no offense by it, and none was taken. Lara had never married, choosing instead to care for their mother after their father's fatal stroke almost twenty years ago.

"Mom said that they would have gotten divorced if Dad hadn't died when he did."

"Those two?" Lindsey said. "Hell would have frozen over first."

Hell *did* freeze over, Lara thought. Leslie's murder had put a terrible strain on the marriage, a terrible strain. It wasn't until after their father's death that their mother had rekindled her love for him. Sadly, she found it easier to love the memory than the man. But in that the Good Lord was kind, for by the time He came for her, her mind was half gone, and she could no longer distinguish one from the other.

"We've talked," Leigh said.

"We're not going to fight you over the house," Lisa said.

"Mom wanted me to sell and split the money between us," Lara said.

"This is your home," Leigh said.

"Keep everything," Lindsey said. "You deserve it."

"All we'd like is a memento or two," Lisa said. "You know, of Mom and Dad."

"Take what you want," Lara said. "I've still got some of Leslie's stuff, too." She smiled wanly. Her sisters were still attractive women, kept their figures, wore their wrinkles well. Not too much makeup, no Botox or boob jobs.

This was probably the last time the L Train would all be together under one roof, until they had to start putting each other into boxes.

Saturday, July 4, 2009

Take away the new cars and modern fashions, and Plainview could be a Polaroid of 1962. Hell, the Motel 6 sign still boasted free color TV. Mike looked out the window of his room as the annual Independence Day parade crawled up Main Street. The high school marching band was wearing the same style of uniform he'd worn when he played trombone with them at halftime of football games in

1973—and the uniforms even then had been fifteen years out of date. He'd heard that due to declining enrollment in the nineties Plainview High School had merged with Ridgemont's. The new blood certainly hadn't improved the musicians any. They were butchering the school fight song just as badly as the seventy-three band had.

The town may be the same, but the teenagers weren't. Crowds lined the sidewalks to watch the parade. Every boy under twenty had a baseball cap turned sideways on his head, an iPod in his ear, and camouflage pants two sizes too big pulled partway up so that his ass was hanging out. Mike couldn't hear what they were saying, but they probably flashed gang signs at each other and talked ghetto, stupid white kids pretending to be black in a town whose entire population wouldn't fill a Chicago block. Most had tattoos and, he imagined, piercings in places no sharp instrument should ever get near.

And then there were the girls…

Beth came out of the bathroom, topless. "Do my boobs sag?" she said.

Mike stepped away from the window and closed the gap in the drapes. "Jesus, Beth," he said. "There are kids right outside."

"Well, do they?"

"You're fifty," he said.

"What's that supposed to mean?"

"It means you look fine, but you're fifty. Everything starts to sag. Who cares?"

Beth put her bra on. "Well, that cheered me right up. So what's so special about Helen Frischel?"

"As a person? Not one thing."

"Then why'd you drag me to the asshole of the universe for her funeral?"

Mike lit up a cigarette and sat on the edge of the bed. "Three girls were killed here in the seventies. Helen was the last of their parents to go, so I came to pay my respects. And while I'm here I thought I'd look up Al Grossman. He was the cop who worked the cases. He and I had some interesting times, I'll tell you. I think he's still alive."

"Killed? As in murdered?"

"Yeah."

"I figured someone running a red light would be big news here."

Mike drew in a long mouthful of smoke. "Used to be." Used to be *any* news was big news, yet in Plainview people barely reacted to Vicky Kajeski's death. Leslie Frischel raised a few eyebrows, but nothing more. It wasn't until Molly Lutz that there was any kind of general alarm, any real police involvement. Even then it wasn't long before Plainview was pretending nothing had happened. Crime might be the norm in big cities, but not here. Here it was an embarrassment. The sooner forgotten, the better.

Beth looked through her suitcase for a White Sox T-shirt. "Who did it?"

"Never caught him," Mike said.

"That's lame," Beth said.

"What do you expect? Grossman was no Sherlock Holmes."

"I meant your reason for coming to the funeral. You just wanted an excuse to drink beer with your old poontang buddies."

Mike smiled. "I never need an excuse to drink beer."

Beth stood sideways in the bathroom door and evaluated herself in the mirror. She cupped her breasts and pushed them up a few inches. "How do I look?"

"You should probably put some pants on before we go out," Mike said.

Sunday, July 5, 2009

Lara poked her head into the sacristy after the service. Evelyn Stigler smiled at her, as she always did. Like her late father before her, Evelyn had time for everybody. "I see your sisters are still in town," she said.

"Leaving tomorrow," Lara said.

Evelyn hung up her robe, smoothing its wrinkles with the palm of her hand. She was wearing a plain white blouse and black skirt underneath. "What's on your mind?" she said. "Trouble with God again?"

Lara always had trouble with God. She was a communion assistant who made herself say the right words and think the right thoughts, but there was a God-sized hole in her soul that no title or words or thoughts could fill. "No," she said. "Leslie."

"Ah, then it is about God."

It was true, in a just world no nineteen-year-old girl should die the way Leslie had, but that wasn't the problem today. "It's my sisters," Lara said.

"Your mother's will?"

"Nothing like that."

Evelyn removed the bookmarks from the passages she'd read in her sermon this morning. "Okay," she said, and sat down. "Tell me."

Lara remained standing. "They've never once mentioned Leslie since they got here. They talk about Mom, and some about Dad, and constantly about their husbands and kids, but not one word about Leslie."

"Your mother just died. Of course she would be on their minds." Evelyn patted the chair next to her. When Lara sat, the woman gently squeezed her hands. "Leslie's been gone a long time, Lara."

"But," Lara said, and for Christ's sake she was behaving as if Evelyn hadn't also lost someone, "they don't act as if she never died. They act as if she never lived."

Evelyn touched the sleeve of her blouse to Lara's cheek, drawing up her tears. "Is it so terrible that they left home?"

"I'm happy for them," Lara said. "I am, but..."

"But it never goes away," Evelyn said.

Sunday, July 5, 2009

Dozens of mourners had attended Helen Frischel's committal service on Friday, but today Mike was alone in the cemetery. The weather was finally starting to feel like summer, the temperature approaching ninety. A few people had been here after church, placing flowers on tombstones and talking to loved ones who could not answer, but the afternoon heat had driven them away. Not Mike. He liked hot weather.

Vicky Kajeski's grave was on the other side of the cemetery, but the Frischel and Lutz plots were within a few feet of one another. If he stood back he could see Leslie and Molly's graves at the same time.

Vicky had been his first, an experiment. Then Leslie, more confident but still feeling his way. But Molly, Molly had been perfection. Divine. Mike knelt before her marker, MOLLY LUTZ, NOVEMBER 11 1956—SEPTEMBER 7 1976, BELOVED DAUGHTER. He ran his hand along the curved edge of the marble. The elements were already starting to take their toll in the form of little dirt-filled chips and cracks.

Mike closed his eyes and remembered, and as he remembered he felt that familiar sense of arousal. It was almost the same, almost.

And yet now there was a numbness in him as well, a coldness that flowed through his veins. The sun beat down on his back and head. He caressed the marble, rubbed his face against it. Vicky and Leslie and Molly. Oh, if he could tear off his clothes and perch on the stone, if he could soak up its heat like a reptile, like a lizard, feeling it radiate through him, warming his blood, making him live again, bringing him back to life.

A woman's voice startled him from behind. "Mike Alexander?" she said.

He looked up from Molly's grave and saw Lara Frischel standing before Leslie's and Helen's and Tom's. He hadn't heard her approach. He was crying.

Lara smiled sympathetically. "She was your girlfriend back then, wasn't she?"

Monday, July 6, 2009

The old Holiday Station had been replaced by a Caseys, but the rest of Plainview looked the same, at least along the main drag. The town had no Wal-Mart, no Target, no Wendy's, not even a McDonald's. Main Street was lined with bars, antique stores, and secondhand consignment shops. The Motel 6 stood across from Weissenfluh's Feed and Farm Implements. Just before the bridge crossing the Marengo River, John's Auto Body and Annie's Alterations faced the Emporium, a dilapidated dollar movie house that showed month-old films after they'd run their course in the bigger cities.

Mom's Diner, a fixture since before Mike was born, was as bland as ever on the outside, but its owners had remodeled the inside, adding a single flat screen TV at the front for locals to watch NASCAR or the farm report.

"Christ, they think they're a sports bar," Mike said.

Beth looked out the window and didn't speak. It was raining.

"Help you folks?" a waitress said. She was a doughy, middle-aged woman with bad teeth and reading glasses tucked over the top of her restaurant frock. Last time Mike had seen her she was a seventeen-year-old with a baby and no boyfriend in sight.

"Suzy?" Mike said.

"Just Sue now," she said. "Do I know you?"

Mike introduced himself and Beth.

"We live in Chicago," Beth said.

Sue put her glasses on and squinted at Mike, then shook her head. "If you say so. Remember the name, but..."

"How's your son?" Mike said.

"Which one? Oldest boy's shacked up with some gal over in Ridgemont. She don't want to get married. Youngest one comes and goes, I can't keep track. Kids, you know?"

"Whatever happened to Al Grossman?"

Sue's face brightened. "Chief? He's in a nursing home up in Lake Center. When Emmy passed, he sort of lost interest in police work. In everything, really. They never had no children to look in on him, so one day he just packs a bag and takes off. When I heard he ended up in the home, I started paying him a visit two, three times a year. Cantankerous old bastard still sings 'Suzie Q' every time he sees me. You remember that old song."

"I like-a way you walk," Mike sang, playing an air guitar riff between lines, *"I like-a way you talk—"*

"Don't you start, too. Your husband's quite the character," she said to Beth.

Beth looked at Mike. She looked at Sue. She looked out the window.

"Think the Chief would mind if I stopped in?" Mike said.

"Can't promise he'll remember you any better than I did," Sue said.

"He at Windsor?"

"That's the only one up there."

"Ought to make it easy, then," Mike said. "You take credit cards?"

"We do, but our machine's broke. Let you write a check, though."

"Couple of burgers and Cokes to go, with fries?"

"*Diet* Coke," Beth said.

"Two number twos coming right up," Sue said, scribbling on her pad.

•••

The drive to Lake Center took forty-five minutes. Beth ate her food and wouldn't speak. Mike tried to make conversation but quickly gave in to Beth's silence. The rain didn't stop. The wind was coming harder now. Thunder and small hail followed, *plinkplink-plink* on the glass and metal of their Explorer. Just inside the city limits Mike pulled up next to the entrance to the Pamida and gave Beth his MasterCard.

"Pamida?" she said. *"Pamida?"*

"It's like a Woolworth's, only more so."

"What the hell would I want to buy in this godforsaken place?"

"You could come with me to see Grossman."

"What's he to you, anyway?" Beth snatched the credit card and an umbrella and got out of the SUV. "If you're not back in an hour," she said, "I'm going home with the first good-looking man I see."

"Knock yourself out."

Beth slammed the door and Mike headed back onto Highway 31. He'd been to Lake Center many times in his youth. Compared to Plainview, it was an exotic big city of almost six thousand. He used to sneak up here on weekends when he wanted to do some serious drinking or buy high quality weed he couldn't get from the pimply losers who sold the stuff in Plainview.

It was en route to here in 1972 that he'd picked up Vicky Kajeski hitchhiking. He was seventeen, she fourteen, if he remembered right. She'd just had a fight with her father.

Windsor was only a few minutes away on Fourth Street Southwest. The building was immaculate, its bricks shiny with a fresh coat of white paint. The lawn surrounding it was a verdant green, but then, for reasons he never understood, grass always looked greener on cloudy, rainy days.

He parked in a spot marked Staff Only and went inside. The nursing station was only too happy to take him to Grossman's room. Other than Sue, Grossman never had visitors. A female orderly in a ridiculously short skirt led him down the hall. Mike was surprised she didn't give the old boys heart attacks wearing an outfit like that.

She knocked on the door to Room 14. "Mister Grossman, you decent?"

"Come look for yourself." The voice was older and thinner but unmistakably Grossman's.

"You have a visitor."

"Oh, Suzie Q," he sang.

"Not this time," the girl said. She opened the door and nodded Mike in.

Grossman, clad in pajamas and a robe, was sitting in a wheelchair watching baseball on TV. "Who the hell are you?" he said. A two-hundred-fifty pounder when Mike knew him, Grossman was probably over three now. He still wore his familiar crew cut, but his jowls were more expansive and fixed, the color and texture of paraffin wax.

"You know me, Chief," Mike said. "Mike Alexander. I spent a lot of time in the back of your old Crown Vic."

Grossman stared at him, looked away, then stared again. His eyes hardened. He knew. He *knew.* "You should've done a damn sight more than that. We had your shoeprints on Frischel and blood type on Lutz."

"Yet you didn't arrest me."

"Prosecutor said no. If we'd had DNA then…And now the evidence is lost."

Mike leaned against the door frame and shoved his fists into his pants pockets. "The blood cools, Chief" he said unsteadily. He thought this would be easier. "I own my own construction business. I have a wife and a daughter. I'm a member of the PTA. I give to Saint Jude's. I volunteer at a homeless shelter. I got an award from Mayor Daley once." He looked down at his feet. "I just wanted you to know. The blood cools."

Grossman raised himself out of his chair. "And you think that's enough?"

"Don't you want to know why?"

"Don't talk to me about *why.* If I had my gun I'd shoot you where you stand."

Mike managed a smile. "Justice at last?"

"There isn't any *justice,* you sick fuck. You got to live your life and grow old. Those girls got to be teenagers, and that's it. No, I'd shoot you just because it felt good. But it wouldn't be justice."

Grossman pushed the button to summon an orderly. "What do you want from me?"

"I don't know," Mike said.

"Get out of here," Grossman said.

DAVE HOING is a Library Associate at the University of Northern Iowa. Although he's a member of SFWA (Science Fiction and Fantasy Writers of America), he rarely writes science Fiction or fantasy any more, concentrating more on literary and historical fiction. His historical novel *Hammon Falls,* co-written with Roger Hileman, was published in 2010, and a collection of fantasy stories, *Voices of Arra* (also with contributions from Hileman) was released in 2011. A collection of his solo short stories, *Tales of Earth,* will be published by All Things That Matter Press later in 2012.

In his spare time he likes to travel, collect antiquarian books, and compose music. He also wins money in the Iowa lottery often enough to keep life interesting—and fund his travel and book interests.

"Plainview" is his first, and so far only, mystery story.

ADDITIONAL COPYRIGHT INFORMATION